CYNTHIA HARROD-EAGLES

Killing Time

An Inspector Bill Slider Mystery

AVON

TWILIGHT

AVON BOOKS, INC.
1350 Avenue of the Americas
New York, New York 10019

Copyright © 1996 by Cynthia Harrod-Eagles
Published by arrangement with Scribner, an imprint of Simon & Schuster
Visit our website at **http://www.AvonBooks.com/Twilight**
Library of Congress Catalog Card Number: 97-26290
ISBN: 0-380-73202-5

First Avon Twilight Printing: February 1999

AVON TWILIGHT TRADEMARK REG. U.S. PAT. OFF. AND IN OTHER COUNTRIES, MARCA REGISTRADA, HECHO EN U.S.A.

Printed in the U.S.A.

WCD   10   9   8   7   6   5   4   3   2   1

Praise for
Cynthia Harrod-Eagles's
Inspector Bill Slider Mysteries

DEATH TO GO

"An accomplished series."
The New York Times Book Review

DEATH WATCH

"A terrifically attractive and sensitive detective hero."
The New York Times Book Review

GRAVE MUSIC

"Delightful characters . . . and an off-the-wall plot
that holds the reader."
San Francisco Examiner

ORCHESTRATED DEATH

"Remarkable . . . Rich . . . Romantic . . . Perfect."
The New York Times

Other Inspector Bill Slider Mysteries by
Cynthia Harrod-Eagles
from Avon Twilight

BLOOD LINES
DEATH TO GO
GRAVE MUSIC
ORCHESTRATED DEATH

With Special thanks to Laurence Cohen for his generous help with the background, not forgetting tea and biscuits.

✦ ONE ✦

Second Class Male

Early on Monday morning, D.I. Carver, about to head downstairs, saw a familiar figure walking away from him along the corridor. "Bill!"

Slider stopped and turned. "Hello, Ron."

"I didn't know you were back." Carver looked him over keenly. "Shouldn't you still be on sick-leave? You look terrible."

"Thanks," Slider said. "I feel a bit under the weather, but Honeyman asked me to come in. We're short-handed, with Atherton in the cot."

"How is he?" Carver's face pursed with a moment's sympathy.

"Still very poorly." Slider marveled for a moment at the word. It was how the hospital had described him yesterday. They had a box of these strange shorthand terms for the varying degrees of human distress—critical, comfortable, stable, poorly—which they used like flashcards. It was kinder than describing reality. Reality was Atherton with a hole in him; Atherton a white face and fragile blue eyelids above a sheet, dips and drains and bags, and a cradle to keep the bedclothes off the wound, so that he looked like Tutankhamun without the gilding.

It was hard to think of clearing up the Gilbert case as a success, though Gilbert was under wraps and the C.P.S. was as chuffed about it as the C.P.S. ever was about anything.

1

But Slider had stupidly allowed himself to be ambushed by Gilbert, coshed, trussed up and, for a harrowing period, kept prisoner and threatened with a knife. When Atherton had come looking for him, Gilbert had jumped him, and the same knife had ended up where Atherton normally kept *quenelles de veau* or designer sausages with red onion marmalade. Slider had narrowly escaped a fractured skull, but Atherton had nearly died, and was not out of the woods yet.

"You've been to see him?" Carver asked.

"More tubes through him than King's Cross," Slider said.

"It's a bastard," Carver said in omnibus disapprobation. "He'll be off a while then."

It was not a question. Slider shifted uncomfortably away from the subject, and said instead, "I hear Mills is leaving the Job?" D. S. Mills, alias Dark Satanic, an old colleague of Slider's, had been a suspect for a time in the Gilbert case.

"Yeah. Well, I can't blame him. It'd be tough after what he's been through. But I'd only just got the extra manpower," he complained. "I don't suppose Honeyman'll roll for it again—not with you being short." He gave Slider a resentful stare as if it was his fault.

"Where's he going?"

"What, Mills? Wales, I gather. What's that place he went on holiday every year?"

"Rhyl?"

"That's it. This bloke he met there, owns his own business, offered Mills a billet. Salesman. Computerized security systems. Thought it'd be a boost to have an ex-dick toting the brochures around."

Poor old Dark Satanic, Slider thought. Going on the knocker was a bit of a come-down from the C.I.D. Or was it? "I suppose it's a job," he said doubtfully.

"I don't think he minds," Carver shrugged. "I think he wants to see a bit of life before it's too late."

"In *Wales*?"

"He's taking his mum with him," Carver said—one of his better non sequiturs. "I dunno but what he hasn't got the right idea," he went on, his face settling into familiar creases of gloom. "The Job's changing, Bill. Every day coppers are getting shot and knifed, bashed on the head and dumped, and for what? We work our balls off catching the villains, and the courts let 'em off with a slap on the wrist, because some social worker says they had a rotten mum and a no-good dad. Yeah, but if one of us makes some pissy little mistake in procedure, it's wrongful arrest and the tabloids start screaming about fit-ups. It makes you wonder why you go on.''

Slider, accustomed to Carver's style, deduced his heart was not bleeding for Slider's bashed head or Atherton's knifed stomach. "Has someone else got hurt, then?"

"You haven't heard about Andy Cosgrove?"

"No. What about him?" Cosgrove was the very popular "community beat" copper for the White City Estate, a PC of the Neo-Dixon school, calm, authoritative, patient, knowledgeable; worth his considerable weight in gold to the Department for the background information he could give on any case arising on his beat.

"He was attacked last night. Beaten up and left for dead."

"Shit," Slider said, appalled. "How is he?"

"Not too clever. He's in a coma, on life-support in St. Stephen's."

"Who did it? What have you got?"

"Sod all," Carver grunted. "He was found on that piece of waste ground around the back of the railway arches down the end of Sulgrave Road, but that's not where it happened. He got smacked somewhere else, driven there and dumped."

"Professional? What was he working on?"

"Nothing in particular—nothing I know about, anyway. Just routine stuff. Like I said, there's nothing to go on." He was silent a moment, sucking his upper lip. He'd had a mustache once that he used to suck, and though he'd shaved it off ten years ago, the habit remained. A bloke and his face-fur, Slider reflected, could be as close as man and wife. "Honeyman's shitting himself. It was the last straw for him," Carver went on. "You going to see him? Reporting back?"

"That's where I was heading."

"He's like a flea in a frying pan. Wants a bodyguard to cross the parking lot."

I don't blame him, Slider thought when he left Carver. Honeyman was only a temp in the post of Detective Superintendent, having been put in as a night watchman when the last Det Sup had died at the crease. Recent events were enough to make anyone nervous, but Honeyman was only a few months short of his pension, and sudden death or grave injury could seriously upset a man's retirement plans.

Through the open door Slider could see Honeyman at his desk, writing. Slider tapped politely and noted how the little chap startled. "Oh, Slider—come in, come in. Good to see you back." Honeyman stood and came around the desk and held out his hand, all evidence of unusual emotion. Slider stood patiently while Honeyman looked him up and down— mostly up, because Eric Honeyman was built on a daintier scale than most policemen. "And how are you feeling now? Quite recovered? I must say we can use you. We seem to be terribly accident-prone recently. You've heard about Cosgrove?"

"Yes sir, just this minute."

"Terrible business." Honeyman shook his head hopelessly.

"Ron Carver's firm is on it, I gather."

"Yes," Honeyman said, rather absently. He seemed to be hesitating on the brink of a confidence. "I've not been feeling quite on top form myself, lately." Slider made a sympathetic noise. "The fact is," Honeyman plunged, "I've asked to have my retirement brought forward. On medical grounds." His eyes flickered guiltily to Slider and away again. "This sort of thing—involving your own men—it takes it out of you. I suppose that must sound to you—"

"You've done your time, sir," Slider filled in obligingly.

"Nearly thirty years," Honeyman agreed eagerly. "It was so different when I joined the service. Policemen were respected. Even the villains called you 'sir.' Now you have respectable, middle-class people calling you 'pig.' And breaking the law so casually, as if it was just a matter of personal choice."

Slider had no wish to stroll down this lane in this company. "Have you got a date for leaving, sir?"

"The end of next week. I haven't announced it yet, but I asked them to relieve me as soon as they could find a replacement."

Honeyman chatted a bit, something about his retirement plans and his wife, and Slider drifted off. A silence roused him, and coming to guiltily he asked, "Is this still confidential, sir? About you going?"

"I don't see any reason to keep it a secret. No, I shall send around a memo later today, but you can spread the word to the troops, if you like."

Start the collection for my leaving present, Slider translated.

"Very well, sir."

McLaren was at his desk, eating a fried egg sandwich from Sid's coffee-stall at the end of Shepherd's Bush Market. Slider knew that was where it came from, because it was the only place nearby you could get them with the yolk in the correctly runny state. You had to be in the right mood to be on either side of a fried egg sandwich, Slider thought. It helped also not to be just out of hospital after a whack on the head.

"Hello, guv," McLaren said indistinctly. "I didn't know you were back. You're looking double well."

"For Chrissake, McLaren, not over your reports," Slider said.

McLaren swiveled in his chair and dripped over his wastepaper basket instead.

"How're you feeling, boss?" Mackay came forward, tin tray in hand. "Can I get you a coffee?"

Slider sat down on the nearest desk—Atherton's, as it happened. "A few days away, and I'm forgotten. You know I don't drink instant."

"Tea, I meant," Mackay said hastily.

"Thanks. No sugar, in case you've forgotten that as well."

Mackay apologized in kind. "We've got some doughnuts."

"From Sid's? Now you're talking."

His eye found a stranger, a tall man in his late thirties, with sparse, sandy hair, plentiful freckles, and that thick, pale skin that went with them. He wore large gold-rimmed glasses and a bristly mustache, and he gangled forward, slightly drooping, with an air of practiced melancholy, as though expecting to be ridiculed.

"We haven't met, guv. I'm your new D.S.," he said, holding out his hand. He had a strange, semi-castrato, countertenor voice and a Mancunian accent. His eyes behind the glass were bulgingly soft, grayish-green like part-cooked gooseberries, but held a gleam of humor. With a voice like that, you had to have a sense of humor to survive.

"Ah, yes, Beevers' replacement," Slider said. "You came last week, didn't you?"

"That's right. Colin Hollis," he offered. Slider immediately felt more comfortable. A C.I.D. department without a Colin in it never seemed quite natural, somehow. "From Manchester Stolen Cars Squad."

"Ah. This'll seem like a bit of a holiday for you, then," Slider said.

"Talking of holidays." Anderson sidled up, a menacing photo-envelope in his hand. "Would you like to see these, guv? My loft conversion. I've done a lot while you've been away."

This was Anderson's latest project—a Useful Games Room Stroke Extra Bedroom. He had decided, unsurprisingly, to line the whole room with pine stripping. "I've got before and after shots," he added beguilingly.

Slider was deeply grateful to be interrupted by the arrival of W.D.C. "Norma" Swilley. Tall, athletic, blonde, gorgeous, and yet with a strangely unmemorable set of features, small-nosed and large-mouthed in the manner of a Baywatch Beauty, she was, according to Atherton, the living proof that Barbie and Ken had sex. She was a good policeman, but she had a low fool-suffering threshold—which probably accounted for why she was still a D.C.—and she swept Anderson aside with the authority of a staff nurse.

"The boss doesn't want to see those. How are you, guv? And how's Jim? All we get is the official report."

"Progressing slowly. I saw him yesterday. He's sleeping a lot of the time, though."

"Drugged, I suppose. It must still be pretty painful."

Slider nodded. "Haven't you seen him?"

"Just once. They're restricting visitors. I suppose you know that. Just one from the firm, they said, so I tossed Mackay for it."

"Doesn't he wish," McLaren muttered.

KILLING TIME ❖ 7

"Of all people," Norma said, ignoring him, "for Jim Atherton to get it in the stomach!"

Slider nodded. He'd thought of that. "It's like a pianist getting his fingers broken."

"Him and food," Norma said, "it's one of the great love affairs. Paris and Helen, Antony and Cleopatra—"

"Marks and Spencer?" Anderson suggested absently.

McLaren licked the last of the yolk and grease from his fingers. "They say he's not coming back. Lost his bottle."

"You've got the most hyperactive *They* I've ever come across," Slider said. "All I know is he's still very sick and he'll be in hospital a while yet, and after that he'll have to convalesce. We're going to be without him a good few weeks. What he'll decide after that no one knows—least of all him, I should think."

There was a buzz of conversation about what Atherton might or might not be feeling, and to break it up, Slider told them about Honeyman leaving. The news was met with a storm of equanimity.

"I know he hasn't been with us long," Slider concluded, "but I think we ought to organize a whip-round. At least buy him a book or something. And a card. Get everyone to sign it."

"I'll do it," McLaren offered, preparing to engage a doughnut in mortal combat.

"Fair enough," Slider said doubtfully. "But try not to get fingermarks on it."

McLaren looked wounded. "I won't let you down, guv."

"There's no way you can," Slider assured him.

He had lunch in the canteen. Chicken curry, which they made halfway decently except that they would put sultanas in it which to his mind belonged in pudding not dinner, and raspberries with *crème aux fraises*, which was cateringspeak for pink blancmange. Slider didn't mind because he actually liked blancmange. He was spooning it up when a shadow fell over him and he looked up to see Sergeant Nicholls bearing a tray. Nicholls' handsome face lit in a flattering smile. "You're back. That was quick."

"Honeyman begged me. I couldn't stand seeing a strong man weep, so—" He shrugged.

Nicholls obeyed his tacit invitation to sit down. "But are you able for it?" he asked, unloading his tray.

"Such tender concern. Yes, thanks. I still get the odd headache, but on the whole I'd sooner be working. Takes the mind off."

"Bad dreams?" Nicholls asked perceptively. "Yes, I'm not surprised. It has to come out somewhere after a shock like that. But I'd feel the same in your shoes: get back on the horse as soon as possible." He reached over the table and laid a hand on Slider's forearm. "Gilbert's banged up tight as a trull," he said, "and there's enough evidence to send him down forever. He's not getting out, Bill. Keep that in mind."

"Thanks, Nutty." They had a bit of a manly cough and shuffle. "I expect I'll be kept busy, anyway, being two men down."

"Och, well, I've some better news for you on that front," Nicholls said. "They're sending you a D.C. as a temporary replacement for Atherton. Someone called Tony Hart, from Lambeth. D'ye know him?"

"Never met him," Slider shook his head. "Ah well, that's better than nothing. But I wonder Honeyman didn't tell me. I was in there this morning."

"Honeyman'd mebbe not know yet. He hasn't got my sources. Did you know he was leaving next week?"

"Yes, he told me that."

"I shall miss him, in a way, you know," Nutty said, thoughtfully loading his fork with Pasta Bake. "He's a real lady."

Colin Hollis stuck his head around Slider's door. "There's some bloke downstairs asking for you, guv. Won't take no."

"Won't what?"

Hollis inserted his body after his head. "Well, I say bloke. Bit of a debatable point, now I've had a look at him. Ey, guv, if a bloke wears woman's underwear, is that what you'd call a Freudian slip?"

"Wipe the foam from your chin and start again," Slider suggested.

"Bloke," Hollis said helpfully. "Come in asking for you, so I went down to see what he wanted, but he says he knows you, and you're the only one he can talk to now that P.C. Cosgrove is gone." He eyed Slider with undisguised interest.

"What does he want?"

"He wouldn't say. But he's nervous as hell. Maybe he's got some gen on the Cosgrove case."

"Name?"

"Paloma. Jay Paloma." Hollis gave an indescribable grimace. "I bet that's not his real name, though. Una Paloma Blanca—what's that song? D'you know him, guv?"

Slider frowned a moment, and then placed him. "Not really. I know his flatmate, Busty Parnell." He sighed. "I suppose I'd better come."

Hollis followed him through the C.I.D. room. "He's got some gear on him. Making a bit, one way or the other. Probably the other. Funny old world, en't it, guv, when the Game makes more than the Job?"

Slider paused at the door. "Every man makes his choice."

"Oh, I've no regrets," Hollis said, stroking his terrible moustache. "I'd bend over backward to help my fellow man."

Slider trudged downstairs, feeling a little comforted. It was early days yet, but it looked as though Hollis was going to be an asset to the Department.

Slider had become acquainted with Busty Parnell in his Central days. She described herself as a show dancer, and indeed she wasn't a bad hoofer, but a small but insidious snow habit had led her into trouble, and she had slipped down the social scale to stripper and part-time prostitute. Slider had busted her once or twice and helped her out on other occasions, when a customer turned nasty or a boss was bothering her. Sometimes she had given him a spot of good information, and in return he had turned a blind eye to a spot of victimless crime on her part. And sometimes, in the lonely dogwatches which are so hard on the unmarried copper, he had taken a cup of tea with her at her flat and discussed business in general and the world in particular. She had made it plain that she would be glad to offer him more substantial comforts, but Slider had never been one to mix business with pleasure. Besides, he knew enough about Busty's body and far too much about her past life to find her tempting.

Her name was Valerie, but she had always been referred to as Busty in showbiz circles to distinguish her from the other Val Parnell, the impresario, for whom she had once auditioned. Slider had lost sight of her when he left Central, but she had turned up again a year or so ago on the White City Estate, sharing a flat with Jay Paloma. The last Slider had heard Busty had given up the stage and was working as a barmaid at a pub, The British Queen. Her flatmate was employed as an "artiste" at the Pomona Club, a rather dubious nightclub whose advertised "cabaret" consisted mainly of striptease and simulated sex acts, and which distributed more drugs than the all-night pharmacy in Shaftesbury Avenue.

Jay Paloma was waiting for Slider in one of the interview rooms. He was beautifully, not to say androgynously, dressed in a white silk shirt with cossack sleeves, and loose beige flannel slacks tucked into chocolate-colored suede ankle boots, with a matching beige jacket hanging casually over his shoulders. There was a heavy gold chain around his throat, a gold lapel pin in the shape of a treble clef on the jacket, and discreet gold studs in his ears. A handbag and nail polish would have tilted the ensemble irrevocably over the gender balance point; as it was, a casual glance suggested *artistic* rather than *transvestite*.

Jay Paloma was tall and slenderly built, and sat with the disjointed grace of a dancer, his heels together and his knees fallen apart, his arms resting on his thighs and his hands dangling, loosely clasped, between them. The hands were well-kept, with short nails and no rings. His thick, streaked-blond hair was cut short, full and spiky like a model's; his face was long and large-nosed, and given the dark eyeliner on the underlids and his way of tilting his face down and looking up under his eyebrows, he bore an uncanny resemblance to Princess Di, which Slider supposed was purely intentional.

He was a very nervous, tremulous Princess Di today, quivering of lip and brimming of eye. He started to his feet as Slider came in, thought about shaking hands, fidgeted, looked this way and that; and obeyed Slider's injunction to sit down again with a boneless, graceful collapse. He put a thumb to his mouth and gnawed the side of it—not the nail or even the cuticle but the loose flesh of the first joint. Probably he had been a nail-biter and had cured himself that way. Nails would be important to him; appearance important generally. Given that he shared an unglamorous flat with Busty and worked at the Pomona, his expensive outfit suggested that he exploited his body in a more lucrative way out of club hours.

"So what can I do for you?" Slider asked, pulling out a chair and sitting facing him. "Jay, isn't it? Do I call you Jay?"

"It's my professional name," he said. He had a soft, husky voice with the expected slightly camp intonation. It was funny, Slider reflected from his experience, how many performers adopted it, even if they weren't T.W.I. It was a great class-leveler. It was hard to guess his origins—or, indeed, his age. Slider would have put him at thirty-five, but he looked superficially much younger and could have been quite a bit older. He had makeup on, Slider saw: foundation, mascara and probably blusher, but discreetly done. It was only the angle of the light throwing into relief the fine stubble coming through the foundation that gave it away.

"It's nice of you to see me," Jay said, with the obligatory upward intonation at the end of the sentence; the phantom question mark which had haunted Estuary English ever since Australian soaps took over from the home-grown variety. It made it sound as though he wasn't sure that it was nice, and gave Slider the spurious feeling of having a hidden agenda, of being persecutor to Jay's victim.

"Any friend of Busty's is a friend of mine," he said. "How do you come to know her, by the way?"

"Val and me go way back. We were in a show together— do you remember *Hanging Out in the Jungle*? That musical about the ENSA troupe?"

"Yes, of course I do. It caused quite a stir at the time."

Slider remembered it very well. It had hit the headlines not only because it was high camp—still daring in those days—

and full of suggestive jokes; not only because of the implication, offensive to some, that ENSA had been riddled with homosexuality; but because before *Hanging Out*, the star, Jeremy Haviland—who had also directed and part-written the show—had been a respected, heavyweight actor of Shakespearean gravitas. Seeing him frolicking so incongruously in satin frocks and outrageous makeup had been one of the main draws which kept packing them in through its short but momentous run. But the gradually emerging realization that Haviland had merely typecast himself had caused secondary shockwaves which had destroyed his career. This was some years before homosexuality had become popular and acceptable. Six months after *Hanging Out* closed, Haviland committed suicide.

"Val was in the chorus, singing and dancing, but I had a proper part," Jay went on. "It was a terrific break for me."

"Which were you?"

"I played Lance Corporal Fender—the shy young lad who had to play all the young girls' parts, and got all those parcels of knitted things from his mother?"

"Yes, I remember. You did that song with Jeremy Haviland, the Beverley Sisters number, what was it?"

" 'Sisters, sisters, there were never such devoted sisters,' " Jay Paloma sang obediently, in a sweet, husky voice. "It was Jeremy got me the part. I really could dance—I'd been to a stage-and-dance school and everything—but all I'd done before was a student review at U.C.L. I was sharing a flat at the time with the president of Dramsoc, and he wangled me into it, because frankly, none of the rest of them could sing or dance worth spit. Anyway, Jeremy saw me in it, liked me, and took a chance. He was so kind to me! I owed him everything. I got fabe reviews for *Hanging Out* and everyone reckoned I was headed for stardom. But then all the fuss broke out over poor Jeremy, and the show folded, and we were all sort of dragged down with him. Tarnished with the same brush, you might say. It was hard for any of us to get work after that, and, well, Jeremy and I had been—you know—"

"Close," Slider suggested.

Jay seemed grateful for the tact. "He tried to help me, but everyone was avoiding him. And then he—" He gulped and made a terminal gesture with both hands. "It was terrible. He was such a kind, kind man."

"I didn't know Busty was in that show. It must have been before I met her."

"She and I shared lodgings. She was like a big sister to me."

"She was at the Windmill when I first knew her."

"Yes, that's where she went when *Hanging Out* closed. It was always easier for women dancers to get work. Well, we sort of lost sight of each other for a long time. And then about eighteen months ago we bumped into each other again in Earl's Court."

By then both had drifted down out of the realms of legitimate theater and into the shadowy fringe world where entertainment and sex were more or less synonymous. Busty was doing a bit of this and a bit of that—stripping, promotional work, topless waitressing. Jay was dancing when he could get it, filling in with drag routines, modeling, and working for a gay escort agency.

"Val was doing the Motor Show—dressed in a flesh suit handing out leaflets about some new sports car. She was supposed to be Eve in the Garden of Eden, the leaflets were apple-shaped. The car was the New Temptation—d'you get it?" He sniffed derisively. "She hated promo work—we all do. Being a Sunflower Girl or a Fiat Bunny or whatever. Humiliating. And the hours are shocking and the pay's peanuts, unless you sleep with the agent, which you often have to to get the job at all. Well, you have to take what you can get. And we're neither of us teenagers anymore. There just isn't the work for troupers like us. Everyone specializes, and the kids coming out of the dancing schools now can do things—well, they're more like acrobats to my mind. It's not what I'd call dancing."

"And what about you? What were you doing?"

"I had a spot at a nightclub in Earl's Court—a sort of striptease."

Slider had a fair idea which club. "Striptease?"

Jay Paloma looked haughty. "It wasn't what you think. In fact, it was my best gig after *Hanging Out* closed. I came on in this evening gown and white fur and diamonds and everything, and did this wonderful routine. Like Gypsy Rose Lee, you know—all I ever took off was the long gloves. Absolutely classical. It brought the house down! Well, anyway, Val and I bumped into each other in the street, and we were so glad to see each other, we decided to share again. We had this place in Warwick Road to start with, and then we moved out here.''

Fascinating though this was, Slider had a lot to do. ''So what did you want to talk to me about?'' he asked, with a suggestion of glancing at his wrist.

Jay hesitated. ''I say, look, d'you mind if I smoke?''

''Go ahead.'' Paloma reached for the pocket of the jacket. The cigarettes were in their original packet, but the lighter looked expensive, a gold Dunhill, Slider thought. ''It always amazes me,'' he added as he watched the lighting-up process, ''how many of you dancers smoke. I'd have thought you'd need all your breath.''

Jay Paloma looked up from under his brows and smiled in a fluttery, pleased way—because Slider had called him a dancer, perhaps. ''It keeps the weight down. You don't—?''

''No, thanks.'' Slider pushed the ashtray across the table and prompted him again. ''Well, now, what can I do for you?''

''I've got a problem,'' Jay said. He puffed at his cigarette. ''I think—well, I suppose you won't believe me, but I think someone's trying to kill me.'' The big blue eyes turned up appealingly at Slider. He was certainly nervous. He was sweating—Slider could smell it, even through what his daughter Kate would have called his anti-shave. Light and lemony: *Eau Sauvage*. Slider recognized it, because it was the one O'Flaherty favored—though O'Flaherty, the patriot, pronounced it O'Savvidge.

''What makes you think so?'' Slider asked encouragingly.

The tense shoulders dropped a little. ''Well, there've been, you know, funny phone calls.''

''Heavy breathing?''

''Not exactly. No. I mean, it rings and I pick it up, and there's just silence. I know there's someone there, but they won't speak. And then, ten minutes or so, it rings again. Sometimes it goes on for hours. I take the phone off the hook, but as soon as I put it back on, it rings again. I can't leave it off all the time because of work. I mean, you never know when someone might want to get hold of you.''

''It could be kids.''

''Kids wouldn't go on and on like that, would they? I mean, they'd get bored and go off and do something else.''

That was a point. This man had obviously thought about his predicament, which made Slider more inclined to believe him.

''Has Busty picked up these calls too?''

''No, that's another thing. It never happens when she's home. It's as if,'' he shivered subconsciously, ''as if he's watching the house, and knows when I'm home alone.''

''Have you seen anyone hanging around? Anyone suspicious?''

He shook his head. ''But it's a block of flats. There are always people around, coming and going. And plenty of places to hide, if you wanted to watch someone.''

''How long has this been going on?''

''Oh, months now. Six months maybe—but I didn't think much of it at first. I mean everyone gets those dead calls, don't they? But about three months ago, the letters started coming.''

''Letters?''

Jay nodded, almost reluctantly, ''At first they weren't really letters, just empty envelopes. Like the phone calls. Sort of unnerving. You tear open an envelope and there's a piece of blank paper in it. But then the messages started to appear.''

''Written? Typed?''

''Cut out of newspapers and stuck on, you know the sort of thing.''

Slider knew. He sighed inwardly. It was so hackneyed. A hoax, he thought. A spiteful hoax by someone who had taken a dislike to Jay Paloma. A homophobe perhaps, or a purity nut with a personal campaign to rid the world of sleazy entertainers.

''And what did they say?'' he asked.

''It started with one word—'You.' Then the next had two words—'You are.' By the end of the week it said 'You are going to die.' ''

"A new letter each day for a week?" This was unpleasant. It was beginning to sound obsessional. Poison pens could be obsessional, of course, without ever meaning to carry out their threats. But there was always the risk that they might convince themselves, steep themselves in their own culture to the point when the unthinkable last step became the inevitable next one.

"Every week." The head drooped. "They got worse—about what he was going to do to me. Cut my throat. And—other things."

"I suppose you haven't brought them to show me?" Slider said, in the tone that expects the answer no.

"I didn't keep them. I destroyed them," Jay said, still looking at the floor.

"That's a pity," Slider said mildly.

"I couldn't bear to have them in the house. And I didn't want Val to see them. I didn't want to worry her."

"You didn't notice the postcode, I suppose?"

"All over the place," he said. "London postcodes, West End, Earl's Court, Clapham—Heathrow once. All different."

"What sort of paper? What sort of envelopes?"

"Just plain white notepaper. Basildon Bond or something. And white envelopes, the long sort, self-sealing. The name and address was printed—you know, like on a printer, on a label. And the words inside, like I said, cut out of newspaper and stuck on."

"Well, if you get another one," Slider said, "perhaps you'd keep it and bring it in to me."

"You don't believe me," Paloma concluded flatly.

"I didn't say that."

"But you're not going to do anything?"

"It's difficult to do anything without having an actual letter to work on." Paloma continued to look at him with a half-defiant, half-angry look—Princess Di at bay, badgered by a *Sun* reporter. "Look, I believe you're frightened," Slider went on, "and that's evidently what the letter merchant wants. It doesn't follow they'll actually do what they threaten." Paloma said nothing. "You haven't told me everything yet," Slider said after a moment. "Something else has happened to trigger your coming here." No answer. "I don't think it was an easy step for you to take."

"You're right," Paloma said, softening at this evidence of Slider's percipience. "I don't like police stations. I don't like police—most of them anyway. But Val said—she said you were different. So I thought—" Slider waited in insistent silence. Paloma swallowed and took the plunge. "A photograph. This morning. Cut out of a book or something. Of a dead body, all beaten up, with its throat cut." He reached out and stubbed out his cigarette with a violently trembling hand, and then quite suddenly turned corpse-white. Slider had been vomited over many times in the course of a long career. It taught you quick reactions. He shot out of his chair, grabbed the back of Jay's neck and pushed his head down between his legs. Jay moaned and dry-retched a couple of times, but didn't actually throw up.

"Breathe deeply. In, and out. In, and out," Slider commanded.

After a bit Jay sat up again, still pale but not quite so green.

"D'you want some water, or a cup of tea?" Slider asked.

"No. No, I'm all right, thanks. Thanks," he added more particularly, eyeing Slider consideringly. He lit another cigarette, and Slider sat down again, keeping a wary eye on him.

"I suppose," Slider said at last, "that you didn't keep this latest mail-shot either?"

Paloma shook his head. "I burned it. In the ashtray." He gestured tremblingly with his lighter. "I couldn't bear it hanging around."

Slider sighed. "It would have helped if you'd brought it to me."

"I didn't know I was going to come in," Paloma said. "I only decided at the last minute. And I felt—I don't know—that if I didn't get rid of it, it might, you know, happen."

Superstitious, Slider thought. Understandable, but not helpful. He said, "If anything else comes, any more of these letters, or anything you're suspicious of, bring it to me unopened, will you?" Paloma assented. "So, now, who do you think is doing this?"

"That's what I've come to you for."

"Quite. But you know more about your life than I possibly

can. It has to be someone you know, someone who knows you." He surveyed Paloma's face. "And in my experience, the victim usually has a pretty good idea who."

"But I don't," Paloma said, his chin quivering with suppressed tears. "I don't have the slightest idea."

"Who have you upset? Who has a grudge against you?"

"No one. I don't know." He drew a long, trembling drag on his cigarette. "I don't know anyone who would do such a horrible thing. The phone calls maybe, but not the letters. Not the—not the picture."

"If you're working at the Pomona, I should have thought you must have rubbed shoulders with plenty of people capable of that sort of thing," Slider said.

Unexpectedly, Jay flared. "Oh, now it comes out! Val was wrong—you're just like all the rest! You despise people like us. You think we deserve whatever happens to us!"

"I'm not in the despising business," Slider said. "Look here, son—" This was chronologically generous, but the blush of anger made him look more than ever like a beleaguered Princess Di, and who would not feel fatherly toward her? "—as long as what you do isn't against the law, it's none of my business. Sending threatening letters is. So why don't you tell me who's behind it?"

"I don't know!" Jay Paloma cried. "I tell you I don't know!" He ground out another cigarette with shaking hands. There were tears on his eyelashes. Slider studied him. He was plainly in trouble, but there was a limit to what sympathy could achieve.

"Well, that's that, then," Slider said, standing up.

Paloma looked up. "Aren't you going to do anything about it?"

"What would you like me to do?"

"Just stop it. Stop him sending things."

"Stop who?" Silence. "If you won't help me, I can't help you."

"I've told you everything I know," Paloma said sulkily. And then he was overcome with his grievance. "I should have known you wouldn't do anything. Who cares if something happens to someone like me? If I was a film star or a famous actor, if I was—" He named a couple of big stars who were prominent homosexual campaigners "—it'd be different then, wouldn't it?''

"I'd say the same to them as I've said to you," Slider said patiently. "Unless you give me something to go on—''

"I've *told* you about the phone calls and the letters. I want protection.''

Slider's head was aching. He grew just a touch short. "A policeman on guard at your door, perhaps?''

"You'd do it for them, all right," Paloma snapped. "But I'm just a nobody. What I do is sordid, but when they do the same thing it's smart and fashionable. Just because they're rich and famous. Some Hollywood bimbo gets her kit off and humps on screen, and she gets an Oscar. If I do it, it's pornography.''

"If anything else happens," Slider said, "come and tell me about it. And if you get any more of these letters bring them in." He walked to the door. "Give my regards to Busty.''

He left behind a seething discontent and a chip rapidly swelling to the size of a musical-comedy epaulette, but there was nothing else to do. When Paloma overcame his reticence enough to disclose who he was afraid of, a discreet visit of disencouragement could be made, and things could go on from there. He was already on the edge; another postal delivery would probably be enough to unseal his lips.

❖ T W O ❖

Cruel as the Grave

A smart rap at Slider's open door on Tuesday morning recalled him from the sea of reports through which he was swimming: the whole of Monday had been spent on paperwork without making any appreciable inroad into it. A young, slight, very pretty black woman stood in the doorway. She had short-bobbed, straightened hair held back by a black Alice-band of plaited cotton, small plain rings in her ears and a gold stud in her left nostril. She was wearing a green two-piece suit and an inquiring look.

"Scuse me, sir, Mr. Slider?"

"Yes?"

"I fink you were expecting me. Tony Hart?" The information failed to connect up across the spaces of Slider's brain, and he merely stared stupidly. She smiled a 150-watt smile. "Don't worry, guv, I'm used to it. It's always 'appening. You were expecting a bloke, right?"

"I—er—yes, I suppose so," Slider managed, remembering Nutty's information at last.

"Well, look at it this way," she said chattily, "you're fil-lin' two quotas at one go wiv me, right? They call me the P.C. D.C. Pity I ain't a lesbian, or I'd be well in demand."

Slider stood up and extended his hand. "I'm sorry, you took me by surprise. I'm very glad to have you here." They shook. Despite her look of slenderness she had a strong hand, and was as tall as Slider. "Is it Toni with an 'i'?"

"No, guv. Would you like it to be?"

"Short for Antonia?"

"No, actually it's just Tony on me birth stificate. I was named after me dad. Me mum's a bit of a weirdo. She called me sister Billy after her baby bruvver. Her older bruvver was called Bernard, so I s'pose me sister had a lucky escape."

Slider suppressed a smile, suspecting that this genial patter served the same purpose as a conjurer's. Major television drama series notwithstanding, women still had a toughish time surviving in the Department, and a joke or two and a bit of camouflage was probably the best defense. "I'd better take you through and introduce you to the firm," he said.

"Rightyoh," she said chirpily. "Is there much on at the moment?"

"Routine. Nothing very exciting. But we're always busy, and at the moment we're short-staffed."

"Yes, guv, I heard about D. S. Atherton. That was a bastard." Slider looked at her, surprised, and she gave him a sidelong look. "Yeah, all right, Lambeth is south of the river, but the newspapers come in once a week on the flyin' boat. How is he, sir, D. S. Atherton?"

"Improving slowly. It'll be a long job."

"And you, sir? You took a bit of a bashing an' all, didn't you?"

Dotty charm was all very well, but Slider was still the boss. "If I think I'm going to faint, I'll let you know," he said, and wheeled her into the C.I.D. room. He raised his voice over McLaren's whistle and Mackay's "Babe alert!" and said, "Listen, everybody! This is D. C. Hart come to join us temporarily." He went quickly through the names and then passed her over to Anderson's care before retreating to the haven of his own room. Why Anderson, he wondered mildly as he walked back. Because he was safe? Less sexist than Mackay and less sticky than McLaren? The least likely to tease the girl on her quota-bility quotient? No, on analysis, it was because he hoped Anderson would try and show her his latest photos. Slider had no doubt she would sort him out.

He could have sworn when he got back to his desk, the pile had grown. What Atherton would have called bullshit on an

Augean scale. He missed Atherton. How was he going to find a *mot juste* for every situation without him? By lunchtime, after a busy morning's shoveling, the heap was larger, word having gone around that he was back. And as if that wasn't enough, Irene had telephoned. She had been mightily peeved that no one had told her he was in hospital until he wasn't anymore, and was still harping on about it.

"After all these years, you've have thought *someone* would have let me know."

"I suppose they didn't know how things stood between us," Slider temporized. Lumps of headache were falling off the inside of his skull like rotting plaster.

"One of the sergeants at least might have thought to tell me," she grumbled. "I mean, I've known them for years. And I *know* Sergeant O'Flaherty has got my new telephone number, because I made a point of giving it to him just in case."

"In case of what?"

She sidestepped that one. "If I'd only known, I'd have visited you in hospital. It's not right. I mean, I am your—" She stopped herself, and her voice fell an octave or two. "I can't bear to think of you being hurt," she said, "and lying there in a hospital bed all alone."

They didn't usually allow sharing beds in hospitals, he thought; but he didn't say it. He felt rather tender about Irene. And of course Atherton would normally have coped with a tactful briefing of his future-ex-spouse, but Atherton too was out of commission. "Well," he said soothingly, "it doesn't matter now."

But it did matter to Irene, and nothing would satisfy her but to see him, so he arranged to meet her for lunch at the Crown and Sceptre. He telephoned the flat to tell Joanna he wouldn't be about—she sometimes dropped in to lunch with him if she was in the area—but the answering machine was on the blink and he wasn't sure the message had taken. So he told Nicholls as well, in case she phoned while he was out.

He was at the Crown before Irene, and stood at the bar opposite the door where she'd see him as soon as she came in. She wasn't really a pub person, having been brought up genteel, and still felt awkward about entering them alone. She arrived punctually, looking both familiar and strange. Familiar because—well, he had been married to her for most of his adult life. Strange because she was wearing a new suit in a style not normally her own, camel-colored with chocolate accessories and the sort of costume jewelry that you see in the windows of high street beauty salons: twirly overbright gold and enormous fake pearls, set around with tiny things that weren't diamonds; patently false and patently very expensive. To Slider the existence of such stuff had always been a mystery on a par with ceramic fruit. Obviously someone must buy it, but *why*?

Her resentment seemed to have dissipated. She smiled uncertainly.

"Hello."

"Hello. Go and sit down over there, and I'll bring the menu. What d'you want to drink?"

She was no fun in a pub—she always had orange juice. But today she said, almost naturally, "Oh, a gin and tonic, please." Gin and tonic, eh? Imbibing at lunchtime? This could spell bad news. He got her drink and took it with his pint over to the banquette where she sat deportmentally, knees and ankles together, hands folded over her handbag in her lap. She was ill at ease and trying womanfully to carry it off. He felt a tug of sympathy for her.

She looked up and smiled uncertainly as he put down her drink on the low table in front of her. "Thanks. You don't look as bad as I expected. I thought you'd be really traumatized after what that terrible man did to you. Thank God they got him."

Traumatized? That was a new word. New vocab, new drink, new outfit. She was not entirely—and he noted it with an odd small pang—his Irene anymore, not the same woman he had been married to for so long, the woman who'd read the *Sunday Times Magazine* adverts with wistful envy. She was wearing a different scent as well, heavy and gardenia-ish, where she'd always preferred the light and flowery before. What was that one the children used to buy her? *Je Reviens*, that was it. Kate used to call it Jerry Vines. "You look nice," he said, sitting down beside her. "New suit?"

She looked down at herself, as though she needed to check what she had on. "Yes," she said distractedly. "Marilyn made me buy it. I'm not sure it's me, really, but she said I ought to—"

Ought to move up a class, Slider suspected. Marilyn Cripps, her new Best Friend, seemed determined to do a pygmalion on her. It was the she-Cripps who had introduced Irene to Ernie Newman, the man with whom she had run away from the marital semi in Ruislip to a five-bedroom detached house in Chalfont. The Crippses lived in Dorney and had a son at Eton. Say no more.

"You look very nice," he said firmly.

"I didn't come here to talk about clothes," she replied, just a little reproachfully. He waited, and she went on at last, "It's getting more dangerous, isn't it? I mean, it seems no time since you were in hospital with those burns after that dreadful Austin case. And this time you were nearly killed. And Atherton—"

"Yes, I know."

"I suppose he is going to be all right, isn't he?"

"I hope so."

She bit her lip. "I worry about you all the time, you know. Madmen with knives, drug addicts, guns. I thought I could stop when I—when we split up. But it doesn't seem to make any difference. I still worry."

"You shouldn't." He tried to say it kindly, not snubbingly—though it would probably be kinder in the long run to snub. He began to see where this might be leading. "You've got Ernie to think about now."

She looked at him doubtfully, wondering if he was being ironic. It was hard not to be, about Ernie. "I don't need to worry about him," she said.

He didn't know how to take that. After a silence he said, "How are the kids?"

"All right. Matthew was really upset when he knew you were hurt. He saw it in the paper—one of the boys at school showed him before I had a chance to talk to him about it. He was more worried than me, even. He thought you were going to die."

That hurt. "He watches too much television." He said it

lightly, but he meant it. "Too many cop shows."

"It's hard to stop him." She sighed. "He's got a television in his bedroom now. Ernie bought it for him."

"You shouldn't have let him. You know I don't approve of kids having their own TVs."

"I know. I don't either, really. It means I can't stop him watching unsuitable programs—violent ones, that give him bad dreams. But Ernie wanted to buy it for him, and Matthew wanted it, and what could I do? I was stuck in the middle."

Slider saw the scenario quite clearly: Ernie wanted to bribe Matthew to like him—and was probably also quite keen to get the children to stay in their own rooms and not clutter up his lounge; and Matthew was being opportunist after the manner of children throughout the realms of time and space. And Irene—Irene wanted to please everyone. Well, that was a new Irene, too. She must be feeling very unsure of herself if she was not insisting on having her own way. He felt a huge and unwelcome surge of pity for her, and thrust it away. "I'll have a word with him, if you like."

"Ernie?" she said in alarm.

"No, Matthew."

She looked at him hesitantly, opened and closed her mouth, and then took the plunge. "He wants to go home. Matthew, I mean. He doesn't take to Ernie. And he doesn't like the house. It's all so strange to him. He keeps asking me, why can't you and Dad get together again?" She swallowed. "He says, you haven't sold the house yet, why can't we just all go home?" Slider could find nothing to say, and into his unready silence Irene said in a small voice, "I've wondered the same thing myself, sometimes."

Slider didn't want to hear this. It was too inexpressibly painful. He saw quite clearly that she felt lost, out of her place, living in Ernie's home, which was not her own, according to his style and manners, which were not what she was used to. The familiar sight of Slider rekindled whatever affection she had once had for him, and blotted out the memory of his inadequacies as a husband, the years of unhappiness she had suffered as a copper's neglected wife. With the slightest encouragement she would ask if they couldn't "try again"; and standing on the brink of that question, he realized with a new clarity that he didn't want to go back. Definitely. Even if he and Joanna didn't make it, his marriage to Irene was definitely over.

But Irene didn't know about Joanna, of course, and this was not the time to tell her, so he changed the subject with a desperate lunge. "How's Kate?" he asked, as if there had been no implied question in her last words.

She reassembled herself with an effort, and said brightly, "Oh, you know Kate. She's agitating for piano lessons now, because her new friend at school, Flora, has them."

"Fancy naming a child after margarine, poor kid," Slider said to amuse her.

She wasn't. "It was one of the names we considered for Kate, if you remember."

Actually, it was she who had considered. He'd expected another boy, for some reason, and had got as far as Michael and no further. When the baby turned out to be a girl, he went blank. Irene had kindly suggested Michaela and he'd roared with laughter and she'd got into a huff, and he'd placated her by saying she should choose, she was better with names than him, and she'd produced a list with Kate at the top, which he'd grasped enthusiastically for fear of what might be lurking further down.

"I always wish I'd learned the piano," he said, to distract her. "It'd be nice for her to learn. I seem to remember seeing a piano in Ernie's lounge, so there'd be no problem about an instrument, would there?"

"But you know what would happen," Irene said crossly. "She'd be all enthusiasm for a week, then she'd slack off, and I'd be the one who'd have to make her practice, and it would be nothing but row, row, row. It was the same with those gerbils. I always ended up cleaning them out—and then you talked about getting a cat or a dog!"

"I only—"

"You got the children all excited about it, without thinking that it would be me who ended up with the responsibility, because you just wouldn't be there when there was a row about it. And then it was down to me to tell them they couldn't have one. I always ended up with the dirty jobs."

Ah, this was better, this was more like it. Slider almost

smiled at her, seeing the steel return to her face, so much easier to bear than wistfulness; but also oddly poignant, because it meant she was *his* Irene again, the disapproving Irene he knew and—well, almost—loved. Best to keep her annoyed, he thought. "You don't have to clean out a piano," he said. "I can't see what harm there'd be in—"

The door opened, and Joanna came in. Perhaps it was because he was in the middle of a familiar-feeling argument with Irene; perhaps it was simply long habit—fourteen years of faithful marriage and two of bowel-churning deception. Perhaps it was Fate sending down a googly. At all events, he panicked.

"Ah, there you are," Joanna said, heading straight for him. "They said I'd find you here."

Nicholls, you die for this, he thought, stuttering to his feet. "Oh, hello, Joanna. Er, this is Irene. Irene, this is Joanna, a friend of Jim Atherton's."

Joanna's smile solidified, and he saw her nostrils flare. Irene said, "How do you do?" nicely, and Joanna repeated her words and even her intonation, while her mind plainly worked furiously behind her mask. Slider's head felt as concrete as her expression; he couldn't think, he couldn't cope. He looked from Joanna, in white jeans, a Greek cotton tunic and sandals, her rough hair held off her face with a pair of sunglasses, to Irene, neat and polished in a suit with matching accessories and a proprietorial smile, and wanted to be anywhere but here, the further away the better.

It was Joanna who spoke at last—it seemed like several suspicious hours later, but it must have been almost instantly, because Irene was still looking social and pleasant. "Yes, they told me you'd be here and that you could tell me the latest on Jim. How is he?"

"Pretty much the same. I saw him yesterday. They say he's improving slowly."

"Is he allowed visitors yet?"

"I'm not sure. He's asleep most of the time, but if you telephoned the hospital I'm sure they'd let you know. Have you got the number?"

He thought he was doing pretty well but she shot him a look of fierce impatience and said, "Yes, of course. Well, I won't interrupt your lunch any longer. I was just passing. Goodbye,'' to Irene, and with a whip-flick glance at Slider, ''it was nice neeting you.''

When she was gone, Irene said, ''Is that Atherton's latest girlfriend? She doesn't seem his usual type—not glamorous enough. And she's a bit old for him, isn't she?'' She chattered on for a bit, until she realized he was too quiet, and said, ''Are you all right? You look a bit pale.''

''A bit of a headache, that's all,'' he said.

She was all concern. ''Do you want to go? Shall we forget lunch? You must be careful, after a crack on the head like that. Look, shall I get you a taxi to take you home? Where are you staying at the moment, anyway?''

That was one question to head her away from. He pulled himself together. ''No, no, I'm fine. Let's have a look at the menu. They do quite good grub here. No, really, I'm all right. I wouldn't drag you all this way and not give you lunch.''

He couldn't wait to get back to the shop and talk to Nicholls; but Nicholls wasn't there. Paxman was on duty, a broad, solid man with a congested face and slow eyes, whose tight curly hair gave him more than a passing resemblance to a Hereford bull.

''Oh, hello,'' he said. ''Did your friend find you?''

''Yes, thank you,'' Slider said with tight irony. ''Where the hell is Nicholls?''

''He's gone to court. He left a message where you were, if your friend asked.'' Paxman always referred to Joanna as ''your friend.'' He disapproved of extracurricular activities, but there was no malice or guile in his face. Plainly he thought he had done what was required. Slider thanked him and went away with an inward whimper. Some days were like this, with a high likelihood of precipitation, dark brown variety; and it wasn't over yet.

Joanna's car was there when he got home, but she had only just arrived: it was still warm and ticking. Her bag and fiddle were dumped on the hall floor, and she was in the kitchen, still in her coat, reading her mail while waiting for the kettle to boil. Oedipus was on tiptoe, his tail straight up, winding himself back and forth around her lower legs. When Slider appeared he started toward him, but got sidetracked by the kitchen table, whose legs he caressed in lieu. He had settled in very well, but they still didn't dare let him out, for fear that he'd try to find his way back to Atherton's flat across ten miles of London traffic. It meant a good deal of dirt-tray cleaning-out, of course, but they shared the burden between them. Slider was a New Man.

Joanna turned and raised an eyebrow at him. Enigmatic, he thought. Could go either way. The fact that she had fallen in with his deception at the pub had puzzled him all day. Did it mean she loved him so much she would spare him any embarrassment, even at the cost of her own dignity; or that she had given up on him and cared so little it was no longer important?

"Are you going to throw plates?" he asked meekly.

"Nah. Too expensive."

She was not going to be angry. A tidal surge of relief. "I'm sorry," he said abjectly. "It was so stupid. I just don't know what came over me. I panicked, I think." She was regarding him with suppressed humor; a sort of exasperated, what-am-I-going-to-do-about-you expression. He could never prejudge what would tickle her sense of the ridiculous. It made life interesting, at least. "I'm really sorry," he said again for good measure.

"Well, it was me who told you not to tell her in the first place," she said. "I suppose I've only got myself to blame. Though I didn't expect you to go on denying me forever. And so automatically, the moment I appeared—like Simon Peter on speed." And then she laughed. "Oh, your face, though, when I came up and spoke to you!"

He didn't think it was terribly funny, though he managed a polite smile. "Well at least you and Irene have met now. It gets the first time over with."

"What d'you mean, first time?" she said suspiciously.

"Well, you're bound to have to get to know each other in the long run. It would be nice if you could be friends—"

"Oh my God, no!" she shuddered. "Don't say that. There's something very weird about men who want to get their wives and their mistresses together."

"You've known many such?" he asked coolly.

"By association. In the nature of things, my female friends have mostly been musicians. And equally in the nature of things, female musicians tend to have to go out with married men, because that's all there is. All that'll put up with their lifestyle, anyway. Inevitably comes the day when the bloke arranges accidentally-on-purpose for the completely unexpected, surprise-surprise, what-else-could-I-do meeting between the two women he's poking. And then the self-satisfied dingbat stands back and gets some creepy thrill out of seeing them talking to each other."

"It wasn't my idea," he said, hurt.

She put an arm around his neck and kissed him casually. "I know. I absolve you of malice aforethought. You're a gent, really. Just don't ever talk about Irene and me becoming friends." She released him and turned to reach for the teapot as the kettle switched off. With her back to him she said, "And if there is another accidental meeting, don't deny me again, will you?"

That was the important bit, the bit she couldn't look at him for. "Definitely not," he said. "Scout's honor." He watched her making tea, knowing there was more to come.

"I was jealous," she said at last. "And I don't like myself when I feel like that."

"I suppose it's quite flattering really," he said lightly. "To think you love me that much."

She gave him a quick glance. "It didn't feel much like love. I wanted to kill her. And then, when she was mashed to a pulp, to kill you."

"Me?"

"For having been married to her. It drives me crazy that whatever happens in the future, I can't change that. She's had you for all those years, and I can't wipe that out, run the film back and erase it. It's a horrible thing to feel that sort of possessive fury. It makes you understand axe murderers. Only obliterating you would have given me relief. Of course, *I* wouldn't do anything about it, but that only makes it worse, because I know I wouldn't, and that just adds frustration to all the other seething acids."

She was serious, and he had to be careful not to say the

wrong thing and offend her. But he couldn't help feeling all the same that it *was* flattering. It might not have felt much like love to her, but he was glad to know, after some of the things that had happened, that she cared that much about him, when he had sometimes wondered whether she couldn't take him or leave him. He touched her on the shoulder, and she turned into his arms. He held her, and felt her relax against him. Then at last he kissed the top of her head, and put his lips against her ear, and murmured tenderly, "I want to obliterate you, too."

It was not until much later, when they were in bed together, that she brought the subject up again. "What was she doing there, anyway? Irene."

"She wanted to see me, to check I was in one piece. She was upset that no one had told her I was in hospital."

"So you asked her to lunch?"

"She more or less asked herself."

After a silence, Joanna said, "What did she really want to see you about?"

"Why should there be another reason?"

"I'll put it another way: what did she really want to see you about?"

"I think she wants us to get back together," he admitted. There was no way around that.

"Oh," she said.

He waited for more, and then said, "She feels guilty and uncomfortable, and the children are unsettled, and since she knows the house hasn't been sold, she thinks it would all be so much easier if we just let bygones be bygones and slid back into the furrow."

"Rut."

"That's what I told her."

"I bet you didn't. I know you, Bill Slider. I bet you avoided the whole issue."

"It wasn't really an issue. She didn't ask outright, only hinted at it. I didn't take up the hint, just changed the subject. So that's that. She'll know it's not on."

"She won't. Women will always believe what they want unless you tell them otherwise in words of one syllable. Have you never heard of being cruel to be kind?"

"I feel sorry for her. And guilty. She thinks the whole breakup is her fault."

"You aren't thinking of it?" she asked warily out of the dark. "Going back to her?"

"Not in these trousers."

"Are you sure?"

He thought honesty might reassure her. "It was realizing that she wanted us to get back together that finally convinced me I could never do it."

"Finally? So you had been considering it?"

"Well, obviously it had crossed my mind on the odd occasion."

"Which occasion?"

"When you're being unreasonable and cruel. When you're away and I think of you frolicking in seaside towns with abandoned musicians."

"I'm never unreasonable."

"I notice you don't say you never frolic," he said suspiciously.

"I have to keep some mystery. How else can I allure you?"

"Allure isn't a verb," he objected.

He felt her smile against his neck. "I miss Atherton, don't you?"

"Of course."

"He is going to get better?" she asked like a child wanting reassurance. Are there bears under the bed? But Atherton was real. The best he could manage was, "It'll be a long job."

There was a long silence. He thought she had gone to sleep, but then she said, "Did Irene recognize me?"

"Recognize you?" He searched the files. "Oh, you mean from that concert?"

"You practically introduced me then."

"No, I'm sure she didn't." He reran Irene's words and expressions. "She said you weren't Atherton's usual type. Not glamorous enough."

"Cheeky mare," Joanna said sleepily. A little while later she was asleep. Slider lay wakeful for some time, his mind jumpy with the unaccustomed stimulation of being back to work. He slept at last, but fell into a nightmare in which he was stalked through the White City Estate by a sweating, knife-wielding Gilbert. If only he could get back to the station he'd be safe, but the blocks of flats proliferated all around him, identical, confusing, every door and corner a possible ambush point, and he couldn't find his way out.

❖ THREE ❖

A Fit of Peaks

The shout came on Wednesday, at a time when Slider, who wasn't going in early, was still in bed.

"A nice murder for you," said Nicholls, who was on earlies. He pronounced it *murr-durr*.

It was a dead body in a flat on the White City Estate. Listening to Nicholls' sealskin-soft Atlantic coast accent, Slider was reminded that the Anne-Marie Austin case had begun just this way, with all its consequences to his private life. Only then, of course, it had been Irene asleep beside him, and she hadn't woken, as Joanna just had, sitting up to look at the clock.

But the flat in question was Busty Parnell's, and the dead body was Jay Paloma's. Busty had arrived home from spending the night away to find the front door open, the keeper of the Yale lock hanging loose from one screw; and inside, Jay Paloma dead in a welter of blood.

Slider's guilt chip had already been overworked with regard to Atherton, and now threatened to go into overload. The poor little bastard knew what he was talking about after all. He had been frightened with a cause. Slider should have done something: his guilt nagged him as he listened to Nicholls with another part of his brain. But what could he have done? Blimey, it had happened so quickly, he could hardly have got him an armed guard for his door even had he wanted to. In the time available, there was nothing he could have done, nothing the system would have let him do, to prevent this. But it didn't change the fact that Paloma had come to tell him he was afraid for his life, and now he was dead. It was breast-beating time, whichever way you sliced it.

"Are you there, Bill?" Nicholls asked into the silence.

"Oh—yes—I was just thinking. I saw him on Monday, you know. The victim. He knew it was coming."

"Chrise, no. That's a bugger," Nicholls commiserated. "And you with your overactive glands."

"My what?"

"Your compulsion to be responsible for everyone's troubles. Global Mammy Syndrome. Ah well," Nicholls comforted him, "this'll keep you busy for a while. Nothing like being run off your feet for keeping your mind off things."

"Thanks," said Slider shortly.

"What is it?" Joanna asked as he put the phone down.

"A corpus," Slider said, pushing Oedipus off his legs and getting out of bed. He turned back to kiss her. "I shan't be back before you go to work. Have a good day."

"You remember I'm on at the Festival Hall tonight?"

"So you are. Well, I'll see you when I see you, then."

"Good luck," she called as he headed for the bathroom.

By the time Slider got there, Busty had been taken away in hysterics, with W.P.C. Asher to lean on, which was one comfort. Hollis was waiting for him.

"I suppose he is dead?" Slider asked, without hope.

"In spades," Hollis said. "Hart's inside."

The flats on the White City Estate had all now been modernized to within an inch of their lives, with double glazing, central heating and solid wood doors—the glass panels in the originals having been a gift for felons. But of course no one locks their door on the mortice when they are at home, and judging by the size and singularity of the footmark on the door, the murderer had been a very large and powerful man, strong enough to kick the door open at the first blow.

The flat seemed tidy and clean. In the kitchen everything was put away, except for two coffee mugs, a saucepan and a plate with a knife and fork lying on it, which were sitting in the sink. Slider examined the evidence. Scrambled eggs, he concluded. On toast. The bathroom was likewise tidy with hand towels neatly folded and bath towels stretched to dry along the shower rail. The bedrooms were tidy with the duvets straightened on the beds. He could tell which was Busty's by the collection of cosmetics spread out on the dressing table, which was larger than the collection in Jay's room; and by the brown-and-red silk Noël Coward dressing gown flung across his bed and the leather mules on the floor by its hem.

Only in the sitting room did disorder reign, and even there only in one small area. The television was on with the sound turned low. On screen a bunch of people with demented expressions were talking nonstop over the top of one another, mugging at the camera, and prancing about a set done out with huge cutouts in primary, not to say dayglo, colors. Someone at TV headquarters had evidently decided that only the brain-damaged and the under-fives watched television at that time of day, and for all Slider knew they could be right.

An armchair near the television had been turned over backward, and Jay Paloma lay sprawled half out of it, cruelly illuminated by the bright sunshine from the window. His head had been beaten to crunchy red-and-yellow breakfast cereal. He was wearing a chambray shirt, jeans and moccasin slippers. The front of the shirt was liberally soaked in blood, which was not surprising because his face had been stoved in by a mighty blow across the bridge of the nose. There were no apparent other injuries, and his clothing was not torn or disordered, his shirt still tucked into his trousers and his slippers still on his feet.

Hart, at Slider's side, turned her head away quickly, swallowing with a clicking sound.

"Feeling sick?" Slider asked. She made an affirmative sound. "Is this your first time?"

"No, sir, I've felt sick before."

He gave her points for trying. "First murder?"

"Not the first, but the messiest," she said.

"You never get used to it," he told her from the depth of his own present misery. "You just have to learn to keep your stomach detached from your eyes. Now, using your eyes, what do you think happened here?"

She looked around, grateful to have her attention taken from the corpse. "He doesn't seem to have put up much of a fight. None of the furniture's out of place, apart from the one chair." There was another armchair, placed opposite the first, both of them facing the television on a slant, and between the two, but set back so that only the end of it was within reach, was a coffee table on which stood a whiskey bottle—White Horse, almost empty—and an empty glass, an ashtray with five cigarette ends in it, and an untidy pile of papers and magazines. Back against the wall was an elderly sofa of the armless couch type, covered with what was nowadays known as a "throw" in a vaguely Polynesian pattern of mutually hostile colors—not so much a throw as a throw-up, Slider thought. Against the wall nearest the door was a large and ugly sideboard in pale highly varnished oak with bulbous legs, dating, judging by its style, from the nineteen-fifties. On it was a collection of framed photographs, mostly black and white, of Busty and Jay in their separate high moments: Jay with Jeremy Haviland in a dinner suit; Busty with a celebrity so blurred it could have been David Nixon or Richard Nixon for all Slider knew; Busty in a lineup of Windmill girls; Jay in an Arran sweater against a wild sea from a knitwear catalogue—and so on. Some of the frames were as old as the photos. Slider touched one gently and its wonky foot slithered on the highly polished surface and collapsed.

"If anyone had bumped against that, the pictures would have fallen over," Hart said.

"So?" Slider encouraged.

"So no fight. The villain must have took him by surprise. Crept up on him and whacked him from behind."

"But the villain kicked the door in. Wouldn't you think he'd have heard that?"

"He might've been asleep. People do drift off in front of the telly."

Slider grunted noncommittally. "Does anything strike you as odd about that ashtray?" he asked her. She looked, bent close to peer, and shook her head. "There are five dog ends in it," he said, "but no ash. How did he manage that?"

"He didn't. Look here," Hollis said. Between the coffee table and the couch there were traces of cigarette ash on the carpet, and an area where it had apparently been rubbed in, with a hand or a foot. "And there's whiskey been spilled here too," he added, sniffing. It was a damp patch which smelled strongly. "Chummy's had the table over."

"Hang about, what's that?" Hart said. It was another glass, on the floor beside the other armchair, but standing upright, as though it had been placed there by someone sitting in the chair. "Maybe the whiskey come from this glass."

"But you can see table's been knocked over," Hollis said impatiently. "Look at the impressions in the carpet where it stood before. It wasn't put back in exactly the same spot."

Hart said, "The table could have been knocked over any time. It didn't have to be the murderer."

"True," Slider said. "But it strikes me that everything is very neat and tidy here. Clean, dusted and polished. Would such a houseproud person knock the table over and then just rub the ash into the carpet? Wouldn't he clean it up properly?"

"All right," Hart conceded, "but if it was the murderer done it, why would he pick everything up again, put the dimps back in the ashtray and all that?"

"No offers," Hollis said with a shrug.

"Well," Slider went on at last, "there's a few things to think about, anyway. Bag up the whiskey bottle and the glasses. And we'll take the ashtray and contents as well."

Certainly, Slider thought, further pondering the room, Jay Paloma was killed there, in that spot, and probably in that chair. Apart from no signs of a struggle, there were no blood-marks anywhere else. No reeling about locked in mortal combat à la Reichenbach Falls. There was blood on the chair, and on the carpet around it, some smears on the end of the coffee table, and a few specks on the TV screen. But why had Paloma sat there and let himself be killed? Asleep, maybe—but wouldn't the kicking in have stirred him, wouldn't he at least have been struggling to his feet?

The worse possibility was trying to suggest itself to him. If Paloma had been pursued to the edge of breaking by a campaign of poison pen letters, it might have bred in him such a conviction of hopelessness that he had simply given up. Believing there was no escape, he had just been killing time here, waiting for the inevitable moment when he would hear the executioner's approaching footsteps. To such a mentality, the crash of the door being kicked in would be almost welcome, signaling an end to the hideous anticipation.

He didn't want to think like that. His global-mammy circuits couldn't take it. Perhaps Paloma had been drunk, and dead to the world. That might do it. Or doped. Leave that, have a wonder about motive, for light relief. It was pretty obviously not robbery. Slider wished the murderer had even made a pretense of ransacking the place. Whoever had killed Jay Paloma had gone straight in and come straight out again—apart from the brief pause to put the coffee table straight. They knew what they wanted all right, and it wasn't loose change or a video recorder.

Busty was waiting for him in one of the interview rooms, W.P.C. Asher in attendance, a cup of tea steaming on the table in front of her. She was dressed in a smart coat with an imitation lucca-lamb collar, which was hanging open over a pink twin-set and a regulation barmaid's black straight skirt. The eponymous udders were discreetly corseted now, but still peaks of splendor; in the first fine braless rapture of their acquaintance, the sight of Busty stepping out down Wardour Street had always set Slider to thinking about Barnes Wallis.

She was not a bad-looking woman still, even in the harsh strip-lighting of an interview room. Asher had escorted her to the ladies where she had had a wash to remove her ruined makeup, and without it she looked surprisingly young, despite her recent bout of hysterical weeping. She was calm now, but looked up at Slider with swollen, brimming eyes and pale and shaking cheeks.

"Busty, I'm so sorry," he said. She nodded, keeping her lips closed. "I have to ask you some questions. You understand?"

She nodded again, and then unlocked enough to say, "You do your job. I want you to get the bastard that did this to my poor—" She lost it a moment. "I want you to get the bastard, and then I want you to let me have five minutes alone with him."

''You've no idea, I suppose, who it might be? Who hated him that much?''

''No,'' she said. ''He was a good, kind soul. He never hurt anyone in his life. He looked after me, Mr. Slider. He was like my big brother. It was him got me the barmaid job, because he didn't like me stripping and such at my age. I haven't turned a trick since we started sharing again, d'you know that? He said to me, Val, he said, you'll never have to do that again as long as I live. *That*'s the sort of person he was. Always thinking of others.''

''I'm sorry,'' Slider said again. He was going to be sorrier when he had to tell her about the poison pen letters, but that was for later. ''Tell me what you know. You'd been away for the night, you said?''

Busty had been visiting her sister who lived in Harlesden. She had set off at about half past eleven on Tuesday morning, taking an overnight bag with her, intending to return at about the same time the next day. ''It was my day off. I wasn't due on again at the pub until this evening. And my sister's not been too clever lately—you know, women's stuff,'' she explained delicately, ''so I went over to give her a bit of a break, let her have a day in bed and an evening out.''

''I didn't know you had a sister.''

''Why should you?'' Busty shrugged. ''We were close when we were kids, but then we weren't all that much for a long time. Actually, I think when I first knew you was when we weren't talking. Well, Mum and Dad didn't approve of my way of life, and Shirley sided with them. It's only since Dad died that we've sort of started liking each other again. She married a real bastard, so I suppose it made her realize there wasn't much to choose between us.''

''Come again?''

She gave him a wan smile. ''Between her and me. Doing it for one man you don't like isn't much different from doing it for several men you don't like.''

''I see. So, you came back from your sister's early. What happened to change your plan?''

''The bastard came back. Her Trevor. He's a lorry driver. He wasn't due back till this afternoon, but he fiddled his tacho and cut his breaks to get through early, and there he was.

Lucky I'm a light sleeper, I heard him parking his lorry outside, so it give me a chance to get out of bed, grab me stuff
and lock meself in the bathroom while I got dressed. Only if
Trevor had come upstairs and found me asleep in his bed—''
She shrugged eloquently.

"In his bed?"

"Shirley's not got a spare room. I was sleeping in with
her.''

"What time was that, when he got home?"

"It must've been about six-ish, a bit before. Anyway, by
the time I get downstairs, Shirl's got the tea on the go, and
Trevor's mellowed out enough to let me phone for me taxi,
otherwise I'd've been stuck. I mean, you try finding a phone
box that works in Harlesden.''

"And you got home about half past six?" Slider said,
checking his notes. The shout was timed at six thirty-five.

"I s'pose so. About then," she said, the animation draining
from her face. "I didn't realize at first. The door looked as
if it was shut. It was only when I went to put my key in the
lock that I felt it move, and then I realized it was only pushed
to. I went in, and—'' She stopped, shutting her mouth hard.

"Yes," Slider said helpfully. "I'm sorry, but I have to take
you through it. Did you expect Jay to be home?"

"Well, yes—at least, he hadn't said he wouldn't. Normally
he'd be asleep at that time, with working late and everything.
Well, he doesn't get back from the club till around four, so
he never usually got up till half-twelve-ish. The only reason
he wouldn't be home would be if he went somewhere with
someone, straight from the club—like, a pickup, you know.
But he hadn't been doing that lately. He'd hardly been out at
all, not socially, and he hadn't had any casuals in months.''

"So you thought he was at home and asleep? Did you call
out to him?"

"No. I'm always quiet if I'm up early, not to wake him.''

"So what did you do next?"

"Well, I heard the telly was on, so I went in to the front
room to see. And there he was.''

"You didn't touch anything or move anything?"

"No. I didn't really go in the room. I could see straight
away, from the door, that he was—that he must be—'' She

shook her head. "I just went straight and dialed 999."

"From your telephone? Which is where?"

"In the hall. Opposite the front door. And then I just stayed by the telephone until the police come. I didn't want to go back in there. I was in a state of shock. I didn't even *cry*. It wasn't until they came and started talking to me that I broke down." She took out a handkerchief and blew briskly.

Slider waited for her. "Would you like some more tea?" Busty made a sound of assent through her hanky, and he looked at Asher, who nodded and slipped out. "Did he often watch television when he got back from the club?"

"Well, no," she said thoughtfully, "I've never actually knew him to do that. But I suppose if he was upset or something and couldn't sleep he might have."

"And the whisky? Was it his habit to have a nightcap before he went to bed?"

"I wouldn't say habit," she said carefully, "but he has done on occasions. Whisky is his drink, but he doesn't have it any special time. I've known him pop down the pub lunchtime and have one, or at home in the afternoon, if there's a good film on. He liked all them old black and white ones, especially if they were about the war. Richard Attenborough and that. Or with his supper, before he went to work. He'd have a pie or a bit of cheese or something, and a Scotch with that."

"When you last saw him—when was that, exactly?"

"When I left for my sister's yesterday. He got up to see me off. He came out in his dressing gown and made us a cup of coffee and sat with me and drank it while I did my makeup."

"And how did he seem? Was he in his normal spirits?"

"Yes." She hesitated. "Well, he's not been all that bright recently. A bit quiet and off it."

"Did he give you any reason?"

"He was worried about something." She hesitated again. "I think it had to do with his friend."

"What friend is that?"

"His gentleman friend," she said rather primly.

"Name?"

"He never told me. He always just called him his friend.

All I know is, he was very rich. Someone important and famous—that's why Maurice was extra discreet.''

"Maurice?"

"That's his real name, Jay's—Maurice McElhinney. Didn't you know? Well, I suppose it's only me that calls him that now. His parents were Irish—from Dublin. I think they were quite well off and that. Anyway, they wanted him to be a lawyer or a doctor or something, and they were really disappointed when all he wanted to do was be a dancer. He persuaded them to let him go to stage school, but when it came out that he was bent as well—well, all he could do was leave home and come to London. I mean, in those days it was hard enough being One Of Them over here, let alone in bleeding Dublin with Catholic parents and everything. And he's never went back. I don't think he's ever even written to them. He said to me only last week, I was all the family he had.'' She began to cry again. Slider left her alone until Asher came in with the tea, and then he gave her handkerchiefs and jollied her along until she was back in control.

"So tell me what you know about this friend of his,'' Slider resumed. "Have you any idea who it was? Any clues at all—where he lived or what he did for a living or anything like that?''

She shook her head. "Usually he talked about his friends a bit to me—not the intimate stuff, just that he'd been to see them and where they'd gone and what they'd done. But this one was different. All I gathered was, if it had got out about Maurice, it could have caused this man trouble.''

"Was Jay—Maurice—in love with him?''

"Oh, I don't think so,'' she said consideringly. "He was generous, this man—gave Maurice presents and money. It was because of that I was able to give up turning tricks—though that was a lot easier on the feet than barmaiding, I can tell you!''

"How long had he known him?''

"About a year.''

"And relations were normally smooth between them?''

"Oh, I think so—except I think the secrecy got on Maurice's nerves a bit. But just recently—well, the last few weeks, I suppose—he hasn't been his usual self. Always very cheerful, he was, and sort of—brisk. Always cleaning the house, singing to himself, nagging me about my appearance. Try this lipstick, Val; have your hair cut, Val; get yourself a new dress, Val. All good-natured, you know. He wanted me to make the most of myself. But lately there hasn't been much of that. He's been sort of quiet and—off it. And then yesterday morning, while he was sitting fiddling with my makeup, I said to him, what's up, Mo darling, you look as if you've got the blues, and he said, oh, he said, my friend and I had a bit of a disagreement yesterday, that's all.''

"He'd been to see him, then, on Monday?"

"Monday lunchtime. He was spending the afternoon with him, but I'd gone to work before he got back. That's why he got up, I suppose, to see me off.'' Her eyes filled. "To say goodbye. If only I'd known. If only we'd both known.''

"Did he say what the quarrel was about?"

"He didn't say quarrel, he said disagreement. He didn't say what about, but they had argued before, so I suppose it was about the same thing. I gather his friend has been objecting to Maurice working at the Pomona.''

That made sense to Slider. "Well, it isn't exactly Rules, is it?''

"Isn't what, pardon?"

Slider waved that away. "Did you know that Jay had been receiving threatening letters?''

"No, I didn't.'' She scanned his face keenly, and then let out her breath in a slow hiss. "So that was it! I knew he'd been keeping something from me. No, I didn't know that, but I knew there was something wrong. I thought at first it was one of those summer colds, you know, that sort of hang on and never come out properly. But no wonder, with that hanging over him, poor lamb! Why didn't he tell me?''

"He didn't want to worry you."

"So you knew about it? He reported it to you, did he?"

"He came to see me on Monday afternoon. Unfortunately, he hadn't kept any of the letters, so there wasn't much I could do. And I had the feeling he was hiding something. I thought he knew who was doing it, but wasn't willing to tell me. I told him to come back if anything else happened.''

She looked at him, her eyes widening. "Do you think—

this friend of Maurice's—do you think he killed him?''

''It's possible, at any rate, that whoever sent him the poison pen letters may have killed him.''

''You knew about the letters,'' she said. ''You could have saved him.''

''I don't know how,'' Slider said abjectly. ''Busty, I'm sorry, believe me. I feel terrible about it. But what could I have done? I had nothing to go on, and short of posting a bodyguard on him—''

But she turned her face away, grieved, and rocked herself. ''If only he'd told me, I'd never have left him. I'd have stayed with him every minute.'' She wiped at her nose and eyes, but they went on leaking, like a slow bleed. She turned back to Slider. ''It's funny, isn't it? He was always so careful—went everywhere by taxi, made me go everywhere by taxi, 'cause he said public transport wasn't safe, especially late at night, and with the kind of places we worked. And always a proper taxi, never a minicab, because he said you never knew who you'd get. There was that time, d'you remember, when I was working at the Nitey Nite Club, what was it, back in 'seventy-eight, when Sandra Hodson got abducted by a minicab driver? D'you remember her? She did that act with the python. Madame Ranee she called herself.''

''Yes, I remember.''

''And she got driven out into the sticks and raped and dumped naked somewhere—''

''Beaconsfield.''

''That's it. Miles out in the country. And poor Sange always hated fields and cows and that. Wouldn't even walk through St. James's Park if she could help it. So ever since then I've never had anything but a proper black cab, and Maurice was the same. That careful, he was. And then they come and get him in his own home—sitting in his own front room, Mr. Slider, watching his own telly. It's not fair. It's—'' She struggled for a word. ''It's like *cheating*.''

''Yes,'' said Slider. ''I know.''

''And I'll tell you another thing,'' she said, flame-eyed with tears and outrage now. ''Just Sunday, he was talking about chucking the whole thing up. He said he was fed up of it, the whole setup, the club, show business, working all night and sleeping in the day, being treated like dirt, being slobbered over by drunks. And he said to me Sunday, he said, Val, he said, let's chuck it up and get out of London while we've still got a bit of life in front of us. Well, he'd got this plan, you see, for us to retire and get a place in the country, in Ireland, and do bed and breakfast for holiday-makers. He'd been saving up ages to buy a little place. It was his dream, but now he said, Val, let's really do it." The animation faded. "He meant it an' all. It's not fair. He deserved a bit of luck, poor Maurice."

He'd had his bit of luck, Slider reflected. It's just that it wasn't good.

❖ FOUR ❖

Fissure of Men

Busty's next-door neighbor was torn between the obligatory reluctance to "get involved," and the temptation of being a star, for if she became a witness for the police, she might get herself on the telly. She havered and wavered, but finally the glamour of potential fame overcame her to the point of inviting Hart in for a cup of tea—a courtesy Hart would have dispensed with. The flat smelled of urine, babies and chip fat. Why didn't humans have those useful nostrils that closed flat, Hart wondered. When her hostess left the room to put on the kettle, Hart sneaked her Amarige out of her handbag and dabbed a bit on her upper lip for protection.

Charmian, was the woman's name, God only knew why. Charmian Hogg. She sat on the sofa opposite Hart, a pasty female, spots at the corners of her mouth and a crop of blackheads on her cheeks like an aerial view of black cattle grazing across a parched plain. Her hair was dirty, her tee-shirt much stained, her short skirt straining into corrugated creases across her belly, her bare legs blotched red and mauve, her feet in broken-down slippers. She pulled a pack of cigarettes out from behind the sofa cushion and lit one, and a dirty child of about three, in sagging, nappy-bulging shorts, wandered in and climbed up next to her, clutching her arm and staring at Hart as if she were Sigourney Weaver. In another room a baby cried monotonously. In a corner of this one, in a playpen, another child of about eighteen months picked listlessly at the tacky bits of trodden-in food on the carpet, and stared out through the bars with its mouth open.

"Them next door," said Mrs. Hogg, "I never had nothing to do with 'em. I told the Council, I don't want the likes of them living next door to me. Disgusting. Well, I don't mind blacks," she said generously, for Hart's sake, "but that lot—! And him! Filthy, I call it. I mean, I suppose some of 'em can't help being that way, which you don't mind when they're nice, like that actor, what's his name, he's very funny, you know the one I mean, the big fat one. But to do it like him next door—just selling himself for money. Just like animals. Not but what he wasn't polite, always looked smart, and said hello nice as you like when I met him on the stairs or anything. Offered to help me up the stairs with the pushchair once, but I wouldn't let him anywhere near my Jason—would I, Jase?" she addressed the odoriferous child beside her, which was now absently exploring its nose with a forefinger, never taking its eyes from Hart's alien face. "You never know what you might catch off someone like that. Riddled with diseases they are—AIDS and that—and I wouldn't have him touching none of my kids."

Hart moved further toward the edge of the armchair she was sitting on, which she had a horrible suspicion was damp. "So you didn't know 'em very well?"

"I never even knew his name until you told me."

"What about your husband?"

"He ain't here. He's got his own flat over Fulham. He don't come here much now. He's got this girlfriend. Right little slapper *she is*!"

"All right, tell me what you heard last night," Hart said, anxious to get her to the point.

"Last night?"

"You said you heard something?"

"Oh. Yeah. Well, there was a noise. Like someone was having a barney. It woke my Jade up, so I wasn't best pleased, I can tell you."

"Woke your what?"

"Jade. Over there." She indicated the child in the playpen. "My little girl."

Blimey, thought Hart. "What time was that?"

"Oh, middle of the night. I dunno exactly."

"After midnight?"

"Well, maybe not. I didn't notice."

"Were you in bed?"

"No, I was in here, watching telly. I might of just dropped off, though," she admitted reluctantly.

"What exactly did you hear?"

"I heard this crash, like the door was being kicked in, and then a load of shoutin' an' crashin' about, like someone was havin' a real barney." She waxed enthusiastic. "All furnicher bein' knocked over and glass broken and that. And then someone shouted, I'm going to kill you, you dirty bastard. And then there was a kind of thud, like a body falling over. And then it all went quiet." She shuddered. " 'Orrible it was!"

In your dreams, Hart thought, making notes with an inward sigh. "What direction did these noises come from?"

"Are you taking the piss?" Mrs. Hogg asked with a derisive look. "Them next door, o' course. That's what you was asking about, isn't it?"

"Yeah, right. But you see, there's no sign of anyone having a fight in there, no furniture turned over or broken glass. So I thought it might be some other barney you heard."

Mrs. Hogg grew sulky. "I know what I heard. You callin' me a liar?"

"I just want you to think carefully about what you really heard. It's not going to help us if you exaggerate."

"I did hear the door bein' kicked in," she said defiantly. "*And* I heard some furnicher crashin'." A pause. "Maybe that was all," she added reluctantly.

"What about the shouting?"

"Well, maybe, maybe not. I can't say for sure."

"And can you help me some more about the time?"

"Like I say, I must of dropped off in front of the telly," she said, eyeing Hart as though she saw her chance of stardom dissolving.

"And it was the noise that woke you up? Do you remember what was on the telly then?"

Further probing brought the admission that Mrs. Hogg had been hitting the Cinzano earlier in the evening, which had caused her to drop off, and the noise next door had only partly woken her. She had dozed again, and it was only when Jade's howling had started off baby Pearse that the combined racket had penetrated her cobwebs. By then all was quiet next door. It was then ten past midnight, so the door-kicking-in could have happened at any time before that.

The neighbors on the other side were harder to coax out, and less forthcoming, but probably more reliable. The elderly couple glared at Hart suspiciously around the chain on the door, and would only open it when she had got PC Baker to come and flash his uniform, and both sets of ID had been carefully scrutinized.

"Can't be too careful," the oldster grunted begrudgingly as he opened the door a little wider. He wore a very sporty home-knitted cardigan of gray wool with a white reindeer-motif border, whose pockets sagged hopelessly under the burden of handkerchiefs, tobacco tin and matches.

"Only you see stuff on the telly all the time," the oldstress added over his shoulder. She was inclined to be apologetic, and would have asked them in, had her husband not blocked the way as robustly as his trembling frame could manage. Hart was quite happy to interview them on the doorstep. Over their diminutive shoulders she could smell the house aroma of liniment, cold roll-ups and dirty bodies, and had no wish to pitch her Amarige against this new Everest.

The old man said their name was Mr. and Mrs. Maple-syrup, but the old lady, whose teeth fitted better, corrected this to Maplesthor as Hart wrote it down. They had heard the door being kicked in all right. It was just before half past eleven, because the film was just finishing, which it was *Assassination* with Charles Bronson, very loud and lots of bang-ing, guns and that, and Mr. Maplesyrup had thought at first the noise was just part of the film, but Mrs. Maplesyrup had said turn the sound down a minute, Charlie, I think it was next door. So he had done, because it was just the whajjer-callums, the titles by then, and they'd listened, and they'd heard a sort of bang next door, or it might have been a thud, maybe, like something heavy being dropped or knocked over. And then nothing, just quiet, so Mr. Fudgefrosting had turned the sound back up because there was that advert he liked, the supermarket one with the little boy and the shopping, he was a laugh that kid, and Mrs. Hotjamsundae had gone to put the kettle on for their cuppa, which they always had one before they went to bed. And while she was in the kitchen it was all quiet next door, and no one had come along the communal balcony past her window. And this morning when she went out to go down for the paper she had just looked next door, just a quick peek, and she'd seen that the door wasn't closed properly and a big footmark on it and sort of splintery-looking at the edge where the Yale was, so she'd known they hadn't imagined it after all.

"I suppose you didn't think of calling the police?" Hart said. Mr. Maplesthorp looked witheringly at her, and said they couldn't go phoning the police every time they heard a thump or a raised voice, or they'd never be off the phone. And the police wouldn't thank them neither, they never did nothing if you did phone them. Anyway, you didn't stick your nose in on this estate, you left well alone as long as *you* were left alone. It wasn't like it used to be in the old days, when you could leave your front door open all day and no bother, and neighbors were neighbors. They were only waiting to be re-housed, but they'd been on the waiting list five years now, so unless they won the lottery—

Mrs. Maplesthorp interrupted to add apologetically that they hadn't thought anything about it really, the noise next door, though they'd always been quiet people, no trouble, and not usually given to fights or kicking doors in, but you didn't get thanked for interfering between man and wife, she'd learned that lesson the hard way when she'd tried to make peace between her brother and his wife, and got an earful from both of them, and they'd never spoken since, except at family funerals and things, though they always sent a Christmas card, which was a bit hypocritical when you thought of it . . .

Satisfactory, Hart thought when she finally made her escape. Three witnesses giving a similar story—you couldn't ask for more than that in an imperfect world.

"Has there been any trouble at the Pomona recently?" Slider asked Sergeant O'Flaherty on his way out to the yard. Fergus was one of his oldest friends, a man of sharp, sidelong wit and vast experience, who lurked, like a birdwatcher in a hide, behind the persona of a joke Irishman, a pantomime Thick Mick. Sometimes Slider suspected that he had slipped so far into self-parody that he had started to believe it.

"Not more than usual," O'Flaherty said. He was on his break and eating a sausage sandwich, washing it down with gulps of tea. "There was a bit of a frackarse Saturday night, but it didn't amount to much—more of a comedy turn in the end. Some animal rights nutters tried to storm the place, but the doormen dusted 'em off."

"Animal rights?" Slider was puzzled. "What were they protesting about?"

"One o' the cabaret acts. Simulated sex with a sheep," Fergus explained with a curled lip.

Slider frowned. "But that's—"

"Asherjaysus, it wasn't a real sheep, it was paper mashy an' a bit o' woolly stuff stuck on; but the animal libbers didn't work that one out until they got in and chucked some paint at the performers. It missed them and hit the sheep, at which point the truth dawned. They was so gobsmacked it give the doormen a chance to grab. They gave 'em no resistance and the doormen chucked 'em out with just a bunch o' bruises. They thought about suing, but when I pointed out what the headlines'd be, sense prevailed and they thought they'd better keep quiet about it, for the sake o' pride." He finished his tea. "D'you know what the Pomona called the act, anyway?" Slider shook his head. "*A Pair o' Sheepskin Slippers*." He gave a snort of mixed disgust and amusement.

"So how come it wasn't all over the papers?"

"The Pomona's owned by Billy Yates, and he didn't want the publicity any more than the animal libbers."

"Ah, of course," said Slider, understanding. Billy Yates was a local businessman with his fingers in almost every pie, and an inordinate influence in the local community.

"He squashed the locals, and they didn't dare syndicate. There was a paragraph in Monday's *Evening Standard*, but it didn't have the interesting details, so nobody else picked it up. Yates was fed up, mind you, having to take off the act, but he couldn't have his *artistes* shagging a green sheep, now could he? O' carse, he'd a' had to take it off anyway, One o' the slippers in question was your man Jay Paloma.''

"Was it indeed?"

"Didn't you know that? I thought that was why you was asking." He looked at Slider keenly. "You think it was some nutter on a clean-up campaign?"

"I'm not sure. Paloma was some bigwig's rent boy, according to his flatmate. He could have been wiped for security reasons."

"Or jealousy. You know what these types are like—incontinent as the moon." Fergus screwed up his greasy bag and potted it neatly in the bin. "How's Little Boy Blue gettin' on?" This was his nickname for Atherton. It was not unaffectionate.

"I rang yesterday. They said the usual things." He tried to be positive. "It's bound to be a long job. It was a massive wound."

"It shouldn't a happened to a bloke like him," Fergus said. "But then, I never thought he should be a copper. Restaurant critic, maybe. It's like seein' a raceharse pull a coal cart."

"He's a good detective," Slider objected. "You're a Catholic, Fergus. Do you believe prayers are answered?"

"Always," Fergus said firmly. He eyed his friend with large sympathy. "Sometimes the answer's 'no.' "

"You're such a comfort," Slider complained, and headed for the door.

Fergus called after him. "D'you know what's headin' the bill at the Pomona in place o' *Sheepskin Slippers*? It's that big fat Vera doin' a strip, all dragged up in Egyptian like Elizabeth Taylor. *Two Ton Carmen* they call it. It's the last bastion o' good taste, that place."

"Oh, you are awake," Slider said. "The nurses warned me not to disturb you if you were resting."

"I can rest all day," Atherton said.

"How are you feeling?"

"Excremental."

Slider studied him from the doorway. "You look like the Pompidou Centre."

"And Honeyman sent a basket of fruit," said Atherton, looking at the thing which lurked horribly in a corner, covered in brittle polythene and topped with one of those vast pale mauve bows beloved of florists.

"Honeyman's an idiot," Slider said, fetching a chair to the bedside. "Can't you give it to the nurses?"

"They won't take it. They keep saying I'll want it later, when the tubes come out. I keep telling them by then it'll be pure penicillin."

"Maybe that's what they mean. Can I get you anything before I sit down?"

"Yeah. Wet my lips, please." There was a container of saline solution and a crock of baby buds for the purpose. Slider performed the task neatly. "You'd make someone a great wife," Atherton said, to cover for the variety of emotions it made him feel.

Slider sat and made himself as comfortable as possible, wondering who they used as a model for these molded chairs.

"How's Jo?" Atherton asked.

"Fine. Busy."

"And you?"

"Ditto. We had a shout. That's why I didn't get in to see you yesterday."

"You don't have to come in every day."

"I do," Slider said shortly. Atherton hadn't the energy to argue with him. He knew Slider blamed himself for the knife wound, because he hadn't let Atherton in on his thought processes, and therefore laid him open (ouch, change metaphor) left him vulnerable to the momentary mistaken identification which had let Gilbert get his blow in. Atherton had even, in his worst moments of despair, blamed Slider himself; but the truth was that it had all happened so quickly, even if he had found himself faced with a complete stranger when the door opened he wouldn't have seen the knife coming. But Slider felt responsible, and visiting every day was one small way of making it up. And Atherton liked to have him visit. It broke up the day a bit.

"Nicholls came yesterday," Atherton said.

"He knew I wasn't going to make it. Did he tell you they've started getting the bill together for Mr. Wetherspoon's charity concert for Children in Need? Nutty's going on in a

KILLING TIME ✤ 55

fright wig and sequins singing 'Hey Big Spender.' He's billed as Burly Chassis.''

Atherton smiled painfully. "Don't. It hurts to laugh."

"Sorry."

"When's that coming off?"

"The concert? September some time."

"Maybe I'll be out for it, then." Atherton sounded so doubtful that it seemed better to both of them for the subject to be changed. "Tell me about the shout."

"The shout?" Slider's mind was elsewhere and he sounded vague. "Isn't it that painting by Munch?"

"Give the man a coconut," Atherton said, secretly rather impressed by Slider's knowledge. "Not *The Scream*—the shout. Your shout."

"Oh! Oh, it was a corpus. In a flat on the White City Estate."

"Blimey, not again," Atherton said. Slider told him about it. Atherton did not know Busty Parnell, and was faintly amused at Slider's seedy Soho and showbiz connections. What a Bohemian past his boss had had! He had heard of *Hanging Out in the Jungle*, of course—everyone had—and of Jeremy Haviland's suicide; but to Atherton it was Theatre History, it was like talking to someone who had actually met Flo Ziegfeld.

"Well, you've got enough there to be going on with," he said. "Seedy connections, mysterious lover, poison pen letters. You won't be bored for a week or two." His voice cracked, and he licked his lips.

Slider looked at him carefully for a moment. "What's the matter?"

"Nothing. Why?"

"Hey, it's me. What's the matter?"

Atherton hesitated, and then, with a hollow sense of helplessness he admitted, "I'm afraid."

"You're entitled," Slider said.

Atherton shook his head slightly. After a while he went on. "I've never been scared before. Not like this. When a bloke pulls a knife on you—"

Slider nodded. "The adrenalin kicks in. Afterwards you think, 'Shit, he might have killed me.' "

"Afterwards. Not before. That's the difference." He turned his head a little on the pillow, looking toward the shadows. "It only happened to other coppers. Now it's us." He licked his lips again. "Aren't you scared?"

It was what Slider had been trying not to think about. But he owed Atherton that, at least. He looked it in the face and said, "Yes. Shit-scared. I don't want to end up a notch on some stupid scumbag's belt."

"So—what, then? Why go on?"

"The odds are on our side."

Atherton closed his eyes.

Slider thought. Yes, the odds were on their side. But the odds were shortening all the time; and anyway, that wasn't it. So what, then? He couldn't do anything else, wasn't trained for anything else. But that wasn't it either. It was what had made him take the job in the first place, that made him stay with it. An inability to do nothing. There were those who, seeing two kids smashing up a telephone kiosk, hurried past, and those who had to protest. His body might have its own views, but his soul sickened at the stupidity and waste of crime, and if he didn't do something, his bit, to stop it . . . It wasn't exactly that he couldn't stop caring. That was perfectly possible, something he was on the edge of every day. It was that he couldn't stop caring whether he cared or not. *That* was the very, very bottom line.

He opened his mouth to share this revelation with Atherton, but Atherton was asleep again.

Freddie Cameron's bow tie of the day was claret with pale blue diagonal stripes, a bright spot in a dark world. Thunder clouds had come up, and an unnatural, yellowish twilight outside made the strip-lighted pathology rooms seem unnecessarily glaring. Slider introduced Hollis, and Freddie shook his hand.

"Permanent fixture?"

"I hope so." Hollis looked around. "Nice setup you've got here. Last time I went to a post there was water running down the walls and the corpse was the warmest thing in the room."

"High Victorian?"

"Low farce," Hollis corrected, and Cameron smiled.

"I know what you mean. Well, there's still a good few of those dear old mortuaries around. You wait till you've attended an exhumation in one. That's when your faith is really tested."

Slider looked around, missing the usual crowd that hung around postmortems. "Where is everybody?"

"Holiday season," Freddie explained.

"Surely not?" Slider said. "They can't all be away at once."

"Tell you the truth, old boy, pathology isn't the draw it used to be. And no one specializes in forensic pathology anymore. When my generation's gone, I don't know who's going to cut up your corpses for you. You know we've lost our only forensic odontologist, don't you?" Slider had heard that the Tooth Fairy, as he was called, had gone to Dublin, where, thanks to the E.C., the livin' was easy. "I tell the students, being a pathologist is a grand life. Easy hours, no stress— and dead men don't sue. Bodies may pong a bit, but it beats being called out in the middle of the night to deliver someone's baby. But they don't listen. To tell the truth, I think they see too many simulated messy corpses on the telly to sustain the thrill. The romance has gone out of it."

"What you've got," Slider said wisely, "is *Weltschmerz*."

"I thought that was a kind of German sausage. How is Atherton, by the way?"

"I hope that's a non sequitur. He's coming along slowly, but it'll be a long job. The wound has to heal from the inside outwards, so it has to be kept open."

"Ah," said Freddie wisely. "That must be a trial. Keeps it always before him, so to speak. How's his morale?"

"Shaky. But he's still very weak."

"Is he allowed visitors? I might pop in and see him, if you think it'd cheer him up. Is this radiant female looking for you?"

Slider turned. "Oh, yes, she's my new D.C., a temporary loaner, though if I'm nice to her she might persuade them to let her stay."

"You should have let her off this post, then," said Freddie the chivalrous. He could never shake himself of the old habit of regarding women as delicate and lovely creatures to be protected and pampered, despite the fact that one of his daughters was a country vet and the other rode a Triumph Bonneville to work. "Shall we begin?"

The body was stripped, and lay pale and faintly shiny on the P.M. table, like something made of high-quality plastic, an illusion aided by the teen-doll perfection of his figure. In life Jay Paloma had been lean and flat-bellied, and, apart from the nest of pinkish-blond curls at the root of the penis, entirely hairless. Even the legs were smooth—presumably the result of hours of agony with hot wax. Because of the leanness, the genitals looked unusually large by contrast, a curious effect Slider had noticed before. He wondered the Government didn't stress that point in its efforts to get the nation to lose weight. It would have had more effect than the health argument.

Freddie spoke into the microphone. "The body is that of a male, apparent age thirty-five to forty years old, well-nourished, of medium build. Height—" He and his assistant measured. "Height is five feet nine inches. Put that into Napoleons, will you, Carol?" he added for the typist. All metric measures were Napoleons to him, just as all foreign currencies were washers. He stubbornly refused to be embraced by Europe.

"No sign of drug usage, no needle marks or tracks. Apart from the injuries to the head and face, which I will come to later, no apparent wounds, abrasions, or bruises. No surgical scars. Estimated time of death—now where did I put my notes? Ah yes. When I first examined the body at the scene of the crime, at—ah—7:15 a.m. on Wednesday, it was cold to the touch and rigor mortis was present in the upper limbs, the trunk and the lower limbs as far as the ankles, but there was still some flexibility in the toes. There was postmortem staining present in the dependent parts of the body. The ambient temperature was 17.2°C and the body temperature 33°C. That was a liver stab, by the way. I avoided rectal testing because of the nature of the deceased's inclinations. The body temperature at 9:30 a.m. was 32.5°C. I estimate that the time of death was between fifteen and eighteen hours before my first examination at 7:15, that is between 1:15 and 4:15 p.m. on Tuesday.''

Slider caught Hart's eye. "Hang on a minute, Freddie," he said. "Are you sure about that time of death?"

Freddie looked up inquiringly over his half-moons. "You know better than that, old boy. Anything over four hours can never be certain. The variations and exceptions are endless. It's my opinion, but I wouldn't stake half-a-crown on it if you know better."

"Well, we've got witnesses—"

"A witness takes precedence over the jolly old Three Signs, you know that. What time do you want, then?"

"Eleven-thirty on Tuesday evening. Not an eyewitness, but two separate witnesses to the door being kicked in and the sound of furniture overturned."

"Eleven-thirty? That gives me not quite eight hours. Well, I'd have thought it was a bit short, but anything's possible. Now I look at him, he's thinner than I first took him for. Nicely built, but not an ounce of fat on him, so he could have cooled and stiffened very quickly, especially lying through the night in an unheated room. And of course," he added with a bland look at Slider, "he's shaved off all his body hair, so he's got no fur coat for insulation."

"Shaved?"

"Or waxed. The things some people will do for love! Let's have him over, John."

The examination continued. "Hypostasis well developed on the trunk and lower limbs. Ah, you see here the evidence that our chap was a practiced sodomite: hairless and smooth as a baby's cheek. Depilatory cream followed by Oil of Olay, I suspect. Epithelium cornfield, smooth and less elastic than normal, and there's a lack of sphincteric tone. No sign of venereal disease, or proctitis. Practiced but careful. Ah, but here, do you see this? Some peri-anal bruising, and a couple of tiny haematomata. Our friend's had a bit of rough sex quite recently. Not immediately pre-mortem, though. Not part of the homicidal attack—twelve to twenty-fours hours before that, I'd say."

"He went to see his lover the day before, apparently," Slider said.

"Did he? You're not worried about this, then? Can we move on?"

"We haven't identified the lover yet. It could be important."

"In that case I'll take swabs."

Freddie came at last to the head injuries, and as he approached them he began to whistle quietly through his teeth, a defense mechanism which caused his typist considerable pain during transcription. "Injuries to the head are consistent with having been caused by repeated severe blows from a hard object. The wounds are considerably overlaid and it is impossible to say with any certainty what the weapon might have been. The blows were inflicted with great force, sufficient to crush the skull."

"In fact," Slider said, "it was our old friend, the frenzied attack."

"Quite." Cameron whistled on. "Let's have him over again."

"Ah, now, this is better. There appears to have been a single blow to the face, across the bridge of the nose, again with enormous force. The clean-cut edge to the wound here— d'you see, Bill?—suggests it might have been something with a straight edge or a square section. A metal bar, for instance, rather than a baseball bat or a knobkerrie."

Slider made a note.

"The blow to the face was the first and fatal one, delivered with sufficient force to drive splinters of bone into the brain. Death would have been instantaneous. The rest of the blows to the skull were carried out postmortem." Cameron paused. "What's up, Bill? With all the blood down the front of the shirt and none down the back, you must have come to that conclusion yourself."

"Yes," said Slider, "but it doesn't make it easier. If you sneak up on someone, it's usual to do it from behind."

"Bit of a breach of protocol," Freddie agreed.

"And there was no sign of a struggle, and no defense injuries—"

"True," said Freddie. "The fatal blow was undefended."

"But if someone had kicked the door in, why didn't he see them coming? Unless he was drunk. Or drugged."

"If he was unconscious through drink or drugs," Freddie said, "it could explain the rapid fall in body temperature and quick onset of rigor. Did he drug?"

"Not according to his flat mate, but she wouldn't necessarily know everything. Or even necessarily tell the truth."

"Well, the blood tests may show something. D'you want the stomach contents analyzed as well?"

"Yes, it may help."

"I'll secure the whole thing and send it off, then."

❖ FIVE ❖

Pom Deterrent

The ground-floor-level manifestation of the Pomona Club was a stuccoed wall painted with a mural of a tropical jungle prominently featuring a grinning snake and an apple. Entrance was via a side alley, and the door sported a state-of-the art neon sign of an apple which flicked back and forth between being whole and having a large, deckle-edged bite out of it. Below the apple little red dots chased themselves around the border of a space which read alternately *Pomona* and *Cabaret*.

Despite the apple theme, Slider happened to know, because an amused O'Flaherty had told him, that the club had been named for entirely different reasons. Billy Yates, the owner, had had a long rivalry with a fellow businessman, Brian Hooper, who being from Sydney himself had referred to Yates's enterprise as "that club with the Pom owner." The name stuck, and Yates, ever a pragmatist, made the best of a bad job and renamed it the Pomona to make it look as though he had thought of it first. Despite his many business interests, Yates seemed to have a particular attachment to the Pomona, spending more time there than might seem warranted.

The neon sign was off now, of course, revealing the secret of its pseudokinesics in an unseemly display of unlit tubes and bulbs. The door below gave access to a steep flight of stairs: the club itself lived in the basement. Hart wrinkled her nose as she descended behind Slider. "Moldy place. How'd they ever get a licence?"

"God knows," Slider said.

"I should've thought it would never pass a fire certificate."

"Contributions in the right boxes," Slider suggested. "Friends in the right places."

"On the square, you mean?"

"You might think that. I couldn't possibly comment."

The club wore an insistent and insincere glamour, an air of having had just enough spent on it to make it appear to a casual or drunken glance to have had a great deal spent on it. It was gloomy now, lit only by the bar lights, and the reflection from the back-curtain to the dance stage, which was made of vertical shimmery stuff like giant Lametta. It smelled of cigarette smoke, spilled alcohol, disinfectant, cellar-mold, and a faint, spicy whiff of something that was either joss-sticks or a certain popular recreational tobacco substitute.

"What a dump," Hart murmured, keeping so close behind Slider he could feel the heat of her body. Nervous, he thought; or perhaps she didn't have very good night vision.

They had not been unobserved. A door revealed itself over beyond the bar as an oblong of light, and a dark figure came through and quickly stepped aside so as not to be outlined. "Can I help you?" a man's voice asked unwelcomingly.

"I'm looking for Mr. Yates," Slider said. There was a click, and fluorescent lights in the ceiling came on, pinning Slider and Hart like bugs on a table.

"If you're tryin' to ge' a job for your daugh'er," the voice said with grim humor and a splendid array of West London glottal stops, "forge' i'. She ain't got the tits for it."

The voice belonged to a tall, very fit-looking young black man—the glossy, dessert-chocolate black of Africa—dressed in a suit of the same cheap-smartness as the club decor, and with his right hand tucked casually in under the left coat of his jacket. The hard eyes had already summed up Slider and Hart as not being dangerous, so the gesture was purely theatrical, meant to impress.

"Detective Inspector Slider, Detective Constable Hart. Mr. Yates is in the back, is he?"

Now the right hand moved with the invisible-lightning

speed of a lizard out from under the coat and down into a pocket. The alert pose became casual. A wide and perfectly false smile decorated the features. "Oh, yeah, he'll be glad to see you. Always glad to see you lot, is Mr. Yates. Come on through."

So, Billy Yates keeps an armed guard at his side, Slider thought as he crossed the room. Now what has he got to be afraid of, I wonder?

The man led the way through into a narrow corridor. He knocked on a door, opened it and said, "Mr. Yates, it's the fuzz. Coupla detectives." He stretched his arm to usher them in, favoring Hart with a salacious look. "F'you want an audition, darlin', I don't mind waivin' the tits if you don't. Geddit?" he added with a grin of delight at his own wit.

Hart looked witheringly as she passed him. "Jerk," she said.

"Shut up, Garry, and get out," a colder, older voice from inside commanded. Slider followed Hart into the tiny room, and the door was closed behind them. Billy Yates sat behind a cheap metal office desk piled high with papers. There were two cheap office chairs and a bank of filing cabinets on this side of the desk, and that was all. The room was so tiny there was only just room between the cabinets and the desk for the chairs. To open a filing cabinet drawer you would have had to lift a chair out of the way.

Yates was a big man who had once been muscular and was going slightly to seed. Still, he was big enough and strong enough to have taken care of himself, especially as, Slider calculated, in any situation he was likely to get the first blow in, and the first blow from him would be the only one in the fight. His face was big-featured, tanned with an expensive, overseas tan which Slider guessed he would sport all year round, and would have been good-looking if it had had a pleasant expression. But there was no smile in the mouth, no humanity in the eyes. It was a cartoon face, just lines drawn around a space, without animation, a representation of a human rather than the real thing. His hair was carefully coiffeured, his cufflinks large and gold, his aftershave filled the small room, but though his suit looked expensive, Slider's eye, tutored over the years by Atherton, saw that it was merely new, and would not last the pace. Cheap-smart again, just a better class of cheap-smart than his henchman's. Was Yates a man who was satisfied with what would pass muster, rather than the real thing, or did he dress down for the venue? If rumor was even half right, he had a wad the size of Centre Point, so he must be spending it on something.

"What can I do for you?" he asked. He waved a hand toward the chairs. Slider sat. Now on a level with him, Yates's face waited for him without expression, his gray eyes stationary as oysters.

"Jay Paloma," Slider said. "He works for you—"

"Not anymore," Yates said sharply.

"Since when?"

"Since he didn't turn up to work. I don't give second chances. Not when there's a hundred people out there eager for his job."

"When did you last see him?"

"Monday night—or Tuesday morning, rather, at about ten past four, when he left to go home."

"Was he alone?"

"As far as I know."

"And when was he due to come in again?"

"Seven Tuesday evening. Seven till four were his hours, with an hour and a half off. He didn't show up, and that was that as far as I was concerned."

"No message or telephone call?"

"Nothing." Yates shrugged. "And after I'd taken a chance on him, given him the job when there were younger dancers I could have had." And paid him accordingly, I bet, Slider thought.

"When you last saw him, did he seem in normal spirits?"

Yates only shrugged, picked up a cigarette box from the clutter of the desk, offered it to Slider and Hart, and then took one himself, making a slow business of lighting it. To give himself time to think, Slider thought, keeping silent. At last Yates said, "As you mention it, he did seem out of sorts on Monday night. Hadn't got his mind on his job. Performed like crap. Fortunately Monday's a quiet night. But I made a mental note that he'd have to pull his socks up or get out."

"Well, you'll be glad to know that you've been saved the

trouble of making the decision," Slider said, watching Yates's eyes. "He's been murdered."

There was no flicker, only a serious, considering look of inward thought. "I'm sorry," Yates said tersely. "When?"

"Tuesday night."

There was no response to that at all.

Slider went on, "I'd like you to tell me everything you know about him."

Yates made a dismissive gesture. "I knew nothing about him, beyond his work."

"Did he meet anyone here? Did you see him with anyone?"

"If I did, I wouldn't have made a mental note of it. The staff are supposed to be friendly to the customers, make them feel at home."

"Who were his special friends amongst your staff? Who did he talk to during his breaks?"

"I don't know that he had any friends. I pay my staff to work, not to fraternize."

"Well, perhaps I can talk to the people he worked with. Perhaps they'd be more forthcoming."

Slider expected Yates to object to that, but after a slow, moveless look into Slider's face, he said, "Do as you please. Just don't do it during my open hours. It wouldn't please my customers to have detectives hanging around asking questions."

I'll bet it wouldn't, Slider thought. He was about to get up when, unexpectedly, Yates spoke again.

"There is something."

"Yes?" Slider said encouragingly.

Yates seemed to be having difficulty in bringing himself to be helpful. At last he said, "I do remember seeing him with someone just recently. For the last few weeks. Not every night, but a couple of times a week. Out in front—in the club. He's been sitting with a man, talking, during his break."

"Did you know the man?"

"No. It wasn't unusual for Jay to talk to customers. But I noticed this one because he wasn't a fag."

"How could you tell?"

For the first time there was a flicker of animation—a with-

ering look. "In my business you have to know. This man
was—" He hesitated. "He wasn't a customer. He wasn't
enjoying the club. He was there on business of some kind."

"Drug dealing, perhaps?" Slider said blandly.

The face went stationary again. "I don't like what you're
suggesting. I think you'd better go."

Slider felt his headache coming on again. "Oh, come off
it, Mr. Yates! You know and I know you get more dealers in
here than Monte Carlo. I'm not here to investigate that. I'm
not here to make trouble for you—but I can, if you won't
help me."

"I doubt it," Yates said with such utter indifference that
Slider wondered anew whose pocket he was into. All the
same, after a moment Yates went on, "But I've no objection
to helping you. I'll give you a description of this man. About
thirty-five, five-ten, well built, clean shaven, dark hair."

"Would you know him again?"

"Maybe. Maybe not. He sat in a dark corner. I got an
impression of him, rather than really saw him. He looked like
trouble."

"Trouble? In what way?"

Yates seemed to have difficulty in defining it. "He was a
professional. He was on some kind of business, and he was
going to get it done, and if anything got in the way—" He
shrugged. "That's why I noticed him; that's why I kept my
eye on him." He tapped his nose. "This was warning me."

"And what do you think Jay Paloma had to do with him?"

"God knows. He wasn't screwing him, that's all I know."

"Could he have been selling him drugs?"

"I've told you—"

"Without your knowledge or approval, of course," Slider
said smoothly. "As I said, I'm not here to make trouble for
you. But a man of your experience must have seen drug dealers at work. So off the record, could this man have been
one?"

"He could have been the type," Yates conceded. "He had
the look. That's all I can say. But Jay didn't use—not to my
knowledge. I wouldn't have anyone who used working for
me. Not worth the risk."

*   *   *

"Someone waiting to see you," Nicholls said as Slider passed through the front shop. The words brought a replay to his mind of Jay Paloma, nicely dressed and sweating through his aftershave with fear, turning up his eyes in appeal. *You let him down.* Cobblers, what could I have done? *Something. Anything. He came to you and you let him down.* And another mind-flash, of the pretty streaked-blond hair pasted into the splintered skull with pink ooze. Flash: the smell of sweat, not Paloma's dainty, fresh sweat, but the old accumulated stink of a man in shorts and khaki socks. Flash: Atherton's eyes widening in surprise and recognition—

"Bill?"

He pulled himself back. "Yes—you said? Someone wants to see me?"

Nicholls watched him consideringly. "You all right, pal?"

"Yes." But Nicholls was an old colleague, and deserved better than that. "That whack on the head I had must have knocked something loose. It'll be a while before it beds in again."

"You came back to work too early." Nicholls was serious.

"Good job I did, as it happens," Slider said lightly. "Where's this bloke?"

It was a slight, wiry man in his fifties, sallow and moley: his face was all over little tags and buttons, some dark, some flesh-colored, as though he hadn't been finished off properly. He had a thick nose, a wide, lipless mouth, milk-chocolate-brown eyes behind large plain glasses, tight crinkly black hair turning gray. He was wearing gray flannels and well-polished black shoes with thick rubber soles, a blue anorak showing a peep of a pale blue polo shirt, and a pair of new pale leather driving gloves, the sort with the knitted string backs. He was wearing the left one and holding the other in his left hand; his right hand showed the two first fingers stained rich amber, and a thick, plain gold wedding ring on the third finger. If he hadn't been under size, Slider would have put him down as a copper off duty.

"Mr. Slider?" He offered a friendly smile with a very large number of small, uneven teeth. "I hope you don't mind. Well, actually, I thought I might be able to help you," he said in the mild accent of North Harrow. "Benny Fluss is my name."

He pronounced it to rhyme with truss. He held out his hand, looking expectantly at Slider as though he expected the name to be recognized.

"Yes, Mr. Fluss," Slider said, managing with the grace of long practice not to notice the extended hand. "What did you want to talk to me about?"

"Well, this awful murder, of course," the man said, reclaiming his hand and comforting it by letting it play with his loose glove. "Didn't Val—Miss Parnell mention me?"

"I'm afraid not," Slider said. "Do you think you might have some information for me? Let's go somewhere quieter, shall we?" He led the way to the nearest interview room and ushered the man in. He seemed nervous—or perhaps on edge was nearer the mark—but eager to please. A friend of Busty's? An ex-customer? Yes, perhaps that would account for the nervousness. A married man, fond of Busty but not wanting any trouble.

"Right," Slider said when they were seated opposite each other, "what do you know about this business?"

"Nothing about the murder, I'm afraid, but I am in a position to confirm Miss Parnell's alibi."

"What makes you think she needs an alibi?"

The man smiled indulgently. "Oh, I don't mean it like that. Obviously Val had nothing to do with it. Anyone who knows her would know that—and I've heard her mention you, Mr. Slider, so I know you *do* know her. But I know how you chaps work. Everything has to be checked and verified, even if it's just to be able to put it aside out of the question. I'm here to put the record straight so that you can tick off that item and get onto something else. That will be helpful, won't it?"

"Any information which bears on the case is helpful," Slider began, and Fluss jumped in again with eager garrulity.

"That's right. That's what I thought. So I popped straight along as soon as I heard about it, to save you the trouble of having to come and find me. Always glad to help you chaps— you're good to us, so we should be good to you. And I don't mind telling you," he went on confidingly, "that, awful though this business is, I can't help being a little bit excited at being involved even in a small way. I've always been interested in the law. It's one of my passions—almost a hobby, you might say. If you were to see my bookcase at home, you'd think it was a solicitor's! Benny the Brief they call me at our garage. That's my nickname, Benny the Brief. They all come to me with their little problems. I'm cheaper than a real solicitor, and I talk plainer English, ha ha!''

Now Slider placed the look of him, the neat appearance, the anorak, the shoes. And, like firemen, they gave each other silly nicknames which were often better known in the business than the real names: a nickname might go all over London if the idiosyncrasy it marked were extreme enough. "You're a taxi driver," he said. "You're the one who brought Miss Parnell home on Wednesday morning?"

"Well done!" the man beamed. "The detective is worthy of his hire! Yes, I'm the man who drove her home—and much more. I'm a very old friend of Val's, and I drive her everywhere. Whenever she wants to go anywhere, she calls me. I'm practically her private chauffeur."

"That's very altruistic of you."

"Oh, she pays the fare. Nothing funny about it, I assure you," he said seriously. "Not but what I wouldn't give her the odd free ride, being as we're such old friends, but she insists on it. 'Benny,' she says, 'you've got your living to make the same as me.' But she goes everywhere by cab, does Val.''

"So she told me."

"Did she? She must have mentioned me then. She didn't? Oh. Well, I met her when she was working in the Nitey Nite Club, and there'd been a nasty case when a colleague of hers got raped by a minicab driver—"

"Yes, I remember," Slider said. "In fact, she mentioned that only the other day."

Fluss nodded. "It was a real shock to her. Well, I said to her after that, you can't be too careful. You make sure you always get a proper cab from now on. 'Benny,' she said, 'if I could be sure I'd always get *your* cab, I'd be a happy woman.' And that was the start of it.''

"How did you meet her in the first place?" Slider asked.
Fluss lowered his eyelids. "Well, if you must know—

strictly off the record—I was working 'round the back' at the time.''

Slider knew what that meant: picking up tourists and taking them to a club on a commission basis. Touting was illegal for licensed cabbies, but—well, lonely Japanese reps looking for a good night out, a taxi driver with a living to make and too many cabs in competition, a club willing to pay £15 a head for customers—it was one of those victimless crimes everyone tried to close their eyes to. Knowing the Nitey Nite and knowing Val, Slider wouldn't be surprised if Benny had also been "going case" as it was called—driving a prostitute and her client from the club to a hotel and bringing the girl back afterward. It was reassuring for the girl to know the driver was looking out for her, and the client would also know that he had been "clocked," and would thus be deterred from any funny business. If that had been the basis of their association, it might well turn into a lasting friendship.

"That's between you and the Carriage Office," Slider said. "I'm just interested in Val and Jay Paloma. So you've been driving her regularly?"

"For the last year or so, I've been the only person to drive her," Benny said with a hint of pride. "I'm on a radio circuit now—Monty's, you know?"

Slider knew. The full title was Monty's Radio Metrocabs; the garage was under the railway arches on the other side of Goldhawk Road, the owner one Monty Green, an expansive man with a figure like Pavarotti and the hackney carriage trade in his veins. Atherton called him Monty Verdi, an obscure joke that made only Joanna laugh.

"So she can always ask for me," Benny went on. "And for when I'm off duty, I've given her the number of my mobile. Any time, day or night, I've told her, you can call me."

"What does your wife think about that?" Slider couldn't resist asking.

"My wife passed away, Mr. Slider," Fluss said gravely. "Six months ago. Cancer of the liver."

"I'm sorry," Slider said. Of course, wedding ring on the right hand—some old-fashioned types still swapped hands to indicate widowhood.

"She went just like that," Benny said, looking down. "I

suppose it was a blessing it was so quick. Thirty years we'd been married, and never a cross word. She was a wonderful woman.''

Slider waited a tactful beat and went on. "So you brought Miss Parnell home on Wednesday morning?"

"That's right." He jumped from Mourning Widower to Perfect Witness suspiciously quickly. "Of course, it was booked for later that morning, to pick her up from her sister's at ten forty-five, but she rang me direct at six o'clock to say her brother-in-law had come home unexpectedly, and could I come and pick her up. She was in quite a state. The man's a brute, Mr. Slider, not to mince words. I can tell you I was around there like a shot. It wouldn't be beyond that man to raise a hand to Val, same as he does to Shirley.'' He gave Slider a significant nod.

"And what time did you get there?"

"About ten past six, it must have been. She was waiting outside on the pavement with her bag, which I—"

"That was quick," Slider interrupted.

"Well, I hadn't far to come. I've got a room in Barlby Road now, just around the back of the North Pole, you know? I sold the house when the wife died."

"But it must have taken you some time to get dressed and so on."

"I was already up, as it happened, dressed and shaved and everything. Well, I've always been an early riser, and since the wife passed on, I don't seem to sleep as much as I used to."

"I see. Well, it was lucky for Miss Parnell, at any rate. And what time did you get to White City?"

"It would be just before half past. Twenty-five past, maybe. That time of morning there was no traffic about, so it was a quick journey."

"And did you go upstairs with her?"

"I wish I had," he said earnestly. "I truly wish I had. I tell you, Mr. Slider, I hate myself for putting her through that all alone. If only I could have saved her the terrible shock! But I didn't usually go up with her, you see, unless she had something heavy to carry, or she invited me in for a cuppa.

And this time she just said, 'See you later, Benny,' and off she went like a bird.''

"See you later?"

"Well, I was to've picked her up to take her to work."

"Did she seem upset about the business at her sister's?"

"No, not really. She knows the score there all right. She was angry when I picked her up that he'd virtually chucked her out, but she was more anxious about Jay, because he'd been rather down in the dumps lately. He seemed a bit under the weather on the Tuesday when I picked her up to take her to her sister's."

"Oh, you saw him then?"

"Saw him, yes. He came to the door. In his dressing gown, and not shaved—which I will say was not like him," he added as if grudgingly admitting that the Krays were good to their mother. Slider gathered he didn't like Jay Paloma. "Always neat and tidy he was as a rule, and kept the flat as nice as my wife kept our house. And like my wife would never have normally gone to the door in her curlers, Jay wouldn't normally have let anyone see him with a stubble and not dressed. So he must have been out of sorts."

"Did he say anything about why he was out of sorts?"

"Oh, he didn't talk to me. Just answered the door and said he'd tell Val I was there, that's all. There was no conversation. But he looked, shall we say, a bit somber. Val said he'd been quarreling with his—*boyfriend.*" The slight hesitation and the emphasis showed what Benny thought of Jay Paloma's inclinations. Then he seemed to think better of speaking ill of the dead and added, "Val was very fond of him. They'd been friends a long time, and he'd been good to her in a number of ways, according to Val."

"Did you drive him, too?"

"I did not," Benny said firmly. "The arrangement I had with Val was special."

"Oh. I understood Jay was very particular about taking cabs too," Slider said.

"I wouldn't know about that," Benny said vaguely. "But, you know, I wouldn't be surprised—" He paused and glanced at Slider.

"Yes?"

"I'm sorry to have to say it, but I wouldn't be surprised if he wasn't involved in something shady that Val didn't know about, and it caught up with him. Sly, these people are. Acting a part all their lives, they get good at deceiving people. Val thought he was a snow-white lamb, but working where he did, and the types he must have been rubbing shoulders with every night—I wouldn't be surprised if he wasn't into something."

"Do you have any idea what?"

Benny smiled apologetically. "No. I'm afraid that's just supposition. No evidence. I shouldn't have said anything, really. I didn't come here to speak ill of the dead, just to assure you that you can cross Val off your list of things to check. I took her to her sister's and brought her back, and there she was the whole time, so she couldn't possibly have had anything to do with it."

Slider raised an eyebrow, Atherton-style. "You don't know that, do you? Unless you were with her the whole time, you don't know that she didn't go back to the flat at some point."

"But she—" Benny looked absolutely dumbfounded, and searched Slider's face for information, his brows buckled with perplexity. "But you can't think that! You can't think *she* killed him! Not Val. It's not possible. Surely you don't believe she had anything to do with it?"

"As a matter of fact," Slider said, amused at the little cabbie's protectiveness, "I don't. I was just pointing out the limits of your evidence. You're very fond of Val, aren't you?"

"I am fond, yes. Yes, I can use that word. I've always liked and respected her, and we've been friends a long time now—"

"More than friends, perhaps?"

Benny's sallow face darkened a shade with—embarrassment? Anger? "I don't know what you mean," he said stiffly.

"Don't you?"

"I don't see," he said slowly, his face clearing and cooling, "that it's any of your business. I came here to help, and I don't see why I should put up with impertinent questions about my private life. If that's the way you treat responsible citizens who try to help you—" He began to rise.

"I beg your pardon," Slider said. "I didn't mean to be impertinent." Lovely word! "It's just that every and any detail can help to fill in the picture, even when it doesn't have a direct bearing on the case. When you're groping in the dark for the light switch, even the position of a chair can help."

Slider wasn't sure the metaphor really meant anything, but it seemed to do the trick with Benny the Brief. He got off his high horse with one bound, and was smiling again, and affable.

"Of course, I understand. You've got a difficult job to do—and a most unpleasant one, as I'm well aware. I've had enough friends in the police force to know that. Well, anything I can do to help, don't hesitate. And I hope my bit of information's been some use to you."

Yes, that accounted for the rapid dismount—he wanted to be the one man with the discernment to understand the Copper's Lonely Destiny. There were people like that, fascinated by everything to do with the Job and longing to be associated with it in some way, outsiders who wanted to be inside. Sometimes they were invaluable and sometimes they were a pain in the neck. Slider was not yet sure which Benny the Brief would turn out to be, but his mother had always told him not to look a gift horse in the teeth.

Snow Use

Busty was staying in a hotel—a large Edwardian house at the near end of Hammersmith Grove. There was a short terrace of them: red brick with white copings, black-and-white checkered front path, stained glass panels in the door, elaborate wooden porch with pinnacles and poker work which put Slider in mind of Hansel and Gretel. They all had names, the sort of names of which Edwardians were so fond, which almost meant something but not quite—Hillsleigh, Holmcroft, Endersby—and all, being too large to accommodate the modern idea of a family, had been turned into hotels. Busty was in The Hillsleigh, suffering from a mixture of shock and frustration, unable to face going to work, unable to go home, trapped in the lethargy of bereavement.

She welcomed Slider's visit as a relief. "Is this social, or business?"

"Bit of both, really," he said. "Business mostly, though, I'm afraid. I want to ask you some more questions."

"Would it be against the rules to take me for a drink or something?" Her haunted eyes pleaded. "Just to get me out of here? This place is driving me up the wall."

Slider glanced around at the awful institutional cheapness of everything in the reception area: the lozenge-patterned carpet designed to repel both stains and the eye; the bland floral wallpaper and framed prints calculated not to trip the taste circuits in any way whatsoever; the furniture intended to discourage sitting around. There were imitation parlor palms which just failed to look like the real thing, standing in plastic pots in plastic Versailles tubs. Even the decorative bark mulch was plastic and almost exactly the wrong shade of brown, though Slider noticed someone had stubbed out a real cigarette in it. It was probably the most exciting thing that had ever happened in here. Poor old Busty would never stand a spell in Holloway, Slider thought, if one day here could drive her to distraction. "Come on, then," he said.

They went to the Hope and Anchor across the road, and Busty asked for a gold watch. Slider got her a double to save time, and himself a Virgin Mary, and they settled into a dim corner. The pub was of the same vintage as the houses across the road, and had apparently used the same interior designer. It was not much of a change, but it seemed to satisfy Busty, who sighed with contentment even before the Scotch touched her lips.

"I want to talk to you a bit more about Maurice," Slider said. "And I want you to be honest with me. Nothing you can say can harm him now, but it may help me to find who did this terrible thing. Do you understand me?"

Busty gave him a wide-eyed look. "I got nothing to hide."

"Don't try and stuff me, Busty. Hiding things from the police is second nature. And I've known you a very long time. But now you've got to go against nature and tell me everything. What was Maurice mixed up in?"

"Nothing that I know about."

"I've had the hint from the Pomona Club that he'd been meeting someone in there a couple of times a week. Dark corner, private conversation. Now who would that be?"

"I don't know. Probably a customer trying to pick him up."

"The boss says this bloke wasn't a ginger."

Busty looked scornful. "Billy Yates? What does he know!"

"Yates said the bloke was a professional, and he looked like trouble. Maybe a drug dealer."

"He ought to know," Busty muttered resentfully.

"Did Maurice drug?" Slider asked.

She kept her eyes on her glass, but she looked a little shaken. "No. Never. He didn't like drugs."

"What about poppers?"

She blinked. "I dunno. Maybe then. I dunno. No, I reckon not. He hated drugs, Mr. Slider. He got quite airiated about it. Said he'd seen too many good people go bad that way. He said—" She stopped abruptly.

"He talked to you about it a lot, did he?" Slider put in smoothly. "Was he getting it for you, Busty? Was that what he was talking to this man for? You persuaded him to get you a little bit of white, just a spot for when you had the blues, or after work when you were really knocked out?"

"No," said Busty.

"Against his better instincts, because he loved you. You wheedled him. He had the contacts and you didn't anymore. Just a little spot of snow to get you through, who could that hurt? Everyone knows it's not addictive."

"No," she said stonily.

"And now it's come back on him, and you feel so guilty—"

She flared. "No! I tell you *no*! I don't do that anymore. Not since I've been sharing with Maurice. He hated it so much, he talked me out of it. He said we had better things to do with our money. We were saving up, Mr. Slider, I swear to you. I could show you the savings book. The Halifax down the Bush. Saving for our retirement. So we could get out. He *hated* drugs. That's why—" She changed track. "He wasn't buying drugs for me, I swear my Bible oath he wasn't." But her face was as miserable as an abandoned dog's, and Slider took her sentences and repieced them.

"Who for, then, Busty? That was why he'd been feeling down, you were going to say. He hated drugs but he was buying them for someone. Why?" He studied her face. "For the money. He was paid a commission, wasn't he? He was the intermediary and they made it worth his while, and the commission went into the savings account. He was doing it for both of you." She was silent, staring into her glass. "He was buying drugs for someone who could afford to pay him well, but who couldn't get them for himself. Maybe couldn't risk being seen buying them. Was it this friend of his, the VIP boyfriend he went to see on Monday?"

She looked up, a quick flicker of a glance. Surrender. "I don't know who he is. That's the truth. Maurice never told me his name or anything about him, except that in his position he couldn't afford any scandal. So Maurice got the stuff for him. He wasn't going to. He said no at first but—but—" Her mouth turned down with misery. "I persuaded him." She started to cry. "I said if he didn't get it, someone else would, and we might as well have the money as someone else. He didn't like it, but I persuaded him. He did it for us. And now—"

Slider handed over a handkerchief and she bubbled and hitched into it for a while. When he judged she was back on line, he said, "So how did it work? He got the stuff in the club, and then what? Brought it home?"

She nodded. "That was another reason he didn't like doing it. He said it was putting me at risk. I told him not to be so daft. No one knew it was there. And it was only for a few hours. He tried to arrange it so he always took it to his friend the next day. He didn't like it hanging around."

In case Busty succumbed to temptation, Slider thought. He changed direction. "He didn't go to work on Tuesday evening, did you know that?"

"No." She seemed genuinely surprised.

"When you left on Tuesday morning, he was intending to go in, was he?"

"He didn't say he wasn't."

"He wasn't ill?"

"No."

"But you said he was upset because of this quarrel with his friend on Monday."

She hesitated. "Well, to tell you the truth—he was at first, when he was telling me about it. Getting it off his chest, sort of. But then he like cheered up. Started talking about the plan—you know, to get a place in Ireland."

"You said you'd been talking about it on Sunday?"

"Yeah. He said on Sunday we nearly had enough, and he reckoned he could get hold of the rest of what we needed. But Tuesday morning he said it was all settled. All we'd got to do was find the place. He was even chatting to Benny about it, telling him where he was going to start looking for a place and everything.''

"So he'd got some more money on Monday, had he?"

She hesitated. "He didn't say so."

"But on Sunday he said he only needed a little more, and on Tuesday he said he had enough. So it sounds—"

"Yeah. Maybe. I dunno about that. All I know was, he was talking like it was all settled. 'Val,' he said, 'we're going to do it.' He was really cheerful about it. Just like a little boy," she added with a sentimental look.

"So when you left, he seemed in normal spirits."

"S'right," she said, but then frowned. "Only—I been thinking—he mustn't of been quite himself, leaving them dishes in the sink. He always washed up straight away after himself. Very tidy, Maurice was, tidied up as he went. Nearly a fetish with him."

"A late supper?" Slider suggested.

"Maybe," she said. "But you said he was sitting watching telly when it happened. He wouldn't normally sit down to watch without doing the washing up first."

"Yes, your tame cab driver told me Jay was a diligent housewife," Slider said. "He came to see me this morning."

"Benny did? What for?"

"Oh, to confirm your alibi."

"Confirm my—? Cheeky sod! But I suppose he meant well. I should've let him know—he was supposed to be picking me up We'nsday harpass five to take me to work, only it completely slipped me mind to cancel him."

"Understandable."

"I suppose he went around and saw all the cops there, and heard about it then. What did he say?"

"Oh, he just confirmed the times you gave me. He mentioned that Maurice opened the door to him."

Busty gave a little snort of laughter. "I don't expect he was best pleased. He'd have hoped to catch me alone. He's sweet on me, you see. Always turning up early, he is, wanting to chat. He even proposed to me a few weeks back."

"Proposed marriage?"

"Yeah. His wife died about six months ago—cancer—and

I will say he had the decency to wait a bit before proposing. But I've known a long time he was sweet on me. Maurice said—joking really—that I ought to accept, to give me security, but I wouldn't want to be married, at some man's beck and call night and day. You can refuse a customer,'' she said, ''but refuse a husband and you've got hurt feelings for days after.''

''So you turned down the offer of matrimony?''

''Yeah, course. I told him I'd promised to stay with Maurice. Not that he really took it in. He still hangs around me just the same, hoping I'll change me mind. Poor Old Benny. I've known him for years, and he's been good to me, but the fact is, even if I wanted to get married, I couldn't get fond of him that way. He's a funny old duck; and my God, his plates don't half pen! That's one thing about Maurice, you could eat your dinner off him—and drink your tea out of his shoes. Of course, being a dancer he's always been dead careful about his feet—'' The tears welled up again as the present tense tripped her up.

Slider deflected her. ''So as far as you knew, Maurice was going to work as usual? And he didn't say he was expecting a visitor?''

''A visitor?''

''There were two whiskey glasses in the front room. One on the coffee table and one down beside the chair.''

She thought about this, and shook her head. ''He never had visitors at home.''

''That you knew about,'' Slider amended, and she looked disconcerted, but continued to shake her head in denial. ''His friend wouldn't have visited him there?''

''Not him! Too risky.''

''Was there anyone at the club he was friendly with? Anyone on the staff?''

''Not that I know about. He never mentioned anyone.''

Slider sighed inwardly. The trouble with someone like Busty was that you never really knew when you'd got to the bottom layer. She probably didn't even know herself when she was concealing things. It was just instinctive with people like her to give nothing away that you weren't certain the other person already knew.

"Well, I'd better be getting back," he said. "If you think of anything that might help me find out who this friend of Maurice's was, give me a ring, will you? Or if you remember the dealer's name, or anything else that might be helpful—"

"When can I go home?" she asked abruptly.

"You want to?"

She shrugged. "All my stuff is there. And where else would I go? There's only my sister's, and I can't stay there. Trevor wouldn't stand for it, even if she had room. And there's no one else. Maurice was all I had in the world apart from her."

And Benny the Brief, Slider thought, but he didn't say it aloud. Benny's feet must be a deterrent indeed if even an ex-hooker couldn't stand them. "I think you ought to be able to go home tomorrow. I'll check when our blokes will be finished there, and let you know."

"All right, people, let's concentrate," Slider said. "Mr. Honeyman would like this cleared up before he leaves—"

"I bet he would," Mackay said.

"We could have a go at his dandruff, clear that up for him as well," McLaren murmured resentfully.

"So let's give him the best goodbye present a Super ever had," Slider went on, "and get it sorted. I'll go through first of all what we know about Jay Paloma's movements. Yes, thank you, McLaren. Right: he was a performer at the Pomona Club, where there was a *frackarse*"—he gave it the Department pronunciation—"on Saturday night, an attack by animal rights campaigners. Paloma was involved, not injured but may well have been upset by it. It was kept out of the papers, except for a par in Monday's *Standard*, which mentioned the club by name but not Paloma, nor the more interesting details of the incident. On Monday afternoon Paloma called at the station to see me, to tell me he was suffering from a poison pen campaign, which started six months ago with heavy-breather phone calls and escalated three months ago to threatening letters. It had escalated still further that morning—that's to say Monday—with a photograph of a badly mauled corpse."

"Guv, the animal libbers," Norma said, "I suppose they

were genuine? It wasn't part of the intimidation?''

Hollis, who was office manager, had the information. "One of them checked out as a paid-up member, but only recently joined. The others seemed to be his mates, and they were all protest virgins. No previous campaign history, and no criminal record.''

"These types usually have enough form to seat a banquet,'' Norma said. "Maybe they were not all they seemed.''

"They didn't seem very much,'' Hollis pointed out. "It wasn't a very bright stunt, and it wasn't ratified by any of the baa-lamb brigades. Going by the interview transcripts, I think they were just a bunch of dickheads acting off their own bats.''

Norma nodded to that, so Slider continued. "On Monday afternoon Paloma went to visit his regular lover, about whom we know nothing at present except that he is some kind of VIP who wanted to keep the relationship secret. They had a quarrel, according to Parnell. They also had somewhat rough sex, resulting in peri-anal bruising, according to the pathologist's report.''

"Because they'd quarreled?'' Mackay speculated.

"It might have been the way they usually did it,'' said Hollis. "We don't know.''

"On Tuesday,'' Slider went on, "Paloma got up and sat with Parnell while she got ready to go out. He was upset at first about the quarrel, but grew more cheerful as he began to talk about his plan to leave London and buy a boardinghouse in Ireland.''

"That sentence would make more sense the other way round,'' said Norma.

"Parnell left the house at eleven-thirty, and she and the taxi driver Fluss are the last people we know to have seen Paloma alive. He was due to go to work at seven p.m. but didn't arrive, nor did he telephone to say he wasn't going in. At half past eleven p.m. we have two separate witnesses to the sound of the door being kicked in, and some kind of further noise suggestive of something heavy being knocked over. At six-thirty on Wednesday morning Parnell arrived home to find the door kicked in and Paloma dead. Any comments?''

There were shrugs all around. "That's plain enough," Mackay said for them all. "Chummy kicks the door down and does him in. End of story."

"Except for the minor question of who chummy was," Norma added with delicate irony.

"Forensic says that from the size of the footmark," Slider picked it up, "we're looking for a very big man, probably over six foot, and powerfully built. The boot had a ridged sole of one of the usual man-made compositions, something like a Doc Marten—"

"Oh, well, that narrows the field a bit," said Norma.

"So if we find a suspect we may get a bit of help there," Slider concluded patiently.

"Guv, I can't believe no one saw this geezer," Hart said. "I mean, with all them flats around—and half past eleven people are coming back from the pub. And what about the block opposite? If you heard a door being kicked in, wouldn't you go out on the balcony and have a look?"

"No," said Anderson. "Ninety-nine out of a hundred, the last thing they'd do is go out and look."

"What about natural curiosity?" Norma said.

"What about self-preservation?" Anderson said. "The immediate neighbors made sure they stayed inside where it was safe."

"Yeah, but that's different," Hart said. "Across the other block it'd be safe enough to go out and have a butcher's. I know I would."

"The estate's not that dangerous," Norma said. "People exaggerate."

"The door was kicked in with one blow," Slider reminded her. "There may not have been that much to hear." Hart shrugged, half convinced. "By all means, interview everyone again. I'm always ready to give instincts a run."

"I've been thinking," McLaren said, and waited for the chorus of whistles and groans to die down. "If this bloke went along there to kick the door in and take Paloma out, why didn't he do it in the middle of the night, when there was no one around? Why choose half past eleven when there could be any number of witnesses?"

Slider looked at Hart. "What's your thinking on that?"

"S'obvious," she said. "Middle of the night he would've stood out like a sore thumb. Half past eleven, pub letting-out time, he passes in the crowd, and if someone sees him kick the door in they probably just think he's forgot his key. Anyone hears a loud bang, they don't pay no attention, just think it's a drunken fight or something and forget it. So when someone asks did you hear anything, they say no, and mean it."

Slider said, "So the killer was a professional, to your thinking?"

Hart looked confused. "Well—"

"Yes? Let's have it."

"Well, guv, the choice of timing and kicking the door open looks professional. And the killing—the first whack across the bridge of the nose killed him instantly, that looks professional. But then he goes onto paste buggery out of the dead man's skull for no reason—that don't look professional. And when he stops to pick up the table and put the fag ends back in the ashtray—that looks plain daft."

"Maybe he wanted to leave everything looking normal," McLaren said.

"Oh, normal—with a dead body on the floor," Hart said witheringly.

"He pulled the front door closed behind him," McLaren defended himself.

"That was to delay discovery," Anderson said. "A front door hanging open in the middle of the night would arouse suspicion."

"I can't see what the problem is," Norma said impatiently. "You've got someone with the foresight to choose the time of day for his murder and the expertise to know how to deal a killing blow. But then he gets carried away with excitement at what he's done and launches—"

She's going to say it, thought Slider.

"—a frenzied attack on the body. When he finally gets his breath back, he's not really thinking straight anymore, if at all. Instinct takes over. He tidies up the table that got knocked over—maybe he had a houseproud mum—and closes the front door after him. I don't see why," she concluded, "you should expect a villain to be consistent—especially in an irrational situation."

"You're talking about this bloke being professional," McLaren objected, "but you don't know he chose half eleven to be clever. Maybe he was dead stupid and never even thought about it. Maybe he had a beef with Paloma, and that just happened to be the time he lost his rag. Rushed around there, kicked the door in, and belted fuck out of him—just happened to get the first killing blow in where it landed, pure chance. That's much more likely."

"And tidied up after himself?" Slider said. McLaren offered no thoughts on that. "Let's move on, shall we? What about this drugs connection? Parnell says that Paloma was buying cocaine for his lover. Billy Yates says he saw Paloma talking to a man in the club who might have been a dealer."

Hollis said genially, "My uncle Fred might stick his wooden leg up his arse and do toffee apple impressions. Might doesn't feed the whippet."

"Quite so," Slider agreed. "However, I have to say that I don't believe Parnell would have mentioned coke at all unless there was something in it. She and I have had a few run-ins in the past on that subject. Now it may be she's not telling me the truth, or at least not all of the truth—in fact, I'm sure of that—but I think we can be sure there's some truth in it. It's possible Paloma was supplying her, and she brought in the lover as a smokescreen. But on the other hand, she did say he was being paid well for it and putting the money away toward this B and B scheme she mentioned. I'm inclined to believe her. I don't think she's got the imagination to make that up."

"It doesn't make the man in the club the dealer," Norma said.

"No. But again, Billy Yates needn't have mentioned him. He certainly wasn't trying to be helpful to me, so presumably he was worried by this man and was hoping I'd act as pest control officer and rid the club of him. And if Billy Yates was worried by the man, there's something about him we ought to know. I wouldn't trust Yates as far as I could spit him, but I trust his instincts of self-preservation."

"Guv," Anderson said, "how about this? Paloma said on Sunday he reckoned he could get the last of the money he needed for the Ireland scheme, right? He goes to see his lover on Monday and arranges to get another supply of coke for him. His lover gives him the cash. He goes into the club Monday night and buys the stuff as usual. Tuesday he knows Parnell's not going to be home, so he arranges to sell the stuff to some local distributor, probably for more than he paid for it. He's waiting in at home for the bloke to call, but word's got around that there's stuff in the flat, and before the right man can get there, someone else breaks in, grabs the snow and whacks Paloma. End of story.''

"There was no sign of anyone searching for anything," Mackay said.

"If he was expecting to sell it, he probably had it sitting there on the table."

"Why didn't he ring in to say he wasn't going to work? Ring in sick, or something?" Hart asked.

"He didn't care anymore. He was leaving anyway, once he'd got this dosh," said Anderson. "Next day when Parnell comes home he's going to say to her, pack your bags, darlin', we're off."

"Very beguiling," Slider said. "But where does the poison-pen campaign fit into this?"

"Maybe it doesn't," Anderson said, wholesale. "Maybe that was nothing to do with it. Given who he was and what he did, there's every chance there were people who didn't like him and wanted to scare him."

Hart spoke up. "Actually, boss, when you come to think of it—you never saw one of the letters. And he never told Parnell about it, either, which you'd think he would. Maybe it never happened. Maybe he made it up."

Slider looked at her. "Why would he go to all the trouble of coming in to see me to tell me about it? He was certainly afraid of something."

"I'd be afraid if I was going to pull off some dodgy stuff with a coke dealer," Hart said. "He came hoping you'd give him protection, put a copper on the door just for long enough for him to get away. Only he couldn't tell you the real reason."

"We're really getting into Hans Andersen country now," Slider said impatiently. "We've got to get more facts. We need to find the man he spoke to at the club, and any other contacts he had there. If the man Yates spotted wasn't a dealer, who was he; and who was the dealer? Paloma had been working at the club for almost a year. He must have talked to other club employees. Who did he know and what did he tell them? Any ideas how we can get the information?''

"Billy Yates's staff won't talk to us," Mackay said. "It's more than their jobs are worth."

"For jobs read lives," Anderson concurred.

Hart snorted. "You don't mean that big ponce Garry, walking about pretending he's got a holster under his arm?''

"Billy Yates has armed protectors, everyone knows that. They're not pretending," Mackay said.

"Yeah, and they're going to go around shooting anyone that asks questions?" Hart said derisively. "Do me a lemon! How long is Yates going to stay in business if he leaves a trail of corpses wherever he goes? If his boys carry shooters, it's to scare people. They're not gonna use 'em. Soon as they use 'em, Yates has got cops crawling all over his place, which is very good for business, I don't think."

"That's the sort of attitude that can get you killed," Norma said sternly.

"This ain't East LA," Hart responded. She turned to Slider. "I reckon I could get that Garry to talk to me, boss. He was fancying me rotten when we was there. If I come onto him a bit—''

Slider shook his head. "I can't let you put yourself in that sort of position. If you lead him on and then try to back out, he might very well force you, or beat you up."

"But, guv—" Hart protested.

"I think you underestimate the danger. He knows you're a copper, don't forget. He'd be glad to humiliate you. And if he got carried away, he might even kill you. Yates may be intelligent enough to know you can't go around offing people, but that's no guarantee Garry is." Slider looked around at the others. "Not Yates's staff, I don't think. But what about the other entertainers? They won't have the same loyalty, and I doubt whether they'll have the same fears. Yates wouldn't waste his energy on them. Find out who they are, and get to them, privately, away from the club.

"Get onto all the known users and dealers in the area and try to get a handle on it from that end. Find out if anyone did know about Paloma having coke on him at any time. And speak to everyone on the block, and anyone who was visiting that evening, and find out if anyone saw the door being kicked in. It's probably worth asking in the local pubs as well.

"Meanwhile," he concluded, "the killer doesn't exist in a vacuum. Someone knows him. Keep your ears to the ground. Ask around all your usual snouts. He came home in a state, probably with blood on him, and if he didn't tell his nearest and dearest why, they probably guessed anyway. You all know that ninety-nine out of a hundred crimes are solved through informers. Get out there and get at 'em."

As the troops were dispersing, Hart waylaid him with a determined gleam in her eye. "Guv, about that Garry—" she began.

Slider's heart sank, but he turned back to give her the benefit of the doubt. "What about him?"

"I know I'm right about him. I'm sure I could get information out of him. He's just pretending to be the hard man. Honest, I know the type."

"Well I'm *not* sure, so we'll just leave it, shall we?" Slider said.

"But you said you were always willing to go with instinct."

"A woman's instinct, is that it?"

"No, guv, a copper's instinct," she returned smartly.

She was so young and so confident she made him feel tired. "How old are you?"

She stuck her lip out. "I don't see what that's got to do with it, sir."

"Of course you don't. One of the nice things about being young is that you think you're immortal. When you've seen a few colleagues go down, you know different. You're not in this job to get your head blown off, Hart."

"I don't reckon to, sir, but—"

"Experience tells when it's worth taking the risk. For this, it's not worth it. Trust me." He began to turn away again.

"You wouldn't say that to Mackay or Anderson," she said sullenly.

His head began to throb. "They would know better than to ask," he said. "If you want to prove you're the same as a man, stick a rolled-up sock down your knickers. I haven't got time to visit anyone else in hospital."

"That's what this is about, ain't it, guv? You feel guilty about Sergeant Atherton and it's making you overprotective to the rest of us. With respect, you ain't got the right to lay that on us—"

"Don't give me that psycho-bollocks. This is not an episode of *Cracker*. And don't ever use those words to me again."

"What words?" she said, taken aback.

"With respect," he said, and left her standing.

"Am I intruding?" Joanna said, and he looked up from his desk to realize she had been standing in the doorway for some time, and he had been half aware of her and trying not to be.

"Oh, no, come in." Joanna walked over and leaned across the desk to kiss him. She had been rehearsing at the Albert Hall for the evening's concert.

"Why so distracted?" she asked.

"I was afraid it was Hart coming back for a rematch."

"Would you care to elucidate?"

He told her. "I don't know why I got riled, except that she's so cocksure, and can't take orders, and wants to go swaggering into the jaws of death like Indiana Jones when it doesn't even begin to be necessary."

"She's young," Joanna said.

"I know. That's the trouble. God, they think anyone over thirty has lost touch with reality. It's part of my job to see they live to realize how wrong they are."

"All the same, she's probably right—about you being overprotective. *Would* you have stopped Mackay or Anderson?"

"They're not female," he said. "It's no good looking at me like that. She was proposing to attempt to seduce a flash, gun-toting club hardman, and, having got information out of him, back out of having sex with him at the last minute. But anything he wanted to do to her, she couldn't stop him doing. It doesn't matter how feisty she is, or how well-trained, he's bigger and stronger than her, and that's the bottom line.''

''But isn't her life hers to risk?''

''No,'' he said, ''it's mine. While she's in the Job and in my firm, she's my responsibility.''

Joanna looked at him thoughtfully. ''You came back to work too soon,'' she said. ''No, don't glare at me, I don't mean your judgment is impaired, I just mean you look tired. And I bet you've got a headache.''

He tried to smile. ''Were you going to suggest having sex on the desk, then?''

''After the rehearsal I've just been through? Lupton and Bruckner? My arm's only hanging on by a thread. God, I hate the Albert Hall! You have to scrub twice as hard to make any impression. But I suppose making it hemispherical seemed like a good idea to her at the time.''

''Queen Victoria?''

''Mrs. Hall. It was named in memory of her husband.''

He gave her a ferocious scowl. ''What do you want anyway, Marshall?''

''I was just going to suggest a spot of lunch. Have you got time?''

''I'll make time,'' he said largely, feeling her different perspective on life like a blast of fresh air from a just-opened window. ''I'll take you to the canteen.''

''Gosh, you know how to spoil a girl,'' she said.

The Special was steak and onion cobbler. ''Aptly named,'' Slider said. It was in fact stew, with things on top that looked like dumplings but were actually a sort of hard pastry, having all the attributes of cobblestones except flavor. Joanna had the fisherman's pie. ''What's under the mashed potato?'' Slider asked.

Joanna chewed thoughtfully for a moment and then looked down. ''Something white,'' she said at last. ''With little bits of something pink.'' She chewed again. ''I am eating, aren't I?'' she appealed for reassurance. ''It's so hard to tell without some sensory imput, like taste or texture.''

''Never mind,'' he said, ''you can make it up with the pudding—they do a wicked jam roly-poly and custard. Atherton says it's the best thing on the menu. You are going in to see him this afternoon, aren't you?''

"Of course. I thought I'd smuggle Oedipus in to say hello. Are you going to be home tonight?''

"Yes. I hope so. I think so.''

"I won't go for a drink, then, I'll come straight home.'' She smiled at him suddenly. "Nice, this, isn't it?''

He looked startled. "Nice?''

"I mean, being able to plan to come home to each other, no tricky arrangements and subterfuges.''

"Oh, that.'' He thought suddenly of Irene, like a low ache of misery, mooning about in Ernie Newman's overstuffed lounge and pining for her own kitchen. "When this case is over I'm going to have to do something about that house,'' he said. "Change agents or lower the price or something.'' It was enough apropos as a comment for Joanna to accept it at face value; but Slider was thinking that if the house were sold, Irene would know there was no going back. But if she was really unhappy with Newman? And if that relationship broke down, what about the children? They'd have to have somewhere to go, they couldn't live in a hotel. Maybe he ought to keep the house on as insurance for them? No, that was ridiculous, he couldn't leave the empty house there forever just in case Irene changed her mind about Ernie. If she could stand him enough to run away with him in the first place—

Joanna's hand rested on his from across the table. "Don't start worrying about that as well. You haven't got room. One thing at a time.''

He looked up, his focus clearing to take in her face, not Irene's, hers, Joanna's. A face so ordinary it was like looking in the mirror, you hardly even distinguished the features; but so important, standing for everything in the last few years that was good in his life, it was like looking at, oh, an authentic photograph of God or something. Skin and lines and hair, eyes and teeth and nose: what was it that made one set of them so different, that nothing in your life afterward could be taken out of their context ever again?

"Are you sleeping with anyone tonight?'' he asked as casually as he could.

"What, after the show? I hadn't booked anyone."

"How about sex and a sandwich with me, then?"

"All right. My place, ten-thirty, on the sofa, bring your own coleslaw."

A furious clearing of the throat whipped Slider's attention to the young PC standing at his elbow with a large brown envelope in his hand and a sappy grin slithering self-consciously about his chops. "This came in for you, sir. Sergeant Nicholls thought you'd like it straight away."

"Thank you, Ferris."

Joanna watched him open it, smiling privately that a man of his age could still be self-conscious about being caught holding hands with his lady-love. And he'd probably use a word like lady-love, too, at least to himself.

Inside the envelope was the forensic report on the whiskey glasses and bottle.

"Ah, now this is interesting," Slider said. "You know that we found two glasses, one on the table and one down beside the other chair?" Joanna nodded. "The glass on the table has Paloma's fingermarks and lipmarks all over it."

"Lipmarks?"

"Oh yes, they're quite distinctive too."

"I must remember not to kiss my victims from now on."

"Not with wet lipstick, anyway. The glass on the floor also has Paloma's fingermarks on it, but they're overlaid by various smudges and marks consistent with its having been held by a hand wearing a leather glove. And it has lip marks on the rim which do not match Paloma's."

"So he had a visitor," Joanna said.

"A visitor who didn't take off his gloves."

"Unusual," she conceded. "Unless he had hives. I suppose the phantom tippler must have been the murderer, then?"

"It's a working supposition. Which suggests that Paloma must have known him," Slider said. "But that doesn't square with his having to kick the door in. It's not the usual way of announcing yourself socially. And why would you offer a drink to someone who'd just done that?"

"Well, look," Joanna said, "maybe Paloma used both glasses at different times. He might have been sitting in the other chair earlier, put the glass down, then later wanted another drink and went and fetched a clean glass. Why not? I've done that myself. And if he was a fastidious sort of chap, the old, greasy glass might not have appealed. And then the murderer fancied a nip after he'd bumped him off, so he just used one of the glasses he found handy."

"But the glass didn't have Paloma's lipmarks on it," Slider said. "It had only one set of lip prints, on one side of the glass, and the rest of the rim was clean."

"Maybe the murderer wiped the rim before he drank," Joanna said. "A lot of people would, quite instinctively, if they were drinking out of someone else's glass."

"Hmm," said Slider. "But there's something else here," he tapped the report. "The whiskey bottle has fingermarks on it too. Two sets. One possibly Paloma's, though they're not clear enough to identify with absolute certainty. The other set is over the top of them: a whole palm and five lovely digits, clear as day. Someone grabbed the bottle firmly in a manner consistent with either pouring or glugging from it—someone with an unusually large hand."

"Didn't you say the footmark on the door was unusually large too?"

"Yes."

"Then presumably they are a set. The glugger was the murderer."

"Presumably."

"So all you've got to do is find him," Joanna concluded happily, "and you've got your proof there all ready and waiting."

Slider turned a page. "Our mystery guest also left his fingermarks on the light switch. Several times."

"It was nighttime," Joanna pointed out.

"Yes, but the light was off in the morning. I suppose he must have turned it off as he left. And again on the front door. That was when he pulled it to, I suppose." He turned back and read it all again. "It's puzzling. Why did he drink out of the glass *and* the bottle? And why did he take his gloves off to pick up the bottle?"

"You want me to solve the whole case for you? He took a drink out of the glass because his nerves were shaken after killing Whatsisname, but that wasn't enough, he needed a good long glug, so he went for the bottle. But he couldn't get the fiddly cap off with his gloves on, so without thinking he took them off. *Voilà!*''

Slider smiled. ''You after a job or something?''

''Well, it's possible, isn't it?''

''Oh yes. There's simply no accounting for the stupidity of the average murderer—thank God, otherwise how would we ever catch 'em?''

He had just got back to his desk when Hart reappeared in his doorway. ''Guv?'' He looked up. ''Sorry.'' She gave him a wobbly grin. ''I dunno what come over me. Must be them testosterone pills I been taking. No, straight up,'' she went on as he began to smile, ''I gotta shave twice a day now. And what you said about rolled-up socks? Don't need 'em. I can write me name in the snow just like anybody else.''

So he told her about the forensic report, as a reward. Hart was jubilant. ''Brilliant! If he's got form, we've got him.''

''Let's hope.''

''In any case, how hard can he be to find, over six foot, massive germans and plates the size of Wandsworth? You see that kicking someone's door in, you don't forget it in a hurry.''

''Off you go then,'' he said indulgently, ''and jog some memories.'' He stood up. ''I've got to see a man about a taxi.''

''How's that?''

''It just came to me. Busty Parnell said that Paloma went everywhere by taxi too. So he probably went to meet his lover in a cab, and if I can find the right driver, he can give me the address.''

''Brilliant, boss.''

''That's why I get the big money.''

SEVEN

Shades of Brown

The headquarters of Monty's Radio Metrocabs was, like every other taxi garage, cramped, chaotic and filthy. It consisted of two railway arches and the tiny cobbled yard in front of them. Under the arches was the repair and servicing workshop for the cabs, and the front right-hand corner was screened off with two walls of wood and glass to make a tiny office for Monty, into which he squeezed himself with his battered desk, his filing cabinets, and an old tin tray balanced on top of a kitchen stool on which the electric kettle and the coffee making equipment stood in a pool of sad spillings and half-melted sugar. There was no ceiling to his corner, and a single lightbulb dangled down, suspended on fathoms of fraying wire from the curved bricks invisible in the darkness far above. In the worst depths of winter a paraffin heater added its stink to that of Monty's cigars and the pervading odor of petrol, but did little to mitigate the cavernous chill. Every surface was tacky with oil, and overhead Metropolitan Line trains passed at regular intervals in a brain-bouncing, tooth-loosening thunder. It was not an office that welcomed visitors, and that was how Monty liked it. He liked his drivers out driving and making him money, not hanging around the depot complaining.

Across the other side of the yard in a new, brightly lit and tropically heated portakabin, the radio side of the operation was worked by Monty's wife Rita and his mistress Gloria in a comfortable atmosphere of tea, bourbon biscuits, knitting, family photographs and refrained gentility. They called the cabbies "dear" and "my pet" and asked tenderly after their wives' ailments, but ruled them with a rod of iron. They would not tolerate the word "can't," and fined them for bad language on a sliding scale from a simple damn upward. "That's twenty pence in the Swear Box, my darling," they would say primly when some benighted cabbie trying to find an invisible fare at a mythical address let loose with a *bloody* over the air; and such was the force of their personalities that the next time the transgressor was in the yard, he would go into the cabin and pay his dues. The box was emptied every week after the lucrative Saturday Night Swear, and the proceeds went toward taking disabled children on an annual adventure holiday.

"Isn't that doing evil that good may come?" Slider once asked Rita, and she primmed her lips and said, "I don't suppose the kiddies mind, dear."

Slider was always amazed by Monty's ménage à trois: he couldn't understand why he bothered. The two women were so alike that people often thought they were sisters. They were the same age, height and build, with the same solid, well-corseted figure and the expensively dull clothes of prosperous middle age. Both wore their hair permed and sprayed to the same style by the weekly attentions of the same hairdresser—Rita's was tinted mauve and Gloria's platinum. Both wore their glasses around their necks on a chain—Gloria's made of pearls and Rita's of little gold beads. Gloria's smile had more teeth in it—she had captured Monty by her vivacity, and was now stuck with it, Slider deduced—but otherwise there was nothing to choose between them. Perhaps that was why Monty hadn't.

The two women were the best of friends, and between radio messages chatted seamlessly in the manner of those who know each other's thoughts. They treated Monty with the same arch and half-affectionate exasperation as they treated the cabbies, corrected his manners, deplored his smoking, doctored his ills and chose his clothes. Slider couldn't imagine what Monty got out of it.

Slider tacked past the cabin, hoping to escape notice,

though he saw through the brightly lit window that Rita turned her head, her jaws never ceasing to move as she talked to the public, the cabbies and Gloria, switching from one to the other as effortlessly as American TV programs switch to adverts. Under the right-hand arch a black cab was up on the lift and one of the mechanics, Nick the Greek, waved a friendly spanner at Slider from the inspection pit as he crossed to Monty's office.

Monty removed a cold cigar from his teeth and struggled courteously to his feet. He was a short, wide man with a thick, collapsing face, despairing hair, sad brown eyes behind heavy glasses, and a full lower lip permanently deformed by having to accommodate huge Havana cigars. They were expensive, and the ladies tutted, so he hardly ever smoked them, just lit them and let them go out. That way they lasted.

He seemed glad to see Slider. "Well, well, well! And what can I do for you today, young sir?"

"Hello, Monty. How's business?"

His face buckled with instant gloom. "*Well* bad," he said confusingly. "When is business anything *but* bad? Heads above, just—that's the best we can hope for. It's a wonder I can sleep at night."

"Come off it, you old fraud," Slider said. "I see you driving about in a new Bentley."

"It's not new, it's two years old," Monty protested. "I only got it to give my bank manager confidence, stop him foreclosing on me. I tell you, Mr. Slider, I'm brassic. What with the cost of cabs, insurance through the roof, rates up fifty percent this year, new Health and Safety rules coming off by the yard every week—it's as much as I can do to turn a penny. And Mrs. Green is not a well woman, you know."

"I'm sorry to hear that. She looks bonny enough," Slider said, glancing toward the cabin.

"My mother," Monty elucidated. "She can't manage the stairs, you see, which means either putting in a stair lift, or making her a bedroom downstairs. Either way, it's all expense. And the mortgage enough to make you faint." He sighed. "I wouldn't wish this life on a dog, I promise you."

So Monty lived with his mother as well as his wife and mistress, did he? Perhaps the one phenomenon accounted for the other. "You know," Slider said, "five minutes talking to you does me the power of good. Makes the world outside seem so bright. You should work for the Samaritans."

"You try getting cabbies to pay up at the end of the week, you'll soon know all about working for charity," Monty said, and busied himself relighting his cigar. Honor satisfied, he went on more cheerfully, "Anyway, what can I do for you? I suppose you're on this business of PC Cosgrove? Rotten bloody shame that was, pardon my French. Is there any improvement?"

"He's still in a coma, but stable, they say."

Monty shook his head. "Rotten business. He's such a nice geezer, too. He was around here, you know, just a few days before it happened."

"Was he? What about?"

"Just chewing the fat. He used to pop in from time to time—have a bunny with Rita and Gloria, cuppa tea, time of day, that sort of thing. It was on his way home. How's his wife taking it? I feel sorry for her, another nipper on the way, can't be easy."

"She's bearing up, I believe. But I'm not on that case—that's Mr. Carver's. I'm here about something else—a murder last Tuesday. I want your help."

"Right you are," Monty said, looking intelligent. "Anything I can do. Always happy to assist the boys in blue."

"I want to trace the cabbie who picked up a fare from the White City on Monday, late morning." He gave Jay Paloma's address and description. "He went up to Town somewhere—I want to know where. It could be one of yours. This bloke went everywhere by cab—nervous type—so it's probable he telephoned for a cab and he may well have used your firm."

"We can soon look that up," Monty said.

"If not I'd like you to put the word about for me."

"Fair enough. You're sure it was a black cab?"

"Yes, he didn't trust minicabs."

"Pity he's dead, then. Can't afford to lose people like that—there aren't enough of 'em. Got a picture?"

"I'm getting them done now. They'll be round this afternoon."

"Right. Let's go and look at the book of words."

They went out into the yard together. "Oh, by the way," Slider said, "I'm interested in one of your drivers, Benny by name."

"Benny the Brief or Benny Bovril?"

"Benny the Brief. Is he all right? Reliable?"

"He's all right," Monty said. "He can be a bit of a pain in the neck—too much of this—" He imitated a yacking mouth with his fingers. "But he's all right. Funny old sort—bit of a reader. Knows a stack about the law. The other drivers take the piss out of him, pardon my French, but they all go to him when they want to know something. Walking encyclopedia. Is he in trouble?"

"No, no. I just wanted to know if I can believe what he tells me."

"Oh, he's honest as the day, old Benny. Had a tough break a few months back—his old lady died. The Big C. Went just like that. Been married a coon's age, as well. He took it really hard—sold the house and everything in it, went to live in lodgings, said he couldn't bear to have her stuff around him, reminding him all the time. Worked every hour God sent. I said to him, Benny, I said, you'll crack up. Take a rest, I said. But no, he wanted to work. Kept his mind off, he said. He's eased off now, though—not been doing much at all, hardly turned in two tanners last week. Just as well, I suppose, or he'd come to grief, and I'd be sorry to lose him. Funny old bugger, but he's all right."

They reached the cabin, and Monty climbed the steps and opened the door onto the Yardley scented, pot-plant-benighted bower. "It's like the hanging gardens of Babel," Monty muttered over his shoulder for Slider's benefit. The women's voices and the squawk of the radio were like birds' cries: Slider had a momentary vision of Rita and Gloria as brightly colored parrots swinging about the tropical branches. But they were nothing if not businesslike. When Monty explained Slider's quest, they consulted the day book for him without ever ceasing to answer the phone and speak their mysterious incantations to the invisible spirits of the cabbies. But there was no record of a call to that address or anything near it, or for the name of Paloma or McElhinney.

Still, Slider was hopeful as he left the yard. Jay had been

as bright and distinctive as his avian namesake, and if Monty circulated the query, someone ought to remember him.

Hart tagged onto Slider as he went past. "Guv, I got a message for you, but I don't know if it's genuine or not. It sounds like someone's pulling our plonker."

"What is it?"

"Well, this bloke said his name was Tidy Barnet. I mean, that's gotta be a joke, ennit?"

"He's a snout of mine," Slider said. Barnet was his real surname. He had had an older brother whose nickname was Scruffy, so Tidy's sobriquet was inevitable. "What did he want?"

"He just said to say," Hart looked down at her pad to check it, "Tidy Barnet says tell Mr. Slider to ask Maroon. Does that make sense?"

"It does to me," Slider said. "He didn't say ask her what?"

"No, guv. That's absolutely all he said, word for word."

"Right," said Slider. They reached his room. "Have those photographs gone round to Monty's garage?"

"Ten minutes ago. And I've got some good news and some bad news."

"Bad news first."

"Them fingerprints off the bottle—all negative. No match in the records. Whoever he is, he's got no recent form."

"Damn," Slider said. "Given the M.O., I wouldn't have thought that was his first attempt at violence."

"Maybe he's too professional to get caught," Hart offered.

"You'd better pray he's not," Slider said. "What's the good news?"

She grinned triumphantly. "We got a witness."

"Eyewitness?"

"I spy with my little eye, something beginning wiv B. A big black bugger in boots kicking the door in at half past eleven Tuesday night. Female living opposite. She does office cleaning at nights, and she's just got home, walking along the balcony feeling in her bag for her key, when she hears this wallop, looks across and sees chummy just kicked the door in and going in the flat."

"You're sure it's the same flat?"

"It's right opposite. She pointed it out to me. Same floor and everything. No mistake, guv."

"She must have been questioned before. Why didn't she say anything?"

"I looked up the notes, and one of the woodentops knocked on her door first time round, but she done the free wise monkeys. When she sees it happen, she just reckons someone's forgot his key, none of her business, right? But when they come around asking about murder, she gets scared. She reckons if she says anything, she's next on the list. So she stays schtumm."

"How did you persuade her to unbutton?"

Hart grinned. "You either got it or you ain't. Plus a few freats."

"You what?" Slider was alarmed.

"Oh, nothing too pointed," Hart said airily.

"What description did she give you? Did she get a good look at him?"

"Not really. Well, those flats are lit up like Colditz on a bad night, but he had his back to her, and she wasn't stopping to stare."

"But you say she thought it was the occupant who had forgotten his key? She thought it was Paloma, in fact?"

"Oh, she never knew Paloma. Never knew who lived opposite. It's like that in them flats. You know the people on your own balcony—sometimes—but that's that. The block opposite's like the other side of a river and the bridge is out. Different country. Strange natives wiv peculiar customs."

"Thank you, Michaela Dennis."

"Who?"

"Skip it. So we've got nothing at all by way of description?"

"Well, she said he was black. And he was big."

"The PC could have told her that."

"Yeah, but I asked her how big, and she said like massive. As he went in the flat, he had to duck his head. Now, I measured and them doors is standard six foot six high."

"If he's more than six foot six tall he'll be easy to find."

"Yes, guv," she said intelligently, "but he needn't be that

big. I mean, internal doors can be anything from six foot, six-three, six-four, yeah? Well, a bloke who's only six-two, six-three can get used to having to duck, and it gets to be a habit. Self-preservation. But there ain't that many blokes six foot three even, and she said he was big with it, like a weight-lifter.''

Slider nodded, thinking. ''Well, if she didn't see his face it's no good trying to get her to come in and look at some pictures. Still, I suppose at least it's further confirmation of the time.''

''That's what I fought. So what's this message, boss? About maroon. Maroon what?''

Slider thought about what had happened last time he went out in the field without telling anyone where he was going, and explained. ''Maroon is a person,'' he said. ''Maroon Brown. She's a prostitute, lives in Percy Road.''

''Appropriate,'' Hart said. ''Is that her working name?''

''Strangely enough, it's her real name. It's short for Mary Oonagh. She had an Irish grandma who brought her up.''

Slider told what he knew of the story. Maroon's grandma at age sixteen had got herself up the duff by a black stoker from a ship which had put in to Cork Harbour for repairs, and shortly put out again. Rather than face her family she had run away to London to have the baby. The war had just ended and the men were beginning to come home, and she had supported herself by working part time in a café and part time on the game. The baby, named Alice, had grown up to show a preference for her father's lineage, and at sixteen had followed family tradition by succumbing to the charms of a West Indian lorry driver and becoming pregnant.

''Of course, by the time the kid was born the father had already disappeared. So Alice did the same.''

''Leaving grandma holding the baby?''

''Quite. So grandma had her Christened with a fine Irish name, and shortened it to Maroonagh, but everybody either misheard it, or thought it was a joke, so she was Maroon Brown forevermore.''

''So how do you know so much about her, guv?''

''Oh, she gets nicked from time to time. I've seen her

around, interviewed her a couple of times. She's not a bad sort.''

"And this snout of yours thinks she knows something about the murder?''

"So it seems.'' He paused, weighing probabilities. "I'm off to have a chat with her. If I take you along, can I trust you to keep your mouth shut?''

Hart looked wounded. "Follow your lead in all things, that's my rule.''

"Ha!'' said Slider.

The house in Percy Road—sounds like a film title, he thought—was one of those miniature grand houses built in the 1840s, semi-detached, three storys including the semi-basement; where once a senior clerk, with a live-in cook and housemaid, aped the style of his immediate superior, who had much the same only bigger and detached. Now the house had fallen on hard times. It stood at the kink of Percy Road, alone of its type, surrounded by meaner dwellings; seedy and paint-lorn, it had sunk to the ignominy of division into a basement flat and four bedsits. Judging by the bell labels, all the occupants were toms. What would Mr. Pooter have thought of that?

Slider gestured to Hart to stand close by the door where the overhang of the shallow porch hid her, and rang the bell. The curtain at the front bay window stirred slightly, and Slider felt himself invisibly considered. He tried to exude unthreateningness. The door did not open, but there was a feeling of activity inside. He rang again. After a further pause the first floor window at the front opened and a female face looked out—black but not Maroon.

"Whajjer want?'' it inquired uninvitingly.

Slider stepped back a little and looked up. "Is Mary there?'' he asked.

"There ain't no Mary lives here,'' the head said scornfully.

"Mary Brown. Mary Oonagh,'' Slider said. The head drew back a little, and seemed to be conferring, if not with its own thoughts then with someone inside.

"You a mate?'' it asked doubtfully.

"Yes, I'm an old friend. It's all right, it's not trouble, I just want a chat with Mary."

"You better come in," the head said at last. "Push the door when the buzzer goes, and wait in the hall, orright?"

After a few moments the buzzer went. Slider pushed the door, gestured Hart inside with a finger against his lips, and let the door close again, flattening himself against it. Almost at once the bay window sash was put up, and a foot and leg appeared. He stepped out of the shelter of the porch to find Maroon halfway out, her leading limb reaching perilously over the short railings for the top step. She gave a squeak like a caught mouse when she saw him.

"Hello, Mary. Going somewhere?"

"Oh, bloody hell," she said, trying to reverse her progress.

"Careful, now, you'll hurt yourself," Slider said. "Come on, love, I just want a chat. You don't need to go all Colditz on me. It's not grief for you." She stared, wide-eyed, and struggled a little, unable to correct her balance so as to pull herself back. "I think it'll be easier for you to come the rest of the way out," Slider said. "Here, grab my hand. And for God's sake be careful. If you fall on those railings you'll never play the cello again."

"I don't need your bloody help," she growled. But he helped her anyway, keeping a firm grip on her upper arm when she was safely on the ground. She wriggled it experimentally, between fear and anger. "Let me go, can't you? What was all that Mary cobblers? Nobody calls me that except my mum."

"Reassurance," he said. "I just want to talk, that's all, I promise. Don't make it difficult for yourself."

She was near to tears, and now that he was close to her he saw that she had been crying a lot recently, and he could smell how afraid she was. She had also been drinking. "All right," she said. "Let's get inside. I don't want anyone seeing you here."

Despite her acquiescence he kept hold of her until she had opened the door and preceded him in. She started like a terrified deer when she saw Hart lingering in the shadows, but Slider soothed her, introduced Hart, and ushered Maroon into the first room on the left. He half expected her to bolt for the bay window again, but she seemed to have resigned herself, and went straight to the mantelpiece to get a cigarette. The room had been the best parlor of the original house. It had a splendid marble fire surround, which had been horribly, carelessly chipped at some time, and also painted red, though the paint was now abandoning it in sheets. It housed a gas fire of extremely, not to say life-threateningly, mature vintage. The rest of the room contained an unmade double bed, a large wardrobe with a mirrored door, two basket armchairs, a chest of drawers, and a tatty chaise longue covered with dirty yellow damask. The room was wildly untidy, a mess of clothes, papers, empty bottles, crockery and glasses and other clutter.

Maroon lit a cigarette rather shakily. Slider sat down on the chaise longue and watched her. "You must be in trouble if you were thinking of running away from me," he said at last. "Do you want to tell me about it?"

"I s'pose that's what you've come for. Oh Gawd." Tears began to leak out of her eyes again, and she puffed rapidly at the cigarette as if that might staunch them. She had been quite good-looking once, but her nose and right cheekbone had been broken at some time, giving her a lopsided look, and though she was only thirty-two or three, drink, cigarettes and her general lifestyle were aging her before her time. She looked entirely West Indian, except for the higher cheekbones and slightly narrower face which was all she had inherited from her grandmother. Her hair was closely plaited into windrows from front to back, finishing off with eight little plaited tails tagged with red beads. Her eyes were bloodshot and heavy-shadowed as she looked at Slider miserably, but without flinching. "I had nothing to do with it, I swear to you. That's the honest trufe. I'd never do anything to hurt Andy. Christ, you must know that."

Slider heard, comprehended, and made the mental adjustment without external sign; willing Hart, standing by the door, not to move or look at him. Not Paloma, then. He had been sent here for the flip side: she had information about Andy Cosgrove. "If you had nothing to do with it, then you've got nothing to fear, have you?" he said.

She moaned and sat down on the end of the bed. "You don't understand."

"Is someone putting the frighteners on you?" Slider asked. "You can't be scared of me, surely?"

Maroon looked up, and Hart saw that indeed, she wasn't afraid of him. How did he do it, she wondered? Must be pheremones. Maroon had already forgotten Hart. Her eyes were fixed on Slider with appeal, but she was going to come across. Hart almost held her breath, not to disturb the delicate balance.

"Oh Gawd, oh poor Andy," Maroon said. "How is he? Do you know how he is? I tried ringing the hospital, but they wouldn't tell me nothing. The word on the street is he's still in a coma. Is that right? Is he going to die?"

"I don't know," Slider said, feeling his way with a sense of eggshells underfoot. "They say he's stable, but of course they're very anxious that he should regain consciousness soon. The longer he's out, the worse it is."

She put her face in her hands. "If I'd known how it would end, I'd never have asked him to help me. But I didn't know. I thought he'd just—you know—start the ball rolling. Pass it over to your side. I never thought he'd go asking questions himself. Oh, my poor Andy!"

Her poor Andy? Slider's ears were out on stalks, but he spoke matter-of-factly. "How did you and Andy first meet? I've often wondered."

"When I lived on the estate of course."

"The White City Estate?"

"Yeah. He arrested me for drunk and disorderly outside the General Smuts one night. I was only nineteen. I was all right then—before I got this." By "all right" she meant in looks. She reached up and touched the broken side of her face delicately, as though it still hurt; probably it still did in her psyche. "I got let off with a caution, and he come back the next day, when he got off duty." She smiled shakily. "Wanted to reform me—talk me into going straight. You could get a job, he said. I didn't know whether to laugh or cry. I mean, me! What could I do? I been on the game since I was sixteen. I don't know nothing else. But he got to me. He was so—" She hunted for a word.

"Earnest?" Slider offered.

"Yeah. Like that. For him it was like, the whole world was

a good guy really, you know? He wasn't long married then, and his wife was expecting their first. Little Adam.'' Her face softened at the name. Blimey, she knows all the history, Slider thought. ''He was so happy, he thought he could change the world. Bleeding sunshine merchant. He even had me believing for a bit.'' She nodded, her eyes round with the wonder of it. ''I tried getting a job, on the checkout down Gateway, just to please him. But I couldn't stand it, getting up every morning and sitting there all day, bloody customers treating you like dirt, yes-sir-no-sir while the manager looks down your front, dirty old git. And the end of the week, what'd you got to show for it? Peanuts. So I chucked it.''

''And what did Andy think of that?''

''Oh, I kept out of trouble in those days, so I didn't see much of him, unless I happened to see him walking down the street. No, it was later I got to know him really well. After I got away from Billy Yates.''

''Billy Yates?''

A look of great bitterness crossed her face. ''Yeah. Him. I'll tell you about him, but you can't use it.'' Now she glanced at Hart, aware of her danger. ''You gotta promise me. He'd have me killed like you'd stamp on a beetle. D'you want to hear it all?''

''Very much,'' Slider said.

''Lock that door, then,'' she nodded to Hart, and got up and closed the window and pulled the curtains. Hart put the light on. Maroon crossed the room and put a rap tape on the cassette player, turning it up to a conversation-covering pitch. She was that scared, Slider thought. Hart had taken out her notebook, but Maroon looked at her sharply. ''Nothing written down. You can stay if he says. But you can't use any of this.''

''I vouch for Hart,'' Slider said. ''Go on.''

Maroon sat on the bed and crossed her legs, putting the ashtray and cigarettes down beside her. Evidently it was going to be a long story.

''Billy Yates,'' she said.

Billy Yates, it seemed, not only ran nightclubs, casinos and amusement arcades, he also ran a string of girls.

"Night after night you lie on your back thinking sixty percent of this is for Billy Yates. I got quite good at sums. Take a fifteen minute blow-job: you're gobbling for Billy Yates for nine minutes." She made a violent sound of disgust. "But you know what was so creepy about him? He never did it himself. If he'd liked girls, if he'd come round now and then and had one on the house—management perks, like his boys used to—you could almost have liked him better. But he's a cold fish, Billy Yates. He never does it—never done it in his life, if truth be known. And it's not that he's the other way, either. He's not queer. He's just cold as a corpse. He looks at you like you're—" She shook her head. "But I've seen him with his business pals, and it's all smiles and big cigars and slap-me-back old pals act. We did this trick once, me and this other girl, Jasmine her name was, at some posh hotel up west, up Lancaster Gate. We was supposed to spend the night with some business contact of Billy Yates's. See them come in together, you'd think they was brothers, arms round each other, laughing and joking. Only his eyes never smile. He's making nice to this Arab, and all the time his eyes are going round like a machine, checking everything in the room. Like he's taking photos. Click click click. The bed, the champagne, the lights, the fruity videos. And he looks at Jasmine and me, click click. That's all we was to him, two bits of gear for oiling up this deal."

But it was unusual for Maroon to see Yates. Normally he ran his girls at arm's length, and that, in its way, was what they resented most. His "boys" did all the hands-on work. They called themselves doormen or drivers or security guards, but Billy Yates just said, "I'll send round one of my boys." They were bouncers in the clubs, croupiers in the casinos, managers in the amusement arcades, and pimps to the girls; they were messengers and chauffeurs and bodyguards and sorters-out of trouble. They collected money and delivered rebukes. They were young, fit, tooled up, and saw themselves as an all-powerful elite. The girls hated and feared them.

"They could do what they liked, as long as they didn't damage the goods." She shrugged. "Some of them just wanted to get their end away, they was no trouble, just get on, do it, get off again. But some of them liked to hurt you. And they worked out ways to hurt you so it didn't show.''

Maroon worked for Yates's empire from 1982 until 1988. ''Six long years,'' she said in a black voice. She was run by one of Yates's top ''boys,'' Jonah Lafota. ''We was his best girls, so we got Jonah for our pimp—only you'd never call him that, not if you valued your skin. Our 'manager' he called himself. He was supposed to keep us in order, and look after us, keep the customers from damaging us.'' She reached up and touched her face again. ''It was him did this. I suppose I should thank him, because it got me away from Yates.'' She gave a bark of ironic laughter. ''I'd kill him if I could,'' she said, ''that's how much I want to thank him.''

It had happened one night when she was about to start work, and Jonah had come in and wanted to use her himself. She had protested she had someone waiting. ''I don't know what came over me,'' she mused. ''You didn't argue with Jonah. But that night, I just turned around and answered him back. I think he was a bit lit up. Suddenly he just lashed out and hit me.'' She demonstrated. ''Backhand, like he was playing bloody tennis. Sent me right across the room and hit the wall. Knocked me out cold. When I came to, I was in hospital with my face all broken.'' She shook her head. ''Billy Yates was furious. If it had been anybody but Jonah, I don't know what he would have done to him. As it was, he just demoted him.'' She shrugged. ''Me, I was let go. I couldn't work for Yates with this face.''

''You didn't go to the police?'' Slider said, more to keep her talking than because he thought she might have.

She looked derisive. ''You kidding? Jonah would have killed me. I was lucky he hadn't killed me as it was, hitting me like that. Like I said, I think he was a bit lit up, because normally he was careful. He never hit people, or if he did he kind of pulled his punch, because he's a monster, is Jonah. Six foot six and built like a brick khasi, with hands on him like—'' She demonstrated with her hands apart. ''So he'd gotta be careful.''

Hart stirred, and out of the corner of his eye, Slider saw her look toward him. Maybe they were here for the Paloma case after all. Maybe there was a connection that hadn't been suspected.

"Do you know where Jonah works now?" Slider asked.

"Oh, he's still with Yates. He's mostly at the Pink Parrot."

"That's another of his nightclubs, is it?"

"Yeah. Down Fulham Broadway. Used to be a gay club, but it's more mixed now." Maroon looked from Slider to Hart and back, the cozy confidence she had built up for herself evaporating. "I don't want him to find me," she said urgently. "D'you understand? He'll kill me if he knows I've spoken to you."

"You haven't told me anything against him yet," Slider pointed out soothingly.

"He wouldn't care about that. If he even saw me talking to you—" She wrapped her arms around herself. "You gotta promise me."

"I promise you," Slider said. "I won't use your name. I'll find some other way. Go on now." She still hesitated, so he primed her with the irresistible. "Tell me about you and Andy."

EIGHT

A Whale of a Tale

When Maroon was still in hospital with her broken face, Andy Cosgrove had come to visit her. He heard the word on the street, and came to see if he could help her.

"He was shocked when he saw what Jonah had done to me. He tried to get me to make an official complaint, so he could arrest Jonah, but I wouldn't. But anyway, after that he kind of interested himself in me. Andy helped me find somewhere to live and—well—he was around a lot and—" She shrugged eloquently.

"You became lovers," Slider offered delicately.

Maroon was pleased with the euphemism. "Yeah," she said. "That's it." Reading between the lines, Slider guessed that from Cosgrove's point of view it was a case of the seven year itch. His marriage was no longer new, and his wife had begun to discover that being a copper's wife was not all roses, which had soured her temper. She had just had another child and sex was off-limits, and the baby was making the nights hideous. Cosgrove had succumbed to the comforts a grateful ex-whore was more than willing to offer. Slider was not surprised—it was a story he had heard many times before—but he was rather shocked that it was Andy Cosgrove, the Father Christmas of W12, who had sinned so callously against his wife. It seemed, however, that an affection had built up between Cosgrove and Maroon beyond mere sexual gratification, and he had done her a great deal of good. The affair had taken on a regular, almost domesticated pattern, and, his needs being satisfied, Cosgrove had begun to be a better husband at home too.

And then Maroon's sister turned up, come to the big city to seek her fortune.

"I didn't know you had a sister," Slider said.

"Nor did I," Maroon said.

It seemed that when Maroon's mother Alice had fled parental responsibility, she had headed up the A1, the Great North Road, which in those days had a romance and glamour to its name, and also led in the direction it was possible to get the furthest away from London. Over the years, Alice kept moving north. Occasionally when conscience bit or good luck came her way, she sent some money for her mother or a birthday card for her abandoned infant, and in that way she and Maroon's grandma kept in distant touch.

Eventually Alice reached Aberdeen, and feeling it impracticable to go any further north, settled down within handy reach of the docks. One day she found herself pregnant again. It was not at all in her plans to bring up a child, and as soon as the baby was born she hastened to her mother, who by then had moved back to Ireland, Maroon having left home. Alice arrived one day with baby Molly and left the next, in the early hours, without her. She had told her mother nothing about the baby's father except that he was Maltese—there was a large community of immigrants from Malta living in Aberdeen. Grandma, resigning herself to another surrogate motherhood, referred to the baby affectionately as "my little Maltesa," and the nickname stuck.

"And you didn't know anything about her until she arrived on your doorstep?" Slider asked.

"Well, I never was one for writing letters, and Gran never got round to it," Maroon said. "Anyway, one day, about a year after I left Billy Yates, this kid turns up and says, hello Maroonagh, I'm your sister. She was just sixteen. Gawd, she was pretty!" Maroon's face softened with remembered delight. "Brown eyes and hair like mine, but not dark like me, kind of honey-colored skin, and sharp little features like a little cat. And she was bright, too, up for everything, always on the bubble. I loved her to death. All I wanted was the best for her. I never wanted her to go on the game like me. I wanted her to get a job and get married, do everything properly, like I never done.''

Everything would have been all right, if it wasn't for Jonah Lafota. He blamed Maroon for his demotion, and wanted his revenge on her, but felt that her close liaison with the local community copper made her a dangerous target. When Maltesa came to town, it looked like the perfect opportunity to make Maroon suffer.

''He went after her. I didn't know at first. He sweet-talked her, showed her the bright lights, told her how much money she could make as a high-class call girl, if she had the right manager. *Manager!*'' She spat the word. ''When I found out, I was furious. I nearly snatched her bald-headed, told her if she wanted to throw her life away, she might as well go and jump off Westminster Bridge and get it over with. Of course, it was the wrong thing to say to Maltesa. She never would take telling. Got on her high horse right away. I tried everything I could, but she wouldn't listen. She said she could make a fortune in a couple of years, and then we could go off and live in Spain or somewhere. Oh, she was full of it!'' Maroon said bitterly. ''Like any little kid dreaming of Christmas, it was all going to be so easy. And she could take care of herself, I needn't worry, she was up to all the tricks, no one was going to take her for a ride.''

There was a heavy silence. ''What happened?'' Slider asked at last.

''Jonah introduced her to drugs. She thought it was all part of the high life, and she could handle it. Of course she couldn't. Gradually she just—disappeared. Jonah made her work for her fixes, and she did things she didn't want to tell me about, so I saw her less and less. I pleaded with her, but it only turned her against me. She changed, that kid—her whole personality. It'd break your heart to see her moody and sullen like she was towards the end. I don't know what she was doing for Jonah at the finish, but he made sure she still got the stuff. She died in 1994. She was only twenty. *He* did that.'' There was a pause while she lit another cigarette from the stub of the current one. ''She was a good kid at heart, just too full of spirit. Ready to try anything. She was easy meat to him. I'd have done anything to save her, but there was nothing I could do. After she died, I just wanted to run away. I think I went a bit mad. I drank a lot. I left the flat and moved around, bedsitters and that. There didn't seem any point in anything anymore. And then Andy found me again." She looked up. "I hadn't told him anything. He didn't know what happened to Maltesa. He didn't know where I'd gone. I should've told him, I suppose. He was worried about me, bless him. Well, he found me, I don't know how. I told him everything, and—and I begged him to get Jonah for what he'd done to my sister. I didn't have any proof, you see. I must have been mad to try and get him involved. I should've known how it would end."

"What did Andy promise to do?"

"First off he went to some boss man in your place," she nodded to Slider, "to ask for a proper investigation. I forget his name, but he was some high-up detective, Barlow or Barnet or some such—"

"Barrington?" Slider said, hiding his astonishment. How had he heard nothing of this?

"Yeah, could be. Anyway, Andy told this bloke everything, and this Barrington or whatever, he told Andy there was no way he could investigate it, and he told Andy to drop it. Absolutely forbid him to mention it to anyone. Andy was really shaken. He thought maybe this Barrington was in league with Billy Yates, maybe they was both masons or something, because Billy Yates has got loads of friends in high places—*you* must know that—which is why he's never got into trouble with the law. But anyway, Andy said to me don't worry, he'd go into it himself, and when he'd got the evidence, this Barrington'd have to do something." She puffed rapidly on her cigarette; her voice was growing husky with too much smoke, taken too hot. "I should've stopped him—except I don't suppose he would've stopped for me, not once he'd got the idea in his head. Stubborn as a donkey, Andy. But I never thought—" She swallowed hard. "Jonah must've got wind of what he was doing, and done him over. And he'll come after me next. That's why you mustn't tell anyone where I am. Don't write it down anywhere. And don't come here again—promise me!"

"Maroon—"

"And get Jonah!" she added fiercely. "Forget the other, just promise me that! I don't care anymore if he gets me, as long as you get him. I'd kill him if I could, but look at me—" She spread her arms. "What could I do against a bloke his size? So you got to do it for me. If he ain't dead, I want him locked up, and throw away the key, for what he did to my poor Maltesa, and my poor Andy!"

When Slider swung the wrong way onto Uxbridge Road, Hart turned to look at him, and wondered at the grim concentration on that usually benign face.

"Guv?" she said tentatively. "Was that straight up, d'you reckon, or was she spinning a yarn?"

"I think she was telling the truth as she knows it," Slider said, his voice vague from the depths of thought.

"But that stuff about Mr. Barrington—he was the Super before Mr. Honeyman, wasn't he?"

"Yes," Slider said.

"Didn't he commit suicide?"

"Yes," Slider said, reluctantly. Hart was silent. "I don't know," he answered her unasked question. "I'd hesitate to think it for a moment. Mr. Barrington had been under a lot of strain, but he never did anything to make me think he was corruptible."

And yet, Slider thought, hadn't he always felt a mental question mark hanging like a dark cloud over the winding up of the Cate business? It was not something he would ever discuss, not even with Atherton, not even with Joanna: but Barrington had been very close to Colin Cate, had hero-worshipped him, and when Cate turned out to have feet of clay, Barrington was shaken to his roots. He had left the building without saying where he was going, returning hours later in a state of nervous exhaustion, without explaining his whereabouts. And it was during those hours that Colin Cate had been shot dead by a marksman with a rifle. Barrington, who had killed himself only a few weeks later, had been a notable shot in the army, and had trophies galore from his shooting club.

Was it possible that Barrington had been as bent as Cate?

That his relationship with Cate was not that of the innocent patsy, which Slider had always assumed? That he had had a corrupt relationship with that other powerful local business-man, Billy "The Pom" Yates?

"You're not to mention this, Hart," he said. "This is ab-solutely taboo, do you understand?"

"Sir."

"I will put an investigation in train as to what, if anything, Cosgrove said to Barrington and vice versa, but it's a very delicate business, and I shall have to tread carefully. So I don't want any gossip muddying the waters. Not a word of this to anyone. If it gets out, I shall know it was you that spread it, and you'll be stuck on so fast your eyes will spin like a fruit machine, savvy?"

"Yes, sir." They rode in silence for a while. Then Hart said, "The other business, sir, the Paloma case—it looks as if it could have been this Jonah that whacked him, dunnit? I mean, Paloma worked for Yates, and there can't be that many six-foot-sixers with humungous plates knocking about."

"It's hard to resist that conclusion," Slider said. "But what did Jonah have against Paloma?"

"If Jonah's one of Yates's hard men, maybe Yates told him to rub Paloma."

"That just moves the question one pace sideways—what did Yates have against Paloma?"

"And where does Andy Cosgrove fit in?" Hart ruminated a moment. "D'you think there's some drugs connection? If Cosgrove was trying to find out where Jonah got the stuff from, Yates might've started thinking he was a nuisance he could do without. And Paloma was supposed to be buying drugs for his friend." She stopped, lost, and finally shrugged. "I dunno. But I can't help feeling there's got to be a con-nection."

"There's no fire without smoke," Slider finished for her. "Well, at least we've got some lines to follow up."

"Talking of following, where are we going, boss?" Hart asked, taking the opportunity.

Slider looked about him. They were in Acton High Street. "Why didn't you tell me I was going the wrong way?"

Atherton was looking much better. "They've taken out some of the tubes," Slider observed.

"I'm on liquids," Atherton said. "No one looks their best with that much plastic around. You, on the other hand, look terrible."

"I'm just tired. I've knocked off for an early night." It was a quarter to eight, but Atherton knew the score and nodded. "Joanna's got a session until nine, but it's only at Barnes, so she should be home by half past. I thought I'd have some grub ready for her."

"Not the Seduction Special? Your spag bol?"

"It's not the only thing I cook. You talk as if I was a one-trick pony."

Atherton looked wistful. "I'd be glad to be able to eat hospital jelly and Dream Topping."

"You will, Oscar, you will. The improvement from last week is amazing. Once they take those drains out—"

"Talking of drains, how's the case coming along?"

"We've got a suspect, one Jonah Lafota. Ever heard of him?"

"No."

"Figures. He's got no record, damn him. And we've got no evidence against him."

"So what makes him a suspect?"

"The fact that he's very big, and whoever kicked in Paloma's door had big feet, and an eyewitness says the kicker was very tall; and that he works for Billy Yates."

"But you've got some fingerprints?" Atherton said. "Then ask him for a set to compare. You've got him either way, then."

"We'd be delighted to ask him, but we don't know where he is."

"Can't you ask Yates?"

"Yates says he sacked him a week ago. Yates has a pleasant knack of sacking people just before they become notorious. We tried the address Yates gave us from his records, but of course Jonah wasn't there. We're watching the place, and we've put out word that we want to speak to him. So we're just on hold as far as that goes."

"Yates must be feeling pretty uncomfortable, if he's got

rid of this bloke so quickly. What reason did he give for sacking him?"

"He says Jonah came to work improperly dressed. No tie and a dirty shirt. He never gives warnings or second chances."

"Nice man."

"It's convenient, if you want to dissociate yourself quickly from anything that niffs a bit."

"Yes, but you can't do that too often and retain your tingling-fresh aroma," Atherton said. He studied Slider's face. "What is it in particular that's bothering you about Yates?"

Slider hesitated; but it was so natural to confide in Atherton, and Atherton had been there all through the Cate business. "This is in confidence," he said. Atherton nodded, and he told him the story of Maroon, Cosgrove and Barrington.

Atherton whistled soundlessly. "Old Andy Cosgrove? Who'd a thunk it?"

"Yes, even I hadn't expected that one. But—well, you know the temptations."

"None better," Atherton smirked.

"The worrying bit is the question of why Barrington told him to drop it."

"You believe this Mahogany?"

"Maroon."

"Whatever. After all, she's only a tom, and you can't believe everything they say."

"She's pretty straight," Slider said. "She's one of the old sort, not like some of the foul-mouthed little bitches you get nowadays. I think as far as this particular business goes, she's telling the truth."

"As she knows it."

"Yes, that's the trouble. Barrington's dead and Cosgrove's in a coma, and who else would know what, if anything, either said to the other?"

"Well, you can't go tramping in asking people like Honeyman or Wetherspoon if Barrington was in league with the villains," Atherton observed. "In fact, I don't see that you can ask anyone on Barrington's side. What about Andy Cosgrove? Who would he be likely to confide in?"

"I've been thinking about that," Slider said. "The trouble is, you get a bit solitary and autonomous being a community cop. No regular partner, no one you work with, and if this was a secret investigation anyway—"

"Did he have any close friends?"

Slider shook his head. "Not in the Job."

"What about his wife?"

"Ah, what? I don't know if he was used to confiding in her, but I wonder how likely it was that he'd chat to her about investigating the death of the addict sister of his prostitute mistress? And given that she's pregnant and spending all her time at his hospital bedside, I hardly like to ask her."

"Well," said Atherton comfortingly, "the Cosgrove case isn't your baby. Why not hand what you've been told over to Mr. Carver and let him worry about it?"

"Hmm. I suppose I must in fairness tell him what Maroon said. But if it was Jonah that killed Paloma, the cases must be connected."

"I don't see why. You don't know it was Jonah whacked Cosgrove. You haven't the slightest evidence or indication. And Cosgrove might not even have spoken to Barrington. He might just have told Maroon that to fob her off."

"How clear and simple you make everything seem," Slider complained.

"It's lying here with a brain untrammeled by the daily grind. If you bring me all your evidence day by day, I'll solve the case for you without ever setting foot outside my own bed."

"Thank you, Mycroft," said Slider.

"Well, if I've got all the brains, it stands to reason you can't have any."

"But you've got the looks, too," Slider objected.

"You'll have to settle for Miss Congeniality," Atherton said kindly. But suddenly he was exhausted. Slider saw it come over him. It was frightening to see the color and animation drain so abruptly from his face.

"Are you all right?"

"Just tired," said Atherton, as though a longer sentence would have been beyond him.

"I'd better go and let you sleep. Shall I call a nurse?"

Shake. "Anything you want?" Shake. "All right. I'll try and get in tomorrow, but even if I can't make it, Joanna will come."

He was almost at the door when he heard Atherton say sleepily, "How's my cat?"

He turned back. "He's fine. Eating like a horse. Well, eating horse, probably. Seriously, he's settled in very well. Misses you, though. He'd come and visit, but they don't let in anyone under eleven."

"He's fourteen," Atherton murmured, his eyes almost shut.

"I'll bring him next time, then, if I can find his birth certificate. They won't pass him otherwise. He doesn't look a day over nine." No response. Slider looked gravely at his colleague's white face for a moment, and then went quietly out.

On the way home, Slider got out of the car at the phone boxes on the corner of Chiswick Lane and phoned Tidy Barnet.

"Can you talk?"

"Hang on." A pause. "Right, all right. You got my message?"

"Thanks, Tidy. It was the goods. Unfortunately it was the goods on the wrong lorry. I'm not doing Cosgrove, I'm doing Paloma."

"No names, Mr. S. Not over the dog," Tidy winced. "You was lookin' for a certain party what smacked a certain iron 'oof, right? Well, the way I 'ear it, this certain other party from Wales, right? was the one what done it. Word is, it was a accident, party from Wales was elephant's trunk, right? Only meant to put the frighteners on 'im. Whacks 'im a bit too 'ard, and lo and be'old instead of frightened 'e's brown bread. But that's who it was all right, right?"

"So I'm looking in the right direction?"

"Right as ninepence."

Now all I've got to do is prove it, Slider thought as he hung up. And find out what the hell is going on. Jonah— party from Whales, he thought further, with a derisive snort, as he climbed into his car. Tidy was a card all right. Right?

*   *   *

Slider was just coming out of the men's room when he met
D.I. Carver about to go in. "Ron, have you got a minute?"
Carver grunted, which might have meant yes or no, and left
Slider to follow him in. "It's about the Cosgrove case. Is
there any improvement, by the way?"

"Nah. He's still unconscious." Carver turned on the tap
and began washing his hands. "It's over a week now. If he
doesn't come out of it soon, they'll transfer him to the coma
wing, and you know what that means. It's poor Maureen I
feel sorry for. That woman's a miracle, sits by his bed hour
after hour talking to him, in case he can hear her. How she
copes with that and two kids as well!"

"I thought you ought to know, some information has come
my way, about something Andy was apparently involved in,"
Slider said. Carver made no reply. He began scrubbing his
nails vigorously, and Slider gathered he was being aggressively uninterested in what Slider had to say—a warning off
from his territory. Carver had been born with a grudge, and
defended it jealously against any encroachment from the mel-
lowing of age or the operation of human kindness.

Slider raised his voice over the ablutions, and recounted
what Maroon had said. Before he could finish, however,
Carver interrupted him.

"Look, Bill, Andy's a good cop, one of the best, and I
don't think this sort of muckraking is going to help him get
well, do you? It's well out of order, to my mind, to gossip
about him when he's flat on his back fighting for his life."

Slider felt for a foothold. "I'm not muckraking, Ron, I'm
bringing information to your notice that might help you find
out who attacked him."

Carver turned off the tap and straightened, meeting Slider's
eye angrily in the mirror. "Oh are you? Well thank you very
much, but when I need your help I'll ask for it. I happen to
know all about his affair with Brown already. It was all over
a long time ago, and considering what poor Maureen is going
through at the moment, I don't think it will help her to drag
it all up again!"

Slider repressed the desire to smack Carver in the puss, and
sought out his most conciliatory tones. "Ron, I'm not trying
to tread on your toes. You didn't let me finish. Maroon ap-

parently asked Andy to investigate something for her, and if he did start asking questions it could have made him unpopular in certain quarters.'' He gave Carver the details, leaving out any mention of Barrington, and was glad to see that Carver was listening intelligently.

When he finished, Carver said in a tone that was at least meant to be reasonable, ''Right. I see. Well, thanks for the info, Bill. I'll certainly take it on board. But if I were you, I wouldn't put too much credence on what a tom tells you.''

''You haven't heard that he *was* asking questions, then?'' Slider said, disappointed.

''I told you, him and Brown was ancient history. He wouldn't put himself on the line for her. If she had any real information, he'd have passed it up to us in the proper manner, and since he didn't, you can take it as read he knew there was nothing in it. It was just a tom's grudge talk. You said yourself she had it in for this pimp. No, Andy would have just said something to soothe her, that's all, and kept his distance. With Maureen in pod again, he's not going to do anything risky, is he?''

Slider nodded, unconvinced. ''Right you are,'' he said. ''But if anything does come up, if you do come across anything that seems to bear on that line of investigation, you will let me know?''

''What's your interest in it, then?'' Carver asked, without agreeing that he would.

Slider said the wrong thing. ''It's Paloma. I'm beginning to get a feeling that the two cases may be connected.''

Carver gave him his most boiled look. ''Oh, I doubt that. I doubt that very much.''

''All the same, I've had word from one of my snouts—''

''You've got your sources and I've got mine,'' Carver said. ''Let's leave it at that, shall we?''

''But if—''

''I'll pass on anything I think you ought to know,'' Carver said, heading for the door. ''Rest assured about that.'' The door sighed closed behind him.

''Bastard,'' Slider said quietly, but with feeling.

❖ NINE ❖

Custardy Sweet

There was excitement in the C.I.D. room. A lift had been taken off the front door of Jonah Lafota's flat, and now the comparison with the whisky-bottle print had come back positive.

"It's enough to bring him in, isn't it, guv?" McLaren pleaded. He had been watching the flat and felt he was due some reward for the boredom.

"How close is the agreement?" Slider asked.

"Sixty percent. But that's because lift off the door wasn't much cop. With a proper set of prints off him, we can get it perfect."

It was the first thing that even approximated to real evidence. "You've still got to find him," Slider pointed out.

Hart, who had just come in, said, "Are you talking about Jonah?" She advanced to the middle of the group and grinned sassily. "I know where he is." When the clamor died down she said, "I got it off a source of mine, that he's got this girlfriend called Candy that he's very hot with at the moment. Candy Williams, supposed to be a bit of a looker—"

"Looker, did you say, or hooker?" McLaren interrupted.

Hart made a rocking motion of her hand. "She calls herself an actress, but basically she's done soft porn, magazines and films, and she's also worked for Yates. Table dancer. She's got a flat in that new block down by the river by Hammersmith Bridge—Waterside Court, I think it's called."

"They're luxury flats," Anderson said. "The knocking business must be good."

"Anyway," Hart concluded triumphantly, "apparently Jonah's been shacked up with her ever since Yates sacked him."

"Who's your source?" Slider asked.

She turned to him, lowering her eyelashes demurely. "I can't reveal my source's name. Fair's fair, guv. He's my snout."

Slider gave her a long look. He suspected she had been hanging around Garry from the Pomona in defiance of his orders. He was going to have to have a heart to Hart with her on the subject as soon as they had time.

"All right. Give me five minutes to have a word with Mr. Honeyman—"

"Oh, guv, talking of Mr. Honeyman," McLaren said, "before I forget, the card's on your desk for you to sign. There's just you left, unless you want Jim Atherton to sign it as well."

"I think he should, don't you?" Slider said. "I'll take it with me, then, the next time I go and see him."

While Slider talked, Honeyman listened at first eagerly, then with growing doubt. "Oh dear, it's not very much, is it? I was hoping you'd manage to clear this one up really quickly."

A quick result on a murder case would be a lovely final flourish on Little by Little's career. Slider stole a glance at his amazing Robert Robinson hairdo and his heart softened.

"I know we haven't got much, but Lafota looks good. One of my snouts has positively fingered him. Once we arrest him we can search his drum, take samples, pin him down. I think we can bring it home, sir."

Honeyman raised hopeful eyes and wagged his tail. "You think so? All right, but bring him in voluntarily if possible."

"If possible," Slider conceded.

Honeyman sighed. "If Billy Yates wants to make difficulties—"

"Mr. Yates seems to be trying to distance himself from Lafota, sir," Slider comforted him. "Could I have a word with you about something else? Something rather—delicate?"

Honeyman looked startled. "Oh—er—yes, by all means."

Probably thinks I want to discuss my matrimonial troubles with him, Slider thought, as he reached around behind him and closed the door. "It's about Mr. Barrington, sir." Slider recounted a brief history of Maroon, Maltesa and Cosgrove. "The difficulty is, trying to establish whether Cosgrove did speak to Mr. Barrington on the subject, and what was said."

"Why should you want to?" Honeyman asked, which was a better reaction that Slider had feared. He had expected an indignant I-don't-like-what-you're-suggesting slap down.

"Well, sir, it occurred to me, if for some reason Mr. Barrington did refuse an investigation, Cosgrove might have carried on under his own steam and buzzed about some people who decided to swat him."

"What does Carver say? It's his case, after all."

"He thinks Miss Brown is making it up. But I don't think she is."

Delicater and delicater—rivalry between firms was not unusual, but it was never comfortable. Honeyman was thoughtful. "I really think you would do better to concentrate on your own investigation, and leave the Cosgrove business to Carver. We won't achieve anything by duplicating efforts."

"No, sir," Slider said. "But I have the feeling that the two cases may be connected—that Lafota may be in the frame for both attacks, and that Yates may be behind it in some way."

"That's a lot of suppositions," Honeyman said, but his eyes were distant, preoccupied. "You were right that this is a delicate business. However, I am prepared to trust your instincts, and I will make some inquiries for you. I shall have to tread carefully, so don't expect overnight results. In the meantime, forget all about this conversation, concentrate on your own case, and don't do anything to get in the way of Carver's inquiries."

"No, sir. Thank you," Slider said. He was agreeably surprised at Honeyman's cooperation, and wondered with a renewed spasm of internal conflict whether his own doubts about Barrington·were shared higher up. It was all too easy to succumb to a conspiracy complex. Honeyman's advice—

or was it an order—was sound. He would do his best to forget about it.

He went back to give the good word to the troops, stopping off at his own room to pick up some papers. Prominently on his desk was the card McLaren had bought for Honeyman. He picked it up. On the front was a grinning pink cartoon mouse, holding a bottle of champagne in its paws. It had evidently been shaking it, Grand Prix style, because the champagne was gushing out behind a flying cork, and bursting bubbles and pink party streamers dotted the rest of the space. Across the top was the word CONGRATULATIONS. Slider opened the card. It had no printed message, but in the middle of the recto page, surrounded by the Department signatures, was written in careful capitals ON YOUR PREMATURE DISCHARGE.

"McLaren!" Slider roared.

In the confined spaces of the custody room, Jonah Lafota looked like Alice in W. Rabbit's house. He was a huge man, not just tall, but massive as well, as if he had been built for a planet with stronger gravity. His muscles moved about in his thighs and upper arms as if on business of their own, and though he wore a fashionable double-breasted suit in a lamentable shade of light gray-green, it seemed to have been cut specifically to prove that you can't get a body like that into a suit. His hair was cropped close, but with the obligatory small thin pigtail at the nape of the neck; his ears were small and set very high on his skull, and he wore tiny gold earrings in the sparse lobes. His huge hands, lightly curled, hung like knobkerries down by his side. Despite his bulk, Slider guessed he would move quickly and lightly.

He was very black, and his wide nose had been further flattened by being broken and, Slider guessed, having the bone removed. Despite noticing this, Slider found it hard to take in his features, impossible to say whether he was good-looking or not, because all the eye would register was his sheer size. Slider had a moment of pity: what must it be like to live all your life with such difference upon you? Men longed to be tall and strong, but Jonah was a freak, a *lusus naturae*. What woman could he lie with without crushing her?

What conversation could he join in with without bending down? Furniture would moan under him, doors admit him grudgingly, clothes and shoes reject him outright. What life was there for him, but to be someone's hard man, a blunt instrument for someone else's anger, but never a full member of the human race?

And then Slider remembered Jay Paloma, turned into something that would put Francis Bacon off his lunch, and hardened his heart.

"I'm Detective Inspector Slider, and this is Detective Sergeant Hollis. I'd like to ask you a few questions about Jay Paloma."

"I don' hafta tell you nuffing," Jonah said without emphasis. Sitting down he was about as tall as Slider standing up, which seemed to make his point irrefutable. Slider decided to ignore it.

"Do you know Jay Paloma?"

"Yeah, know him. He use come downa club." He slurred his words, not as a drunk does, but in the manner of one who does not have to say very much to get his message across. He sat back on the small chair, his fists resting on the table, looking in a lordly way at the wall or the ceiling, anywhere but at Slider. He didn't seem nervous, angry or afraid. He didn't seem anything at all, really, except big.

"Which club?"

"Pink Parrot."

"When did you last see him?"

"Jay? Dunno."

"Roughly when? Give me some idea."

"I don't see him there no more. He works downa Pomona."

"When were you last at the Pomona?"

"Dunno."

"Days ago? Weeks ago?"

"I go there sometimes. If Mr. Yates wants me. I ain't been there a long time."

Slider noted the use of the present tense. "I understood that Mr. Yates had sacked you."

That produced a reaction. Jonah's eyes flicked toward Slider, and a sort of spasm clenched his face and his fists for an instant. He seemed to go through some internal struggle before saying, "Yeah."

"When was that?"

"Tuesday morning. I finished four o'clock. Mr. Yates told me not to come back."

"So Mr. Yates was at the Pink Parrot?"

"He come round jus' before closing."

"Was that usual?"

"He goes round all the clubs."

"Every day?"

"Nah," Lafota said scornfully. "What jew fink?"

"Every week?" Lafota shrugged. "So why did he sack you?" Lafota didn't seem to be able to answer that. His eyes were fixed on the wall beyond Slider and he was breathing like a karate exponent psyching himself up for a pile of house bricks. "Was it for improper dress?"

"Yeah," Lafota said at last, on an exhaled breath. Clearly resentment was fighting with some other emotion. "He said my shirt was dirty."

"What did you do then?"

"I wen' home, didn' I?"

"To your flat in—Star Road? That's off the North End Road, isn't it?" Jonah shrugged. "What time did you get there?"

"Half four maybe."

"And what did you do?"

"Went to bed, man, wha' fink?"

"Alone?"

Lafota clearly wanted to tell Slider to mind his own business, but an alibi was an alibi. "Candy was there. My girl-friend. She been staying wiv me."

"And what did you do for the rest of the day?"

"I got up about half one, messed around, had summing tweat, watched the telly."

"What time did you go out?"

"I never went out, man."

"Not at all?"

"I stopped in. Candy was wiv me. I stopped in and watched telly, went to bed about half eleven, went to sleep. Candy will tell you."

"I'm sure she will," Slider said politely. "And what happened the next day?"

"I got up about half nine, and Candy and me went over her pad. She got stuff to do. All right?"

"Did you at any time go to Jay Paloma's flat?"

Lafota looked contemptuous. "I don' even know where he live, man."

"Oh, surely you do."

"What is all this, man? Get off my back, right? I don't know nuffing about Jay, 'cept he use' come down the Parrot an' he don't no more." He stood up, an effect like a bedside cabinet growing into a double wardrobe before one's very eyes. "I come here, I answer your questions, all right? And now I'm going. You got nothing on me."

"I'm afraid we have," Slider said. "We have your fingerprints, found inside Jay Paloma's flat, which you say you never visited. So I'm afraid I shall have to ask you to sit down and answer some more questions."

He didn't sit down, and Slider felt the hair rise on his scalp for an instant; but he could see Jonah had been shaken. His brows drew together and his eyes dothered as he engaged in frantic thought—wondering what he might have touched, perhaps?

"I ain't answering no more questions," he declared at last. "And I ain't staying."

"Then I'm afraid I shall have to detain you," Slider said. He was surprised that Jonah had come voluntarily in the first place. Perhaps he was under orders from Billy Yates. If so, would Yates spring him, or continue to distance himself? It would be interesting to see.

Candy Williams looked both nervous and depressed. She was young—judging by the curve of her cheek and fullness of lip, Norma thought she was probably only about nineteen—and adequately pretty, though her face seemed puffy and her eyes red, despite the thick, disguising makeup, as if she had been crying a lot recently, or alternatively had been on a bender. She moved, Norma noted, with a certain upright inflexibility which did not go with the profession of dancer, table or otherwise. She wore a miniskirt and her long, young legs were bare, but she had on a large, baggy, concealing jumper. She had not seemed surprised when she opened the door to the police. Now she sat with passive docility in another interview room, her eyes moving anxiously from face to face, licking her lips occasionally. She would clearly like to be elsewhere, but just as clearly was under orders to do what had to be done.

"Your full name is Candy Williams, is that right?" Norma asked. Easy questions first, to get her relaxed.

"Clare," she said. "My real name's Clare. Candy's my stage name."

"How sweet," said Norma. "And you're an actress, I understand?"

"Yeah, that, and I dance. Model a bit. Whatever."

"An all-round entertainer. And you live at Flat Twelve, Waterside Court, Hammersmith?" A nod. "You work for Mr. Yates, don't you?"

She licked her lips. "Sometimes."

"Your last job was table dancing, at the Manhattan Club in Clapham?" Candy did not dissent. "Is that how you met Jonah Lafota? At the club?"

"Not at the Manhattan. I was at the Pink Parrot. Filling in."

"Filling in as what?"

"Waitress," Candy said.

"Topless?" Candy shrugged. Prostitution was the name of the game, Norma thought, but that was not what they were here for. "How long ago was that? When you worked at the Pink Parrot and met Jonah?"

"About three months."

"And you started going out together then?" Candy looked up for a moment, as if struck by the incongruity of the expression. Norma smiled. "That's when you became his girlfriend," she amended. "I don't suppose you had much choice. He's not someone I'd like to have to say no to."

Candy's eyes met Norma's. Her expression did not change, but contact had been made. We're all sisters under the skin, said Norma's smile, and men are all bastards. It's only a matter of degree. "Does he knock you about, Candy?"

"He's all right," Candy said expressionlessly.

"He isn't," Norma said. "Don't worry, I'm not going to give you away to him. Tell me about Tuesday last week. You'd been staying at Jonah's flat, is that right? Since when?"

"The weekend. Satdy. I went over Satdy afternoon. He was working Satdy night and Sundy night, but he likes to have me there when he wakes up. So I stopped on."

"Were you there on Tuesday morning when he came home from work? And what time was that?"

"About half past four."

"And what did he do?"

"He come straight to bed." All this was easy to her, straight from the script. She answered without hesitation.

"What time did he get up?"

"It was about half past twelve when he woke up. I brought him breakfast in bed."

"You were already up, then?"

"Well, I slept in the night, so I got up when he fell asleep."

"I see. So you brought him breakfast, what then?"

"He et it. I got back into bed." She shrugged to indicate the reason for that. "Then we got up about half one."

"And what time did he go out?"

Her eyes moved cautiously. "He didn't go out."

"He must have gone out at some point in the evening."

"He didn't. He didn't go out at all."

"But how would you know? You weren't there the whole time, surely?"

"We both stopped in. He was with me all evening, all night."

"Come on, you must have been out at some point between half past one in the afternoon when you both got up, and half past nine the next morning when you went off to your place. That's twenty hours."

The mathematics seemed to upset Candy, and she looked uncertain, but still she said, "I was in the flat all that time. And Jonah was with me."

"Every minute?"

"Yeah."

Norma looked at her consideringly a long time. Candy shifted a little under the gaze, but returned the look defiantly.

Norma changed tack. "Tell me what you know about Jay Paloma."

"I don't know him," she said, easily again, back on script. "I never even met him."

"But you know who I'm talking about."

"It was in the papers. Jonah's talked about it. He got murdered."

"So Jonah knew him?"

"He worked for Mr. Yates. Jonah's met him a couple of times, I think. He didn't know him well."

"Why did Mr. Yates sack Jonah?"

"I don't know. He didn't say."

"He was upset about it, wasn't he?" Candy hesitated. "He must have been furious. Did he take it out on you?"

"No," she said, but absently, as though she was thinking about something else.

"Candy, I think Jonah had something to do with Jay Paloma's death. I think he's told you to say that he was with you, to give him an alibi for when he was at Jay Paloma's flat. That makes you an accessory. Do you know what that means?" No reply. "It means that when we get enough evidence to charge Jonah, you can be charged with him. And we're going to get that evidence, believe me. It's only a matter of time. Jonah's going down. Surely you don't want to go down with him?" No answer. Candy stared sullenly at her hands. "I've seen your flat—very swanky. Nice bathroom, nice kitchen. Soft toilet paper. You wouldn't like it in Holloway, believe me. It's a dirty, horrible place." No response. "Help me, Candy. If you tell me the truth, I can help you. You'll be all right."

"You don't know Jonah," she said abruptly, and then folded her lips tight, as though she hadn't meant to say as much.

Slider felt a certain sympathy with that. He spoke for the first time. "If Jonah's inside, he can't hurt you, can he? Help us put him away, and then you'll be safe. It's the only way you *can* be safe. If he walks out of this police station, he's not going to be in the best of moods. Even if he thinks he's got away with it, he's going to be fed up with having spent all this time in here, and who d'you think he's going to take

it out on?'' Candy looked at him resentfully but said nothing.
''Just tell me the truth, Candy. He wasn't really with you all
Tuesday evening, was he? He went out. Tell me what time
he went out.''

Candy didn't hesitate this time. ''He was in all evening,''
she said. But to Slider's ears it had a hint of wistfulness about
it.

Billy Yates's brief was a quick-talking, smiling, rotund man
called David Stevens. He had small, twinkling brown eyes
and thick glossy hair, and exuded such enormous vitality he
was like something out of a Pedigree Chum advert. He also
had suits to die for, and the sort of wildly expensive red
BMW coupé that successful pimps liked to drive. As he rep-
resented all the worst criminals on the ground, Slider knew
him very well. The trouble was, Slider liked him, which made
it harder to resist him. He thought Stevens liked him, too, but
Stevens had the lawyerly knack of being able to think one
thing and do another.

''How come you represent Yates as well as the scum of
the neighborhood?'' Slider asked. ''Is there some connection
I should know about?''

''You'll have to be careful what you say to me, or I might
have to sue you for defamation of character,'' Stevens said
cheerfully.

''Definition of character, did you say?''

Stevens whistled soundlessly. ''Ooh, Bill, that's another
hundred thousand. Mr. Yates is a prominent local businessman of impeccable probity, who does a great deal of good in
the neighborhood and gives generously to charity.''

''Yes, of course, silly me, that's what I meant to say,''
Slider said. ''And what can his interest be in Mr. Lafota, I
wonder?''

''Mr. Yates takes an interest in all his employees.''

''Mr. Lafota is unemployed,'' Slider pointed out sweetly.

Stevens was unshaken. ''You didn't let me finish,'' he said
smoothly. ''The end of my sentence was—even when they
have left his employ. Mr. Lafota needed a solicitor—Mr.
Yates asked me if I would act for him. So here I am.''

''I can't say I wasn't expecting you,'' Slider said resignedly. "Though I didn't think you'd get here so quickly. Jonah hasn't even had his phone call yet. So tell me, how did Mr. Yates hear that Mr. Lafota was helping us with our inquiries?"

"There isn't much Mr. Yates doesn't hear." Stevens gave Slider a canny look. "Now, Bill, don't be obvious! You can't bring in a seven-foot giant built like a brick shithouse unnoticed, y'know. Anyone could have told him that."

"I suppose so," Slider sighed. "You're such a nice bloke, Dave, how can you square it with your conscience to spend your life trying to get creeps like him off the hook?"

"Not that old chestnut!" Stevens chortled. "You must be feeling tired, old chum!"

Slider eyed him resentfully. "Where did you get that tan? The Bahamas?"

"In my own little old back garden, mowing the lawn. It *is* summer, in case you hadn't noticed. And now I want Mr. Lafota out. You've got sweet FA, and you know it, so you'll have to let him go. Much better not to struggle against the inevitable, as the actress said to the High Court judge."

"Oh, gimme a break, Dave," Slider said with faint, uncharacteristic irritation. "We're not playing Scrabble, you know."

Stevens only looked merrier. "I know you want a result before Little Eric says bye-bye, but that's your problem, not mine. You've got nothing on my client, and I want him sprung."

"I've got the fingerprints," Slider pointed out.

"On a bottle of whisky, not on a murder weapon. Paloma bought his Scotch from the club, staff rate. Lafota's been in the storeroom there. The prints could have got on the bottle any time. You'll have to do better than that, sweetheart. It's not proof. It's not even evidence."

"And the prints on the light switch, in the flat he claims he's never visited."

"They're very poor prints, less than fifty percent agreement."

"It's enough to hold him on, while we look for something better," Slider said.

Stevens shrugged. "Temporarily. The Muppets will let me have him. You know that."

"That gives me thirty-six hours. I'll take what I can get."

Hart looked in. "You still here, guv? I wondered when I saw the light on."

"I was just thinking of going," he said. He eyed her thoughtfully. "Come in a minute, will you?" She came and stood before the desk, eyeing him perkily. Didn't these youngsters ever get tired? "I don't generally interfere with my people's intelligence gathering, but then they know the rules I like to operate under. You're new to the ground, and you're new to me, and I have the feeling you also like life to have an element of excitement. This information you got on Jonah Lafota—"

She grinned. "S'all right, guv, it wasn't Garry. Listen, just because I'm black, female, and I talk wiv a gorblimey accent, it don't mean to say I'm stupid."

"I didn't think you were stupid," Slider said mildly. "I thought you probably felt you had something to prove."

She became serious for once. "You're dead right. You've heard of accelerated promotion? I got the opposite. People like me don't start from the starting line, we start from back in the pavilion." Then suddenly she grinned again. "And d'you know the worst fing of all? If I do get on, get promoted, even if I get commended, I'll never know if it's because I'm any good, or because some git's trying to prove he's not prejudiced. I can't win. *He* can't win. I hate positive discrimination. It's a bastard. At least with the old sort you knew where you were. If it wasn't happening to you, you knew everything was all right. Now they've invented the other stuff, you'll never know. You'll never, ever know."

There was a short silence. "You don't leave me with much to say," Slider said. "I was going to tell you there's no discrimination in my firm, but now if I tell you that, you won't be able to believe me."

"Yeah," she said with sympathy. "It's like this—" She took hold of the skin of her cheek between finger and thumb. "Once you got it, you just have to learn to live wiv it. You look tired, guv. An' I bet you ain't had anything to eat all day.''

Slider tried to look stern. ''You're not my mother.''

''That'll be a relief to my dad.''

Slider stood up, hesitated, and then said, ''D'you want to go and get something to eat? Now you've reminded me, I am hungry.'' Joanna was away for the night, a concert in Leeds. He didn't want to go home to cold bread and cheese.

''Yeah, great,'' Hart said easily.

''Right then. Oh,'' he remembered, ''I've just thought, I ought to go and look at my house first. My old house—I'm not living there. I have to drop in now and then to make sure it hasn't been burnt down or taken over by squatters. It'll take about half an hour.''

''No problem,'' she said. ''I'll come with you, if you like, and we can get a bite after.''

''Okay. There's a decent curry house not far from there. I'd be glad of the company, make sure I don't drop off at the wheel.''

He wouldn't, he was aware, have said that to Atherton, would not have felt the need to offer a justification. Was that another form of prejudice? He supposed it was, in a way, because he wouldn't have said it to McLaren, either—supposing he had ever been likely to invite McLaren's company. Why couldn't he treat Hart like a male colleague? He had never seen himself as a crusty old M.C.P.—hadn't he always said Norma was the best policeman in the department? And that wasn't because she was a woman, but because she was the best. Ah, but then, had she been a man, would he have ever felt the need to say it? Bloody hell, this prejudice business was a minefield! No, be fair, he had only said that about Norma out loud when someone had attacked women in the police generally as being inferior in some way. And privately he thought about her no differently from his male troops: her physical difference was a trait attached to her like McLaren's eating habits or Mackay's football fanaticism or Atherton's finickitiness.

He didn't think he was prejudiced, not in any direction. He worried about Hart because she was a rookie and because she was a wild card—he didn't know what she might do. On the subject of which—

"By the way, who was your informant, if it wasn't Garry?"

"It was another bloke I met down the club. He's a regular, he knows everybody. S'all right, guv," she added as Slider looked at her in alarm, "nobody knew who I was. That's one advantage of being black and female, you can dress up outrageous so no one recognizes you. I walked right past that Garry in the doorway and he never clocked me. Mind you, he is as fick as pig-dribble."

"And that's supposed to reassure me?" Slider wanted to forbid her to go there again, but in the wake of all this talk and thought about prejudice, he felt his hands were tied. After all, he wouldn't have tried to stop Mackay. He wouldn't even have tried to stop Norma.

✤ TEN ✤

Taking Hart

There was a slight fog, just enough to catch in the lights: the new halogen street lamps with their down-directed beams looked like a double row of shower heads. The gibbous moon was an extraordinary color, a most unnatural-looking dark yellow. Lying on its back low in the sky, it looked like a half-sucked sherbet lemon.

"Where do you live?" he asked Hart. She had snuggled into the seat beside him, drawing her legs up and wrapping her arms around them. Her generation was so much more at ease with everyone than his had been. In her place at that age he'd have sat up straight and worried about pleasing.

"Streatham. I share a house. But I'm stopping with me mum and dad while I'm at Shepherd's Bush. They live in North Wembley."

"Is that where you were born?"

"Near enough. Willesden."

"So you're a northerner?"

"Am I?"

"North of the river. That accounts for why you seem so normal. Atherton has this theory that London north of the river and London south of the river are utterly alien to each other. He calls it Cispontine and Transpontine London." It didn't mean anything to Hart. But then it hadn't to Slider until Atherton explained.

"You miss him, don't you?" she said.

"It was another complication in my life I could have done without."

"What's this house we're going to?" she asked. So he told her. He meant to give her the briefest outline of the house situation, but her questioning was so adroit he found himself telling her more, about Irene now apparently having second thoughts and his worry about the children being brought up by Ernie Newman.

"It's not that I've anything against him, except that he's a boring fart. It's that they're *my* children, my responsibility. If anything goes wrong, it'll be my fault, but now there's nothing I can do to control the situation. I hate responsibility without power. It's—frustrating," he ended mildly, suddenly aware of how much he was giving away.

"Yeah," she said, in a tell-me-about-it voice.

He glanced at her. "Have you got a boyfriend?"

"Not at the moment," she said.

"It's hard for women in the Job—particularly in the Department. That's one of the unfairnesses."

"S'right. And at least when you get married you can have a wife. If I get married, I've got to have a husband." She made a face.

"Would you like to be married?"

"Not now. I want a career now. I like the Job, I want to get on. But I'd like to have kids too. I wanna have my career now, then when I'm forty-five ease off a bit and do the other. A bloke could do that. I can't. It's like *this*." She tweaked her face again. "So tell me about frustration," she finished. "The way I see it, we all got disabilities. It's like we're all cripples, one way or another. Blind people, people with no legs, they got to adapt. But when you got all your bits and pieces, you expect too much. We got to start thinking like cripples."

"Count your blessings," Slider said. "They used to tell us that when I was a kid. There was even a Sunday School hymn."

"If I was you, guv," she said gravely, "every morning when I got up I'd look in the mirror and thank Jesus I'm not McLaren."

Slider laughed, and pulled off the A40 into the slip lane.

"Soon be there now. It won't take long. I've just got to make sure nothing disastrous has happened. Then we'll go for a Ruby. I'm assuming you like curry?"

"Do lemmings like cliffs?" said Hart.

When they got to the house he'd have expected her to stay in the car, but she got out when he did, so he didn't say anything. She followed him up to the front door. "Nice," she said.

He concealed his surprise. "You think so?"

"My mum and dad'd love this."

"They can have it," he offered promptly.

"They couldn't afford it."

"Neither can I," he said, but he thought it just showed you, one man's meat is another man's McDonald's. Everything looked all right, no obvious broken windows or signs of squatters. He unlocked and stepped inside. The air smelled dry and stale, like packet soup. At first when he had come back it had seemed like his home, though deserted. Now he had been away long enough for it to seem alien to him: the spaces no longer fitted the geography of his eye's expectations. They say if you shut your eyes while walking you retain an image of where you're going to tread for eight paces, after which your brain loses confidence and you have to look again. It took longer to get unused to your old home, but he could no longer have confidently negotiated it in the dark. Not that it was ever completely dark. The street lamps filled it at night with a ghastly pinkish-yellow glow.

He left Hart in the hall and went upstairs to make sure there was no water where water should not be, and that the windows were all still locked. It was such a waste for the house to be empty, he thought, even though he didn't love it. And the mortgage hurt more now that he wasn't getting any use from it. Maybe, he toyed, he and Joanna should move into it. He had forked over those greens before, though, and knew the caterpillars. Even if he could live with Joanna where he had lived with Irene—and anyone could do anything if they put their minds to it—Joanna would hate it. He didn't suppose for a moment that she'd consent to it, so he had never even suggested it. He had put the house on the market and she had not demurred, so that was that.

Maybe, he thought, she had not demurred because she thought he would not consider it? She usually kept herself a firm pace out of his former life, deeming it to be his own business. Maybe he should have put it to her? Perhaps, like Hart, she would think it nice?

No, he couldn't be *that* wrong about her. But it made no sense to be paying for two properties. Maybe he should accept that he was not going to be able to sell it, and try to let it instead. But it would need a bit of capital spent, and who would provide that? Ernie was the only one with cash. Wherever he stepped, his foot landed in Ernie. The fact was that the easiest solution to everything would be for him and Irene and the children to move back in here. He shuddered. He hated being here, and prey to thoughts like that. Better get out fast and have a restorative curry.

He went downstairs again, switching off the stairs light at the bottom. The other downstairs lights were off, but there was enough coming through the glass door to see by. In the ghastly sodium dusk he looked around for Hart. She had wandered off somewhere.

"Where are you?"

She appeared silently in the doorway to the lounge, right beside him.

"Are you ready, then?" he asked.

"Mmm," she said. She was very close, and as she turned her face upward toward him he realized, suddenly and shockingly, that she wanted him to kiss her. Or, rather, that if he kissed her she wouldn't object, she would respond. He looked down, saw the gleam of her eyes, the full firmness of her lips, and he learned what a large variety of thoughts could bound through the head simultaneously—and at a moment when he was having enough trouble controlling his instant hormonal reaction, without having to sort a panic-stricken babble into order of importance.

She was *attracted* to him? He had never thought of himself as sexually attractive, though Joanna evidently found him so, but that was different, wasn't it, that was the whole bit, troo lurve? But as for Hart, oh my God, had he led her on, did she think that was what he brought her here for? Hadn't anyone told her about Joanna? He was right after all, you couldn't treat a female colleague exactly like a male colleague. Now what was he going to do?

The most horrifying aspect of the situation was that the lawless stirring in his loins was whispering that he could do it, yes he could, why not, he was a free agent wasn't he, why waste a golden opportunity? And simultaneously in yet another subsection of his brain he remembered that Kate had always got loin and lion mixed up and had long believed that loin chops had a much more exotic origin than the sheep or the pig.

Sometimes Fate takes pity. He did not have to discover how he would have got out of *that* one, because a shadow appeared behind the glass of the front door, and a key was slipped into the lock. It was Irene, of course. Apart from her, only the estate agent had a key. She said, ''Bill?'' inquiringly, and a little nervously, as she opened the door. The front door obscured her view of them at first, but the hall was so small that once the door was opened flat against the right hand wall, he and Hart were immediately before her as she stepped in.

She stopped and stared at them. Slider saw immediately how it must look. He and Hart were standing very close together, all the lights were off, and the air was sulphurous with maculate conceptions.

''I saw your car out there,'' Irene said falteringly, ''but there were no lights on. I thought—I wondered—''

Thanks a lot, Fate, Slider thought. Out of the doodah into the whatsname.

''We were just leaving,'' he said. As an answer it left a lot to be desired—which was evidently also how Irene viewed Hart. Slider could see her bristling. ''I just popped in to check that everything was all right,'' he said. ''This is Detective Constable Hart. My wife Irene.''

''How d'you do?'' Hart said politely, but she did not move away from Slider's side. She looked at Irene curiously. The staging was all wrong, he realized: Hart was standing in a position of belonging, looking at Irene-the-outsider.

''Am I interrupting something?'' she asked icily.

''Of course not,'' he said. ''Don't be silly. As I said, we were just leaving.''

"Don't go on my account," Irene said.

"Look, we've been working late and we were going to get something to eat, but I remembered I had to check on the house, so we stopped here on the way," he said. He felt Hart stir beside him, and knew she was right. Never explain. It only made things worse—as if, paradoxically, it proved there was something to explain.

"Working late. Yes, of course," Irene said, looking with operatic contempt from Slider to Hart and back. "I should have remembered that's what it was always called. I was a policeman's wife for long enough."

"Irene—!" he began, exasperated.

"Oh, I don't blame you," she said bitterly. "I've no right, when it was me that—" She couldn't quite say it. "You're a free agent after all. I just would have thought that you'd— not in this house—" She choked and turned away. Slider felt a monumental annoyance that was only intensified by the knowledge that (a) she actually felt those things, despite the hackneyed words, (b) it was really he who was the guilty party, and doubly guilty because he went on letting her think it was she who had sinned first and (c) that she had hit on some of the same words, free agent, that he had been thinking himself only seconds before.

"Irene, will you stop talking like a Barbara Cartland heroine. Nothing is going on here."

"It's none of my business if it is," she said, maddeningly. "I won't hang around here getting in your way. I just—" She dissolved into tears.

Slider pulled out his handkerchief and stuffed it into Irene's hands. "Yes, what were you doing here, anyway?" he asked, trying for a mixture of briskness and kindness.

"I was just passing," she said, muffled as she mopped, "and I saw your car."

"Just passing? From where to where?"

"Don't interrogate me!" she said with a flash of her old spirit. "I'm not one of your criminals."

"Sorry. But really—"

"All right," she said angrily, "I sometimes come here. When I'm feeling—when I don't feel right at Ernie's, I come here and just sit. It's my home, and I miss it, all right? I sit here and think—think that maybe we could get it together again, maybe you would forgive me and come back. Like a fool, I thought perhaps you missed it too. I see how wrong I was.''

"You were wrong," he said, "but not for this reason. W.D.C. Hart is a member of my firm, that's all, and I don't think we should discuss our private lives in front of her."

"I'm sorry," Irene said, though he had no confidence that she believed him. "Like I said, I've no reason to complain. I was the one—" She stopped again. He hated her to feel so very bad about her lapse.

"We'll talk," he promised. "We've got a lot of things to say. But not now, not here. I'll ring you, all right? And we'll meet and talk."

"All right," Irene said, muted.

Hart seemed to shake herself free of her paralysis—or was it just curiosity? Everyone was nourished on soap operas these days. "I'll go and wait in the car, guv," she said, thought about saying goodbye to Irene and wisely thought better of it, and took herself off.

"She's a pretty girl," Irene said.

"She's a colleague, that's all," Slider said wearily.

"It doesn't matter," Irene said. She looked at the handkerchief in her hand. "I'll wash and iron this and send it back to you."

"I wish you wouldn't talk like that."

"I'll give it to you next time I see you, then."

"Are you all right now? Can you drive yourself home all right?" The moment he said it, he cursed himself. She was going to say "this is my home" and start it all off again.

But she just nodded. "You'll phone me?"

"I promise."

She started to go, and then stopped and said, looking up at him, "I miss you, Bill."

He knew he had to say, I miss you too, but wondered what effect it would have on her expectations; and in wondering hesitated just too long. She lowered her head, turned, and trudged off.

He locked the house up and went back to the car. When he was in, Hart said, softly and feelingly, "Christ."

And then some, he thought. He started the engine.

"I'm sorry, guv," she said.

"It's not your fault. I'm sorry you came in for it."

"D'you want to just drop me off at the tube or something?"

He looked at her, surprised. "We haven't eaten yet. I don't know about you but I need a curry. A Madras at least, after that."

She looked at him for a moment, and then grinned. "Yeah," she said. "Me too."

The taxi driver's name was Leonard Marks. "Lenny," he simplified it, offering his hand to Slider. He was a tall, well-built man with a large, handsome, fleshy face, thick wavy hair, and brown, steady eyes. Everything about him seemed calm, open and facing forward, like a lion gazing out over the veldt. "Lenny the Lion, they call me," he added on the wake of Slider's thought. "From Sniffy Wheeler's garage in Homerton. Anyone'll tell you."

"Right," said Slider, accepting the bona fides. "Thanks for coming in." Monty had telephoned first thing to tell Slider he had found his man for him.

"It's the business all right," Monty had said proudly. "Good as gold, Lenny. Everyone knows him."

"So you think you can tell me something about this chap?" Slider went on, tapping the print of Jay Paloma's photograph.

"That's right. It was Monday morning, last week, about half eleven—quarter to twelve. I'd done a book job to Paddington Station, but I don't generally like ranking up, unless I can see a crowd waiting, and there was nothing doing at the station rank. So I was cruising. I came down Edgware Road, around Marble Arch, down Park Lane. There was a fare outside the Dorchester, but I got overtaken—some smart-arse butterboy in a brand new cab who doesn't know the rules. I've got his number!"

He wagged his head significantly. Slider knew that to overtake—to take a fare who was signaling another cab—was a heinous crime, and no mercy was shown to the sinner. "Go on," he said.

"Right," said Marks. "So I get down to Hyde Park Corner and it looks like the Lanesborough Hotel rank is running, so I go round and put on. Anyway, just as I got up to point, your friend here appears."

"He came out of the hotel?"

"No, he was a walk-up. But funny enough, I saw him in my rearview mirror, paying off another cab at the corner. That's why I remembered him particularly. I wasn't really looking at him, of course, I only glanced, but I got that impression."

Slider nodded. This man's impression was probably sure enough. "You didn't see whose cab it was?"

"No," he said apologetically. "It was just a black cab. I didn't see the number or the company or anything. Well, anyway, this bloke comes up to my window and asks for Chelsea Embankment. I says to him, 'Any particular part, sir?' because a lot of people call it Chelsea Embankment all the way along, from Cheyne Walk to Vauxhall Bridge. And he says, 'Oh, yes, Flood Street, please.' "

"How did he seem? What was his manner?"

Marks considered. "A bit vague, maybe. Had his mind on other things."

"Nervous?"

"Could have been. Maybe a bit. Preoccupied, is what I'd say."

"Did you have any conversation with him?"

"Not a dickie. He just sat there looking out of the window. Anyway, soon as I turned into Flood Street off King's Road, he tapped the glass and said, 'Anywhere here,' so I pulled in, he nipped out, paid me, and walked away."

"Did you see where he went after that?"

Marks smiled a slow, handsome smile. "Well, as a matter of fact, I did. You see, I drove on down to the end of Flood Street, but the Embankment was chokka, so I did a u-ey and came back up to get back on the King's Road again. And there he was, standing on the steps ringing the doorbell. And as I get opposite, the door opens, and I see the householder all smiles letting him in. And I thought to myself, so much for all your cloak-and-dagger stuff, chum, changing cabs and getting out at the corner! Because it was obvious this bloke's a ginger, and the house he's visiting doesn't belong to Jimmy Nobody.''

"I don't suppose by any wild chance you saw the number of the house?" Slider asked.

"I didn't need to," Marks said. "I know the address very well. I've been there a few times, I know who lives there. It's Sir Nigel Grisham.''

"What, the M.P.?"

"Cabinet Minister," Marks corrected significantly. "Practically the Grand Old Man of the party. So how d'you like them apples?''

"Good God," Slider said. "You're quite sure about all this?"

Marks nodded. "I saw him. I'd recognize him anywhere. Hurrying your bloke in, he was, hand on his elbow, peeping past him to make sure no one was watching." He mimed it graphically.

"But *you* were watching. If you were just opposite the house, surely he must have seen you?"

Marks shook his head. "Seeing's not a matter of what's there, is it? It's a matter of what your brain takes in. And a black cab in London—well, it's part of the furniture, like a pillar box or a lamppost. Your brain kind of edits it out. Unless you're looking for one, you just don't see it. I've noticed it time and again.''

"Sir Nigel Grisham," Slider said wonderingly. Paloma had certainly been sinning above his station.

Marks grinned. "Who's a naughty boy, then?"

"You're willing to make a statement about this?"

"Sure. Anytime you like. Always willing to help. And I'll put out the word on that other cab, if you like, the one I saw your friend getting out of. Chances are he changed twice if he was trying to be clever, took his local cab to somewhere no one'd think anything about. I'll see what I can do."

"Thank you," Slider said, "but I don't think it's important. We needed to know where he went rather than how he got there.''

"I'll ask around anyway. It's no trouble," Marks said, brushing his mane back with a casual paw. "Anything you want, just ask for Lenny the Lion.''

*   *   *

As he went into the C.I.D. room, heads flew apart. The two closest were Hart's and Norma's, and Slider felt a low, depressing sensation that they had been talking about him, that Hart had been describing the marital scene on the doorstep. Or was that indigestion? He shouldn't eat Madras, or at least not after six p.m.

Norma and McLaren were back from searching Lafota's flat. "We haven't got much," Norma confessed. "We've got a boot with a sole that matches the footmark on Paloma's door, but they're ten a penny."

"Not in that size," McLaren pointed out.

"True, but turning it up the other way, I doubt whether you'd find many blokes that tall under the age of, say, thirty, who didn't wear boots like that."

"Every little helps," Slider said. "It all adds to the picture. Did you find anything else?"

"A packet of drinking straws in the kitchen cupboard," Norma said, "and I'll bet they weren't for Coca-Cola. Forensic is going over the place for any traces, but unfortunately he didn't leave any packets behind when he and Candy struck camp. Which for a careless man was awfully careless of him."

"So it's back on the streets, then, boys and girls," Slider said. "Knock on those doors and ask those questions. If Lafota left his flat on Tuesday night to go to Paloma's, someone must have seen him. And people must be talking about it."

"Guv, it must have been a hit, mustn't it?" Mackay said. "I mean, why else did Lafota do it? He didn't have a beef against Paloma, did he?"

"Don't ask me—ask around," Slider said. "The staff and regulars at both clubs—the Pink Parrot and the Pomona—have got to be our best bet. I'm getting some uniformed help as of today, so I'll put them on the local stuff and you lot can concentrate on the clubs. I want everyone followed up and asked about both of them. Who did they know, where did they go, what did they do."

"It's gotta be a drugs connection," Mackay said. "Stands to reason."

"I hate to say it," Norma said, "but I agree. And my bet

is that Yates is behind it; and if he is behind it, he's going to take a lot of winkling out." There was a mutter of agreement.

"Nobody has special protection in my book," Slider said firmly. "If Yates has been a naughty boy, Yates is going to get his hand smacked. Meanwhile, we mustn't lose sight of the victim. We don't know nearly enough about what Paloma got up to when he wasn't tucked up safe at home with Busty Parnell. Although we do now have a line on his special boyfriend, for whom he was putatively acquiring the recreational sugar." He told them about Lenny Marks's evidence.

Hollis whistled. "Sir Nigel Grisham? Oh my oh my. That's bad news for the Government."

"I never would have thought Grisham was an iron," Norma said. "He's got a wife and kids, hasn't he?"

"In the country," Hollis said. "And if this gets out he'll be spending a lot more time with them."

"What about protecting a political career as a motive for murder?" Hart said.

"Don't get carried away," said Slider. "We've got Jonah on ice, remember."

"Maybe we've been maligning him. How tall is Grisham?" Mackay wondered.

"Paloma could have been blackmailing him," McLaren helped him out.

Slider said, "I'm going to interview Sir Nigel Grisham myself—"

"And when he interviews people, they stay interviewed," Norma concluded. "Who're you taking with you, boss?"

"Hart," he said. "It's likely to be a delicate interview, needing subtle techniques."

Hart was grinning broadly and the others were looking faintly baffled. It was good to keep your troops from growing too complacent, he thought.

Research into Sir Nigel Grisham's background proved he was eminently blackmailable. Besides the house in Flood Street he had a large country house near Chenies, in a part of Buckinghamshire long favored by the upper echelons of government and the civil service for its pretty, unspoiled countryside and good fast roads into London. Grisham had married the daughter of a Cotswold landowner with the bluest of blood and the blackest of bank accounts and had raised four attractive children, the youngest just at university age. His Parliamentary career had been solid rather than fast-track, but in a Parliament increasingly filled by the callow and the indistinguishable, he had now in his early fifties attained an elder statesman status which was almost better than talent.

"And he's tipped to get Foreign Secretary in the reshuffle," Hart said as they headed westward—a simple phone call had established that Grisham had left Chelsea for his country house, or "done a bunk" as Hart put it. "A bum-scandal'd put paid to that, all right."

"How do you know that?" Slider asked.

"Well, s'obvious. It's all right coming out of the closet if you're an actor, but the public don't like turd-burglars representing 'em at international summits."

"I didn't mean that, I meant how did you know he was tipped for Foreign Secretary?"

She looked at him, wide-eyed. "It was in the news. Blimey, guv, don't you read the papers?"

"When do I have time?" he countered irritably. "I can't even get through all the stuff on my desk."

"Yeah," she said placatingly. "Well. Anyway, the papers'd have a field day if it got out about him and Paloma, even without the murder. They don't like anyone in the foreign office to sleep around, ever since Profumo."

"But that was prostitutes."

"So was Paloma. And arse-bandits is even worse. It looks as though Grisham's got the wind up, anyway, making a run for it."

"It is summer, you know. People do go out of London in summer. And he has a wife and children in the country."

"He's bound to have seen Paloma's death in the papers."

"Then he ought to think he's safe," Slider pointed out. "Dead men tell no tales."

Hart only grunted, unconvinced. "I bet he's in a panic," she said. Slider agreed with her. If Grisham had seen Paloma's death mentioned in the papers, he must wonder whether he ought to come forward and disclose his relationship, or whether that would be exposing himself needlessly. Well, he was soon to find out.

Edge House, Grisham's country place, was closed off from the road by a high wall. The ornate gates were shut; through them was a view of a gravel sweep around a well-tended piece of lawn, to a handsome Palladian house in softly red old brick with an ancient wisteria climbing up one corner, and modern but tasteful single-story additions on either side. A million upward, Slider guessed, depending on how much land was attached.

"Lifestyles of the rich and shameless, eh?" said Hart. "I've never been this close to the seat of power before. Are you sure it's all right to come asking him questions? We won't be slapped in the Tower for Les Majesty or summink?"

"Cabinet ministers have no special immunity, not like diplomats," Slider said. "He's got to account for himself just like anyone else. At least, if we can get past these gates," he added, looking in vain for a handle.

"There's an intercom," Hart pointed out. "Shall I ring?"

"No, I'll do it," Slider said.

She grinned. "Afraid they won't let us in if they hear my accent?"

Slider frowned at her. "Get in the driving seat."

It was a woman's voice that answered when he rang; even distorted by the intercom, it was middle-aged and cultured in accent. "Who is it, please?"

"Detective Inspector Slider, Metropolitan Police. I'd like a word with Sir Nigel, if you'd be so kind."

There was a pause. A conference going on, or simple caution? "I don't know an Inspector Slider," the voice said. "You're not our usual security liaison."

"It isn't about security, ma'am. I'm from Shepherd's Bush C.I.D. I'd like a word with Sir Nigel on a private matter."

"Well I don't know. It sounds very odd. Are you alone?"

"I have Detective Constable Hart with me. May I suggest you telephone my Area Commander, Mr. Wetherspoon, at Hammersmith Police Station for confirmation of my identity?"

Another pause. It was like holding a transatlantic telephone conversation. "Very well," the voice said at last. "Please come in, Inspector."

There was a buzz and a click and the gates swung eerily open. Hart drove in over the scrunching gravel, and before they reached the front door, the gates had swung closed again with a solid electronic clunk. Someone must have been watching—there was a security camera mounted above the door—for the front door opened as soon as they reached it. A woman stood there, a well-preserved, well-dressed, well-coiffeured lady in her fifties, with a face schooled over a lifetime of public work to show no emotion. The eyes, however, were quick and anxious. They surveyed and summed up Slider and Hart with rapid professionalism.

"I'm Lady Grisham," she said. "Please come in."

They walked past her into a lovely hall with a polished wood floor, a Sheraton side table bearing a *famille rose* vase, and a staircase of airy beauty rising like an invitation to the delights of the first floor. The walls were robin's egg blue and weighted with old and expensive oil paintings; the air was cool and faintly scented with lavender. An ancient and outrageously shapeless black labrador waddled up with a clicking of nails and swung a polite tail, his blue-filmed eyes scanning in vain for faces through his own personal mist. Lady Grisham stood with her hands lightly clasped before her, elegant in a floral silk dress, pearls and a carefully selected brooch, as she had stood on a thousand platforms and sat on a thousand committees: being what was expected of her, waiting to cope. Slider felt a deep reluctance to be here. He felt like a vandal. He had come to smash this sweet order to bits; but he saw in her dark, unhappy eyes that Lady Grisham had been expecting this moment, perhaps for years.

"I'm sorry to have to disturb you like this," Slider said when he had shown his identification, "but it is very urgent."

Lady Grisham was ready to fight a rearguard action. "I know you have your duty to do, Inspector, but it really is a very inconvenient time. My husband is far from well, and he had a sleepless night. I persuaded him to try to take a nap in the library, and I really don't wish to disturb him just when he may have managed to get off to sleep. He has a very crowded schedule for the next few days, and in this present state of health—''

''It's all right, my dear.'' The right-hand door which led off the hall, which had been standing slightly ajar, opened fully and Sir Nigel himself appeared. In tweed trousers, checked shirt, knitted tie, olive-green cardigan with leather buttons, and highly polished brogues, he was perfectly dressed for leisure in the country—if you were a public figure, that is. The old dog turned its head at the sound of his voice and staggered across, wagging everything in delight. Behind Sir Nigel was a glimpse of another lovely room, book-lined, with an Adam fireplace and comfortable old leather chairs. ''I wasn't asleep,'' he went on. ''And I'm sure the inspector and his colleague wouldn't be here if it were not important.''

''But Nigel, oughtn't we to telephone Roger?'' she said urgently.

''I don't think so. I don't think he can help at this stage. Won't you come through to the library, Inspector?'' He looked bleakly at his wife. ''Don't let anyone disturb us, Annie. And no telephone calls.''

She met his eyes with some message, to which he shook his head just perceptibly; as if she had said, *run away, there's still time*, and he had said, *it's too late, there's no escape*. Slider was perfectly well aware that this was fanciful on his part, but he wished the minister hadn't called his wife Annie, and he wished the old dog hadn't tried to go with his master into the library and been gently, firmly repulsed. ''No, no, old fellow, not you. Go with missus, go on.''

''Jasper, come here,'' Lady Grisham called. The dog pivoted stiffly and lumbered reluctantly to her, and Grisham closed the library door.

''Can I offer you sherry?'' he asked, ushering them to seats.

''No, thank you,'' Slider answered for both. He felt bad enough without drinking the man's liquor.

''You won't object, I hope, if I have one?'' Grisham said. ''I usually do at this time. Sure I can't tempt you? Quite, quite. On duty, of course.'' He made a slow bustle of getting out decanter and glass, pouring and putting away, and Hart flung a couple of urgent looks at Slider—*thinking out what to say*—but Slider let them pass him by. Grisham was trying to steel himself for the ordeal to come, that was all. Finally he came and sat down opposite Slider, took a large sip of the sherry, put down the glass and said, "Now, what can I do for you?" in a bland and friendly manner as if they were constituents come to talk about road planning. But his voice wavered slightly, and he looked haggard. Lady Grisham had probably spoken no more than the truth when she said he was unwell and hadn't slept. His face, familiar from the television and newspapers, handsome in a presidential way, looked lined and exhausted; his mouth drooped wearily at the corners and his eyes were baggy with lack of sleep.

"I'm very sorry to have to broach this subject with you, Minister," Slider said, "but I imagine that you must be aware that Maurice McElhinney, also known as Jay Paloma, was found dead at his flat on Wednesday last week."

Grisham was breathlessly still. "Why should you think I would be aware of that? Am I supposed to know this—"

"To save you trouble, Sir Nigel, I should say that Jay Paloma was traced to your house in Flood Street on Monday afternoon last week the day before he was murdered, and that you were seen to let him in and greet him in a friendly manner. And that he told his closest friend that he had spent Monday afternoon with his lover."

Grisham started to tremble. He moved his lips a few times, but couldn't seem to speak.

"We have taken in custody one Jonah Lafota, who works at the Pink—" He stopped, because Grisham had gone quite suddenly to pieces. The meat of his face began to quiver uncontrollably, his mouth sagged so that a thread of saliva slipped out of one corner, his eyes rolled around and upward. For a thrilling second Slider thought he was going to have a stroke or a heart attack, but it was only despair and grief. Grisham put his hands over his face and hunched forward, chewing at his brow with his fingertips, moaning quietly. Hart looked at Slider but he shook his head. Behind Sir Nigel's hands, the doglike moans blurred into words.

"I knew this would come. Oh God, I've been such a fool. I can't bear it. I didn't mean it to happen. Oh God, I'm ruined.

I'm finished. Oh God, what's going to happen to me? Annie. The children. They'll never live it down. It's horrible. I never meant anyone to get hurt. It was a mistake. I didn't want him hurt. What's going to happen to me? I'm finished. Oh God, I can't bear it.''

This went on for some time while Slider and Hart waited in silence, Slider feeling a familiar blend of emotions, pity for the writhing victim before him, relief that they were obviously on the right track, hope that he was going to come across with the goods. At last, when the paroxysm seemed to be waning, Slider got up, went to the cupboard where the sherry had been stored, sniffed out the brandy, and poured a large slug. He took it back to the cabinet minister, laid a kindly hand on his shoulder, and said, ''Here, try this. It will steady your nerves.''

Grisham removed his hands from his face reluctantly, but he knocked back the brandy and then busied himself with his handkerchief, wiping his eyes and blowing his nose.

''Another?'' said Slider. Grisham nodded. After the second stiffener, he seemed back in control. He sighed, sat up straight, clasped his hands together in his lap for comfort, and said, ''I suppose I must tell you all about it.''

''It would be better if you did,'' Slider agreed.

Grisham looked at him, half pathetic, half resentful. ''But I swear to you, I never meant any harm to come to him. You must believe me. I was as shocked as anyone when I saw in the papers that he—that he—''

''That's all right, sir,'' Hart said gently. ''Why don't you tell it from the beginning? It'll flow easier that way. Just start at the beginning, and see how it comes.''

And, oddly, it was to Hart rather than to Slider that Sir Nigel Grisham told the tale. As though she would understand better. One minority to another, perhaps? But he told it, that was what mattered.

❖ ELEVEN ❖

Rich and Shameless

"I don't want to you to think—I haven't lived a double life, you know," Sir Nigel said. "What I mean is, I haven't made a habit of—" He paused, and the words *this sort of thing* hovered unspoken. The trouble with the unspeakable, Slider thought, was that there were no words for it.

"You're a happily married man," Hart said helpfully, and Grisham looked rescued.

"Yes, very happily. Annie is a wonderful person. Without her I could never have got where I am today. I love her very much. We love each other very much. It's important to understand that."

"Yeah, okay," said Hart, willing to be convinced. "So where does Jay Paloma fit into it?"

"I don't know," he said. He stared away bleakly. "It was an extraordinary thing. It was not something I expected. I'm not—I haven't ever been—"

"Were there others before Jay?"

"No," he said quickly. "That's what I'm trying to tell you. Oh, I got up to the usual things at school, the way boys do, but it didn't mean anything. At that age it's just eroticism, not homosexuality." There, the horrid word was out. Grisham seemed the better for it. "As a teenager I had all the normal urges. I went out with girls. I planned to get married. There was nothing different about me."

"So Jay was the first male lover you ever had?"

He hesitated. "The first lover, yes. But I did—have encounters. Just a few. Over the years." Hart nodded, easy, uncritical, simply interested, and Grisham unfolded a little. "The first time was when I was in Frankfurt on a business trip. A group of us went out for the evening, rather overdid things, ended up in a nightclub. I started chatting to a gorgeous-looking female—well, she looked gorgeous in that light. I was rather drunk, you know, otherwise I wouldn't have—"

"Yeah, I know."

"We ended up going back to my hotel room. I don't honestly remember all that much about it. But I suppose you can guess the rest."

"The female turned out to be male."

"Yes. And—well—he seemed to think I'd known that all along, and I was—I don't know—it was rather exciting in a strange way. So I—"

"Done it," Hart finished for him. He looked at her carefully, to see if she were mocking or disapproving, and she made a tiny movement of her hands, shoulders and head which said as clearly as words, *c'est la guerre*—or, since it was Hart after all, *vese fings 'appen*. "So that was the way it went after that, was it?"

"I didn't make a habit of it," he said with a little sharpness. "I felt very bad after that first time—mostly for being unfaithful to Annie. But over the years—the stresses of the job—I wasn't proud of myself, but I don't want you to think I was ashamed, either. We dedicate ourselves to public service, and we live a life of unnatural strains, terrible hours, long periods away from our loved ones—"

"Yeah, tell me about it!"

"Of course, you would understand." And for the first time he looked at Slider, including him in the "you." Slider nodded slightly. "Well, when you live that sort of life, something has to give in the end. And I think Annie preferred it this way, rather than—well, I never gave her a rival, you see. She has been the only woman in my life. And I was always discreet. What I did harmed no one."

"And it was always like that, was it?" Hart prompted. "A casual pickup in a club. Just a one-night stand."

"Anything else would have been dangerous—and unfair to Annie. And it wasn't all that often, you know—once or twice a year. Half a dozen times at most. In any case, I've hardly had the time or energy in recent years. You can't imagine how ministerial work has multiplied in the last decade. I'd been living like a monk for years when I met Jay." He paused at the sound of the name, as if re-realizing the purpose of this cozy chat.

"So how did you meet him?" Hart picked up the thread easily and passed it back to him.

"One night, about a year ago, I was at my London house, alone and at a loose end. A meeting had been canceled at the last minute and I suddenly had nothing I had to do. No one was expecting me anywhere. I can't tell you what a heady sensation that was! It was the first time in months. Of course, I thought at first of coming down here, and I was on the point of telephoning Annie to say I was coming, when I suddenly thought, no, damnit, I'm going to take a little time for myself, be unaccountable for an evening—"

"Cut yo'self a little slack," Hart supplied.

Grisham seemed charmed with the phrase. "Cut myself a little slack, just so! That's exactly it! After being tethered head and foot for so long, the idea was intoxicating. So I went to the Pink Parrot Club."

"How did you know about it? Had you been there before?" Slider asked.

"Only once, and a long time before, but I'd heard about it. If you go to clubs at all, you hear about others. And it was conveniently close. That's why I chose it, because it was the nearest."

He seemed struck by the idea, and dropped into silent thought. Slider guessed what it was: by such random, meaningless decisions our fates are determined. If you listen very carefully, he thought, you can hear the gods laughing.

"And it was that night you met Jay Paloma?" Hart prompted after a moment.

Grisham came back from his distance, and seemed older, colder, grayer. The dance was over. This was the morning after. "Yes," he said. "It was—do you know the expression *coup de foudre*?"

"Yeah," said Hart, rather than break his rhythm.

"The moment I saw him, I was lost. And I knew it was the same for him. It wasn't like anything I'd ever felt before. Not even for Annie. I love her dearly, but this was something different. It was like meeting the other half of my soul after a lifetime of searching—except that I hadn't been searching. I hadn't even known I was incomplete. I fell in love with him, even though he wasn't a woman. It didn't matter what he was, what body he happened to be in. I just fell in love with *him*. Can you understand that?"

"Yeah, I can understand."

Grisham shrugged as though the story was finished. "So we became lovers. Whenever I could make time, we met. It was the start of a new life for me."

"It couldn't have been easy," Slider said, "given how busy you were." Grisham looked at him. "And given that he was living in a place where you couldn't visit him, and that he was working as well."

"You know all about it, I suppose."

"I understand that you had—disagreements. About his working at the Pomona Club."

"I wanted him to give it up," Grisham said. "If only he'd listened to me, none of this would have happened. I wanted him to give up work and move into a place nearer the center, so that we could see each other more often. So that he could be more flexible about when we could meet."

"So that he would always be available when you found yourself with time to spare," Slider filled in.

"Is that unreasonable?" He addressed the protest to Slider, but then looked at Hart. "He wanted to be with me as much as I wanted to be with him. I had enough money. I told him, he would never want for anything. I'd always been generous with him. Whatever he wanted, he only had to ask, he knew that. But he said he didn't want to be a kept man. He said it was humiliating. As opposed to what he did at the Pomona, I asked him? A kept man. How could he talk like that? When you love someone, you don't think like that."

"So you quarreled," Hart said neutrally.

"Oh, not really quarreled. We had arguments. Disagreements. It was something that came up from time to time.

Mostly we were happy, very happy. But I did worry about the Pomona for other reasons, security reasons. And just recently—with the reshuffle coming up—I told him he *must* give up working there. If it got out, it would mean—'' He stopped. ''Well, that's all over now,'' he went on flatly. ''My career is over.''

Slider stopped Hart with a look and said evenly, ''Tell me about the cocaine that Jay bought for you.''

''Oh, you know about that, do you?'' Grisham said with a bitter look. ''What do you want to know, then?''

''Whose idea was it? Did you ask him or did he offer? Did you use it together?''

''We didn't use the damned stuff! I've never taken drugs. I've smoked a little pot now and then, but only abroad in countries where it was legal. In my position you can't be too careful.'' He did not seem to see any irony in the words. ''And Jay hated drugs, hated everything to do with them. He was passionate on the subject. I think if I'd ever suggested we took something together he'd have walked out on me there and then.''

''Nevertheless, he did buy cocaine for you.''

''Yes, he got it for me, under protest. He didn't want to do it. I had the devil of a job to persuade him. But it was—necessary.''

''What for?''

Grisham frowned. ''I suppose I have to tell you. At least then you won't think I took the beastly stuff. I don't want that slur laid on me, along with everything else. The truth is that I got it for a colleague. A fellow Member of Parliament. He was blackmailing me.'' He looked from Slider to Hart and back. ''That's the sort of person we get in the House nowadays. Nice, isn't it? This—*colleague*—found out about Jay and me. He came to me and said that if it got out it would be the end of my career. At first I brazened it out. Told him to publish and be damned. But he said it wouldn't hurt *him* to spill the beans, and that if I wanted to make sure he couldn't do so without implicating himself, he'd tell me how. I couldn't think what he meant—I thought he was suggesting some disgusting *ménage à trois*—but it turned out that what he wanted was cocaine. He reckoned that Jay would know how to get hold of it, and if we formed his supply chain, he would never be able to split on us. A painless kind of insurance, he called it.''

"And did Jay know how to get hold of it? Slider asked.

"He found out. After a lot of persuasion. I gave him the money, he got the stuff and passed it to me, I passed it to my colleague and collected the cash. What he did with it I don't know. I hoped fervently that he would poison himself with it, but he hasn't so far.''

Sold it, probably, Slider thought, in single fixes to fellow ravers. At a profit. "Do you know where Jay got it?''

"He found some contact through the club. That's all I know. He wouldn't tell me any names, and I didn't want to know them.''

"He actually bought it from someone at the club?''

"He wouldn't tell me any of the details. I suppose he thought it was safer for me not to know.''

"He was taking a considerable risk," Slider said.

"I hated putting him in that position," Grisham said, "and he hated doing it, but he did it for me. That's the sort of man he was. He did it to protect me. Because I couldn't see any other way out. Oh, I've made such a mess of things!'' He put his head in his hands.

"Tell me about the last time you saw him. The Monday, wasn't it?''

Grisham raised his head wearily, and obeyed. "It was all arranged. We had the whole afternoon together, the first time in weeks that we'd had a decent amount of time. I can't tell you how much I was looking forward to it. But I could see as soon as he arrived that he was not in the best of moods.''

"How do you mean? Depressed? Worried?''

"I don't know quite how to put it. On edge, perhaps. Restless. He kept walking about the room, wouldn't settle. Did dance steps and stretches against the furniture. He did that sometimes to—to distance himself from me. Emphasizing his independence.'' This was addressed to Hart again.

"Why'd he wanna do that?'' she asked.

"Oh, I don't know. He was upset about something and wanted to take it out on me. I didn't inquire too deeply because it didn't pay. I didn't want to quarrel with him, and I thought he'd just come out of it once he relaxed a bit. So I said what's wrong, and he said nothing, and I left it at that. But he kept picking at me, finding fault, wanting to quarrel. I let it all bounce off me. But then he picked up the newspaper and glanced through it and said, 'Oh look, there's a bit about us in here.' "

"I bet that gave you a fright," Hart said.

"I can't tell you how my heart jumped. I thought he meant him and me. And when I looked at it, it was a news paragraph about some brawl at the Pomona Club. I—I'm afraid I just snapped. My temper was already frayed. He had been—"

"Winding you up?"

"Yes, winding me up. And I was always worried about the Pomona Club, and his connection with it. And I hated the fact that he went on working there in preference to a more civilized life where we could see more of each other. We had the most dreadful quarrel—"

"On that subject?"

"Mostly. It spread, as quarrels tend to, but it had its roots firmly in the Pomona Club. It ended with me giving him an ultimatum, and him telling me to go to hell, because he didn't need me. And he said if he got out of the Pomona Club, it would be for his own reasons, and he'd get right out of my life at the same time."

"Oh dear," said Hart, in response to Grisham's look of appeal.

"It was like having a bucket of cold water thrown over me. I stopped shouting and tried to placate him. I begged him not to say things like that. I said things should be whatever way he wanted. Well, he calmed down, and after a bit I thought the best way to make things up would be—"

"To go to bed."

"Yes. Yes. But it wasn't like before. I was—I was angry with him. I wanted him to admit that he *did* need me, that it wasn't all on my side. But he wouldn't. In the end it was—rather horrible."

Hence the rough sex. Slider could imagine it, rather more graphically than he liked. Grisham was afraid of losing Paloma, and fear made him angry. The one situation where he felt he had control was between the sheets, and he was going to prove he was master.

"So what happened after?" Hart prompted after a tactful silence.

"He left early. I'd arranged everything so that we could have a long time together. I begged him not to waste it, but he wouldn't stay. He looked at me so coldly."

"And afterwards——?"

"Afterwards, after he'd gone, I wanted to punish him." Grisham's voice was very quiet, and Slider was almost holding his breath. He had come to find out the cocaine connection and what exactly Jay Paloma had done on his last full day of life; but something else was coming, something unsuspected, and if Grisham were disturbed in any way he might realize what he was doing and shut up. "I didn't want him hurt, you must understand that. Not hurt, just frightened."

"Right, just frightened," Hart agreed.

"To punish him for frightening me. And to make him see he couldn't leave me. After he left I had a lot of drinks rather quickly, and then I went out, I walked around—up and down the Embankment for hours—thinking what to do. And then I went to the Pink Parrot."

"Yeah, 'course."

"There's a man there—a sort of bouncer, I suppose, though he's always smartly dressed and carrying an expensive mobile phone. I suppose he might even be more of a manager than a bouncer. But he's huge, absolutely huge."

"Yeah, I know. Jonah Lafota."

Grisham blinked. "You know him?"

"We've got him tucked up in custody, back at the station."

"Ah." It was a long, terminal sort of sigh. "Then you know all about it."

"From his end. Not from yours. You asked him to go and give Jay a smacking for you, did you?"

"No! I made it very clear I didn't want him hurt in any way. I gave Jonah money. To tell you the truth, even at the time I didn't really think he'd do it. He knew I was drunk—good God, it was obvious to anyone. He took the money and just grinned at me, as if he found the whole situation highly amusing."

"Did he know about your relationship with Jay?" Slider asked.

"He'd seen us there together, in the Pink Parrot. And I expect Jay had told him. Anyway, I had another drink or two, and then I went home, and fell asleep like the dead. And the next morning, I thought it must all have been a horrible dream, except that I had a terrible hangover, and the money had gone all right. My anger was gone too. I just felt miserable. I didn't want Jay frightened, I just wanted him to come back to me."

"Didn't you try to get in touch with Jonah?"

"Well, no." Grisham looked a little dazed. "In the clear light of day the whole situation was farcical. It never occurred to me for a moment that he'd do anything. I wouldn't have known where to find him, in any case, except at the Pink Parrot, and that's closed during the day. I did think about giving a ring in the evening, just to ask if he'd put the money away safely for me until I could collect it, but I realized that would only make me look more ridiculous." He looked at Slider, pleadingly. "I was quite sure he wouldn't do anything. I mean, why would he, even if he did think I meant it?"

Yes, why, Slider thought.

"In the afternoon I telephoned Jay's flat. I wanted to make it up with him. He didn't usually bear grudges. I thought I might even tell him about my little adventure, as a sort of joke. I thought it might amuse him—or at least prove how much I loved him. But there was no answer, so I supposed he'd gone out."

"What time was that?" Slider put in.

"I left it until the afternoon, because he doesn't usually get up until about half past twelve. I telephoned at about half past one, but there was no answer. I was busy then for some time and couldn't get to a telephone, but I called again at about half past four, and again at six, but there was still no answer. After that I couldn't ring again because I had to go to the House—there was an all night sitting—but in any case I knew there'd be no point, because he leaves for work at about half past six."

"Didn't he usually put the answering machine on when he went out?"

"Yes. I did wonder about that. But he might have guessed I would ring, and didn't want me to be able to leave him a message."

"Yes," said Slider thoughtfully.

"And then the next day I saw it in the paper—"

"Yes," said Slider again.

Grisham looked at him grayly. "Can you tell me what happened? There were no details in the papers. I keep thinking—wondering—"

"We're still trying to find out exactly what happened," Slider said. "Jonah Lafota apparently went to the flat on Tuesday night, kicked the door in, and killed Jay Paloma with a single blow from some heavy instrument. There doesn't appear to have been any struggle, so it must have been quick. I doubt whether Jay had time to realize what was happening."

"He killed him," Grisham whispered.

"We have Lafota's fingerprints inside the flat, and we have a witness who saw the door being kicked down by him at half past eleven on Tuesday evening—"

Grisham sharpened. "But he should have been at work at that time. Why wasn't he at work?"

"We don't know. I'm afraid there's a great deal we don't know yet."

"But he's dead," Grisham said. "Jay is dead. That's the bottom line." He rubbed his face with his hands, looking desperately tired now. "What's going to happen to me, Inspector? Am I going to be arrested for murder? I never meant him to be hurt, I swear it. Will that make any difference? Mitigation, or whatever it's called. I loved him. I never meant him to be hurt."

"It will be taken into consideration," Slider said circumspectly. "And the fact that you have cooperated with us, and haven't tried to hide anything, will tell in your favor."

"Cooperated," Sir Nigel said blankly. He shook his head slowly. "I've been the most god-awful fool. And I'm responsible for Jay's death—I can't get away from that. I almost wish we hadn't abolished hanging. I ought to pay the penalty. It would be a relief, in a way." His voice dropped to a whisper. "I loved him so much."

Slider could only take so much. "I don't think it would be

a relief to your wife and family to see you hanged.''

Grisham snapped out of it, though it was the frayed snap of very elderly celery. ''You're right. I must think of Annie and the children. I suppose there's no way of keeping any of this quiet? I don't want to escape my punishment, but the scandal would be a punishment to them, too, and they don't deserve it.''

You should have thought of that a long time ago, Slider thought, but not being one to kick a man when he was down, he didn't say it. ''That's not in my hands,'' he said instead.

''Are you going to take me away?''

''I don't think that will be necessary. You aren't intending to run away, are you? What I'd like you to do is to make a full statement of everything you've just told us, with some extra details about times and dates that I'll ask you about. Then we'll leave you alone for the time being. Later it will be necessary to interview you again, perhaps here, perhaps at a police station, and the question of charges will arise. Your fullest cooperation will be in your best interests; and I'm sure I don't need to advise you not to talk to anyone about any of this.''

''No,'' Grisham said. ''You can be sure I'll keep my mouth shut.''

''Now I expect you'd like to have your solicitor present while you make your statement, wouldn't you?''

Grisham gave a faint smile. ''I imagine Roger's already on his way here. Roger Tagholm is my solicitor. Annie wanted me to call him when you first arrived, and I don't know my Annie if she didn't call him as soon as the library door closed behind us.''

Slider found Joanna by Atherton's bedside. Their heads were close together in absorbed conversation, but first Atherton looked up, and then Joanna turned her head and saw him, and they both smiled. ''It's the man himself,'' Joanna said.

''Shall I leave?'' Slider asked plaintively. ''You looked so cozy when I came in, I wouldn't want to be in the way.''

''We were just talking.''

''What about?''

"Jim has this theory that everyone in the world is a character out of *Winnie the Pooh*."

"What I said," Atherton corrected her, "was that the characters in said book are such archetypes that you can categorize all the people you know by them."

"That's what I said," Joanna objected. "And we were just arguing about which character *he* was."

"I'm Christopher Robin," Atherton said quickly. "The wise outsider, the adjudicator who takes no part but sees all; the Great Narrator."

"Also known as God," Joanna said sarcastically. "Whereas I said—"

"He's Piglet," Slider said.

She looked delighted. "Yes! You see it too!"

"I shall sulk," Atherton said. "I won't be Piglet. Joanna's Rabbit, of course—"

"You swine!"

"But you, Bill," he went on solemnly, "are hard to define."

"He's Pooh Bear, living under the name of Slider," Joanna said.

"But with just a touch of Eeyore, do you think?"

"Is this the best you can manage by way of intellectual exchange?" Slider asked.

"From where I'm lying, it's a Socratean Dialogue," Atherton said. "Do you know what the absolute worst thing about being in hospital is?"

"I'm sure you'd like to tell me."

"It's the relentless baby talk. At some point in history all the medical staff jointly decided that they could cope with the revoltingness of sick people if they treated them like subnormal seven-year-olds. 'We're just going to pop you down to X-ray and take some pictures of your tummy.'" He made a sound of disgust. "They all do it. It's always 'just': we're *just* going to do this or that—we're *just* going to cut your leg off—as if that makes it better. And 'pop.' Everything's 'pop.'"

"Pop?" Slider inquired mildly.

"Pop you down to theater. Pop you into bed. Pop this thermometer in your mouth." He assumed a whining falsetto.

" 'Would you just like to pop yourself over onto this trolley for me?' No I bloody would not!"

"You're feeling better," Slider concluded. "Your word sensitivity's returned."

"It never went away," Atherton said. "I just hadn't got the energy to talk about it. How's the case coming along?"

Slider frowned. "I've got a whole lot of new information."

"You don't seem too happy about it."

"Because it doesn't make *sense*," Slider said resentfully. He told them about Grisham. "It looks like another couple of loose ends tied up, but it just makes things worse."

"But you've got this Jonah bloke already, haven't you?" Joanna said. "You thought he did it, and now Grisham says he paid him to do it. What's the problem?"

"As Grisham himself said to me, why should Jonah do it?" Slider said. "Look, a man comes up to you in a club and shoves a wad of banknotes in your hand and asks you to go round and frighten a friend of his—why would you do it?"

"For the money," Joanna said.

"A couple of hundred?" Slider shook his head. "Not worth the risk, especially if you're working for Billy Yates. Besides, you've already got the money. The man's tired and emotional, and you're four times the size of him. If you want the cash, you've got it. You don't have to do anything for it. It's very unlikely the bloke will ever come back asking for it, and if he does, you've only got to smile menacingly and say you don't know nuthin' 'bout no money. What's Grisham going to do?"

"You're assuming Jonah's bright enough to think of all that," Joanna said. "What if he's really, really dim, and just does what he's told?"

"If he's merely obedient, why *kill* Paloma? That's just crazy."

"He could have been drunk. Or lost his temper," Joanna said.

"Or just overenthusiastic," Atherton said. "You said he's huge—maybe he doesn't know his own strength."

"Or maybe he'd always hated Paloma and was glad of the excuse," Joanna added.

"And another thing," Slider went on, "where do the poison pen letters come in?"

"Maybe they never existed. You never saw any. Maybe Paloma just made them up."

"But he was afraid of something," said Slider. "Maybe there weren't any poison pen letters, but he was afraid of something."

"Maybe this, maybe that," Atherton said sleepily. "Anything's possible. Maybe Jonah didn't kill him."

"Thanks," said Slider. "You said you were going to solve this case for me from your bed."

"I can't make bricks without straw. Bring me more facts."

"Facts," Slider said crossly. "What are facts? You think you know something, and then you turn it round another way and it means something entirely different."

"Nothing is what it seems, and reality is up for grabs," Atherton said sympathetically.

"That reminds me," Joanna said, "did I ever tell you my favorite Bob Preston story?"

"You have so many," Slider said. "Go on."

"But this is a true story. You know Bob Preston, who used to be our co-principal trumpet? Right, well, Bob studied composition at university, and for his finals he had to write an original piece of music which would be marked by his professor. His professor was—" She named a famous English composer. "He was so brilliant he scared the shit out of Bob, though he admired him tremendously. Anyway, when it came to it, Bob couldn't write a note, hadn't an original thought in his head. Complete blank. He was in despair, because everything depended on this composition. Then a streetwise friend gave him a tip. 'Take a piece of your professor's own music,' the friend said, 'turn it upside down and write it out in your own handwriting. Your prof won't recognize it, but it'll fit his brain patterns well enough for him to think it's good. He'll love it, he'll give you top marks." Bob thought this was a brilliant idea, so he got hold of a Fantasia which he happened to know his prof was particularly proud of. He turned it upside down and wrote it out—and discovered that what he had was the first movement of a Sibelius symphony."

Atherton shouted with pleasure.

"I never know whether to believe your stories," Slider complained.

Joanna smiled seraphically. "Everything I tell you is either true, or bloody well ought to be."

✤ TWELVE ✤

Quinbus Flestrin

Slider faced David Stevens in the corridor outside the tape room.

"Look, Dave, you've got to get him to come across. It's not doing him any good, this refusing to say anything."

Stevens shrugged his bouncy shoulders. "I can only take my client's instruction. If he doesn't want to talk—"

"Have you explained to him about the change in the law over the right to remain silent?"

"Who d'you think you're talking to here? Of course I have."

Slider struck off points on his fingers. "We've got the footmark on the door, fingermarks inside the flat, an eyewitness who saw him kicking the door down. And now we've got Sir Nigel Grisham's statement that he paid Lafota money to put the frighteners on Paloma. There's no doubt we'll get custody extended."

"I agree," said Stevens easily.

Slider blinked. "I've got enough to charge him."

Stevens smiled. "So charge him." He was eyeing Slider closely. "Charge him," he said again.

"I want him to tell me what happened!" Slider burst out in frustration. "Grisham only asked him to frighten Paloma. Why did he kill him? Was it an accident? Why did he wait until the next evening? How did he know Paloma was at home? Keeping silent now is pointless—can't you make him see that?''

Stevens grinned his predator's grin. ''Ah Bill, Bill, the great poker face! You've got doubts, haven't you?''

''Don't get clever with me. I just told you that.'' He rubbed his eyes. ''If there's anything he's got to say in mitigation, he's weakening his position by not telling me now. *You* know that. Make *him* understand it.''

Stevens laid a hand on Slider's shoulder. His shirt was crisp, his suit unwrinkled, his aftershave a poem; and his eyes twinkled with that wholehearted enjoyment of life only solicitors can afford. ''I will do my best, old son,'' he pledged. ''Angels can't do more.''

Jonah, seedy, rumpled and smelling of sweat, lit another cigarette and coughed through the first drag. His eyes were bloodshot from smoke and lack of sleep. He glared at Slider defiantly across the table.

''I didn't do it, right?''

''You didn't do what?'' Slider asked.

''I didn't kill Jay.''

''Then who did?''

''I dunno. How should I know?'' All I know, 'e was dead when I got there, right?''

''That's not very original. If I had a fiver for every time someone's told me that—''

''Itsa trufe!'' Now Jonah sounded frightened. His voice cracked a little. ''I never done nuffing to him. He was dead when I got there.''

''All right, tell me about it,'' Slider said.

Jonah was no orator even when he wanted to speak. It was like pull-out toffee, getting his story, but assembled it amounted to this: he had driven from his flat to White City, timing it to arrive at about twenty past eleven when the pubs were turning out, so that he wouldn't be noticed. He went up to Paloma's flat, kicked the door in with one mighty blow of his right foot, went straight to the sitting room, from which he could hear the sound of the television. Paloma was sprawled dead on the floor with his overturned chair.

''How did you know he was dead?''

"Aw, come on, man!" was Jonah's reply to that.

"Did you go right up to him and look?"

"Nah, I could see from the door he was dead all right."

"So what did you do?"

"Nuffing. I never done nuffing. I just got out, right? It wasn't no business of mine."

"Hmm. But you see, the people next door who heard you kick the door in also heard you knock over something heavy. They heard a thud, as if something heavy had hit the floor. Now what was that, I wonder, if it wasn't Jay Paloma?"

"I never touched him! I tell you I never touched nuffing!"

"Nothing at all?"

Jonah stared at him, eyes wide, his mouth open to repeat his panicky denial. But Stevens beside him stirred like the first faint dawn breeze ruffling the willows, and Jonah's mouth remained open and silent as he tried to capture the thread which had been spun for him.

"The bottle!" he cried at last. He might as well have pronounced it *eureka*. "I was shakin', man, an' I needed a drink, so I grabbed the bottle. The whiskey bottle on the table."

"So you did go into the room, then? Just now you told me you stayed by the door."

"Look, I just went to look at 'im, right? Like anyone would. I never touched 'im. And I was so shook up, like I said, I grabbed the bottle and took a drink, and when I turned around to put it back, I knocked the table over."

"You knocked the table over?"

"Yeah." Lafota seemed to feel relief at having reached sure ground. He looked at Stevens for approval. "That's what these people must of heard, right? An' everyfing went on the floor. So I picked it up and put it back, and then I took off."

"Why did you pick everything up?" Slider asked.

"I dunno," Lafota said, floored by the question.

But in Slider's mind the scenario played true. What could be simpler for a man-mountain in a normal sized sitting room than to knock the table over? He might have done it at any point while he was whacking Paloma; or it might actually have happened as he said, when, shaky from the killing, he had fortified himself with a drink. It had the sappy ring of truth about it, that bit. The killing he had planned and vis-

ualized, but the mess as the table went over, spilling magazines, whiskey and the contents of the ashtray on the floor,
was something unexpected, and it threw him. In his panic,
wanting to leave things as he had found them, wanting to
leave no trace of his having been there—other, of course, than
the dead body—the big lug had tidied up after himself, put
the table back, rubbed the ash into the carpet so that no one
would notice it, entirely forgetting that he had left his dabs
all over the whiskey bottle. It was the sort of stupid thing a
person would do, when they were not accustomed to thinking
things out, and found themselves in an unexpected and frightening situation.

"So why *did* you kill him?" Slider asked at last, conversationally.

"I never," Jonah said stubbornly. "I told you. He was
already dead when I got there."

"All right, then what did you go to the flat for in the first
place?" No answer. "Why did you go to the flat and kick
the door down?" No answer. "Did you do it for the money?"

Jonah looked contemptuous. "You call that money? I
wouldn't spit on a beggar for that." Stevens stirred, and Jonah
glanced at him anxiously, and then said, "I never killed him.
He was dead when I got there."

"But then *why* did you go there?"

Now Jonah looked sullen. "I ain't saying no more. I never
killed 'im, that's all. I ain't done nuffing." He turned resentfully to Stevens. "You get me out of here, right? They got
nuffing on me." And he folded his massive arms across his
chest and ostentatiously closed his mouth.

Hollis was in Slider's room, reading something he held in his
hands. He looked up as Slider came in. "Any luck?"

"I ain't saying nuffing," Slider said, going around his desk
to sit down heavily. "Now he says he found Paloma already
dead when he got there, was so upset he took a drink of
whisky, and knocked the table over putting the bottle back."

"Really? Well, I don't know about you, but I'm convinced," Hollis said brightly.

Slider gave him a look. "It means he's talked his way out
of the fingerprints."

"It looks like an open and shut case to me, guv," Hollis said comfortingly. "I wouldn't worry. He'll come clean in the end."

"With Stevens as his brief?" Slider said. "What's that you've got there, anyway?"

Hollis proffered it. "It's the additional forensic report."

Slider took it. The lab had typed the anal swab ready for cross-matching if requested. Well, that should keep Sir Nigel straight and true to his story. There was no trace of any known recreational drug in the bloodstream, and the alcohol was low, 40mg per 100ml, so Paloma was neither drunk nor high at the time of death. And the stomach contents had been analyzed as scrambled eggs and toast, eaten less than one hour before death.

"Well, that's consistent with the dirty dishes in the kitchen," Slider said, throwing the paper down on his desk. "No surprises there."

"The hearty man ate a condemned breakfast," Hollis said.

"A late breakfast, anyway," Slider said. "What else have you got for me?"

"Oh—this, sir." Hollis passed over the envelope with an abstracted air of having forgotten he was holding it. It was large, square and stiff, and Slider guessed what it was before he opened it.

"Mr. Honeyman's farewell party," he said aloud. "The official brass one, complete with speeches and presentation."

"You're invited, sir?" Hollis said with a smirk. "Congratulations."

"Not so fast," Slider said. "I've got to take someone else from my firm." He passed the invitation back. "As the only sergeant still upright, that means you. If I've got to suffer, I don't see why you should get away with it. I'm not a well man, you know."

Hollis bulged at him. "Me, guv? They won't want me. I'm a new boy, hardly know Mr. Honeyman."

"Don't grovel," Slider said coldly. "You're It."

"But it says black tie! My dinner suit's twenty years old. It's got twelve-inch flares and eight-inch lapels. The Fred West Wedding Suit look. I don't even know if I can still get into it."

"Hire one," Slider said brutally.

"Guv, listen, take Swilley. Give yourself a bit o' credit."

"I wouldn't do that to Swilley," Slider said.

"Hart, then." Hollis seemed struck by his own idea a moment after voicing it. "That's it—take Hart. Not only will it give you street cred, having a bird on your arm, but think how much it'll annoy the high-ups."

Slider looked at him narrowly. "White man speak with forked tongue. But you've got a point."

"That's right, guv." Hollis relaxed ostentatiously. "She doesn't mind what she says to anyone, and she's cracking-looking. And being an ambitious female, she probably won't mind going."

"All right, you've made your point," Slider said. "I shan't forget, though, how you abandoned me in my hour of need."

"That seems fair," Hollis said happily, "I won't forget it either." He got as far as the door and turned back. "Guv, I was just thinking—I suppose Lafota couldn't possibly have been telling the truth?"

"Meaning?"

"Well, you remember at the postmortem, the pathologist bloke started off thinking the death were much earlier? It was you saying late breakfast made me think—well, it *is* more like a breakfast meal, scrambled eggs, in't it?"

Slider was silent. The wrong time of death? Two men on the scene? Could that be the answer to all the anomalies? There was something else, something that made Hollis's suggestion chime harmoniously rather than jar. He looked back through his mental filing cabinet, and Hollis waited, watching him. What the hell was it? Something he had noticed without noticing, right at the very beginning. Something about the room in which Paloma was found.

"You were at the scene before me," Slider said at last. "Were the curtains in the sitting room open or closed when you arrived?"

"Open," Hollis said without hesitation. "The sun was shining in."

"You didn't open them?"

"Not me."

"Who was first on the scene? It was Baker, wasn't it? He

wouldn't have pulled the curtains back. He'd know better than that.''

"Shall I check, guv?"

"Yes, do that. If the curtains were open—"

"Yes."

"It isn't impossible that someone should sit and watch television at night with the curtains open, particularly in summer—with the long twilights people do sometimes forget to pull them. But—"

"Yes, guv," Hollis said.

Slider met his eyes unwillingly. "If there's anything in this, we're back at square one, you realize that. We'll have it all to do again. We'll have to go over every statement, re-examine the witnesses, reinterview all the neighbors with a new time of death in mind."

"No nice goodbye present for Mr. Honeyman, then?"

"Go and track down Baker. And if he says the curtains were open, you'd better assemble the troops to start looking at the statements."

"Right, guv."

"Oh—Hollis!"

"Guv?"

"That television program that was on when we arrived at the scene. What channel would that be?"

"That's *The Big Breakfast*. Channel Four."

"Right. Thanks," said Slider.

Honeyman seemed ill at ease. "Ah, Slider," he said vaguely. He stared at and through him, frowning.

"You sent for me, sir?" Slider reminded him tactfully.

"Yes. Yes." A pause. "Oh yes. You've had your invitation to my farewell party?"

"Yes, sir."

"And who are you bringing?"

"I thought Hart, sir, if that's all right."

"Hart? Oh yes. Yes, good idea. Bring a little life into it. These do's tend to be stuffy. A lot of men together, slapping backs and talking shop." He cleared his throat as though embarrassed. "You know of course that I'm not leaving?"

"Not, sir?"

"No. Well, not this week, anyway. I had hoped we could bring this Paloma case home by today, but as we haven't—well, I couldn't go in the middle of it. Especially given the sensitivity of the Grisham connection."

"I see, sir. So how long will you be staying on?" If the case went into extra time, what then? Would they just slip little Eric in the non-active filing cabinet years hence and forget him?

"I've asked for another fortnight," Honeyman said. "If there's nothing substantial by then I shall have to hand it onto my successor, but I did want to give it a reasonable chance. I look to you—er, Bill—to send me out in the right style." He used Slider's name with all the ease of a Victorian virgin naming a private part.

"I'll do my best, sir," Slider said. "So—what about the party?"

"Oh, we had to go ahead with that. There are some very senior people coming, and it's difficult to get them all in the same place at the same time. It would have been impossible to reschedule at this late stage."

"I see."

Honeyman looked at him almost pleadingly. "And what is the latest movement on the Paloma case?"

Slider felt a cad to be hitting him when he was down. "There seems to be some possibility of doubt that Lafota is our man, sir," he said; and explained.

Honeyman's face, which had sunk at the opening words, rose again from the waves toward the end. "Oh, I'm sure that can be got over. You must look into everything, of course, but there's no doubt Lafota was there, and he must remain our best suspect. And while we're on the subject," he hurried on, as though afraid Slider might voice some more inconvenient doubts, "I have some information for you concerning an inquiry you put to me." He raised his eyebrows and gave Slider a significant nod. "Shut the door, will you?"

Slider obeyed. Honeyman sat down behind his desk and gestured Slider to sit opposite him.

"This is confidential and very sensitive. I'm sure I can trust you?"

"Yes sir," Slider said, a little intrigued.

Honeyman seemed to relax. "I know you're a good chap. The thing is—" He hesitated, and, leaning forward a little, adopted an unburdening posture. "Senior rank has its social aspect, and I'm not very good at being pally. It's held me back to a certain extent. But I've always believed in being open, and I dislike—yes, I dislike very much—the sort of keep-quiet-and-do-as-you're-told attitude that's rife amongst some of the higher echelons."

Slider was now mystified. He could only look receptive and hope that the unburdening wasn't going to get too sticky. Deeply personal confidences tended to involve a morning-after hangover of the do-you-still-respect-me variety, which Slider had no wish to be on the wrong end of.

Honeyman sighed. "I've been in the Job thirty years, all but," he confided. "I was never a high flyer. I was interested in police work, that's why I joined. But there comes a point when you have to decide whether you're going to have a career structure, or settle for being PC Plod and going out in a blaze of obscurity. And a career demands a certain amount of compromise. A certain amount of put up and shut up. Tact, diplomacy and the occasional—" He hesitated again, lost for the right word. Slider could think of plenty, but plumped for tact and diplomacy and waiting in silence. "Fudge," Honeyman said at last. "Well, perhaps not quite that. A blurring of the outlines."

"Yes, sir," Slider said, to help him along.

Honeyman looked at him sharply. "I don't mean abandoning one's principles. I don't mean doing anything wrong. But sometimes one has to be, well, pragmatic." He stopped, internally digesting something, and then seemed to come to a decision. "I've taken my share of stick over the years. When you aren't a high flyer, it's expected. But when it comes to being spoken to like that—"

"Sir?"

"Look here," Honeyman said, "I've been told to keep my mouth shut about this, but I don't see how you can carry on an investigation without all the information, and it is my personal judgment that you ought to be told. So I am going against orders. But this must go no further."

"I understand, sir."

"Yes, I think you do." Honeyman scanned his face keenly. "Cosgrove did put an inquiry to Mr. Barrington. And Barrington did tell him to drop it. He had orders from higher up. There was—and is—a special Scotland Yard investigation going on into a very large drugs network. It is a very major investigation indeed, and they're hoping to bring down some very major players. The whole thing is very sensitive and very expensive, and if anything were to happen to disrupt it there would be repercussions at the highest level. The Drugs Squad has got undercover people in all over the place—"

"Including at the Pomona Club, sir?" Slider put in.

"Got it in one. That's why Cosgrove was warned off, and that's why I've been told to warn you off. Any snooping around the Pomona or Yates is likely to tread on certain toes, and it won't be tolerated."

"Warn me off without explanation?"

"Exactly. That's what gets my goat," he added with sudden animation. "Don't ask questions, just do as you're told. What kind of way is that to run a department?"

"I appreciate your telling me all this, sir," Slider said. "Can I ask you—is Yates one of the big players they're after?"

"I can't tell you that. Oh, not because I've been warned, but because I don't know. But I suspect he is. There's something not quite right about friend Yates, or my name's not Eric St. Maur Honeyman."

Slider took that without a blink. "It occurs to me to wonder, sir, whether Cosgrove was whacked because he was asking questions about Yates. His girlfriend said he told her he wouldn't be put off by Mr. Barrington's warning, and that he'd go on asking questions on his own."

"It occurs to me to wonder that too. But I've been told to keep my wondering to myself. Any questions that need asking will be asked by the great and good at Headquarters," Honeyman said with undisguised sarcasm. A spot of color appeared in each of his cheeks. "But Cosgrove's one of *my* men. I may not have been with you long, but Shepherd's Bush is *my* ground and *my* responsibility. Well, that's it," he concluded. "You know as much as I do now. I'm not going to tell you to leave well alone. But I will tell you to be careful.

Your career could be on the line if you foul the scent for the Drugs Squad. Those special posting boys are impatient of locals and arrogant as hell.''

"I suppose,'' Slider said tentatively, "you don't know the name of the undercover officer who's been targeting the Pomona?''

"If I did, I wouldn't be allowed to tell you. And if I told you, it would be strictly against orders for you to contact him.''

"Of course, I see that. It's just that, if we knew what he was up to, we could make sure not to get our lines crossed. It's easy to blunder into snares when you don't know where they've been set. We might already have caused some upset, simply by arresting Jonah Lafota. If only we could ask him,'' he finished wistfully, "I'm sure the officer on the ground would see the sense in keeping us informed.''

Honeyman eyed him through a blend of righteous indignation, years of resentment, and a touch of holiday rapture. "I am absolutely forbidden to tell you Detective Sergeant Richard de Glanville's name,'' he said firmly.

"Of course, sir. I understand.''

"It would upset Mr. Wetherspoon very much if he were to hear you had approached D.S. de Glanville. Very much indeed.''

"I wouldn't dream of letting him hear that, sir,'' said Slider. He and Little Eric looked into each other's eyes. It was a moment of contact, of tentative warmth between them. He wasn't a bad old boy, Slider thought, for an impossible bastard.

"Good, good. Well, off you go, then,'' Honeyman said briskly. "I'll see you at the party later on.''

"Yes, sir. Thank you.''

"At least they can't touch my pension,'' Honeyman said as Slider headed for the door.

Slider sat down at his desk, hesitated a moment, and then picked up the phone and dialed Scotland Yard. "Detective Superintendent Smithers, please.''

It rang a long time before a woman's voice answered.

"Pauline, it's Bill Slider. I didn't interrupt you in the middle of someone, did I?"

"Fat chance," she said. "I was in the loo, that's all. Is it trouble?"

"Why should you think that?"

"When else do you ever ring me?"

It was a deserved barb, Slider realized. He had known Pauline Smithers for most of his career, but her seniority, his diffidence, and Irene had prevented him from seeing much of her socially—which before Joanna might have been just as well. There had been a definite tenderness between them at one time.

"Congratulations on your promotion," he said.

"Thanks," she said. "But you know I only got it because they're abolishing the D.C.I. rank. They had to do something with me. Shove me up and shove me sideways."

"Bollocks. You deserve it. You've deserved it for a long time."

"You could have had it if you'd wanted it," she said seriously. "You've got the talent, and you haven't got my disadvantages."

"Disadvantages?"

"Two of them. Front upper body, left and right."

"From what little I know of them, I'm sure they're a positive asset."

"Chivalrous but inaccurate. The point is, if I've got this far despite being female, you could have been a chief superintendent by now if you'd wanted."

"I suppose that's it. I didn't want."

"Then you're a fool, Bill," she said briskly. "Who d'you think you are, Peter Pan? You want to retire on that salary grade, do you?"

"It's not a question of money," he began.

"Then you've got a Gandhi complex, which is worse."

"I'm good at what I do," he said. "It ought to be possible to be rewarded—to get the promotion and the pay increases—without—being moved into a different job that you wouldn't be so good at."

"Yes, there's a lot of things ought to be different from what they are. You've just got to work with what there is.

It's a fool who complains about the system when he can't change it.''

"I wasn't complaining. I'm happy being a D.I."

"You won't be for much longer, chum, when the kids start being promoted over your head, and you've got some spotty youth giving you orders. Still, it's no concern of mine. What did you want, anyway?"

That didn't sound very promising. "I just phoned to congratulate you. How are you enjoying the new posting?"

"Don't stuff me, Bill. What do you want?"

"I need your help, Pauly," he said meekly.

"I'd guessed that much," she said. And then, more kindly, "Are you in trouble?"

"I've got a case. It was difficult from the start, but now I've come up against official silences, it's escalated to impossible."

"All right, tell me the worst."

He gave her a rough outline of the case, and told her what Honeyman had told him. "It occurs to me this undercover guy may have been the one Yates saw talking to my victim. I need to find that out so that I can strike it off my list. And I could use a little more information about what my victim was getting into. I'm groping about in the dark here."

Pauline said slowly, "And what do you want me to do about it?"

"Tell me how to get in contact with this de Glanville without blowing his cover or upsetting the brass."

"But why ask me? I'm not in the Drugs Squad."

"You're at the Yard. And you have contacts everywhere, I know you have. You've told me yourself plenty of times that you've had to play it sneaky to get on. The Ladies' Loo Network you used to call it. Female solidarity."

"You're forgetting I'm brass myself now. Senior ranks solidarity—what about that? What you're asking me could get me demoted so fast I'd get friction burns on my arse."

"But it's crap, this blackout. I'm far more likely to mess up their investigation through ignorance than if I knew where not to tread. Help me. Can't you help me?" There was a silence. "Please, Pauly. I think I'm losing it."

"I don't like it," she said.

"It's in his own interest. If he was the man Yates mentioned, that could mean he's clocked him. He could be in danger."

"I wish you wouldn't come to me with this sort of thing," she said, and he knew from her tone of voice that he'd won. "I don't mind helping you out, when it doesn't mean breaking the rules. But I'm in a vulnerable position now. You wouldn't believe the cabals that operate up here. And there are no women on the Square, that's another thing."

"No one need ever know. You can do it. I wouldn't ask you if there was any way I could do it myself. And it's for a good cause."

"Yeah. Your promotion. If only. All right," she said at last, "I'll try and get him to contact you. That's the best way. But if nothing happens, it's because I haven't managed it. Don't chase me up, or bother me, or leave me messages."

"Hey," he said, wounded, "it's me."

"And you owe me, after this."

"Anything."

"I won't hold you to the anything," she said drily. "But a bloody good nosh, anyway."

"Just pick the date and the restaurant," he said.

He put the phone down feeling happier. Women C.I.D. officers were so beleaguered that they tended to stick together and help each other out; and there was also that curious solidarity that women of all ranks show each other in front of the mirrors in the loo. Information he was confident Pauline could come by. The cooperation of the unknown de Glanville was a different matter. But he had done his best; now he could only wait.

❖ THIRTEEN ❖

There's Many an Old Tune
Played on a Good Fiddle

The estate sat in its daytime quiet, all the kids in school, all the workers at work, just a few mums and tots about, and the occasional dog busily trotting its rounds. With the new universal affluence, even council tenants had cars, and parking had become a severe problem on an estate built for people who walked or went by bus. The roadsides were always occupied; the yards around which the blocks of flats were built had been divided up with raised flowerbeds and marked out into parking spaces, which were allocated to specific flats for fairness. Slider found an empty one easily enough, for in the daytime a lot of people took their cars to work, but in the evening the yards were full. It occurred to him to wonder where Jonah parked on the murder evening; and if Jonah wasn't the murderer after all, where had the murderer parked, and had anyone noticed an alien vehicle in their space?

As he got out of the car and locked it, he felt that inexplicable crawling of the skin that comes from being watched. He made a business of fumbling with the key and testing the handle to give himself time to look unobtrusively around, but he couldn't see anyone. The owner of the space, perhaps, debating whether to come out and challenge him? It was probably nothing, but being whacked on the head by a murderer had concentrated his instincts of self-preservation wonder-

186

fully, and instead of going straight up to Busty's flat, he did a walkabout, going up the stairs of the block opposite, walking along different balconies, looking out all the time for the tiny giveaway movement. But he saw nothing, and, chiding himself for overreaction, he crossed the yard and went up to Busty's flat.

Busty answered the door to him with a blank look which endured for a moment before recognition tuned in. She was in full working fig—black skirt and a tight vee-neck mauve jumper with lurex threads woven through it. Her hair was fully coiffed and her makeup daunting, but behind it she looked sad. Slider thought that was really sadder than if she had looked haggard or grief-stricken or riven with despair. You could get sympathy, drugs or even—*absit omen*—counseling for desperate grief, but sad you have to do all on your own, and it goes on so much longer.

"Oh. Mr. Slider. I was just getting ready to go to work," she said.

"Hello, Busty. I thought you were poshed up. You look very nice."

"Only will it take very long?" she asked, not responding to the compliment.

"Not long. I want to ask you some more questions. Are you up to going back to work?" he asked as she walked ahead of him to the sitting room.

"I got to do something. Can't sit around all day. Especially not here." She paused a moment at the door of the sitting room like a horse balking at water. "I make meself come in here, but I still see him, you know, lying there."

He put his arm around her shoulders. "You're very brave," he said. "If it's any help, I think it must have been very quick. I doubt if he would even have known what happened." Who had he said those same words to recently? Oh, yes, Sir Nigel. Jay Paloma had two mourners who had loved him sincerely. There were worse epitaphs.

"Thanks," she said after a moment, and got out a handkerchief, carefully to dab her eyes. "Don't get me going. I can't do me warpaint again."

"Are you managing all right for money?" he asked her, wondering if that was why she had to go back to work.

"Yeah," she said. "I got me wages, and there's all the savings. Lucky Maurice put it in a joint account, so it come to me automatic. There was 'ell of a lot of it." A thought struck her, and she looked at him with alarm. "It won't be took off me, will it?"

"No. Why should it?"

"Because of Maurice buying the stuff for his friend."

"I don't think that's going to come into it. Anyway, who could say that was where the money came from?"

She relaxed. "Only he'd want me to have it." A look of bitterness crossed her face. "I've had his mum and dad on the phone. They want to take him back to Ireland to bury."

"Ah."

"Them what've never spoken to him in twenty years."

"Yes. I'm afraid they are his next of kin. Did he leave a will?"

"Not that I know of. He wasn't expecting to get murdered."

"No, I suppose not. Well, I'm afraid if they insist, the law's on their side. Does it matter very much to you where he's buried?"

"It's not the *where*, but I'd've liked to be there, to see him off. They won't invite me, though. Not someone like me." She blew her nose carefully. There were little rings of white now on her nostrils where she had pinched the makeup off. "What did you want to ask me, anyway? I got to get on, or I'll be late."

"I'd like you to cast your mind back to the way the flat was when you came home that day. What I'm trying to do is establish exactly what time of day Maurice was killed."

She stared. "I thought you knew. Half past eleven at night, didn't you tell me?"

"I'm testing out a theory," Slider said. "There's a lot that doesn't add up, and it's possible we've been proceeding on the wrong assumption. Now you told me that Jay was very tidy—houseproud even?"

"That's right. It was him that did all the housework." She looked around the room, and he looked with her. It was tidy, but there was dust on all the surfaces, and a cold smell of disuse. "Everything was always spick and span."

"What was his routine? What did he do when he got up?"

"Well, he'd have a cup of coffee, then he'd go to the bathroom. Always spent ages in the bathroom. Bath, wash his hair, shave—ever so particular about shaving, went over his chin with a magnifying mirror and tweezers after. And he had to do his legs and that." She gave him a sidelong look and he nodded understanding.

"So all that would take him—how long?"

"An hour, I suppose. More even."

"And he always bathed before breakfast? Never the other way round?"

"He liked to get clean first. Always wash and everything, get dressed then have his breakfast."

"But that last day, the Tuesday, his routine was rather put out, wasn't it, because he got up to see you off?"

"That's right. Well, he'd've normally got up about half twelve, but he got up about eleven."

"And what did he do?"

"Well, he made us some coffee, and he sat with me and drunk it while I finished getting ready."

"In his dressing gown and slippers?"

"That's right."

"And he hadn't done his bathroom routine yet?"

"No. Well I was still in and out."

"Quite. So when you left at half past eleven he would probably have gone straight to the bathroom?"

"Oh yes. Bound to. He wouldn't hang around dirty, not Maurice."

"Which would take him to half past twelve-ish. And then he'd have breakfast?"

"I spect so."

"What did he usually have?"

"Oh, all different things. Toast or cereal or something hot. Depended on how hungry he was."

"Scrambled eggs, maybe?"

"Yes, he sometimes had that."

"What did you have for breakfast that morning?"

"Me? I never had nothing. Just the coffee. I was going to have lunch at Shirley's, I didn't want to blow meself out."

That would account, Slider thought, for two coffee mugs

and the single plate and pot in the sink. It was looking possible.

"What about washing up? Would Maurice have left the breakfast dishes in the sink?"

"Oh no, he'd have washed up straight away. Never liked leaving things." She looked at him, trying to follow his train of thought. "Them things in the sink—"

"One plate, two mugs. If they were his supper things, why two mugs? Unless one was left from earlier in the day."

"No, if he'd had a cup of coffee on its own some time, he'd have washed up the mug. Anyway, he was sitting watching telly, wasn't he? He wouldn't have sat down and watched telly without washing up first." Slider saw something dawn on her. "And another thing, I've just remembered, and now you come to mention it does stick out—the bath towels."

"Yes?" Slider thought. "There were two stretched out on the shower rail."

"That's right. Mine and his. He hung them like that to dry, and then later on he folded them up and hung them on the towel rail with the others. He'd never have left them like that all day."

Slider nodded thoughtfully. Even people with strong routines could deviate from them. It wasn't proof of anything, but it was suggestive. The eggs might have been supper, he might have had a rogue cup of coffee earlier and been distracted from washing up the mug, he might have forgotten to go back and fold the towels. Any one of them—but all of them? Unless he had gone out on urgent, unexpected business, and been out all afternoon—then he might not have got around to completing his morning tasks. And Grisham said there was no answer from the telephone. But that could be evidence either way, in or out. "Did Maurice ever forget to switch the answering machine on when he went out?"

"I've never known him to," she said.

Of course that wasn't proof either. He *might* forget. Or he might simply not answer for some reason. But it was another little grain to add to the scales.

"One last thing," he said. "The television was on when you found him?"

"Yes."

"So whatever channel it was on must have been what he was watching when he was killed."

"I suppose so."

"My sergeant said it was set on Channel Four. Now, I've got here—" he felt in his pocket "—the schedule for that day, the Tuesday. Will you look at it, and tell me what there is on Channel Four that he might have been likely to watch."

She took it, peered, crossed the room to her handbag for her glasses, and looked again. "Well, the film, of course. He'd have been up for that. *In Which We Serve*—that was one of his favorites. He loved all that sort of thing, old black and white films, especially about the war."

"Would he have known it was on? Do you have the television listings anywhere?"

"No, we don't get a paper or anything. But we got Teletext. And anyway, there's always some daft old film on Channel Four in the afternoon. Maurice knew that."

"Let's see, that was on at one-fifty-five. Is there anything before that he'd be likely to watch?"

She peered. "Hmm. I don't think so. He wasn't a great telly fan really, except for the old films. He'd sooner read a book, he always said. Me, if I was home, I'd watch anything, especially the soaps, but he'd always tut at me and say it was rotting my brain and couldn't I find anything better to do. But he did like the movies."

"All right, what about later in the day? In the evening?" She looked at the programs rather hopelessly. He tried to help her along. "What about the news? Would he have watched the Channel Four news?"

"Oh no, I don't think so. Well, there's not a lot here I could say for sure he'd watch. He wasn't really very big on telly, like I said."

"Assuming for the moment that he was killed at half past eleven while he was watching television—what do you think he'd have been watching?"

"The film I should think. He quite liked Charles Bronson."

"That was on I.T.V."

"Yes. That'd be the best bet."

"Not the documentary on Channel Four?"

192   ❖ *Cynthia Harrod-Eagles*

"What, this one, about women in industry? Ooh no, I don't think so."

"All right, thanks," Slider said, taking back the schedule. Busty looked at her watch and he did likewise. "Have I made you late?"

"Well, it is late. But Benny's not come yet. That's not like him to be late."

"Perhaps he's waiting downstairs for you?"

"He always comes up and knocks. Wouldn't miss a chance." She smiled a little. "But maybe he saw you come up. He wouldn't want to intrude. He's like that. Very discreet, is Benny."

"I'd better go and leave the path clear for him." He walked to the door, and she followed him. "Has he asked you to marry him again?"

"What, Benny? Nah. I wouldn't be surprised if he was working up to it though." She sighed. "I think I'll have to get rid of him. Stop using his cab. Now I haven't got Maurice to come between us, it could start getting awkward with old Benny. I mean, he's a nice bloke and everything, but it could get a bit embarrassing. And my eye, his feet don't half pen!"

Slider laughed. "You make me nervous about my own. I shall go back to the station and investigate."

"Oh no, you're not niffy," Busty said.

He opened the door and stepped out onto the balcony, and, in his new caution, leaned briefly over the balcony wall to scan the area. Everything looked the same, safe and serene.

Busty came out, too, folding her arms across her twin peaks, blinking a little in the sunlight like a vast back-combed bushbaby. A wave of affection came over Slider. People like Busty were all right. They were never any trouble. They just got on with things.

"If there's anything I can do for you, Busty, you know just to ring, don't you? You've got my number."

"Yeah," she said. "Thanks." She seemed touched, and blinked a little more moistly. "You're all right, Mr. Slider," she said, echoing his thoughts, and then leaned forward and kissed his cheek. "Ta frevrything."

Downstairs Slider got in his car, backed out of the space and drove off down the yard. He kept an eye on his rearview mirror, but he saw nothing untoward, no sudden movements, or cars casually pulling out of parking spaces to follow him. Just plain, old-fashioned paranoia, he supposed. Everyone in the universe had that, according to Atherton.

In spite of his odd appearance—or perhaps because of it—Hollis came across as reassuring to members of the public. He sat on Mr. Perceval's sagging sofa with his knees nearly up around his ears, his tufty, uncertain head appearing between them like an elf peeking out from the trees. There was a curious humility about him, as though he had come to learn: Plato at Socrates' feet.

Mr. Perceval, who lived in the flat directly underneath Busty Parnell's, was both reassured and flattered. It was a long time since anyone had wanted to learn anything from him. He had been wise in his time—he had actually led a very interesting life—but he was old now, and quite alone in the world, and he moved very slowly and whistled when he spoke because his false teeth were too big, so not many people had the patience to listen to him. His teeth were too big because his gums had shrunk, along with everything else. He had been a magnificent five foot six in his full manhood, now he was only five foot two. Where had his four inches gone, he wondered? He pondered the question sometimes as he moved slowly around his flat. The flat was too big for him now he was on his own, especially as he'd sold most of the furniture over the last few years, so that it was practically empty. He was like a shriveled kernel rattling about inside a walnut shell. Back in history when they'd moved the calendar along to catch up with the rest of the world, people had gone out in the street and marched with banners shouting ''Give us back our eleven days!'' He'd learned that in school. Sometimes as he walked about the kitchen, heating up his supper and setting out the tray (he still liked to do things properly, it helped fill the time), he would find himself chanting ''Give me back my four inches!'' inside his head.

He'd left school at fourteen, though he reckoned he'd still learned more than they knew at eighteen these days. He was apprenticed to a violin maker in Ealing. Nineteen twenty-four, that was. He loved violins; it wasn't that he was musical, but he liked the feel of the wood, and the smell of the shavings and the varnish, and the slow, tender creation of something which was so much greater than the sum of its parts. They were all different, all beautiful in their own way, like women, and you had to know how to get the best out of them. When his apprenticeship was over, he went to Guivier's violin workshop up in Town. He'd met a lot of famous people. Sir Edward Elgar—he'd met him once. A real gentleman, he was, but sad, so sad it made you shiver. And that Yehudi Menuhin had come in once for a repair to a fiddle, and he'd chatted to Mr. Perceval just as nice as you like. And although he wasn't musical, Mr. Perceval had started going to concerts—well, it made sense, to see what it was all about, the work he put in. That was how he met his wife, Violet, at a concert at the old Queen's Hall. They went to the Proms together that summer, and one evening, after the concert, outside the Stage Door at the Albert Hall, Sir Edward Elgar had come out and passed right by Mr. Perceval on the way to his car and had recognized him and touched his hat to him. A real gentleman. Mr. Perceval was so pleased and Violet was so thrilled that later that evening he had popped the question to her, on top of the number twelve bus going home, and she had said Yes.

Three children they'd had, and would have had more, except that the war broke out, and though being the father of small children Mr. Perceval could have got out of it, he didn't think it was right to. Violet agreed, and he joined up straight away. It was all right at first, they didn't send him overseas, so he was able to get back and see Vi and the kiddies now and then. They would listen to concerts on the wireless together. The old Queen's Hall got blitzed—that was a shock. Then later in the war he got sent out to the Far East. That was bad enough; but he ended up in a prisoner of war camp, and that was—well, you just didn't talk about it. Still, he survived, and you had to be grateful, didn't you? He lost most of his hair because of it, though, and nearly all his teeth. When he got home after the war, the first thing he did was have the rest out and get a nice set of false ones on the Beveridge, as they used to say then. Well, it was only fair to Vi. He looked a sight with all those gaps.

There was no place for a violin maker in the New Britain,

so he had to begin again. Bicycle repairs he went in for. He reckoned with petrol rationed, everyone'd be using bikes, and he wasn't far wrong. Then he got interested in watchmaking, just as a hobby to start, but soon he was mending people's watches and clocks on the side, so to speak, and pretty soon that was the best part of the business. In the Sixties when everyone started getting cars, and bicycles went pretty much by the board, he dropped that side of it and started taking in wirelesses as well. It was just common sense and nimble fingers, he told Violet. There was nothing much to it.

Nimble fingers. You wouldn't think it to look at him now. He was lucky if he could make a cup of tea now without spilling it. And when you were old, people thought you were daft as well, that was the worst of it. He still had all his marbles, thank you, but they would talk to you that soppy way, like talking to a parrot. Not that many people talked to him at all now. Vi was gone—taken suddenly, didn't even make it to his retirement. They'd looked forward to his retirement, doing things together. And the children were all gone too, Jim to Canada, Peggy to Australia. Kevin, the youngest, had gone out there too, but to Sydney—Peggy was in Brisbane. He hadn't heard from Kevin for sixteen years. Kevin never married. He never married, and then he just—stopped writing. Well, you had to wonder, didn't you?

And so here he was all alone in this flat. The pension didn't go very far, but he didn't want much at his age. If he'd saved a bit while he was working, maybe he could have gone out to Canada or Australia and been near the kids. He should have saved, really. But he didn't know that he'd really want to live abroad, even if it was Commonwealth. You were better off with what you knew. No, if he won the Lottery, he didn't know that he'd go. What he would do, if he won the Lottery, was go to a concert. He'd like to go to a concert again. Maybe one of the Proms—hear a bit of Elgar. He'd like to do that once more before he went Upstairs.

Hollis listened courteously, attentively, his hands still and no notebook in sight. And only when Mr. Perceval had wound himself down and come to a stop did he raise the question of the bumps upstairs. "It seems you mentioned when we talked to you before that you heard a noise upstairs earlier in the day—in the afternoon, sometime?''

''Ah, well, you didn't want to know about that, did you?'' Mr. Perceval said with a canny look. ''Young policeman, all impatience, wants to get on and get done with it. I'm an old fool and I speak too slow. He didn't want to know.''

''I want to know,'' Hollis said.

''All interested in late at night, weren't you?''

''That's right. But now I'd be very interested in anything you could tell me about this other thing. A heavy thud, did you say?''

''A crash and a thud, I'd call it. Like something big and heavy falling over.''

''And do you remember what time it was?''

''Course I do. Twenty past one. I looked at the clock.''

''And why did you do that?''

The old man whistled a ghostly laugh through his vast china teeth. ''Clever, aren't you? 'Cause I thought someone might want to know, that's why!''

''Really? So what did you think had happened that some-one might want to know about?''

But Mr. Perceval only went on laughing to himself, his shoulders shaking. At last he stopped, sighing, and got out his handkerchief to wipe his eyes, a process of agonizing slowness. When he had succeeded in getting the handkerchief folded and back into his pocket, he straightened his shoulders a little and said, ''Right, I'll tell you all about it, if you've got the patience.'' Hollis nodded, and grew still and earnest again. ''Middle of the day, see, it's quiet. Everyone out at work, kids are at school. I like the quiet. I sit here and just listen. I got me library book, but mostly I just listen. You'd be surprised what you can hear. Metal frames, these flats are built on, did you know that?''

''No, I didn't.''

''Not from round here, are you?''

''No, I'm from Manchester.''

''I guessed that, from your accent. I was born and brought up in Shepherd's Bush. I saw these flats being built. Great steel frames, just like Lego it looked. And the metal carries sound, like the strings of a violin, you see, and the inside of the flats are like the sound box. I listen and try to work out what the sounds mean. Shut my eyes and visualize, see 'em walking back and forth, pulling out a chair, shutting a cupboard. Sounds were important in the jungle. It was all you had—nothing to see. Just the snap of a twig—and you got to know which direction it comes from. That takes practice.''

He paused, his eyes fixed, listening to something—in memory, perhaps. ''So anyway, this day you want to know about. *She'd* gone out, I knew that. I heard the front door slam. She's a heavy walker, and she will slam doors. *Him*, now, he's soft on his feet. You don't hear his feet, except when he goes over the creaking boards. I know where all of *them* are.''

''He was a dancer,'' Hollis offered.

The old man lifted his head a little in attention. ''Was he? Was he? Now that's interesting. That accounts for the exercising, I suppose. Ballet, was it?''

''Something similar,'' Hollis answered discreetly.

''He exercised in the evening, half past five to six o'clock. It took me a while to work it out, what it was. Anyway, this particular day, I'd heard him in the bathroom—you can hear the water rush out of the bath—and then in the bedroom— over that way—and then it all went quiet. Prob'ly in the kitchen. They got stone floors, the kitchens—fireproof, see?— so you can't hear walking about in the kitchen. Then about one o'clock I heard him come in above me. I was sitting in here, in the front room. There's a board about there.'' He pointed to the ceiling near the door. ''It creaks when you step on it, no matter how soft-footed you are. He walked across, and then I heard the telly come on.''

''You can hear the television?''

''When it's turned up. *She* has it up loud. A bit mutton if you ask me. She'd had it on the night before. So when he turns it on, the sound's still up loud, you see? But then he turned it down. You know why? He had a visitor.''

Hollis felt his scalp prickling. They were onto something. He knew it. ''A visitor? How did you know that?''

''They've got a doorbell, just the right pitch to carry. He turns the telly down, crosses the creaker.'' He pointed again. ''I didn't hear the front door open and shut. He doesn't slam like her. But then a moment later he comes back into the front room with someone else. I hear them come in, first the visitor, then him.''

"You're sure of that?"

"Two different treads. The visitor's a heavier walker. Visitor sits down over there, him upstairs goes over there. Anyway, then it goes quiet again—they're sitting down, right, chatting? Then about five minutes later he goes out and comes back in—gone to fetch something. He's not made a cup of tea—not gone long enough. Fetched something to show him, maybe.''

"Or fetched the whiskey bottle and two glasses,'' Hollis said.

"Oh, is that the way it was?"

"I don't know. I wasn't there. But there was a whiskey bottle and two glasses on the coffee table.''

Mr. Perceval nodded several times, piecing the knowledge into his soundtrack. "Right. Right. Then, twenty past one, it happens, a crash and a thud, just over there.'' He pointed at the ceiling, and Hollis noted that he was indicating just about the position of the chair and the body. If Perceval had never seen the inside of Jay Paloma's flat, it was a good piece of evidence, because his own easy chair and television were in a quite different position. "And then,'' Perceval went on, "some banging and trampling in about the same place—''

"What sort of banging?"

"Like D.I.Y., but muffled. Like somebody hitting something with a wooden mallet, maybe, rather than a hammer. And he's moving his feet, the heavy-footed one, trampling about, like I said, but all on the spot.''

The repeated blows to the skull, Hollis thought. The frenzied attack. D.I.Y. was about the mark: Paloma had had the loft conversion to end them all.

"Then there's a silence, and then he goes out, back across the creaker, and there's nothing more. I didn't hear the front door close. He did it quietly. And then there's silence up there all afternoon. Which is why,'' he said, fixing Hollis with a stern eye, "I reckoned someone would want to know. Because I listened for him to go out of the room, but he never did.''

"Are you sure it was the visitor who went out?"

"Course I am. Different tread. Anyway, *he* was found dead up there, am I right?"

"Yes, he was, but not until the next day. He could have been killed any time. And we know—you know too because you heard it—that someone broke into the flat that evening."

"He was already dead by then," Mr. Perceval said with calm certainty. "Must've been. Else why wasn't he walking about? Why didn't he answer the phone when it rang? And why didn't he do his exercising? Always did his exercising, regular as clockwork."

"That's a good point," Hollis said. "But why didn't you tell us all this before?"

"I told you, that young constable didn't want to know. In too much of a hurry."

"You could have told someone else. Called at the police station. You should have come forward with important information like this, you know."

"And would you have believed me?" Mr. Perceval said. "You were all stuck on half past eleven, and fair enough, with the door being broken down. If some doddery old josser came tottering in talking about creaky floorboards at twenty past one, you'd have shown him the door. Politely, all right, but that would have been the way of it, am I right?"

Hollis had to admit, unwillingly, that he was right. The ill-fitting teeth, the whistle, the slowness, would hardly have cut the mustard in the frenetic pace of modern station life, and without time and space to expand and justify his story, Perceval was barely believable. Even now, Hollis was wondering how you would ever present his evidence in such a way that a court would accept it. He was pretty sure the C.P.S. wouldn't even want to try.

FOURTEEN

Honeyman: I Funked the Skid

Candy Williams looked frightened to death, but though her little chin quivered she faced Slider and Hart resolutely.

"I ain't got nothing to say. You got my statement. Why don't you leave me alone?"

"Hmm, yes, I know," Slider said, "but—can I sit down? Thanks. Yes, your statement. It's giving me problems, and do you know why?"

Candy didn't evince any desire to be told. She had sat down opposite him on the edge of a chair, her bony knees together and her ankles well apart, her hands clutched together in her lap. She looked about thirteen. She turned her face from him and stared at the window.

"I'll tell you," Slider went on. "Well, I knew you weren't telling the truth. And you knew that I knew, didn't you? I mean, nobody was fooling anybody in that interview room."

"Candy, we're trying to help you," Hart interposed sharply. "Pay attention." Candy's face remained averted, like a child refusing to take her medicine.

"The thing is this," Slider went on conversationally, "I know Jonah made you give him an alibi. I suppose he threatened you with all sorts of things if you didn't. I expect he gave you a few smacks as well, just to give you a taste." Candy's mouth moved at that, a little, bitter downturn. "So you lied about him being in the flat with you all that time. I don't blame you. But now something new has turned up, and that lie isn't going to help him anymore. To help him you've got to tell me the truth.''

Now she turned her face back, looking at him, puzzled, trying to understand.

"You see, I don't think Jonah did murder Jay Paloma."

She stared.

"But I can't prove it unless you tell me the truth. You've got to admit to me which bit of your story was a lie, so I can be sure the rest is true, do you understand?''

"You're lying," Candy said, looking from one to the other uncertainly. "You're tryna trick me. You're tryna to get me to drop him in it."

"No. Absolutely not," Slider said. "Listen to me: Jonah doesn't need an alibi for half past eleven at night. But if you go on lying about that, I can't accept your evidence at all, on anything. You can't be his alibi for any other time. And that means you'll be useless to him."

"You don't want him to think you've let him down, do you?" Hart suggested.

Candy began to sweat. She seemed confused. She looked at Hart and let drop an appalling facility of abuse.

"It's no good swearin' at me, sweetheart," Hart said. "I'm not the one on the spot. Big Jonah give you a job to do, and if you fuck it up—" She shrugged eloquently.

"You bastards," said Candy. "You pig bastard slags. What you tryna do to me?''

"Just tell me the truth, Candy. Tell me what really happened on Tuesday," Slider said with gentle insistence.

She looked at him now, and there was appeal under the defiance. "You don't understand. You don't understand *nothing*!"

"Then make me understand." Slider became brisk. "Come on, Candy, I'm trying to help you, but if you won't help yourself—"

He stood up, gesturing Hart before him. He thought it wasn't going to work—Candy let him get right to the door before she spoke—but at last she said uncertainly, "Wait a minute." He turned back inquiringly. She was chewing her lip, and there were beads of sweat like cloudy tears lying in her eye sockets. "Gimme a minute. Lemme think. I can't think!'' she protested. Slider nodded to Hart to stay by the door, as if ready to leave on the instant. He took a step back into the room and waited, holding his breath.

''Are you telling me straight—about Jonah? That you don't think he did it?''

''Straight,'' Slider said. ''I don't think he did. You'll be doing the right thing by him, telling me the truth.''

Her mouth turned down. ''I don't care about that black bastard. I hate him! Y'wanna see how much I care about him?'' With a violent movement she dragged up her baggy sweater. She was naked underneath, and her small bare breasts flipped rubberily as the hem caught them. The sweater held up around her neck, she turned herself this way and that, like an art dealer tilting a painting to catch the light. Her narrow back and grayhound ribs were an impressionist sunset of black, red and yellowish green. She looked like a late Turner. ''He done this to me. He said he didn't hafta be careful 'cause I wasn't working.'' She dropped her sweater and turned to look straight into Slider's eyes. ''He don't leave no marks, usually. He knows a lotta ways a hurtin' you without it showing.''

''You don't have to take this sort of thing, you know,'' Slider said. ''You don't have to put up with it.''

Tears stood out suddenly in her eyes. She held her arms out from her sides, turning her palms up. ''What are you talking about? Look at me! He's four times the size of me. *How d'you fink I'm gonna stop him, you stupid, shit, fucking, man, copper!''*

She flopped down on the settee and put her head in her arms and sobbed loudly. Hart watched impassively, her arms folded. After a moment Slider sat down beside the girl and put a tentative arm around her, and she flung herself with a fresh burst to cry noisily on his shoulder. Slider waited. She was so small and bony and young, so young to be already one of the Lost and Damned. It wasn't the prostitution that bothered him. Unlike some of his colleagues, he had no problem with prostitution: providing it was all consenting, he thought it was people's own business. It was her hopelessness, the fact that so near to the beginning of her life she had decided that there was nothing to be had in life but money and the comforts it bought; that there was nothing to be done about anything, nothing to strive for or stand against.

Eventually she stopped, sat up, groped about her hopelessly for a tissue. The box on the coffee table was empty. Slider was about to part, sighing, with another handkerchief, but Hart the practical darted out and in again with a handful of bog roll from the bathroom. When the mopping up was done, Slider said to Hart, "Make us some coffee, will you?" The tiny kitchenette was off the lounge, the door just beyond the end of the sofa: she would be able to both see and hear while in there.

And Candy Williams turned to Slider and said, "All right, I'll tell you what I know, but it ain't much." And she scanned his face for response, for approval perhaps, or at least for some sign that he was taking charge of her. She was born to be a victim, he thought. Chronically unable—either congenitally or because of her upbringing—to take responsibility for herself, she was there for the taking for anyone who would tell her what to do next, and by humping her, hitting her or buying her presents give some sense of structure to the terrifying formlessness of existence.

The first part of her story had been true. Jonah had come home from work at about half past four, his usual time after work. He hadn't been sacked by Yates. "That was balls. He was just told to say that. It made him mad. He didn't want to have to tell anyone he'd been sacked. And not for wearing a dirty shirt. I fink Mr. Yates said that just to put him on."

"So he came home in a bad temper?"

"No, that wasn't then. All that come later. Listen." She seemed distracted by his lack of understanding.

"All right, I'm listening. What did he do when he got home?"

"He went to bed, like always. We done it—"

"You had sex?"

"Whajjer fink? Then he went off to sleep. I fell asleep as well, but then the phone rang about eight o'clock. Not his flat phone, his mobile. That meant it was Mr. Yates. He started talking to him, and it was yes, Mr. Yates, no Mr. Yates at first. Then he started to get annoyed. He got out of bed and was walking up and down and like clenching his fists. And then he kicked a chair out of the way. I knew I was in trouble then.''

"Was he arguing with Mr. Yates?"

"You don't argue with Mr. Yates," she said flatly. "But I could tell he didn't like it. He was saying why, and why's it gotta be done that way, and stuff like that. And when he finished he threw the phone across the room and shouted 'Bastard!' And he looked at the clock and he shouted, 'He waited till I was asleep, the bastard!' and then he threw the clock across the room an' all.''

"Why would Mr. Yates do that? Wait until Jonah was asleep, I mean?"

"Just to make him mad. He'd know he'd be deep asleep at eight o'clock and it'd be the worst time to wake him. He's like that, Mr. Yates—especially with Jonah. He likes annoying Jonah, 'cause he knows Jonah can't get back at him. He thinks it's funny. He'll laugh out the other side of his face one day." She looked seriously at Slider. "Jonah'll kill him one day, I mean it, and I just wanna be around to see it.''

There were too many painful implications to that thought for Slider to comment on. He put her gently back on the track. "Did Jonah tell you what Mr. Yates wanted him for?"

"Did he! I got the lot. He ranted and raved about it." She frowned, trying to put the story in order. "Apparently this bloke come in to the club the night before—posh geezer— and give Jonah a load of money, just shoved it in his hand, four hundred, all in twenties—to go round this other bloke's house and give him a real fright. Like, maybe rough him up a bit, but nothing too bad, just scare him."

"Yes, I know about that. I've had it from the posh geezer."

This seemed to reassure Candy. "Oh, you know him, do you?"

"I know him. And was Jonah intending to do what he asked?"

She looked scornful. "Was he buggery! Jonah thinks it's all a big joke, seeing he's four hundred up. This bloke was well plastered, and Jonah reckons he's never going to remember next day where he left the dosh. Apparently he was swaggering round the club telling everyone, the great stupid bastard, and Terry—he's the manager, one of Mr. Yates's spies—he tells Mr. Yates about it. Because apparently this posh geezer's somebody really important?"

Slider gave a nod in response to the slight question mark.

"Well, anyway, apparently Mr. Yates phones Jonah to tell him he wants him to do what this geezer asked after all. Jonah asks him why but Mr. Yates ain't telling. He gives Jonah chapter and verse how to do it and when, and then he says—this is what really makes Jonah mad—he says that Jonah mustn't be working for him when he does it. So that's when he tells him to say he was sacked at four o'clock, and about the dirty shirt an' all. I bet it was that Terry thought that one up."

"If Jonah hated the setup so much, why would he do it? What was in it for him?"

"Well, he's one of Mr. Yates's boys, isn't he? And Mr. Yates would see him all right."

"But he'd sacked him."

"I told you, that was just the story. A course he was still working for him, only it hadn't to be official, so that if there was any trouble it wouldn't come back on Mr. Yates. Like I say, he'd see Jonah all right. And if there was any trouble, Mr. Yates's solicitor would get him out."

This was a nice angle on Stevens, Slider thought. "Go on. So what was the plan?"

"Well, Jonah was spose to go round there at eleven, so as to mix with the chucking-out crowds. And I was spose to give him his alibi. That's why he told me about it, see?"

"And what did you say?"

"I was scared. I said I never wanted nothing to do with it."

"But if the plan was only to scare this man—where was the harm?"

She shook her head, folding her arms around herself as if she was cold. "I see the temper he was in. I fought this bloke was gonna get a pasting, and I never wanted it coming back on me. I told Jonah I wouldn't do it, and he started shouting at me, but I was so scared I said I was going, and then he really went mad. He punched me in the stomach and knocked me across the room, then he picked me up and banged my head on the ceiling, and whirled me round and round over his head, and I fought he was gonna chuck me out the window. I was shit scared. I fought I'd had it. But he only frew me on the bed and jumped on top of me and started hitting me. That's when he said he didn't need to be careful 'cause I wouldn't be working for a while. But he was careful not to hit my face—nothing that wouldn't be covered by my clothes.''

She told it so matter-of-factly, as though she was describing the steps of a dance. Perhaps in a way that's what it was to her.

"Go on," Slider said. "What happened next?"

"Well, hitting me give him a hard-on, so he did—you know what. And then he wanted to go to sleep. But he said he couldn't have me sneaking off while he was asleep, so he tied me up to the bottom of the bed, and tied a rope round my neck and went to sleep holding the other end.'' She examined Slider's expression. "It wasn't so bad, 'cause he couldn't tie the ropes too tight, in case they left a mark. Only I was desperate for a pee, that was the bad bit. Anyway, when he woke up he untied me and let me go to the bathroom, and told me to bring him breakfast in bed.''

"What time was that?"

"About half past twelve. And then when he'd et it I had to get in with him 'cause he wanted sex again, and then he got up and had a shower.''

"And what time did he go out?"

"Not till evening, about half past ten.''

"You're sure about that? You're quite sure? You're telling me the truth now?''

"Yeah," she said, and the word was a sigh, like someone accepting a sentence.

"He didn't get up until half past one, and he was indoors, in your presence, all day?''

"I should know," she said succinctly. "He watched the telly all afternoon. He started drinking as soon as he was dressed, and by the time ten o'clock come he was steaming. I was shit scared. If I could've run away I would've, but he never let me get near the door, and the one time he thought I was trying he thumped me again. Then about half past ten he got up and turned the telly off. He was so lit up and so mad by then, I thought meself, this is gonna turn bad, he ain't never gonna be able to stop himself. I mean, he's that strong he can break your arm just shaking your hand if he's not careful—and he wasn't in the mood to be careful. I thought he was gonna go out there and kill this bloke, whether he meant to or not. So he went, anyway, and he locked me in so I couldn't run while he was gone.''

"Did you try telephoning anyone?"

She shrugged. "Who was there to telephone? I just waited. Anyway, about half past midnight he comes back, and I knew straight away it had gone bad. I never seen him like that before. He was jumpy and weird, laughing one minute, scared the next."

"Did he tell you what had happened?"

"Nuh. He just said, Candy baby, you and me's going for a little trip. And he reminded me what I had to say if anyone asked, and then he said let's go to bed."

"And you went to sleep?"

She gave a short, unamused laugh. "I wish. He was really wired up. I never seen him like that before. He was just humping me all night. I could hardly walk the next day. He fell asleep in the end when it got light, and then he woke up about nine o'clock and we left the flat about half past and come here."

She came to a halt and was silent a moment, and then she looked at Hart, remembering where she was and who she was telling. "When I saw in the papers, I thought he'd done it. He never said nothing to me, but when he saw me looking at the news about it, he just laughed, like a really weird laugh. He never said it wasn't him. I thought I was living with a murderer. I mean, he went out there and come back—and now you say it wasn't him?"

"I don't think so," Slider said.

She looked bewildered. "Then what the bloody hell's going on?"

"I don't know," Slider said. "Did he talk to Mr. Yates at all, after he came back that night?"

"He'd been talking to him already, in the car, driving back after doing it. When he got in he said he'd got his instructions. That's all he said. And he never talked to nobody after that.

He never left the flat, and that's the truth. I tell you, it was a relief when your lot turned up. It was like being shut in a cage with a mad animal.''

Slider tried to look solid and reassuring, though his mind was going around like a hamster on speed. What the hell was going on? ''You've done the right thing telling me all this, Candy. Don't worry, everything's going to be all right.''

''If you want to make a complaint against Jonah, we'll go all the way with you,'' Hart put in.

Candy looked from one to the other. ''You don't get it, do you? It's not Jonah I'm afraid of, not now.''

If there was anything in the world that demonstrated the futility of human endeavor, Slider thought, it was a Function in a Hospitality Room. The characteristic feature of hospitality rooms is their inhospitableness; and a gathering for social purposes of a group of people who have nothing in common but business is bound to be dysfunctional.

''Why do I get the feeling I've been here before?'' he muttered to Hart. She, he noted with a strange pang, was looking eager, as though expecting to enjoy herself. She had changed in the loo at the station, and was now extremely fetching in a black dress so short and so full-skirted she looked like a nineteen-twenties illustration of Violet Elizabeth Bott, but in negative.

''There ain't many females here,'' she muttered back to him. ''Are you sure you should've brought me?''

''Quite sure,'' Slider said. Having a pretty young woman beside him at a do like this was the only point of difference: the weary staff, the wearier canapés, and the choice between white wine that tasted like thinner and red wine that tasted like turpentine, were all too familiar. A rapid scan of the room, however, revealed that he didn't recognize a single face, which was a little odd. He couldn't even see Honeyman, though he supposed he must be lurking where the guests were thickest. He was still hovering uncertainly when a youngish man he didn't recognize approached him and addressed him in French, with the colonial accent of Croydon.

''Sorry?'' Slider said.

"Oh, sorry," the stranger said. "I thought you were one of the French delegates."

"Are we expecting French delegates?" Slider asked, puzzled.

"What?" said the stranger, upping the stakes to bewildered.

"Guv," Hart said, tugging Slider's sleeve and gesturing toward the door. The parting of crowds had revealed the notice board—one of those fuzzy black slatted things with white plastic letters pressed into it. "We're at the wrong bash."

The management of the hotel, the board announced, was welcoming an international electronics firm to the Chiltern Suite.

"Oh, are you the police?" the stranger said, relieved. "You're next door, in the Pennine Suite. All look the same, these places, don't they?"

Slider and Hart stumped next door. Directly in line of sight of the entrance was Ron Carver so deep in conversation with Mr. Wetherspoon that he practically had his tongue down his ear. Slider did not find that immediately reassuring. A waitress with a hopeless expression offered a tray of filled glasses and Hart took one of white wine.

"Better not," Slider said. "You'll be running all night. Safer to wait and have a pint later."

"I'll be all right," Hart said. "I'm black, enni? Guts of iron. Drink anything."

Honeyman came up and formally shook hands with both of them. "Nice of you to come," he said. He teetered a little on his tiny toes—from inebriation, it was plain, as well as nervousness. "And I see you've brought W.D.C.—er—"

"Hart," Slider supplied.

"Hart. What a good idea. Very dull, these affairs. Middle-aged men in suits talking shop. You'll brighten us up, er—" He had forgotten Hart's name again already. "Pity there won't be any dancing. I'd have made sure I put my word in, stolen you from Slider here. *Droits de seigneur*, eh, Slider?"

Slider could feel Hart seething at this ponderous non-PC gallantry, and kicked her discreetly before she could jump down poor old Eric's throat. "That's right, sir," he said pleasantly. "There's a good crowd, isn't there?" He glanced around at the assembled barons of F District. There were even some Area demigods—easily distinguishable because their dinner suits fitted them. Did they all know they had been brought here under false pretenses, that the farewell was premature?

Honeyman intercepted the glance and looked even more nervous. "Yes, very gratifying. The most senior ranks will be going to dinner downstairs later, after the presentation, of course, but meanwhile, I want everyone to enjoy himself. And herself, of course. Themself. Oh, you haven't got anything to drink," he noticed, with obvious relief at being able to interrupt himself.

"I'm driving, sir," Slider said quickly.

"Ah. Yes." Honeyman blinked. Since when did the C.I.D. worry about that? "Commendable. Commendable. Well, I must circulate." He turned away, and then back. "Er, Slider—that confidential matter we spoke about earlier? You didn't—er—" He cocked a significant eye at Hart.

"You said it was confidential, sir," Slider said reassuringly.

"Ah yes. Good. It's just that—well, with so many senior ranks present—you understand."

"Yes, sir, perfectly."

When he was gone, Hart said, "I fink he fancies you, guv. D'you want me to make myself scarce? I don't wanna be a gooseberry."

"How would you like to spend your days tracing stolen cars?" Slider said coldly.

Hart grinned. "All right, I'll be good. Who's that Mr. Carver's so thick with? If he gets any closer they'll have to get married."

"That is our Area Commander, Mr. Wetherspoon," Slider said impressively. "Curtsy while you think what to say; it saves time."

"Oh, is that Weverspoon?" Hart said. "Yeah, I've heard a lot about him. He's getting up this charity concert, ain't he?"

"He was born getting up a charity concert. He's very keen on that sort of thing," Slider said. A waitress arrived at his elbow with a silver tray of pieces of chicken tikka each speared with a cocktail stick. Slider and Hart both took one to get rid of her. The pieces were nicely calculated, just too large to put in the mouth whole, and just too small to bite without the remainder falling off the stick. They were also very hot. Hart evidently favored the "one go" approach. She chewed briefly and swallowed. "I see you've got an iron throat as well as an iron gut," Slider said.

Hart twirled the cocktail stick. "What you sposed to do wiv these things, anyway?"

"No one's ever come up with a satisfactory solution to the problem."

"They can be lethal, you know," Hart said. "Wedding reception down our way, once, this bloke ate a bit of quiche or whatever without taking the stick out. His wife said, 'ere, y've been and swallered your stick, yer daft get. Oh blimey, so I 'ave, he says. They were just 'aving a good laugh about it when the stick goes right frough his windpipe and he chokes to death, before you can say vol-au-vent." She eyed him defiantly. "It's true. Put a bit of a crimp on the party, I can tell you."

"I really needed to know that," Slider said. "Here—" And he relieved her of her stick and put it with his own in his top pocket, whence they would later, no doubt, return to haunt him. Wetherspoon finished with Carver, looked around, spotted Slider and started toward him. Significant? Slider wondered. Wetherspoon was a very tall, rather angular man, with grizzled, tightly curling hair that grew upward above the temples, giving his head a strangely square look. He always reminded Slider, for some reason, of an Airedale terrier. It was rumored of him that he had once, as a young man, smiled, but disliked the sensation so much he had resolved never to do it again. Some said that the one time he had smiled it had been at a woman, which had led to his having to marry her, hence his disillusionment. Slider, who had once met Mrs. Wetherspoon, was inclined to believe the story.

"Ah, Slider—a word," said Wetherspoon.

Slider obediently gave him one. "Sir."

Wetherspoon turned on Hart a smile that would have freezed the tassels off a stripper. "If you'd be so kind," he said. Men who packed his amount of firepower did not need to specify the kindness. Slider jerked his head at Hart and she moved reluctantly away. "Yes, Slider," Wetherspoon continued when they were alone. "You've made certain inquiries about Mr. Honeyman's predecessor, in connection with a case."

"Yes, sir." Even allowing for Wetherspoon's designer charmlessness, Slider felt there was some little hint of disapprobation in the tone.

"The case is not, in fact, one of yours."

"No, sir, but—"

"There are reasons," Wetherspoon trod over him, "very serious operational reasons, why your inquiries cannot be answered. In fact, your inquiries must not be pursued. Do you understand me?"

The words *yes, sir* hovered obediently at Slider's lips but he resisted them. "I appreciate that it may be a delicate area—"

"No, I don't think you do appreciate," Wetherspoon said. "Mr. Honeyman has passed on your thoughts to me, and I don't see that you have any evidence at all that your case and Carver's are connected in any way. It is for Carver to decide what is or isn't relevant to his own case. In any case, I have told him what I have just told you—that there must be no inquiries along the particular line you raised with Mr. Honeyman. He understands that. Do you?" Slider drew breath to argue and Wetherspoon leaned his head a little closer and lowered his voice threateningly. *"Do you understand?"*

"Yes, sir," Slider said.

Wetherspoon straightened up. "Good. Now that that's out of the way, we can concentrate on enjoying this splendid party. But you haven't got a drink."

"I'm driving, sir."

"Ah. Very commendable," said Wetherspoon, almost duplicating Honeyman's reaction. He glanced down at the glass of red in his hand. "Pity though—I chose the wines myself. Do you like wine?"

"Yes, sir."

"Good. Good. You don't have any sort of talent I haven't heard about, I suppose?"

Slider had lost him. "Sir?"

"My concert, man, my concert. Singing, dancing, conjuring? Comic monologue? Play the piano, at all?"

"Not even slightly," Slider said.

"Pity. Well, you must do your bit by selling tickets. Set a good example. I expect every officer, inspector and above, to sell at least twenty tickets. Friends, neighbors and whatnot. Get in among 'em." He paused on the brink of a monumental descent into the vernacular, a jocularity aimed at winning the common soldier's heart. "Bums on seats, that's the name of the game! Must make it a raging success. For the kiddies, you know."

"Yes, sir," Slider said. Wetherspoon gave him one more deeply unfavorable look, nodded, and went away. Slider felt the side that had been nearest him begin to thaw.

Hart reappeared. "Trouble, guv?" she murmured.

"No, just being told there are things it is better for a detective inspector not to know," Slider said. He looked across at Carver and saw Carver's gaze quickly averted. He'd have liked to know what Carver had been saying to Wetherspoon, though—and vice versa. "I wonder if he was told the same thing. It didn't look like it."

"Come again?" said Hart.

"Do you ever get the feeling that everyone else knows something you don't?"

"That's paranoid," Hart said.

"You'd be paranoid if everyone was plotting against you," Slider complained.

A waitress thrust another tray at them, and Slider took what appeared to be a cocktail sausage on a stick, but which proved—as he discovered when he bit it—to be merely a tube full of boiling fat, which instantly glued itself to the gums behind his upper molars and inflicted third degree burns. "Bloody hell!" He grabbed Hart's glass and swilled desperately.

"Not your night, guv," said Hart sympathetically.

"Why didn't I join the fire brigade when I had the chance?" Slider said bitterly.

The party ripened like a mold culture. Officers were getting drunk. The noise grew. Slider got separated from Hart. He got buttonholed by an agonizingly boring man from Hammersmith nick who seemed to know him a great deal better than he ought considering Slider couldn't remember his name and only recollected ever having spoken to him once, and who wanted to talk to him about crime statistics. He ripped himself free at last like sticking plaster, and began to push his way slowly but purposefully through the crowds, trying to look as though he was on his way somewhere, in the hope of avoiding anymore conversations. He was beginning to get a headache.

And then suddenly Honeyman was at his side again, clutching two glasses of amber fluid. His cheeks were flushed and his eyes were shiny. "Look here," he said, "I'm having a proper drink." He proffered one glass. "Join me? You weren't serious about that not drinking because you're driving business were you?"

Slider hesitated. Honeyman seemed to have become almost human. "I didn't fancy the wine, sir."

"Sensible man. Filthy stuff. But for God's sake, don't call me sir. Not here. Chance to let down the barriers for once." He jerked the glass at Slider, swilling the liquid dangerously up the side. "Whisky. Scotch, in fact. Took you for a Scotch man. Was I wrong?"

Slider took the glass just in time. "I prefer a pint, sir, but I like Scotch."

Honeyman leaned toward him with a fascinating smile. "Between you and me, Wetherspoon fancies himself as a wine buff. Hasn't a clue! Reads the Sunday supplements, watches the TV, takes it all as gospel. And the man's the most frightful bore about it. Never accept a dinner invitation to the Wetherspoons'," he warned solemnly. "He's got a sign over his front door." Honeyman drew it in the air. " 'Welcome. This is what death is like.' "

Slider wasn't sure whether he was supposed to laugh. "I don't think I'm ever likely to be invited," he said.

"No, I don't suppose you are. Welsh claret," he added from a bitter memory all his own. "Afghanistan Côtes du Rhone. Nuits St. Bogota. What was that advertisement? 'Not a drop sold till it's five weeks old.' Ah, this is more like. Well—cheers."

"Cheers," Slider said obediently.

Honeyman sank half his Scotch, glanced quickly around, and then looked at Slider. "I suppose you're wondering what's got into me. I suppose you're thinking, my God the old fool's finally flipped his lid."

"I wasn't thinking that."

"The thing is, you see, that I'm suffering from a sort of last-day-of-term—oh, what's the word?"

"Euphoria?"

"That's it. Together with a dislike of being poisoned. And being talked to like a half-witted schoolboy. This is all strictly confidential, mind," he added with belated caution. "Where's that lovely young girl of yours? You won't repeat anything I say?"

"Of course not."

"Being talked to like that. That's what gets my goat. I'm going to have another of these." He drained his glass, looked around as if wondering where the bottle was, and then turned back to Slider. "Talked to like an idiot schoolboy. At my own retirement party. After thirty years in the Job. It's not on."

"No, sir."

"So I wanted to tell you, Slider, that I'm on your side. You do what you have to, and I'll back you up. To the hilt. All the way." He swayed suddenly, and had to shift his feet to regain his balance. "Fuck it," he said. Slider couldn't believe his ears. Honeyman looked at him almost gleefully. "Didn't think I had it in me, did you? I know what you chaps think of me. But I tell you this—I'm a policeman, first and last. Not a politician. Not a businessman. Not a civil servant. And you are too. That's what I like about you, Slider. You're a good egg. D'you want that?" He gestured abruptly toward the tumbler in Slider's hand.

"No, sir," Slider said, and gave it to him. Honeyman took a gulp.

"I'd like to bring this one home before I go. This case. Sir Nigel Grisham's involved. It's high profile now, you know."

"Yes, sir." High profile now, because of Sir Nigel—but who cared about Sir Nigel's friend, the dancer-cum-prostitute he paid for and exploited? Fame was all, fame excused all. Jay Paloma had been right.

"Do it for me," Honeyman said, "and I'll back you all the way."

"I'll do my best, sir."

"I know you will. Good man. Not many of us left. Not like that lot." He gestured with his eyes in the vague direction of the rest of the world. "Got to go. Presentation and speeches next, and then I've got to go and have dinner with *them*. Well, I won't be leaned on. They'll find out. I'll sweet-talk all they like, but I won't be leaned on."

And with a nod he swayed away. Slider watched him go and wondered if it was possible to be drunk just on noise, because the world wasn't making much sense to him just then and his head was reeling, but he hadn't touched a drop. Not even the Scotch, more was the pity.

❖ FIFTEEN ❖

They Eat Horses, Don't They?

Hart had left her car at the station, so he drove her back there. "Are you all right to drive home?" he asked.

"I only had two glasses," she said. "You were right. It was like urine re-cyc."

"How would you know?"

"Anyway, I got to get changed, then I'm going up the canteen for a cup a coffee before I go home," she said. She looked at him hopefully, but his mind was elsewhere, and he merely grunted. In his office he found a message asking him to call Det Sup Smithers, giving her home number. He telephoned Joanna first.

"What are you doing there?" she asked. "I thought you were at the farewell party."

"I was. But I've come back here to do some thinking."

"Are you coming home? I was just going to have some supper. Oatcakes and cheese and a very large malt whisky. In the bath."

He visualized it. "Which one?"

"We've only got one bath."

"Which whisky."

"The Macallan." But she had already guessed that he was going to say no. "I've got no clothes on," she added hopefully.

"I was just ringing to say don't wait up for me, I might be late," Slider admitted.

"Oh."

"Is everything all right?"

"Just peachy," she said. "Except that I've been getting funny phone calls."

"What sort?"

"I say hello, they put the phone down."

"How many? How often?"

"Three this evening."

"Oh. Are you worried?"

"No, not really. It's annoying, more than anything."

"Don't answer anymore. Put the answering machine on," he advised.

"What if you want to call me?"

"You'll hear my voice on the machine, and you can intercept."

"But I'm not sure it's working properly."

"I thought you were going to get it fixed. Oh, never mind now. Look, put it on anyway, and if I want to phone you—it picks up on the fourth ring, so I'll let it ring three times and stop, and then ring you again immediately."

"All right. Are you onto something? Is that why you're staying late?"

"I wish I were. Every new bit of evidence I get seems to make things foggier instead of clearer."

"It'll come to you," she said. "Virtue brings its own reward."

"That's a misquotation," he said.

"Just testing."

He pressed the receiver rest to get a new dialing tone, and dialed Pauline's Richmond number.

"Pauline? It's Bill."

"Oh, hi. Well, I've done it for you. Don't ask me how. He's going to ring you—but not at home and not at work. Give me your mobile number."

Slider told her.

"Right," she said. "I'll give this to him, and he'll contact you and arrange a meet."

"When?"

"He knows it's urgent," Pauline said. "That's all I can

tell you. He's got to watch his back. Leave it to him. And—Bill? Be careful.''

"I always am.''

"No you're not. I heard about that attack on you, and your sergeant—what's his name?''

"Atherton.''

"That one. It's a dangerous game now. That's why our friend agreed to contact you. He wants to keep you out of it, to save his own skin.''

"I'll be careful,'' Slider repeated. "Pauline, thanks for doing this for me. I really appreciate it.''

"That's all right,'' she said. "All part of the service. D'you know why I never got married?''

"No,'' Slider said, puzzled.

"I didn't think you did. When you've got this case out of the way, I'll hold you to that meal. But I warn you, it'll be a credit-card job.''

"Nothing's too good for you,'' Slider said.

Almost immediately he put the phone down it rang again. He answered it and was greeted by silence. He thought for a moment it was one of Joanna's "funny phone calls,'' but after a moment Irene said, "It's me.''

"What's the matter?'' he asked.

"Why should anything be the matter?''

"I know all your tones of voice. What's the matter?''

She seemed to have difficulty voicing it. "I've been trying to ring you all evening,'' she said at last.

"Well I've only been here about a quarter of an hour. I was at Honeyman's farewell bash.''

"I don't mean there. I was trying to ring you at home.''

He prickled with advance warning of a storm. "Where?''

"Where you live, of course,'' she said shortly. "Sergeant Paxman gave me your home number.''

"Oh, did he?''

"I told him it was urgent. Anyway, why shouldn't he?'' Irene said sharply. "He knows I'm your wife. Is it supposed to be a secret?'' Slider couldn't answer that. "So I rang there, and a woman answered.''

"And you hung up, of course. That explains it. She thought you were a heavy breather.''

"Who is she?" The question was both naked and urgent. Slider dithered over what was best to do or say, what would hurt all involved the least.

"No one you know," he said at last.

"She didn't sound like a landlady."

"You can tell that from 'Hello'?"

"Bill, don't torment me," Irene said. "You're living with someone, aren't you?"

"I should have thought that was self-evident."

"You know what I mean. You've got another—you've got a woman."

No way out of it. "If you must put it that way—yes."

"It's that black girl, isn't it? That's why you took her to see the house. You're going to move in there with her."

"Irene, for God's sake! I told you W.D.C. Hart is one of my firm, a loaner until Atherton's on his feet again. I'd just gone to see the house was all right, that's all, and she happened to be with me."

"You don't have to lie to me," Irene said pathetically. "Why shouldn't you have another woman? It's only natural. You're an attractive man. I couldn't expect you to be a monk for the rest of your life. I just wish you'd had the courage to tell me, and not make me find out that way."

"Why do I feel I've strayed into a Celia Johnson movie? Watch my lips: I am not having an affair with Hart!"

"Well it looked like it, from what I saw. And you said you're living with someone."

"You're the one who can tell everything from one word on the phone. Couldn't you tell that wasn't Hart?"

Irene made one of those extraordinary and devastating leaps of logic that women seemed to be capable of when sniffing out infidelity. "Oh my God," she said with the horror of absolute conviction in her voice, "it's that woman at the pub, isn't it? When I had lunch with you. The one who came in, and you said she was Atherton's friend."

"She is Atherton's friend."

"Yes, and the rest. I *knew* she wasn't his type. My God! No wonder you seemed so put out when she turned up. I thought it was because you were ashamed of being seen with me."

"Oh *Irene*—!"

"But why did you have to lie about her? You could have told me. I've got no right to complain, after all."

"You were in the middle of telling me that Matthew wanted to go home. I thought—" That was a sentence too delicate to finish.

"Well, obviously," she said bravely, "there's no question of that now. I'm sorry I embarrassed you by mentioning it. I had thought that maybe it wasn't too late, maybe we might be able to get back together—for the children's sake if nothing else—but obviously it's too late for that now." She drew a slightly quivering breath. "If only I'd spoken earlier, maybe it would have been different. But I suppose you couldn't have forgiven me even then. I've made a mess of everything, haven't I?"

"It's not your fault," he began, but she interrupted him.

"It is. I never knew when I was well off, that's what it was. And I suppose I didn't really think, when I walked out, that it was an irrevocable step. It was a sort of cry for attention, really, I suppose. I was just trying to make you notice me. I never thought properly about the consequences."

"Oh, Irene," he said helplessly.

"It's all right, I know, I've made my own bed and all that. Do you love her?"

"Look, I don't think—"

"You can tell me that, can't you? She's not much to look at," she said dispassionately, "so I suppose it must be love. Or was she just available? She wasn't really Atherton's girlfriend, was she? I'd hate to think you were getting yourself involved on the rebound. I mean, don't rush into something with the first female to come your way, just because she's desperate and you don't like being alone. It would all be such a waste if we both ended up unhappy."

This was terrible. He was on hot coals. "Are you really unhappy?"

She paused before answering. "Does it matter if I am? I mean, if there's nothing to be done about it? If you've got someone else and it's serious, we're never going to get back together again. Or is it," she added hopefully, "just a passing thing?"

"It's serious," he said unwillingly.

"How can you be sure? You can't have known her long. You've only just met her."

It seemed an ideal moment to begin setting the record straight. "I've known her a long time," he said.

"What, because she was a friend of Atherton's?"

"A friend of both of us."

There was a silence in which he could hear her computer grinding to a conclusion, but he couldn't think of a thing to say to interrupt the process. He wanted to tell her the truth, but couldn't break the habit of subterfuge which had built up around his relationship with Joanna. He found it intolerable that she should blame herself entirely for the situation, but feared bringing down her wrath on his head by confession. But they were adults, weren't they? And now that they had parted, surely the truth could be borne? It must be the best option, so that everyone knew where they stood, and a final and amicable arrangement could be made.

"Look," he began—the most fatal, incriminating word a man could ever say to a woman.

"You were having an affair with her," Irene said with chilling certainty. "Before. Weren't you?"

"Look, I—"

"I *knew* there was something going on! I just couldn't fathom out what. But I told myself I was imagining things. And then, when Ernie started getting interested in me—" She found her anger. "You let me feel guilty! You let me take all the blame, and all the time you were having an affair! You were sniggering behind my back with that—with that—"

"Irene, for God's sake, it wasn't like that."

"How long? *How long?*"

"It doesn't matter. Surely it doesn't matter now. We've both got someone else. We've both got new lives. What does it matter whether—"

"What does it matter? You let me go through agonies of guilt about breaking up our marriage, and all the time you were messing around with that—that—*bitch*—and you ask me what does it matter? My God, she isn't even good-looking! How could you do it to me? It'd be bad enough if she was a dolly bird, but how could you betray me for that fat cow?''

"Don't talk like that. All that recrimination stuff is over—''

"Oh, don't you believe it, chum! I haven't started yet!'' Irene spat, incandescent with rage. "There's a few things going to be different from now on, I can tell you! I've been treating you with kid gloves, thinking I was the guilty party. Now you're going to find out a few realities of life. By the time I've finished with you, you're going to wish you'd never touched that bitch with a ten-foot barge pole. Your feet won't touch the ground, I promise you that.''

"Irene—''

"You'd better get yourself a lawyer, Bill Slider!'' she yelled, and slammed the phone down.

Slider replaced his receiver and contemplated it in unhappy silence for a while. "I don't think I handled that very well,'' he said at last.

"You all right, guv?'' Hart asked from the doorway.

He looked up sternly. "Have you been listening?''

"Not me,'' she said indignantly. "I just got here.'' She eyed him with interest. "You look a bit down. I was just going off. D'you fancy a drink?''

He thought of Irene phoning up for a rematch and being told he'd gone down the boozer with Hart. Or even coming to find him and walking in on them. In any case, he had to be alone for when the Scotland Yard man rang. "No, thanks all the same. I've got some thinking to do. You go on home. I'll see you tomorrow.''

When she had gone he sat a bit longer, staring at nothing, frowning in thought. And then he got up, making sure to grab his mobile, and went out. He was parked on the corner of Abdale Road—he couldn't get into the yard—and as he came out onto the street his mobile rang. There seemed to be no one around. He stepped back against the wall and answered it.

"Yes,'' he said into it.

"You were expecting a call from me,'' said a voice. It wasn't a question.

"Yes.''

"I can meet you now. Mention no names. You know where they found the P.C. who got hurt?"

"Yes."

"There. Ten minutes. Don't get followed." He rang off. This was a very cautious fellow, Slider thought. Ten minutes didn't give him long to make sure he wasn't followed—no time to drive circuitously. He hurried to his car. He decided to park in Hammersmith Grove and walk the rest. He saw nothing in his rearview, nothing suspicious when he parked and got out. There were people about, but no one seemed to be paying him any attention—or deliberately *not* paying him attention—and he had no sense of being watched. Besides, this was his home ground, and it seemed absurd to be taking all these precautions on these ordinary streets. He walked without elaborations down the quiet back streets, only keeping an ear open for footfalls, and snatching a look behind when he abruptly crossed the road. There was no one about.

When he reached the waste ground he felt more ill at ease. The lighting came only from the railway line above: there were deep shadows everywhere and blackness under the arches. He did not know what de Glanville looked like. Or sounded like, come to that—he was assuming the call came from him, but supposing someone else had got his mobile number, someone who had a grudge against him? There were plenty of those in his past, let alone the present case. He stepped onto the waste and kept close to the wall, and reaching the first arch backed just inside it and stood still, listening and watching.

He smelled him first. As soon as the man moved, and before the moving air brought a sound to his ears, Slider's nose picked up the cologne. Subtle, expensive. He put his back to the wall and looked into the darkness for the movement and said softly, "Who's that?"

"De Glanville." It was the voice on the phone—one worry down, anyway. "It's all right. You weren't followed." The voice came closer as it spoke, and now he appeared beside Slider in the entrance to the arch. Taller than Slider, but not by much; well-built without being heavy. A handsome, dark face with designer stubble making it look darker; thick, long-ish dark hair, brushed back and bronze-tipped and styled in a classy salon—or at least an expensive one. He was wearing the undercover cop's favored blouson-style jacket, in suede—new enough for Slider to smell that now, too—along with dark trousers and black leather casual shoes with thick soles. He had a gold and jet stud in one ear, expensive and discreetly unconventional. The intelligent brown eyes were watchful in a face made firm by responsibility. A man who could look after himself and expected to win. To Slider he had copper stamped all over him. No wonder Yates had clocked him.

"Why here?" Slider asked.

"It was the only place I could be sure you'd know without my naming it. Mobiles are not secure. That's why I called this meet."

Called this meet, Slider smiled inwardly. How they all loved playing cops and robbers! He had the strong desire to call de Glanville "son"; but probably the danger de Glanville faced was real and desperate. "You're going to tell me what's going on?" he said hopefully.

"I was in favor of telling you in the first place," de Glanville said. He had a slight accent: Slider couldn't decide what. There was something about the "e" in "telling" and the "th" in "the." "I don't want local boys trampling all over my investigation, busting in on me and blowing my cover."

"Believe me, I don't want to do that either," Slider said patiently. "If I know where the land mines are, I'll know not to tread on them, won't I?"

De Glanville smiled, a brief flash of very white teeth in the dark lower half of his face. Slider thought women would find him attractive. Perhaps it was necessary to his job. "I've already had your oppo under my feet. What's his name? Carver? Why don't you people ever talk to each other?"

"Beats the hell out of me. Look what I had to go through to get to talk to you," Slider said.

"True. All right. Let's get on the park. I'm in at the Pomona—I guess you know that." He used "guess" as a foreigner uses it, not an Americanism. Could it be that he was a real Frenchman? But he didn't quite sound French.

"Are you after Yates?"

"Yates is a player, but he's not the biggest. That's why we don't want him flushed out yet. It's his bosses we're after.

But I had contact with the man you're interested in—Jay Paloma.''

"You met him in the club? Several times?'' De Glanville nodded. "You were spotted. Yates told me about you. He said he thought you were a dealer.''

"He was supposed to,'' de Glanville said with a touch of complacency. Stand aside, redneck, and let the big city experts in. "Paloma was buying snow—you know that, don't you? I'd seen him sniffing around a dealer I was interested in and for operational reasons I didn't want him hanging around that particular area, so I told him I'd supply him.''

"How did you get the stuff?''

"You don't want to know that. I knew who he was getting it for, so I supplied him for some time. I thought there might be some important connection that way. It did seem for a time that our big player might be an M.P. and using Parliamentary privilege to shelter under. But it turned out to be a false lead. So I dropped Paloma.''

"Wait a minute, let me get this straight. Did Paloma know who you were?''

"Not *who*—but what.''

"He was working for you, in fact.''

"Effectively. I got him the stuff, he passed it onto his bumchum and reported back to me. I primed him with the questions to ask and what to look out for. But as I said, it was a dead end.''

"How did you persuade him to spy for you?''

"It wasn't hard,'' de Glanville said with a short laugh. "I was giving him the stuff at a fraction of the price, and he was pocketing the difference. He was perfectly happy. Plus I leaned on him a bit.''

"Really?'' Slider said neutrally.

"I had the goods on him, didn't I? And you saw him: he was a bit precious—very dainty in his ways. He wouldn't have liked a spell inside with all those nasty rough boys.''

"Yes, that would scare him,'' Slider agreed. "When you dropped him, you told him you wouldn't supply him anymore?''

"Of course. But he said he was getting out anyway. Saved enough of Grisham's money to go back to Ireland. I said that was a good idea. Didn't want him hanging around and maybe letting the cat out of the bag. Gave him a bit of a push in that direction, if you want to know. But as it happened, it wasn't necessary.'' He shrugged. ''Best result all round, really, when he got topped.''

Slider nodded politely. ''I suppose you don't know who did it?''

''Nope,'' de Glanville said. ''That's your business.''

''I told you that Yates had spotted you for a dealer, and you said he was supposed to. But it occurs to me that he might have blown your cover.''

''Because Yates sent one of his goons around to hit Paloma?''

''How the hell did you know that?''

''It's my business to know things. But I want Yates left alone. We're very close now. I don't want him spooked. And I want that gorilla of his sprung.''

Slider saw no reason to reveal his hand. He shrugged. ''If you say so. But what about Cosgrove?''

''Cosgrove was a worse problem to me because everyone knew he was a copper. He was clodhopping after Yates, and I had to get him warned off. I couldn't have him hanging around the club.''

''But do you know who whacked him?''

''Nope. I got him off my back, that was all that mattered to me. He hadn't been around there for weeks when it happened. But I doubt, frankly, if it was anything to do with Yates. Yates is too fly to put out a hit on a copper—and if he did, he'd do it more professionally than that. It had all the hallmarks of an amateur to me. But it's not my case,'' he finished with a shrug.

''It's not mine, either,'' Slider said. ''When did you last supply Paloma with any white?''

De Glanville considered. ''It was the Thursday before he was killed. Thursday night stroke Friday morning. I suppose he gave it to his friend on Friday or Saturday and a happy weekend was had by all.''

''And that's when you told him you didn't need him anymore?'' De Glanville nodded. ''So he knew before the weekend.''

"Certainly. Now I've told you everything you need to know. You'll stay away from the club and Yates from now on. I want everything to settle down again."

"What will happen to him?" Slider asked.

"Yates? Why, have you got some beef against him?"

Slider thought of Maroon, and Maltesa, and Candy, and all the other pathetic toms nobody cared about. Thank you, Mr. Gladstone. But they had rights, like anyone else, and what they did was not illegal, that was what got him. Prostitution was not illegal—living off their backs, like Yates and his gorillas, *that* was illegal.

"He's responsible for beating up a girl I know," Slider said. All right, it was Jonah who broke Maroon's face, but it was Yates who made Jonah possible.

De Glanville hesitated, but then his face softened a little in sympathy. "He's going down. Don't worry about that. We've got enough on him to send him away forever and ever. As soon as we've sprung the trap on the top bosses, we'll clean up the scumbags like Yates."

"And Jonah Lafota?"

"Him too." Dark eyes gleamed in the darkness. "My promise on that."

"Thanks," said Slider.

De Glanville looked out of the arch at the quiet night. "It's safe enough. You can go now."

Slider said, "There is just one other question." De Glanville looked at him a little impatiently. "What *is* your accent? I can't place it. I thought at first it was French, but now—"

The teeth whitened across the dark face. "What are you, Professor Higgins? Belgian Congo. Zaire. I was born there. My dad was in the diplomatic. But my mum's British."

"Thanks," said Slider gratefully.

He went a long way around to get back to his car, for safety's sake, but he saw nothing and felt nothing. He got in and drove. It looked after all as if there wasn't any connection between the Paloma murder and the Cosgrove case, except stupid concurrence. He didn't mind being wrong, but he absolutely hated Carver to be right, to say nothing of Wetherspoon. He thought about Carver and Wetherspoon at Honeyman's party. It hadn't looked terribly much like Wetherspoon telling Carver to back off and Carver saying yes sir, certainly sir. It had looked a lot more like Carver getting his hand down Wetherspoon's trousers, and Wetherspoon saying I'll pull strings for you, Ron, just don't stop loving me. But as Hart had said, that was just paranoid. Anyway, Cosgrove was not his case and not his business. He must put it out of his head entirely.

So he drove to the pub where Busty was barmaid, to ask her the only other thing he hadn't asked her—whether she knew Andy Cosgrove.

The pub was crowded, and Slider, scanning the bar for Busty, was surprised and amused to see that one of the bar stools was occupied by the trim, moley person of Busty's tame taxi driver. What was his name? Oh yes, Benny the Brief. He had one hand wrapped around a half-pint jug and the other was supporting a lighted cigarette, and as Slider came up behind him he saw that his eyes were fixed adoringly on the heavenly shape of Busty Parnell, serving down the other end of the bar in a pink sequined sweater, low-cut enough to leave everything to be desired.

"Hello there, Mr. Fluss," Slider said, remembering his name at the last moment. "Drinking and driving? Tut tut."

The little man started violently, and then smiled his crooked, multidentate smile as he recognized Slider. "Oh, I only have the one when I'm driving, don't worry. I nurse it. I'm a great nurser. Can I get you one?"

"No, thanks, I just came to have a quick word with Busty."

Benny looked pained. "Valerie, please, or Miss Parnell. She's not—that horrid name—anymore. That belongs to the past. That's all over. She's a respectable woman now."

"Of course. I'm sorry," Slider said, amused. "It just slipped out. So you're still on duty, are you?"

"Not as such," Benny conceded. "But I'm keeping a clear head for driving Miss Parnell home when her shift finishes. That's a sacred duty to me, so you don't need to worry about me having too much, I can assure you." He burbled on a bit, but Slider wasn't listening. Busty looked around at last and he caught her eye, and she came down to him with an eager look.

"Hello! Have you got some news?" she asked.

"I'm afraid not. I just popped in to ask you something. Could I have a quick word?" He flicked a warning glance Bennywards and she picked it up with commendable quickness.

"Come down the other end, then, where it's quieter," she said. "George, can you serve for me for a minute? Just five minutes. Thanks, love."

At the other end of the bar she propped up the hatch and made a little quiet corner for them. Slider eased himself in beside her. "I see you've got an escort laid on for later," he said.

She made a face. "Oh, I can't seem to shake him off. He's been ever so kind since Maurice died, can't do enough for me, but he gets on my nerves a bit. I'm thinking of setting George on him."

"That's a bit cruel, isn't it?" George the barman was a low-browed, long-armed creature who looked like a genetic experiment gone horribly wrong. He was kindness itself, but his terrifying looks were too useful to the management for them to admit it publicly.

"Well, just to tell him he can't sit in here all evening nursing the same half," Busty said. "Anyway, what did you want to ask me?"

"Do you know Andy Cosgrove?"

"What, the copper? Of course. He got beaten up, didn't he, poor soul, and left in a coma. Just before Maurice got— you know." She moved her head as though she could avoid the pain with the word.

"That's him. But I mean did you know him personally?"

"Everybody on the estate knew him," Busty said. "He hasn't gone and died, has he?"

"No, there's no change. You knew him to speak to?"

Busty smiled. "Oh yes. Well, he used to go out with a working girl, didn't he? He always took a special interest in us."

"Did you know Maroon Brown, his girlfriend?"

"Oh yeah. She used to live on the estate, did you know that?"

"Yes, I knew that."

"And she used to come in here quite a bit. Met Andy here sometimes when he come off duty. Course, I haven't seen her lately."

"So you knew Andy quite well?"

"Oh yeah. Like I said, he had a soft spot for working girls." She glanced back down the bar at Benny the Brief and lowered her voice—unnecessarily—to say with a sporting grin, "Old Benny thought it was terrible—about Andy and Maroon."

"How did he know about them?"

"I told him, a course. He didn't half tut. Well, Andy's a married man, and Maroon's a full-time prostitute. And he didn't like me mixing with bad hats like that. He's a real old woman, sometimes, Benny."

Slider was not interested in Busty's guard dog. "So when did you last see Andy?"

"Couple of weeks ago. Not long before he was done over, as a matter of fact. He came to see me at the flat one afternoon, when Maurice was out. Doing a bit of sniffing around, he was, not that he came straight out with it. But I know when I'm being pumped."

"What did he want to know about?"

"Oh, I dunno. Something about Billy Yates and Maurice. I didn't get it at first. I thought he was after Maurice—you know, because of the stuff." She lowered her eyelids daintily at the mention. "But thinking about it later, I think he was hoping Maurice might have something on Mr. Yates, to incriminate him. He had a down on Billy Yates for some reason, did Andy. It wasn't official police business," she added cannily, " 'cause he didn't come straight out with it. Just hinting around, you know."

"Did you tell him anything?"

"And drop Maurice in it? What d'you think I am? Of course I didn't. Well, anyway, Andy stayed a bit and had a bit of a chat and then he went, and that's the last time I saw him."

"Had he ever called on you before?"

"What, at the flat? No. No, he hadn't. Come to think of it, I suppose that must of meant it was important. But I didn't make anything of it, really. I mean, I know what you coppers are like. Always lonely, always wanting a chat.'' And she smiled fondly at Slider, remembering.

Slider cleared his throat. He had enough woman trouble already. ''Can you remember exactly when that was—the day he visited you? You said it wasn't long before he was attacked.''

''That's right. It was the week before. On the Thursday or Friday, I think. Let me see.'' She furrowed her brow willingly but evidently without much hope.

''You said it was while Maurice was out,'' Slider prompted. ''Where had he gone, do you remember that?''

''Oh, to see his friend, of course. Wait a minute, yes, I've got it now. It was the Friday afternoon. And poor Andy got done over on the Saturday night. Well, there! With all the trouble over Maurice I never thought, but it was just the day before. It makes you think, don't it?''

''Why didn't you mention this to me before?'' Slider said.

''You never asked,'' she said with a touch of indignation. ''Anyway, it's got nothing to do with Maurice, has it?''

''No,'' Slider sighed. ''No, I don't suppose it has.''

''Anyway, what did you want to ask me?'' Busty said. ''Only I can't leave George holding the baby.''

''Oh, that was it. About Andy Cosgrove. It was just a loose end I wanted tying up.''

''And has it helped?'' she asked, eyeing him keenly.

No, Slider thought, it hasn't. ''*You've* helped,'' he said. ''Thanks, Busty. When all this is over, I'll take you out and buy you a curry. Like the old days.''

''Only this ain't the old days anymore,'' she said sadly. ''In the old days everybody was shocked if a copper got hurt. Now it don't even make the front page. We didn't know when we was lucky.''

Ain't it the truth, Slider thought. On an impulse he laid his hand briefly over hers as it rested on the bar, and leaned forward to peck her on the cheek. ''See you, Busty.''

Outside, on the way to his car, he passed Benny's black cab. Or he assumed it was Benny's—he wouldn't expect there to be two Monty's Metrocabs parked down the side of the pub. It was interesting that he hadn't noticed it on his way in. It was like Lenny the Lion said—you didn't see black cabs unless you were positively looking for them. They were street furniture, and the brain edited them out.

He got in his car and just sat, wondering what to do next. He toyed briefly with the idea of going home, but knew he couldn't bear to. When he needed to think he had to be out; home had too many other connotations to be conducive. If he went home he'd have to tell Joanna about Irene and the phone call, and he didn't want to think about that yet; couldn't afford the brain space, with so much else that needed to be sorted out. So there seemed nothing for it but to go and see Atherton. It was late, and even with flexible visiting hours the nursing staff might be unwilling to let him by. But he knew a back way in, and if challenged he could always flash his brief and claim official business. Which it was, in a way. Cot-case or not, Atherton was still his partner.

❖ SIXTEEN ❖

Waste Not, Want Not

He parked down the narrow service road behind the hospital, and when he got out and turned to lock the door, he got that prickling feeling again of being watched. It was just the loneliness of the road, he told himself, and the multiplicity of shadowy places. The backs of hospitals were always unlovely: all downpipes and dirty windows of frosted glass, and always a single mysterious plume of steam rising from somewhere into the yellow sodium-lit sky. He thought briefly of the waste ground, and de Glanville, and de Glanville's extensive caution. Well, he was after big players, and big players did sometimes get carried away. But they wouldn't be interested in Slider. His head was aching a bit, and he wondered if thinking you were being followed was a sign of brain damage. Perhaps he had come back to work too early. If he hadn't come back, this whole Paloma mess would have landed on someone else's desk and he wouldn't have Busty Parnell on his conscience. He should have taken more sick leave. He yearned to be lying on a beach somewhere instead of here, slogging it out with this grubby mystery; but now he had taken hold of it, he couldn't put it down. Unless his head actually fell off, he would have to see it through.

His unofficial way in was across the backyard and past the dustbins. There was a metal fire door, one of those push-bar-to-open jobs, which was slightly warped and would only shut properly if you yanked it hard, which porters in a hurry often did not bother to do. If you just let it go to close by its own weight, it simply rested shut without the lock catching. So it was now. Slider worked his fingers under the rim and pulled it open. It gave onto a stone-floored corridor with dark-green glazed tiled walls lit by a single sulky bulb in the high ceiling. To the right a much scarred metal door gave access to the incinerator room, where they burned the infected waste and the bits of people that people didn't want anymore. Slider hurried past it with a superstitious shudder. At the far end was a pair of black rubber swing doors, and he pushed through these into a corridor of the brightly lit hospital proper, with its white noise of air conditioning and its smell of you-don't-really-want-to-know-what-this-is-covering-up. Here was the goods lift and a series of storerooms, and a little further along a granite staircase with metal hand rails, alongside a branch corridor which led to the mortuary and the old postmortem room. He had been there more times than he needed to remember, in the company of Freddie Cameron, which was how he knew this back way in. He clattered up the stairs, meeting no one and reflecting how easy it was to bypass security in a hospital. But of course hospitals had not been built with security in mind. Who would ever have thought there would be a need?

Coming at Atherton's room from the wrong end, as it were, he didn't even encounter a nurse. He could see by the glass panel in the door that the light was on, and looking through he saw Atherton sitting up in bed; and in a chair beside the bed, chatting to him, was Hart.

He went in. "What are you doing here?" he asked as Hart looked around.

"Just visiting," she said. "Why not?"

"It's late," Slider said. "How did you get past the nurses?"

"One of 'em's a friend of mine," Hart said simply.

"Good evening. Yes, thank you, much better, thank you for asking," Atherton said to the wall.

"I was going to ask if you minded being disturbed so late," Slider said, "but I got thrown off track. You're *looking* better."

"You look terrible," Atherton reciprocated. "Are you having headaches?"

"Does Salman Rushdie have life insurance?"

"Has something happened, guv?" Hart asked, searching his face. "Some new information?"

"Why should you think that?"

She grinned. "Deduced it, din' I? You ain't bin home, and it's ages since I left you at the factory."

"Pull up a chair," Atherton said, "and tell all. I need mental stimulation. Now I'm not drugged all day long, I'm bored to death."

So Slider brought Atherton up to speed, and told them both about his interview with de Glanville and the truth about where Jay Paloma had got the cocaine.

"It's ironic," Slider concluded. "At one end of the chain there was Grisham being blackmailed into getting the dope from Paloma, and at the other end Paloma being blackmailed into getting it for Grisham."

"It's pafetic when you fink of it," Hart said. "When you remember, guv, how that Grisham was going on about true love and finding his soulmate, and all the time poor old Paloma was spying on him and putting his money aside so he could get enough saved up to leave him."

"But it does look as though the drugs can be ruled out as a motive," Atherton said. "Obviously he wasn't whacked for bilking a dealer or anything. He wasn't really a threat to anyone."

"It might still have been someone who knew he had the stuff and just wanted to nick it," Hart said.

Slider shook his head. "That won't work. There was no sign of the flat being searched; no sign even of anyone going through the victim's pockets. If some local lowlife or addict did it just to get a single packet, they wouldn't have left without even looking for what they came for."

"I suppose not," Hart conceded unwillingly.

"Then what does that leave you with? Yates?" Atherton said. "He's into some serious naughties somewhere. And he definitely sent Jonah Lafota round. Though we still don't know what he wanted Paloma done for."

"*I* do," Hart said.

Slider looked at her narrowly. "Have you been hanging around that club again?"

"No, boss," she said in wounded tones. "I din't need to. I got my snout wound round my little finger now."

"You're a bleeding contortionist, that's what you are," Atherton said admiringly.

"I ain't been wasting my time," she said with a sidelong look at Slider. "My snout got it all off that ficko Garry. Apparently Yates knew Paloma had been scoring white in the club and he didn't like it, 'cause the dealer wasn't one of his. Well, we know now it was one of ours. Anyway, Yates don't want any outside dealing on his patch, and he don't want any trouble spoiling the spotless reputation of his fine establishment. So when Grisham comes in and makes the fuss, Yates sees a way of putting the frighteners on Paloma, and if anything comes back at him, he lays it off on Grisham, because there's witnesses that the daft bugger give Jonah money to do it. Jonah don't like it, of course, because it's his spuds on the barbecue, but he's got to do as he's told. If Yates says it's Christmas they all sing carols."

"Is that the way it was?"

"Yeah, and when we come in asking questions, Yates comes over all helpful and puts us onto the dealer to keep us off his back. Probably hoped we might scare him off the patch, as well."

"Well, that ties up an end. But I rather think Yates is ruled out for the murder," Slider said regretfully. "I can't see him sending two men to do the same job. And if he'd had Paloma killed in the afternoon, he wouldn't have sent Jonah round in the evening."

"Are you definitely accepting Jonah's story, then?" Atherton asked. "That Paloma was already dead when he got there?"

"It agrees too well," Slider said. "Look." He counted the points out on his left hand. "For a start, Freddie Cameron originally put the death much earlier—between one fifteen and four fifteen. He accepted the later time because we had witnesses to the breaking down of the door, and an eyewitness outweighs the science of rigor. But that was his first opinion."

He extended the forefinger to join the thumb. ''Then there's the old man who lives underneath.''

''Sounds like the title of a children's story written by the Prince of Wales,'' Atherton commented.

Slider ignored him. ''His evidence is very detailed. The visitor, the heavy fall, the trampling and banging as the body was repeatedly struck—it all agrees.''

''He could be making it up to get attention,'' Hart said. ''Old man, living alone, no family—''

''We've all seen *Twelve Angry Men*,'' Atherton told her.

''That's always a possibility,'' Slider conceded, ''but he did point out the exact spot where the body fell, without ever having seen inside the flat. And his background and his explanation make it plausible that he was listening, and that he could distinguish what he heard. Hollis believes him, and Hollis is no monkey. The old man also says that Paloma didn't do his practice at the usual time that evening; and we've got Grisham's word that he telephoned several times in the afternoon and got no reply.''

''Paloma could have guessed it was Grisham ringing and just not answered,'' Atherton said.

''Of course. But add it to the rest of the evidence, and it starts to tell. Point—where have I got up to? Three?''

''Four, if you count Grisham,'' Hart said.

''Four, then. There's the forensic evidence about the stomach contents. Scrambled eggs on toast eaten less than an hour before death. That ties in with the crockery left in the sink, and it could have been eaten any time. But Busty expected him to get himself breakfast after she left, and she says he always washed up immediately. So look at the timings: she leaves him in his dressing gown at half past eleven. He takes an hour-plus to get shaved, washed and dressed—half past twelve, twenty to one. He cooks himself some breakfast and eats it. Puts the dirties in the sink to wash. Then he goes into the front room to put the television on—''

''He ain't done the washing up,'' Hart objected.

''I have to guess here, but maybe he just popped in to check the time of the film. It was one he didn't want to miss, and they start at a different time every day. He and Busty didn't have a newspaper or a *TV Times*, but they did have

Teletext. It's possible he just went in to check the time, meaning to go straight back to do the washing up before settling down. But at that very moment, the visitor arrives.''

"It makes sense," Atherton conceded.

"They sit and talk, Paloma gets them both a drink, then at twenty past the visitor jumps up and whacks him."

"But—"

"Bear with me," Slider said, lifting his hand. "See how this works out. Paloma's dead. So the washing up doesn't get done. The bath towels don't get folded and hung up as usual. He doesn't do his practice. He doesn't answer the phone. He doesn't go in to work. The television's on and tuned to Channel 4 for the afternoon film—a black and white wartime job of which he was very fond. Busty says if he'd been watching that night he'd have had it on I.T.V. for sure. The curtains are open—if he'd been watching at night he'd have drawn them.''

"It's all circumstantial," Atherton said.

"Yes, but it adds up. Nothing jars yet. All right, come eleven-thirty Jonah Lafota turns up to scare the bejaysus out of Paloma. He's drunk and furious about the whole thing. He kicks the door in and storms into the front room, where the telly's on. By the light of the screen he can't see much. So he turns on the light, leaving his fingermarks on the light switch. He sees Paloma lying on the floor. He walks over, sees the mess someone's made of the man he's been sent to scare, and realizes the creamola he's in. He grabs a drink, knocking over the table, panics, picks everything up and puts it straight and leaves, remembering—for he's intelligent, our boy—to put the light off again as he goes, and pull the front door to so that it won't be seen until he's well away.''

"Brilliant, boss," said Hart enthusiastically.

"Hm," said Atherton. "But Jonah's supposed to be professional. Why didn't he wear gloves?"

"Because he didn't go there to murder Paloma, only scare him; and having been scared Paloma wouldn't have brought charges, not even for the bust-in door. So there was no need to be careful.''

"It explains why there was gloved fingermarks on the glass and ungloved on the bottle," Hart approved. "The visitor at one o'clock came to murder, so he wore gloves. He had a drink with Paloma, and he used the glass.''

Slider nodded, looking from her to Atherton. "We decided from the start that Paloma had been taken by surprise. There was no sign of a struggle. But how could he have been taken by surprise—and from the front—if the door had been violently kicked in? But if he was sitting having a chat with the murderer, who suddenly sprang up and whacked him across the bridge of the nose, killing him instantly—it fits all right. Lafota was telling the truth, Paloma was already dead when he got there, and the scrambled eggs were breakfast, not supper.''

"But who?" Atherton said. "And why?"

"That, as somebody once remarked, is the question." Slider rubbed his forehead. "I think we need to sleep on it. We're missing something.''

Atherton caught Hart's eye and made a gesture toward the door with his head. She took the hint and stood up. "Well, if it's all the same to you gents, I fink I'll go and have a chat with my mate. While I'm here. Got to keep her sweet or she won't let me in again. How did you get in, guv?" she added with interest.

"I've got a private route," Slider said, "but I'm keeping it to myself.''

"It's a secret passage," Atherton said. "Starts behind a concealed panel in the library and comes out in the crypt of the ruined chapel.''

"Garn," said Hart, and departed.

Atherton looked keenly at Slider. "What's up, boss? Is it the case?''

Slider hesitated, but it was habit to confide in Atherton. "Mostly that. But now I've got trouble with Irene as well. At least, I think I have.'' He told Atherton briefly about the phone call.

"You are a plonker when it comes to women," Atherton said. "How could you get yourself into such a mess?''

"Your own relationships with women are notably successful and well-managed, of course," Slider said with a touch of resentment.

"I don't have relationships with women, that's the whole

point. I flit like a butterfly from flower to flower. A little sip here, a little sip there, and—''

''Has Sue been in to see you?''

''Yes, she's been in,'' Atherton said shortly.

''Just once?''

''Who's counting?'' His tone was brittle. ''I keep telling you, there's nothing between Sue and me.''

''Yes, you tell me that, but you don't tell me why,'' said Slider. If he was having his tender parts probed, he was going to probe back some. ''You and she were very hot, and then suddenly it all stopped. Why?''

Atherton was on the brink of snapping ''Is that any of your business?'' when he paused and reflected that it just about was, or at least it had the right to be, and said instead, ''Look—''

''Ha!''

''What d'you mean, 'ha!'?''

''Prevarication alert. When a man starts by saying 'look,' it's a sign he's wriggling. *Why* did you stop seeing Sue? Plain answer.''

''Because it was getting heavy. She was getting too serious.''

''*She* was?''

''You know what women are like,'' Atherton said unconvincingly. ''You go out a couple of times and they start wanting to leave stuff in your bathroom. Then they want to know what you're doing every minute of the day. Before you know it, they're talking about looking for a flat together.''

Slider looked at him sadly. ''You're crazy about her.''

''I just don't want to get involved. Anyway, we're supposed to be discussing your problems, if you don't mind.''

''At least mine are positive problems, not negative ones.''

''Is that supposed to mean something, or was that a bit of your brain I just saw fall out of your ear?''

''It means,'' Slider said, ''that if you're not 'involved,' as you call it, you're nothing. It's like saying life is difficult, so I'd sooner not be born.''

''Very profound.''

''You can sneer all you like, but what else is there? Bonking a series of bimbos you don't give a damn about? You might as well masturbate and save the money.''

"I'm quite happy as I am, thank you,'' Atherton said with dignity.

"You aren't,'' said Slider. They eyed each other for a while in tense silence. "How are you, anyway?'' Slider said at last.

"They're going to try me on solid foods next week,'' Atherton said, not with unalloyed bliss.

"That's good, isn't it?''

"Theoretically.''

"Are you in much pain?''

"Oh, it comes and goes. No, it's a lot better now.''

"But?''

"I don't know,'' Atherton said with evident difficulty, "if I'll be coming back.''

"Oh,'' said Slider. He sought careful words. "That would be—a waste.''

"The thing is,'' Atherton went on, looking bleakly at the wall beyond Slider's shoulder, "I don't know what else I can do.''

"But you're intelligent. You've got A levels and everything,'' Slider said. "You'd easily get a job.''

"At my age? Anyway, it's the only thing I ever wanted to do, be a copper.''

"Really?'' Slider said with some surprise. He had always thought Atherton became a policeman out of general indifference.

Atherton smiled faintly. "My pose of languid insouciance is not meant to fool you, oh great detective. Since I was a kid reading 'tec novels, it's all I ever wanted. It disappointed my father and broke my mother's heart, but I always knew it was the one thing I could do well, and be happy at.''

"So why—er—?''

Atherton looked at him. "I've seen bits of me God never meant to be seen. I lie here every day and look at *this*.'' He gestured toward his wound. "And I think, 'I never want to be in this situation again.' And next time it could be worse. I could be shot. I could get killed.''

"Oh, come on—'' Slider began, but having screwed up his courage to say all this, Atherton wouldn't be stopped.

"It could happen. You know the chances. Seven officers killed in the last five years. God knows how many thousand wounded, some of them disabled or scarred for life. I don't want to end up with a plastic nose. And the thing is, they'll know. The villains. They'll know I'm afraid, and that'll make it all the more likely. I'd be endangering other people. I can't go on, Bill. I've—lost my nerve."

Slider didn't know what to say to comfort him. "Don't think about it now," he said. "Think about it later."

"Thank you, Scarlett," Atherton said, managing a smile.

"You're still under the weather. Everything will seem different when you're on your feet and out of here."

"How do you cope?" Atherton asked, eyeing him.

Slider said, "I don't really think about it until it happens."

"You've had your share," Atherton observed.

"Of course, it's your first time. That's always worse. And some coppers do take it harder than others. I suppose you've got more imagination, or something."

Atherton winced. "You make me sound like Patience Strong."

"My advice would be, don't make any decisions on the basis of how you feel now. Get fit again, see how you feel then. Don't rush it. Run yourself in gently with a shoplifter or two, just to get your hand in, then move onto an underage burglar—"

"What's your interest in all this, anyway?" Atherton demanded.

"I should miss you," Slider said.

It was the sort of moment when men get gruff. Atherton said gruffly, "Well, you've got a new partner now. What's she like?"

"You've seen her. Slender waist, firm, pouting breasts, legs that go all the way up to her shoulders—"

"You could be describing me," Atherton said, and the moment was past.

A nurse put her head around the door. "I thought I heard voices. You shouldn't be here, you know," she said to Slider. "How did you get past the desk without me seeing you?"

He didn't want to give away his secret route in case he

needed it again. "I expect you were answering a call," he said.

"I hope this is urgent, official business," she said sternly.

"It was. I've finished now, though. I'll be off," Slider said, obeying the insistently held-open door. "I'll look in again tomorrow," he said to Atherton.

"Don't bother," Atherton said. "Send me Hart instead."

"You'd only burst your stitches," said Slider.

Because the nurse was watching he had to go out past the desk and to the main lift, but he got out at the first floor and made his way back to the stone stairs. If he went out at the front he'd have to walk right around the hospital to get to his car and he was tired now. There was a smell of pallid food wafting up the staircase: the kitchens must be somewhere up this end. It was funny, he thought, how often the kitchen and body parts incinerator were close together. Mackay said it was a case of waste not, want not, and amplified the thought if given any encouragement—or even without it.

Slider pushed open the rubber swing door and found the corridor past the incinerator room was in darkness. Holding the door open, he looked for the light switch on the wall just inside, and clicked it. Nothing happened. The bulb must have gone. He didn't fancy groping his way down the passage in the pitch dark. But at the far end the metal door was slightly open—letting the rubber door close behind him to cut out the light, he could see two edges of the door outlined by the orange glow from the lampposts in the street. It was enough. It wasn't as if he could get lost anywhere.

The corridor was only thirty feet long, but five steps into it he suddenly got a very bad case of panic. The hair stood up on his scalp and he wanted to run. For an instant he stopped himself, manly-wise; and then he thought, yeah, what the hell, panic! And ran. At least, he flung the first running step forward, but that was all he had time for before the wall fell on him and knocked him down. He sprawled on the cold rubber floor, smelled a terrible smell of gas, felt someone looming over him; and a terrible, unmanning despair swept over him. This was it. He was going to die. And in his last moment, he thought of Atherton, so near but just too far away to help him.

* * *

The looming shape was gone. He wasn't dead. Someone ran past him. He dragged himself partway up, propped on one elbow, feeling sick. The outline of the metal door changed shape, there was a dark figure framed in it, looking out; looking back. A metallic scraping noise—whoever it was was forcing the door all the way out so that it stayed open. The figure ran back. Slider flinched; but it was Hart. He smelled her perfume on the gusted air before her.

"Sir, are you all right? Guv?"

"I'm all right. Get after him," Slider croaked.

She was away again. He saw her darken the door briefly. He dragged himself into sitting position and leaned against the cold wall, glad of the little light, glad he was not in darkness. The nausea was passing, a numb, throbbing pain tuning in behind his head. He reached up shaky, flinching fingers and located the area of extreme tenderness around the lowest cervical vertebra, which woke to jangling when he touched it. The fact that he had flung himself forward had saved him from having his neck broken; amazing thing, animal instinct. He would never scoff at it again.

Hart came running back, and was on her knees beside him, her hands all over him. "Nothing," she panted. "No sign of anyone anywhere. He's had it away down the road by now. Are you all right, guv?"

"I think so," he said.

"What was it? Where did he get you?"

"He hit me with something. Back of the neck. My jacket collar cushioned it."

"Who was it, guv? Did you see him?"

"No, he was hiding in the dark. The light didn't work. He must have taken the bulb out. Did you get a look at him?"

"No. Just a sort of dark shape at the far door. I must have scared him off."

"Thank God you came." He winced. "Leave that alone. I'm all right, just leave me alone." She desisted. "Why did you come? What were you doing here?"

"I followed you," she said. "You left your mobile behind."

"I did?"

"I just popped into Atherton's room to say goodbye, and he said you'd left your mobile. He told me about your back way in so I ran after you, down the back stairs. As I pushed open *that* door, all I saw was the dark shape as he scarpered out of *that* one."

"He was standing over me, ready to finish me off. You saved my life."

"Oh, that's all right. Any time," she said, sounding embarrassed. "Who was it, though? Someone to do with the case?"

"Unless it was a homicidal hospital porter, I should think that's a fair bet."

"Sorry, guv. I'm a bit rattled."

"How d'you think I feel? Give me a hand up, will you?" He got to his feet, leaned against the wall, and had an experimental moan. It felt good, so he repeated it. "I'm too old for this sort of thing," he said. Maybe he'd join Atherton in retirement. They could go shares in a chicken farm.

"Put your arm over my shoulder and I'll support you," Hart said, slipping her lithe body into the operative position. "Let me take your weight."

"It's all right, I can walk," he said.

"No, come on, guv. No sense in taking chances. I'll help you to a chair and then I'll go and find a nurse or someone."

"What?"

"To have a look at your head. You'll need an X-ray or something."

"Oh no you don't. I'm not getting caught up with all that again. I've done my hospital stay for this year."

"But, guv—"

"He didn't hit me on the head, and nothing's broken. Just a bit bruised." He tried an experimental rotation of the head and it hurt, but not by that much. "I'm going home."

"Suppose he's still out there?"

"You said he'd gone."

"I could be wrong."

"You can walk me to my car, if you're worried. But he won't attack again tonight."

"How can you be so sure?" she said indignantly. "If he really wants to kill you—"

''You don't know it's a man,'' he said, to sidetrack her. ''It could be my wife taking vengeance.''

''Then she'd attack me, wouldn't she, not you?'' Hart said with a cheeky grin.

He was glad to have distracted her, but he didn't want her continuing in this delusion. ''You take too much upon yourself,'' Slider said grimly. ''Walk with me to my car, and then I'll drive you to yours, just in case. And from now on, we both avoid dark alleys. Will you stop flapping, W.D.C. Hart! If he'd wanted to take on two of us, he wouldn't have run off when you came on the scene, would he?''

❖ SEVENTEEN ❖

State of Affairs

"All the same," Joanna said, easing arnica into the spot, "she had a point."

"Atherton reckons she's got several," Slider said. "Ouch."

"That'll teach you not to be facetious. What in the name of Jupiter did he hit you with?"

"It felt like a smallish building," Slider said. "But I wasn't knocked out, just groggy. And nothing's broken. It's just a bruise. I don't want to spend any more time hanging around a hospital if I can help it. I've got things to do."

Joanna came around the front of him and sat down, knees touching his knees, face inches from his. She looked pale and tired and worried, and he suddenly had a very glad and lifting awareness of how much he loved her, which was reassuring in this world of uncertainties. "Suppose he tries it again, whoever he is?"

"Well, being in hospital wouldn't help me, would it? I proved how easy it is to sneak in."

"I was voicing a different worry that time," she said. "I'd moved on from (a) you might have delayed concussion to (b) there's a murderer prancing about trying to invalidate your ticket." Her eyes were anxious. "I don't want to lose you, Bill."

She laid a hand on his knee and he placed his over it. This would be a good time, he thought to give her something else to worry about. A nice go of stomachache to take her mind off toothache. "Irene knows about us," he said.

It worked. "What? You don't mean you told her?"

"It sort of came out."

"Wait a minute, wait a minute, let's get this straight. When you say you told her about us, what exactly did you tell her?" Her eyes widened so far her eyebrows made her scalp shift backward. "You told her everything?" He nodded mutely. "Oh, bloody Nora, now what have you done?"

"Bloody Nora?" he said, amused. "You sound like a policeman."

"Laugh while you can," she said grimly. "Let me guess how pleased she was to find out the true state of affairs, if you'll pardon the pun."

"She told me to get a lawyer," Slider admitted. "Her parting words before she slammed the phone down."

Joanna jumped to her feet and paced about. "Phone! It was her on the phone, putting it down when I answered! Of course, why didn't I guess?"

"How do women do that?" he marveled. "Yes, she was the phantom phone caller. She'd been trying to get hold of me—to discuss our getting together again, I imagine—and when she kept getting a woman's voice, she rang me at the office."

"I don't know why you're being so flippant about it," Joanna said crossly.

"It's less antisocial than crying," he said, "which is what I feel like doing."

She sat down again abruptly. "I'm sorry. I know you care about her—about them. But really, Bill, why on earth did you—I mean, what good did you think it could do her to know?"

"I just couldn't bear to hear her blaming herself for everything. Anyway, she'd have had to know sooner or later. It would have come out."

"I don't see why."

"Because whatever you think now, you and she are bound to meet from time to time in the future, and things slip out. You can't keep a guilty secret forever. And the later she found out, the worse it would be."

"After the divorce would have been good. I'd have settled for that."

"I hate lying to her. I hate lying about you. I'm sorry, I didn't set out deliberately to tell her, but it just came out, and I can't help feeling it's for the best."

"As if your life wasn't complicated enough already," Joanna sighed. She leaned forward and kissed his forehead. "You really are a clot, Bill Slider. She's going to have your balls for jewelry now, you know that? She'll divorce you for adultery, and it'll all be adversarial instead of amicable. She'll have the house off you, and every penny she can screw out of you, and refuse you access to the children on the grounds that you're an unsuitable influence."

"Thanks."

"I just thought I'd mention it."

"Anyway, she won't. How can she, when she's gone off with another man?"

"But now she can say you drove her to it."

"Oh, it doesn't work that way nowadays. The courts know what's what. It'll all be settled half and half in the end—these things always are."

"But you'll have to fight for your half now, instead of being given it."

He lost patience. "What do you want from me?" he snapped. "It's done now. Don't go on and on about it."

She looked at him whitely. "I'm just pointing out—"

"Perhaps you'd prefer me to go back to her? That would save you a lot of trouble."

"Of course, your divorce is none of my business," she said neutrally. "You must settle it your own way." And she went out of the room.

Slider sat and cursed, softly but fluently, and hit his knees with his fists a few times. Then he got up and went after her. She was in the kitchen standing over the kettle, waiting for it to boil.

"You haven't switched it on," he observed. She pushed the switch in without answering. He put his arms around her from behind and kissed the back of her neck. "I'm sorry," he said.

She turned inside his arms and looked into his face carefully—to see if he meant it, perhaps—and then sighed and leaned into the embrace.

"I'm sorry," he said again. "I'm upset and worried. I shouldn't snap at you."

She rested her head against his cheek. "I worry about you. I wish we could just get away from all this."

"I know the divorce is your concern too—"

"Oh, bugger the divorce. The divorce is a pleasant itch compared with having a maniac on the loose trying to kill you."

"He won't try again," Slider said soothingly. "He'll have scared himself too badly by nearly getting caught."

"Do you really think so?"

"Really," he said. He felt her relax. "Boy, I'm getting good at this lying, aren't I?"

She began to laugh. "Oh, you bastard."

He set her back from him and kissed her, and said, "I'll be all right. I'm a survivor. It's Atherton you ought to worry about. He thinks he's lost his nerve. He's too sensitive to be a policeman, really. I think you should do everything in your power to boost his morale and get his pecker up."

"Not until his stitches are out," she said. "Ah, but then! I want you to remember it was you who suggested it."

He slept late the next morning, and went on dozing when Joanna got up, waking properly only when she came in with a breakfast tray. He dragged himself up. "Let me pee first." When he came back she had pulled the curtains, letting in the sunshine, and was sitting cross-legged in bed. He got in, and she settled the tray between them. Oedipus appeared from nowhere and jumped up on the bed, sat precisely with his tail around his feet, and closed his eyes against temptation. His purr gave him away, though. Slider felt like purring too. Scrambled eggs with Parma ham, toast, fresh peaches cut into easinosh slices, a jug of juice. He sniffed it. "Squeezed?"

"For a treat. There's a grapefruit in there too."

"Everything I like best. What's the celebration?"

"Oh, this and that," she said. "How's your neck stroke head?"

"It's been worse."

They ate without talking much, and then she put the tray aside and they made long, slow love; the best for ages, which made him realize how much of their lives together was snatched between his duties and hers. Coordinating two schedules of unsocial hours took determination and dedication—but it was worth it. Afterward they lay entwined and, eventually, talked.

"Shouldn't you be going to work or something?" she asked.

"I was just going to say that. What have you got on today?"

"Concert tonight in Newbury, but there's only a seating rehearsal. It's the repeat of the one we did in Leeds."

"So what time d'you have to be there? Five?"

"Five-thirty. So I've got all day. I had thought of cleaning this place up a bit and doing some shopping. The joys of domesticity. You can help me if you like."

"I'm onto you. You just want to keep an eye on me."

"Do you blame me?"

"As soon as this case is out of the way," he promised, "I'll take the rest of my sick leave and we'll go away somewhere. If you can get the time off."

"Watch me. But what about the case? Did anything happen yesterday?"

So he told her what he'd told Atherton and Hart already. Going through it again was never a bad idea.

"So you know all about who didn't do it," she said when he had finished.

"That's right. We've run out of false trails at last. Now we've just got to find who did."

"It must be someone he knew, because he let him in."

"People let in people they don't know," Slider said. "Meter readers, insurance salesmen."

"You don't sit and drink whiskey with the meter reader," she said. "Well, I do, but I'm unusual."

"True. But then you do it in the nude. Paloma was fully dressed. I think it's fairly safe to conclude that he knew the visitor."

"Could it have been his lover? Grisham? Come to try for

a reconciliation? He pleads, Paloma resists, they argue, Grisham loses control and bashes him.''

"With?"

"Whatever," she said evasively. "Something he found lying to hand.''

"Whatever the weapon was, it was taken away, and Busty didn't say anything was missing.''

"She might not notice. Well, something he brought with him, then. A walking stick."

"Very gentlemanly, but not heavy enough. But anyway, we know it wasn't Grisham. He had an alibi. He was telephoning Paloma from his office in Westminster at half past one.''

"Why didn't you tell me?" she said indignantly.

"I didn't want to short-circuit you. I thought you might say something useful.''

"Everything I say is useful. So what about this weapon?"

"Whoever did the job, it had to be something small enough to be concealable when he left the flat, and heavy enough to be that small. Probably metallic. Possibly with a square edge.''

"Like a spanner?" she suggested.

"Yes, a heavy spanner would do it.''

"So you're looking for a man who owns a spanner. That narrows it down.''

"Ah, but he might have bought it specially.''

"True. So you've got to use your brains.''

"Don't say that as if it was a disaster.''

"Why not try a different approach," she said, propping herself up on one elbow. With her short bronze hair tousled, she looked like a show chrysanthemum past its best. "It seems to me you haven't considered the poison pen letters.''

"Not recently. But of course we thought we had the right man in Jonah, so the letters seemed incidental—if they existed. He didn't bring any in to show me, remember.''

"But I can't see why he would make them up. Assume they did exist—isn't it likely that whoever sent them was also the murderer? That it was an escalating campaign which went to its logical conclusion.''

"It's a possibility." Slider sat up. "The escalation is certainly there. Six months ago, according to Paloma, it started with phone calls; three months later the letters started, and increased in menace week by week. Of course, these things don't usually end in murder, but it's not unheard of. But who hated him with that sort of concentrated hatred?''

''Didn't he give you any hint as to who he thought it was?''

''He said he didn't know. I got the impression he had his suspicion, but he wouldn't say anything. At the time, I thought he suspected Grisham.''

''But why would Grisham—?''

''Oh, because of the Pomona Club—refusing to stop working there. But that was before I talked to Grisham. The man really loved Paloma; and I just don't see him as the kind to work in that underhand way. When he really lost it he acted very directly—rushing into the Pink Parrot waving fistfuls of quids. A poison pen is a different kind of character—slow, brooding, insidious and mean.''

She shivered. ''And now he's after you.''

''Well he won't get me. But what intrigues me is why did the campaign go so suddenly from the letters to murder? I'd have expected some buildup of physical attacks before the final one—broken windows, vandalism, arson attacks, that sort of thing. To make him suffer as much as possible before killing him.''

''Presumably he did something that speeded it up,'' Joanna said. ''What happened in the days just before the murder? Could it have been something to do with that animal rights business?''

''I don't see what,'' he said, frowning. ''That was a pukka AL job, though unauthorized, and none of them had any connection with Paloma—we checked. And the only person who was likely to mind about the publicity was Grisham, and we've investigated that. All the same,'' he went on, putting his legs over the side of the bed, ''I think you're right. Something he did in the days before his death—over the weekend, perhaps—sparked it off. We've got to work out what.''

''You're getting up?''

''Mm. I have to go in,'' he said absently, heading for the bathroom.

She saw he was off on his other plane. "I wish I hadn't started you thinking. I thought we were going to go shopping together," she said.

"Oh yes, let's have lunch," he said vaguely over his shoulder.

"No, that was the Eighties," she called after him; but he didn't hear her.

As he entered the C.I.D. room, Norma, without looking up from her desk, began to sing very softly an old C.I.D. melody.

> *They called the bastard Stephen,*
> *They called the bastard Stephen.*

The rest of the team joined in with increasing volume.

> *They called the bastard Stephen,*
> *'CAUSE THAT WAS THE NAME OF THE INK!*

"I gather Jonah Lafota has departed," Slider said when they'd stopped.

"Not this life, unfortunately," Norma said.

"Sprung last night," Hart said resentfully. "Pity poor Candy."

"The fact is, ladies and germs," Slider said, "much as we may regret it, Jonah was telling the truth and Paloma was dead when he got there."

"We can still nail him for conspiracy can't we, guv?" Anderson pleaded.

"And that filth, Billy Yates," Norma added. "We can't let him off."

"I'm afraid there are bigger things afoot, and we are under orders not to frighten the rabbits." Chorus of groans. "But I am assured," he raised his voice over the woe, "that they will be going down and that deserts will be just. Eventually."

"Mushroom time," Anderson commented. "Get your heads down, here it comes."

Slider ignored him. "So let's concentrate our minds on the problem in hand, which is still who killed Jay Paloma. We're back to basics. Whoever it was, it wasn't the invisible man,

so let's get out there and ask questions. I can't believe that
nobody saw the murderer arrive and—more importantly—
leave. However calculating he was, he'd have been in a state
of nervous tension, and maybe blood-spattered when he left.
Someone saw him, they just haven't remembered it yet.''

They dispersed, muttering. He called them back. ''Oh, and
some good news, to speed you on your way. The latest report
from the hospital is that Andy Cosgrove's coma seems to be
lightening. So there's a good chance he's going to come out
of it.''

That at least produced a spatter of lighter expressions.
McLaren, unwrapping a Topic bar, said, ''If he does come
out of it, and he's still got all his marbles, he'll be a fool if
he doesn't leave the Job. Once you've been in a coma like
that, any little bump on the head can send you back down,
and the next time you never come up again.''

Norma, who had a street gazette in her hand, threw the
book at him.

Slider had all the documents of the case spread out over his
desk, and when the phone rang it took him a minute to find
it.

''Inspector Slider? My name's Larry Mosselman.'' When
Slider didn't react he went on, as if it explained everything,
''They call me Mr. Atlas.''

''Sorry?''

''You know—Mosselman, muscle-man?''

''Ah! You're a taxi driver?''

''That's right. I thought you were expecting me to call.
Lenny Cohen's been putting the word out that you've been
looking to contact the driver who picked up a certain party
on Monday the fifteenth?''

''You know Lenny, do you?''

''Everyone knows Lenny the Lion. We've played golf together once or twice, but he's bit out of my league now. Well,
he does a lot of nights, so he gets the practice.''

''You're not with the same company as him?''

''No, I work for Jack Disney's garage in Old Road, Hackney—just behind the Victoria Park?''

''Yes, I know it.''

"Anyway, in connection with your inquiry, I heard about it when I went in yesterday to settle up, and I think I might be the cabbie you're looking for. As far as I can tell from the picture, my fare was the same man, and I did put him down at the Lanesborough rank about twenty to twelve that Monday."

"Did you see where he went then?"

"He walked on up the street, as if he was heading for the hotel entrance. That's all I saw, because I wasn't putting on myself, so I pulled away. But what made him stick in my mind," Mosselman went on intelligently, "was that when I picked him up, he'd just got out of another cab."

"Had he? Well, we did suspect he might have. He was trying to be cautious, cover his tracks."

"Not very good at it, though, if he let me see it," Mosselman said. "And Lenny saw me drop him as well. Mind you, he looked like a bit of a daft ponce, if you don't mind me saying so."

"Talking of which, can you give me a description of your fare?" Slider said, to be on the safe side. He took down the details, which as far as they went fitted Paloma. "And where did you pick him up?"

"Hammersmith Broadway, about ten past eleven. On the gyratory, outside the new building where the post office used to be. He was standing on the curb, on the wrong side of the railings. He waved me down, but traffic was slow so I'd had plenty of time to clock him as I approached, and I'd seen him get out of the other cab and pay it off. Anyway, he got in and asked for the Lanesborough, and I took him there."

"Right," Slider said. "Thanks. Well, it may not turn out to be important now, because we've found out where he ended up that day, but we're always glad to have the loose ends tied up. It all adds to the picture."

"Right you are. Glad to help," said Mosselman. "Do you want me to come in and make a statement or anything?"

"I don't think it'll be necessary, but I would like to take your address and phone number in case we need to contact you." He wrote to Mosselman's dictation, and then added, "By the way, I don't suppose you saw the driver of the cab this man got out of?"

"No, I didn't see the driver, but I saw the name on the side of the cab. It was one of Monty's Radio Metrocabs."

"Was it, indeed? Thank you, Mr. Mosselman," said Slider.

Monty was not in his hutch, for once. Winston, one of the mechanics, said he had gone to hospital.

"Nothing serious, I hope?" Slider said.

"Nah, s'just 'is checkup. It's routine, right? Like, 'e 'ad this 'eart attack, like years ago, an' they make 'im go, right, like, every six months, reg'lar."

"I see. I'm glad it's nothing bad. Wouldn't want to lose another good man," Slider said. Winston stared at him with his mouth open, and Slider hoped he was better in the motor mechanical field than he was at deciphering human speech. "I'll just go and speak to Mrs. Green," he said clearly, and left the mechanic to work on that.

Rita was also missing, and the bower was surprisingly peaceful without her. Gloria gave Slider a toothy smile and invited him to sit down, offering him tea and biscuits with an eagerness that suggested she could not stand the near-silence. "She's gone with Monty to see the specialist," she explained when he asked after Rita. "I think she wants to persuade him to make Monty give up the cigars."

"But he doesn't really smoke them. He lights them and they go out. He probably just likes something in his mouth."

Gloria wrinkled her powdery nose. "They stink. I hate those things," she said. "Is there something I can help you with, or did you particularly want Rita?"

"No, you can help me," Slider said. He told her about Mosselman's information. "I'd like to check the day book again, in case we've missed anything."

But the day book produced nothing that looked remotely like Jay Paloma. "He's sure it was this cab company?" Gloria said at last.

"He said he saw the name on the side."

She shrugged. "Then I suppose someone was doing him a favor."

"But the cabbie saw him pay," Slider said.

"Well, it couldn't have been on the clock," Gloria said. She looked at Slider. "It could have been Benny the Brief, I suppose. He was always round there, wasn't he, round the flat, 'cause he was friends with that woman.''

"It crossed my mind," Slider said, "but why wouldn't he have mentioned it to me?"

"Maybe because he didn't put it on the clock, and didn't want to get into trouble. Is it important? That wasn't the day the chap got killed, was it?"

"No, it wasn't. Probably it isn't important." He thought a moment. Gloria was low man on Monty's totem pole, and had to toe the party line when Rita was around. This was a golden chance to get her views un-iced. "What do you make of Benny Fluss?"

"He's all right," she said indifferently.

"D'you like him?" She made a face. "Tell me what he's like."

"He's a boring old fart," she said, surprising the hell out of Slider, who almost looked around for the Swear Box. She saw his surprise and blushed a little. "Well he is," she said defensively. "Jaw, jaw, jaw. And never admits he doesn't know something. Makes it up as he goes along, and if you catch him out he bullshits and makes out he said something different. Can't be in the wrong, you know the sort; and patronizing? Rita and me might be moron slaves.''

"I gather you don't like him," Slider said mildly.

"Oh, he doesn't bother me, really. Don't see enough of him to get worked up. Monty thinks he's a hoot, plays him along, you know, to get him to talk. But there's a side to him I don't like." She lowered her enormous, lavvy-brush lashes and looked at Slider sidelong. "He was in trouble once, did you know?"

"Police?"

"It didn't come to that, but it ought to've, in my view. You see, Benny had a half-flat in those days—about ten years ago, this was."

Slider nodded. Half-flat was the arrangement where two drivers shared the same cab, one driving days and one driving nights.

"Anyway," Gloria went on, "he found out that the other driver was seeing Gwen—Benny's wife, Gwen—while Benny had the cab. There was a terrible to-do. Benny went round to Sam's—Sam was the other driver, Sam Kelly—and beat him up. Did a real job on him. Terrible it was. Well, I know Sam was in the wrong, but Rita and me thought Benny went too far, and the police should've been told. But Sam wouldn't make any complaint against Benny, so I suppose he thought it was coming to him, but as soon as he was out of hospital he moved right away and we've never seen him since. But after that I could never really laugh about Benny like Monty does. I mean, it's in him somewhere, isn't it? And who'd have thought he could be that jealous about Gwen? I know they'd been married a long time, but I never got the impression he cared tuppence for her, seeing them together. It's a funny thing, jealousy, isn't it?'' she finished on an academic note.

"It certainly is," Slider said, substituting it at the last moment for how would you know?

He sat in his car and made the necessary calls. There were several of them, and by the time he got to the corner of Wood Lane, Hart was waiting for him.

"I'm spose to give you this," she said, waving the warrant as she climbed in. "What's cooking?"

"Benny the Brief," he said.

"The tame cabbie?" she said with evident surprise.

"I've been thinking about time scales," Slider said. "Six months ago, his wife died. At the same time the silent phone calls start. Three months ago he asked Busty Parnell to marry him and she turned him down. From that point Jay Paloma starts getting threatening letters."

"You think he sent them? What for?"

"Jealousy," Slider said. "The oldest, blackest, meanest emotion. He's been looking on Busty as his own property for years, but while he was married it never occurred to him to do anything about it. After all, he was comfortable as he was. But once he's a widower he starts to think he could have her all to himself, marry her and take her home for keeps. He's so confident of the outcome he sells the marital home so that they can get a new place together. He hasn't even asked her yet, but he's sure she'll jump at the chance of changing her unsatisfactory life for security and Benny's fascinating company. Only when the moment finally comes, she refuses him. She prefers to live with a painted popinjay who earns his living doing unspeakable things in a basement club.''

''Bit of a bummer,'' Hart agreed.

''He can't hate her for it, of course: his hatred is aimed at Jay, his rival for Busty's affections.''

''So he starts sending poison pen letters, you reckon? I s'pose it makes sense.''

''I don't know whether he hoped to scare Paloma into leaving Busty,'' Slider said, ''or if it was just venting his feelings. Bit of both, maybe.''

''The letters was posted from different places all over London, wun't they?'' Hart remembered. ''A cabbie'd have no trouble sorting that side of it.''

''Yes, and living in lodgings rather than in a shared home he'd have the privacy to make them up.''

''So if it was him, what d'you think triggered the murder?''

''Jay Paloma was going to take Busty away from him. Jay had been saving money for them to buy a place together in Ireland—his dream plan. It might have remained a dream, except that he had reached a crisis in his life. He'd hated having to buy drugs for his lover, but now the supply was cut off he was probably worried about what would happen to Grisham. He must also have worried for his own skin—could he trust the supplier not to bust him? There was the paint-throwing incident at the Pomona which upset him; and the poison pen letters were getting him down. His quarrel with Grisham was probably the last straw. He was now so fed up with his situation that he decided their savings were enough for him and Busty to get out and put the plan into action. And Busty was happy enough to go along with it.''

''Yeah,'' said Hart, staring forward. ''We saw Paloma going was reason enough to make Grisham mad, but we never fought about Parnell and Benny Fluss. Good one, guv.''

''I should have got onto it before,'' Slider said. ''I should have picked up on the discrepancy in the statements. You see, Busty told me that on that last day, Jay was chatting cheerfully to her *and* Benny about his plan, but Benny said Jay didn't speak to him at all, and that he was low and depressed. I think Jay had probably told him they were definitely going when Benny drove him to Hammersmith the day before, and that was when Benny decided to do it. So he didn't mention that journey to me—in fact, he said he never drove Paloma—because in his own mind it was connected with his guilt. And he projected his negative emotions onto Jay the next day, and remembered him as being low and depressed.''

"Well, you would be, wouldn't you, if you was gonna get done that day?"

"Quite. Of course, all this is conjecture. But Paloma let the murderer in and sat and chatted with him, which meant he must have known him well; and Busty said he hadn't any friends, and never saw people at home. Also, Benny was the one person who knew Paloma would be at home alone. He drove Busty to her sister's, and he knew she would ring him to be collected from there when she wanted to come home, so there was no danger she'd walk in on them.''

Hart nodded. "What about the weapon?"

"Joanna suggested this morning that it could be a heavy spanner. Something Benny would have to hand in his cab. Also we know the murderer wore leather gloves; and when I first met Benny he was wearing a pair of brand new ones.''

"The gloves'd get messed up."

"And you can't get bloodstains out of leather. You can wash a spanner, though, as long as you haven't got a wife at home to ask you awkward questions.''

Hart sat thinking it through. "D'you really think he'd do that, just for the sake of old mother Parnell?"

"She's not that old," Slider protested. Actually, she must be about the same age as him. "Anyway, he was obsessed by her. And jealousy is a strange thing.''

"It was a frenzied attack," Hart said. "If the first blow killed him, there was no need to bash his head in like that. It didn't make sense when we thought it was a pro job, but if it was jealousy—well.''

"That's what I thought. And given the way Paloma's head was battered, I think he could be dangerous. If he has moved from threatening letters to actually killing Paloma, the next step could be that he decides he can't keep Busty to himself any other way than by killing her—and then probably himself.''

"Yeah," said Hart thoughtfully. "I seen that sort a thing before."

"We've got to get him banged up before he hurts someone else. But so far it's all guesswork. That's why we've got to have a look at his room and see if we can find something a bit more solid."

"Like bloodstained gloves?"

"Or the makings of the poison pen letters—a pot of glue, some mutilated newspapers."

"We should be so lucky!"

"And I've asked Norma to check his mobile phone account for the numbers he's called. We might be able to correlate something from that. Ah, this is it."

❖ EIGHTEEN ❖

Hell Toupée

It was a stunted, two-story house, one of a terrace built between the wars, and set below street level—there must have been a hillside there—so that you went down a flight of steps set into a bank to gain access. One flight to each pair, whose doors stood side by side, set back in arched porchways. Slider rang the bell, while Hart stood two steps up keeping a look out for homicidal black cabs, and eyeing the road as if it might bite her.

The landlady was a woman shrunk with age, with white wispy hair, National Health glasses, a thick nose, pendulous lip, and folds of heavy skin hanging loose about her face and neck like elephant's trousers. She wore a green nylon overall of the sort that Woolworth's assistants used to wear in the old days—for all Slider knew it might have been one, nicked in her heyday—and those tartan slippers with a fawn fold-back collar and a fawn bobble that boys used to buy for their fathers for Christmas back in 1962. She rolled a ferocious eye up at Slider and snapped, "Yes?" in exactly the tone of voice in which she might have said, "Bugger off!"

Slider got as far as introducing himself and showing his brief when she interrupted. "Is *she* with you?" she said with a glare in Hart's direction. "Tell her to get off the steps. I washed them this morning."

Slider cut to the chase. "I understand you have a Mr. Fluss staying with you."

"I've a lodger of that name," she corrected aggressively, as though he had impugned her chastity. "What's it to you?"

"I'd like to see his room, please, Mrs.—?"

"Bugger off!" she snapped. Slider blinked. "And it's Miss. Miss Bogorov."

"Ah," said Slider. "Well, could you show us his room, please?"

She looked at him a moment longer, and then turned and went into the house without a word. One thing to be said about eastern Europe, Slider thought, it taught people not to argue with policemen. He beckoned to Hart and followed her in. The entrance passage was dark, and so narrow it might have been designed for a different race—which, in a way, it had, the working classes in the twenties and thirties being generally smaller and slighter than today's chunky breed. The smell of dust came up from the carpet as he trod; and mingled with a composite house-smell of dog, tea, cooked rice, metal polish and incense. The stairs were straight ahead, as narrow as the hall, with a dogleg passage going past them to the rear of the house. At the foot of the stairs, on the wall, was a rather beautiful icon with a beaten silver surround, of a melancholy saint with his eyes rolled up and his head so far over on one side he looked like a Guy Fawkes effigy without enough straw in the neck. The missing straw seemed to be leaking out through his body in hedgehog spikes.

Miss Bogorov, one foot on the stairs, glanced back and saw what he was looking at. "Saint Sebastian. My mother brought it over." Her voice for a moment became liquid. "That's all I've got left of her things. Everything else got sold."

"Over?" Hart murmured behind him, but he silenced her with a gesture. Now was not the time, and he was a Dutchman if he didn't recognize a deep vein of Russian melancholy just waiting to be mined, preferably across a table over endless tea. He left Saint Sebastian with a glance. Living with him, he reflected, was enough to make anyone scratchy.

"How many lodgers do you have?" he asked as Miss Bogorov climbed before him.

"Just the two. There's three rooms upstairs, but Mr. Johnson has one for a sitting room." She turned her head all the way back and fixed him with a terrible eye. "I live downstairs," she said, to make sure he knew there was nothing louche about the arrangements. It occurred to Slider that here after all was Benny the Brief's soulmate, if he did but recognize it. He could marry her and move downstairs and they could swap Crying Shames to their hearts' delight.

Miss Bogorov reached the top, turned right and stood with her hand on the doorknob. The upper hall was dark and depressing, with a polished wood floor and a strip of patterned carpet down the middle. The walls were painted brown up to the dado and grubby cream above, and the doors were varnished dark brown with brown mottled Bakelite doorknobs. It couldn't have been redecorated, Slider thought, since it was built.

"Nearly six months he's been with me, Mr. Fluss, and no trouble at all," she said, looking from Slider to Hart and back as if searching for a clue. "A very nice gentleman, respectable and quiet. With very proper views. Otherwise I shouldn't have taken him in. And Mr. Johnson's been with me eight years. This is a respectable house. Trouble enough we had when I was a girl, and all through the war. I don't want anymore trouble now. Remember that. This is my house. If you've got to do anything, do it quietly and don't make a mess."

Then she turned the doorknob and pushed the door open, and stood back for them to go in, folding her arms across her chest and sinking her chin, in the manner of oppressed peasants the world and time over, when the commissars come to steal their pigs and slit open their grain sacks.

Slider nodded. "Thank you," he said pointedly. She sighed and went away down the stairs.

Slider surveyed the room. A single bed with a candlewick bedspread under the window. Cheap beige wall-to-wall carpet with a rug of nineteen-fifties vileness covering it in the middle—black with a pattern of red, yellow and green lightning jags. Very contemp'ry, he thought. A washbasin and mirror in the corner. A window so small and inadequate it seemed to be letting in darkness rather than light. An oversized wardrobe and chest of drawers using up the space. A pink basket chair on spindly legs jammed between the chest of drawers and the sink. A table and kitchen chair jammed between the wardrobe and the door. A low bookcase jammed between the foot of the bed and the wall.

The chest of drawers was five feet high, and a good four feet long, and drawers all the way. "You start on that," Slider said. The table was very small, its surface about two feet six by eighteen inches, and covered with marble—presumably it had been a washstand of some kind—and on it stood an Anglepoise lamp whose springs had gone, which was held in position by an ingenious arrangement of strings fastened to a hook on the picture-rail above. This, perhaps, was where the work had been done. Slider switched on the light and bent to examine the surface closely, hoping for a trace of glue or a stuck scrap of newspaper. But Miss Bogorov was too good a housekeeper, and the surface was perfectly clean. He went over to the sink. Here, perhaps, a bloody spanner was washed—too long ago, now, for any traces to remain in the waste-pipe. A Duralex glass held a toothbrush with a brown and shaggy head and a tube of toothpaste with a messy cap. He ducked his head this way and that to see if there was a lip print. There were marks enough on its surface. They would take it, anyway. He straightened up. What was that smell, a cold, old smell, almost metallic, which hung about the room?

"Guv?" said Hart at that moment. "Have a goosey at this."

He joined her at the chest—o would that t'were!—and looked into the top right-hand drawer which she had opened. Inside—among a useful litter of things like string, playing cards, boxes of matches, Elastoplast, Sellotape, rolled crêpe bandages, the recharge lead from an electric razor, sundry loose 3-amp fuses, and a very old souvenir corn-dolly with Southwold painted across it which was losing its hair everywhere—sitting there mutely pleading for clemency was a bottle of Copydex, the sort that has a little brush attached inside the lid, and a pair of cutting-out scissors. Stacked neatly toward the back of the drawer was a couple of hundred white self-seal envelopes—"the long sort" as Jay Paloma had put it.

"Of course, it don't prove anything," Hart said in the sort of voice that expects to be contradicted.

"If only that dickhead Paloma had brought in an enve-lope," Slider mourned, "we could have done a match. Bag 'em up, anyway—oh, and the tooth glass. One way or another we've got to get something hard."

"How were the envelopes addressed, again?" Hart asked.

"Printed labels. I suppose he had them done at a Pronta-print somewhere. Now if we could find which one—!"

"He'd have thrown any left away," she said. "Incrimi-nating."

Slider looked around. "Keep looking for the gloves. I'll have a look at the books."

The bookcase was so positioned that you had to crane around the wardrobe to see the books at the end of the shelf. Very eclectic selection, he thought, using an Atherton word. Was eclectic right? Or was it eccentric? Or did they mean the same thing perhaps? Legal books, medico-legal books, a wor-rying collection of Arrow True Crime books, *Great Court Cases of History*, *F. E.—a Memoir*, Richard Gordon's *The Medical Witness*, Henry Cecil and John Mortimer, *The Lay-man's Guide to English Law*, a pocket Latin dictionary and four London A-Zs in various stages of decrepitude. Wedged in at one end of the top shelf and protruding slightly was a Basildon Bond writing pad. "We'll have this as well," he said, pulling it out with an effort. It brought with it a large format paperback which hit the floor with a thud before Slider could catch it. He picked it up. *A Practical Guide to Forensic Examination*. He put his thumb to the back and scrolled through it. Sets of black and white photographs, of clinical equipment, of weapons, close-ups of wounds, part-dissected bodies, and some whole-body shots of multiple mutilations. A brief sampling of the text proved it was a serious book aimed at the professional—a starter volume for the newly appointed police surgeon, perhaps—which accounted for the unexpurgated photographs. Photographs? A thought struck him, and he examined the sets of photographs more closely. Plates seventeen and eighteen were missing, neatly razored out flush with the fold. He turned to the front. *List of Illus-trations*. He looked up number seventeen: *The Waddington Case—Frontal View of the Injuries*. And number eighteen was the same case, the injuries to the head. A close-up presumably. What had Paloma said about the photograph that had been sent to him? A dead body, all beaten up, with its throat cut.

"I think we've got him," Slider said, straightening up. "This can't just be a coincidence. We've got him, Hart. Come and have a look."

What *was* that smell? He heard a wooden creak and turned to look, just in time to see Benny the Brief in the doorway launch himself forward with his arm raised. Hart beat Slider's reactions off the mark by twenty years, hurling herself in hard and low like a rugby forward, hitting Benny amidships and carrying him by her impetus backward to hit the doorjamb. He rolled around it and fell out into the passage with her on top of him, hitting wildly but largely ineffectually (thank God!) at her back with whatever he was holding. Slider threw himself at them, grabbing Benny's business arm and slamming it to the floor with all his weight. The spanner—for it was he—jumped from Benny's hand and hit the floor, skidding along it with an interesting scuffing sound like an ice skater on a rink.

"Get his other hand," he panted to Hart, trying to get his knee over the leg nearest him and hold it down. Benny was bucking like a teenage horse, but completely in silence. Slider supposed he had had the spare breath knocked out of him. Between them they managed to get him subdued and rolled over on his face, and Slider sat on him while Hart got his handcuffs out of his pocket and snapped them on. Once he was cuffed, Benny fell silent and still, so still that Slider thought for one rippling moment he might have snuffed it. But when he was dragged up to sitting position, he proved to be alive enough to bare his tiny hampsteads and spit at them. His aim, fortunately, proved faulty, though Slider wondered what Miss Bogorov would think of spittle on her carpet. It seemed ungrateful after she'd taken him in and ignored him so nicely.

"All right, I'll watch him, you phone for the cavalry," Slider said to Hart, and keeping a wary eye on Fluss he chanted the coppers' hymn of triumph at him. "You do not have to say anything, but your defense may be prejudiced if you do not mention while being questioned something you

later rely on in court . . .'' It didn't quite have the swing of
the old one, or the punch of the more informal "You're
fuckin' nicked, mate," but it sliced the same way.

And at last he realized what the smell in the room was, the
cold metallic ghost of the smell he was now getting hot and
fresh in waves, the smell which, when he was sprawled on
the hospital corridor floor, his nose had translated as escaping
gas. It was Benny's feet, clad for sneaking-up purposes in a
pair of tropical-swamp trainers. He could easily have qualified
as the only man in history to get his money back from the
Odoreater company. As Busty had said—and Slider could see
now why she hadn't wanted to marry him—they didn't half
pen and ink.

He was still doing the formalities, of course, when Joanna
arrived to have lunch with him; she obligingly went out to
fetch sandwiches so that he could eat at his desk, and came
back with an inspired roast beef and mustard with salad in a
granary roll.

"Where did you get this?" he marveled. Sid's coffee stall
only had white bread; the only granary Sid knew about was
his grandad's wife.

"New sandwich bar just opened—you know, where the
shoe repairers used to be?" Joanna put down another bag with
an air of minor triumph. "And they had a rather nice-looking
banana cake. And I got you tea."

"You're a wonderful woman. Your price is above rubies."

"I haven't charged you yet," she said. "I'm thinking of
adding on something for wear and tear to my nervous system."

"I thought you were looking a bit peaky. But you should
be glad we've got him under lock and key."

"Only just. You could have been killed."

"I was quite safe with Hart," he said. "You should have
seen her! Across that room like Linford Christie. When we
were reporting to Honeyman he asked her what steps she took
when she saw chummy in the doorway and she said 'Bloody
long ones, sir.' What a guy!"

Joanna eyed him. "You know she's got a crush on you?"

"Nonsense," he said through a mouthful of heaven. Of all

sandwiches in the whole world, roast beef was his absolute favorite. "I'm old enough to be her father."

"That's the point."

He swallowed. "Anyway, I think she fancies Atherton. She seemed to be hanging around the hospital room last night."

Joanna sat on the edge of his desk and took the lid off her coffee. "Yes, and what *about* last night? I suppose that it was this Benny creature that thumped you?"

"Yes. I didn't see at first how it could have been, because I left him at the pub with Busty, waiting to drive her home when the pub closed. But after I left Monty's and before Hart and I went to his place, I rang Busty, and it turns out that after I left, she had a row with him, and told him she didn't want him to drive her home, that she'd get a lift from the barman."

"How come?"

"Oh, he didn't like her chatting to me secretly up the other end of the bar. And I compounded my sins by kissing her goodbye—only on the cheek, but it was enough to rouse all his possessive instincts. She wouldn't have it, and virtually chucked him out."

"So he, seething with jealousy, followed you with malicious intent? But how did he manage that? I mean, if you left before him—"

"I did, but I didn't drive off straight away. I sat in my car for a bit, thinking what to do next. I suppose when he'd finished having his row he came out and saw me."

"And you didn't see him? You didn't notice him follow you?"

"I haven't seen him following me at any time, but he's been doing it for several days. That's how he turned up while Hart and I were going through his pad—he followed me all the way from Monty's. And he had his own front door key, of course, so he could let himself in quietly and creep up on us. Miss B, his landlady, shut herself in the kitchen and resolutely ignored the whole frackarse, even when the three of us were rolling about on the floor, and when the troops arrived with wailing sirens. We had to go and winkle her out to tell her we were taking him away—she didn't want to know. You'd think we were the *Cheka* the way she looked at us.''

Joanna took a sip of her coffee. ''So how did he square all this following people with earning a living?''

''He didn't. I should have picked that up, really, except of course that I wasn't looking at him for a suspect. But Monty told me, when I first asked if Benny was pukka, that after his wife died he worked every hour God sent, but that for the last couple of weeks he hasn't been turning in much money. Not surprising if he'd been driving about on his own business.''

''Presumably with the 'for hire' turned off, so he didn't get hailed.''

Slider nodded. ''Of course, a black cab is the perfect vehicle—pardon the pun—for spying on people. You're highly mobile, and you're inconspicuous. Nobody notices you, or thinks anything of it if they do. All black cabs look alike to a layman, and nobody ever looks at the reg number. You don't have to hide, or have an excuse to be there. And from the other side, nobody knows where you are supposed to be at any particular time. You're unaccountable.''

''Perfect for having extramarital affairs,'' Joanna said.

''Yes. I understand they do have a high divorce rate. Occupational hazard.''

She screwed up her sandwich bag and leaned over to drop it in his bin. ''Like musicians and policemen.''

''Talking of policemen,'' he said thoughtfully. ''Fluss is on the brink of confessing to the Cosgrove attack as well.''

''*He* beat up Andy Cosgrove?'' Joanna said in surprise. ''What on earth for?''

''The same thing, jealousy. Cosgrove visited Busty at her flat on the day before he was attacked. Fluss had got so obsessed by then he spent a lot of time hanging around just watching her door. He knew who Cosgrove was, and Busty had told him about Andy's affair with Maroon. Busty thought it was a charming story, but Benny disapproved strongly. So when he saw this lecherous reprobate coming out of his angel's flat, it was too much for him.''

''How did he manage to get him alone?''

''I haven't got to the bottom of it yet—I'm going to have another go at him this afternoon. He's still at the stage of hinting things, and only admits openly what he thinks I already know. But Cosgrove often hung around Monty's garage, and he'd been making inquiries about something he was investigating. All Benny had to do was to get a message to him that he had some information, and arrange a meeting. I think,'' Slider said, staring reflectively at his banana cake, ''that he probably didn't mean to hurt him. From what he's saying at the moment, I think he probably only meant to frighten him off, possibly by threatening to tell his wife, but finding himself alone with the bearded pillager he lost his temper and laid him out. He thought he'd killed him, so he bundled him in his taxi and dumped him on the waste ground.''

''He must have been a little discomposed to hear that Cosgrove wasn't dead,'' Joanna said mildly.

''Yes, and I do wonder whether pulling him in when we did might not have saved Andy from being finished off. That, and the fact that Ron Carver's been dealing with the case. If I'd been on both cases, and it had seemed that anyone was connecting them—''

''But you did,'' Joanna said. ''You've had the feeling all along they were connected.''

He smiled ruefully. ''Yes, but that was just my dumb luck. I thought Yates was involved with both, and it turns out he was involved with neither. I haven't won any bouquets for that, you know.''

''You win mine,'' she said. ''And I'm glad you're not going to be a sitting duck anymore.''

''It may have served a good purpose. If he hadn't been following me around, he'd have been brooding over Busty's continued refusal to have him. I think she may have had a narrow escape.''

''I'm supposed to be glad about that? Sooner her than you, for my money.''

''But I'm paid to run the risk, she isn't.''

''I don't buy that. She got herself mixed up with the bloke in the first place. She should have had better taste.''

''You can be very harsh sometimes,'' he complained.

She looked at him. ''I can't tell you what it feels like to think every time the phone rings it's going to be the hospital, to say they've got you there in more pieces than an IKEA flatpack waiting for an allen key.''

''You sounded just like Atherton then.''

She wasn't distracted. ''Though these days I suppose if the phone rings it's as likely to be Irene as anyone. What do I do, by the way, if she turns vengeful and arrives on the doorstep to batter me with a baseball bat?''

''She won't,'' he said.

''You have no idea, Bill Slider,'' she said solemnly, ''the strength of emotions you arouse in women. Well, I suppose I'd better go away and leave you to it.'' He looked at her gratefully, and she smiled. ''I know. I don't suppose I'll see you before I leave for work tonight? No, I didn't think so. Oh well, at least after this you'll have some time off.''

''I promise,'' he said.

''And watch out for your little W.D.C. Don't go sending out the wrong signals. I'm telling you she fancies you.''

''I'll prove you wrong,'' he called after her. ''It's Atherton she's after.''

So he wasn't entirely surprised, when he arrived almost drunk with weariness at Atherton's room that evening, to find Hart there, sitting on the edge of the bed; nor to hear that Atherton was chatting her up—evidently inviting her to dinner at his place when he got out of hospital. Here it comes, Slider thought, the old infallible method. He got a female into his little bijou nest, laid a gourmet nosh in front of her, and once she got a sight of his cuisine, she melted into submission. How many women had he pulled that way? Well, about the same as he'd had hot dinners, by that reckoning.

''Are you fond of fish?'' Atherton was saying.

''Yeah, we eat it a lot at home,'' Hart said, unconscious of the approaching huntsman. ''My mum was born in Jamaica. They eat fish there all the time.''

''Well, you must let me cook you my special lemon sole,'' Atherton said. ''I do it with lime and black butter, and it's absolutely delectable. I call it my Sole Raison d'Être.''

Slider felt it was time to intervene. ''You must be feeling better,'' he announced himself.

Hart jumped up. "I fink he's tryna get off wiv me. Is that all right, guv?"

Slider spread his hands. "What have I got to do with it? I'm not your dad. Actually, I'm your debtor. I haven't had a chance to say this properly to you, Hart, but your prompt action in Benny's room probably saved both our lives."

She looked pinkly pleased. "I didn't even fink about it. It was just instinct."

Slider looked at Atherton. "She shot across the room like an actor hearing the phone ring. Old Benny didn't stand a chance."

"Yes, I've been hearing the denouement," Atherton said.

"One bit Hart won't have told you about, because I only heard it just before I left, is that Cosgrove regained consciousness this evening."

"That's terrific. Does he remember anything?"

"They don't know yet. He's still very dopey, of course, but at least he knows who he is, and he recognized his wife all right. They haven't been able to question him about anything yet."

"We can only hope," Atherton said.

Slider went on, "Ron Carver's at his bedside even now, hoping he's going to disprove my contention that Benny the Brief did Cosgrove too."

"But Benny's put his hand up for it!" Hart said indignantly. "You put in a hard afternoon's work on him to get that confession, guv."

"Mr. Carver wouldn't let a little thing like that get in the way. He's got a whole lineup of spare villains that he'd like it to be, and psychotics make false confessions every day of the week. He's praying the forensic team aren't going to find any traces in Benny's cab, but my money's on blood down the back of the seat." He chuckled at the thought of Carver's rage when it did turn up. "How that man does detest me, to be sure!" He oughtn't really to say things like that in front of Hart, but euphoria was eroding his native caution. She'd find out the truth of it sooner or later, anyway.

"Never mind," Atherton said, "I bet old Honeyman's pleased to get the Paloma case sorted."

"As a dog with two willies," Slider said. "It might have

been difficult to bring home without Benny's attack on Hart and me, though we had the lip print match, plus all the circumstantial, the discrepancy in his statements and so on. But now he's dropped himself in it, plus he's made a full confession, so it's all over bar the party-poppers. And Mr. Honeyman can depart in peace, with a defiant digit in Wetherspoon's direction. Absolutely in confidence, but I gather the powers that be have been suggesting poor Honeyman's about as much use to the Department as a chocolate teapot, and that he couldn't bring a case home if it was strapped to his wrist."

"It won't do you any harm either," Atherton observed.

"Do I note a hint of envy in your voice?" Slider asked. "Can it be that you are beginning to feel a restless urge to get back to work?"

Atherton smirked a little. "Oh, well, I can't help feeling that if I'd been around we'd have got a result in half the time."

"Bloody sauce," Hart said indignantly.

Slider said, "No, he really means he *can't* help feeling it. It's in his genes."

"She doesn't yet know what I keep in my jeans," Atherton reminded him. "Besides, if our firm is going to be illuminated by her presence, I can't wait to get back."

"Sadly, Hart is only a temporary loaner, as your replacement. Unless I can get the new boss to buy her for us—assuming she wants to stay, that is."

"You bet," said Hart economically.

Slider refrained from asking why. Discounting Joanna's unwelcome speculation, did Hart want to stay for the joy of working in Shepherd's Bush, or for the heady prospect of getting into Atherton's boxers? Poor Sue, he thought, and wondered how Joanna would take it if Atherton did start something up with Hart.

But he had his own love life to worry about. He hadn't heard from Irene since she slammed the phone down on him, and he was wondering whether he ought to ring and try to placate her, little as he relished the prospect. The alternative was to wait for the solicitor's letter—though he couldn't altogether dismiss Joanna's suspicion that she might get a visit from his ex-wife-elect, to rant if not to bash. Jealousy was a strange and potent thing. There had been times when he had wanted very badly to batter Ernie, and he wasn't even in love with Irene. Actually, he didn't know that Irene was in love with him, or ever had been, but there was that possessive demon that lurked in everyone, which said if I can't have you, no one else is going to. What Atherton called *canis praesepis*. One way and another, he was going to have to pay for his sins. Perhaps Atherton was taking the wiser part after all by not getting involved.

"Actually, I have got a bit of news on that front," he said, coming back to the present. "Mr. Honeyman sent for me this afternoon to tell me that they have named his replacement at last."

Atherton sat up. "Really? Fantastic. Who is it, anyone we know?"

"Oh yes, we know him. I should think everybody knows Detective Superintendent Fred Porson."

Atherton's eyes widened. "Oh bloody Nora! Not The Syrup! What have we done to deserve that?"

Hart was looking lost. "Who's this? The what?"

"Fred 'The Syrup' Porson," Atherton elucidated. "Famously foul-tempered and notoriously the bearer of the most unconvincing hairpiece ever to leave the back of a cat!"

"I crossed paths with him briefly when I was at Hampstead," Slider said. "We used to call him The Rug From Hell. He doesn't like it to be mentioned, so I warn you," he said to Hart. "Or looked at."

"Trouble is, you can't look anywhere else," Atherton said. "But it's not just the rug: he uses words like a blind man swatting wasps at a picnic. Ernie Wise crossed with Mrs. Malaprop. It's going to drive me mad. You know I've got a low threshold for language abuse."

Slider was quietly pleased that Atherton was assuming he would be there to be driven mad. Talk of taking another job seemed to have been dropped. Things were definitely looking up.

"D'you know where he's coming from?" Atherton was pleading. "Where's he been lately? Somewhere taxing, I hope."

"He's been on a Commissions Office posting at the Yard," Slider said. "Traffic Planning Unit. So he'll be full of beans, raring to go, ready to get his teeth into an operational again. Ready to take out all his frustrations on us for being CO'd for three years."

"Look on the bright side, guv," Hart suggested. "Maybe he'll be so glad to get out again he'll be in a sweet and pliant mood."

"In the pig's eye," Atherton said elegantly.

London Rhyming Slang

Nobody really knows for sure the origin of London rhyming slang. It is said to have been invented by the underworld to prevent the police understanding what was being said; if so, it was obviously counterproductive, since the police have always been among its prime users. It had been in use certainly since the beginning of the nineteenth century, and possibly longer.

Rhyming slang simply uses a common phrase which rhymes with the word in question. But sometimes only the non-rhyming half of the phrase is used, so that there is no apparent connection between the original and the slang. Thus "feet" become "plates," via "plates of meat." This makes the code much more difficult to penetrate—and, of course, makes the whole thing much more fun.

Glossary

Brassic (for boracic)	boracic lint	skint (i.e. broke, penniless)
Brown bread	dead	
Bunny (for rabbit)	rabbit and pork	talk
Butcher's	butcher's hook	look
Dickie	dickie bird	word
Dog	dog and bone	phone
Elephant's	elephant's trunk	drunk
Ginger	ginger beer	queer (i.e. homo-sexual)
Gold watch	scotch (whisky)	
Hampsteads	Hampstead Heath	teeth
Iron	iron hoof	poof (i.e. homo-sexual)
Mutton (for Mutt'n')	Mutt and Jeff	deaf
Pen	pen and ink	stink
Plates	plates of meat	feet
Ruby	Ruby Murray	curry
Syrup	syrup of figs	wig

Fall Victim to Pulse-Pounding Thrillers
by *The New York Times*
Bestselling Author

JOY FIELDING

SEE JANE RUN   71152-4/$6.99 US

Her world suddenly shrouded by amnesia, Jane Whittaker
wanders dazedly through Boston, her clothes blood-
soaked and her pocket stuffed with $10,000. Where did
she get it? And can she trust the charming man claiming
to be her husband to help her untangle this murderous
mystery?

TELL ME NO SECRETS   72122-8/$5.99 US

Following the puzzling disappearance of a brutalized rape
victim, prosecutor Jess Koster is lined up as the next
target of an unknown stalker with murder on his mind.

DON'T CRY NOW   71153-2/$6.99 US

Happily married Bonnie Wheeler is living the ideal life—
until her husband's ex-wife turns up horribly murdered.
And it looks to Bonnie as if she—and her innocent,
beautiful daughter—may be next on the killer's list.